THE SCRATCH DAUGHTERS

ALSO BY H. A. CLARKE

The Scapegracers

THE SCRATCH DAUGHTERS

H. A. CLARKE

EREWHON

THE SCRATCH DAUGHTERS
Copyright © 2022 by H. A. Clarke

First published in North America and Canada by Erewhon Books, LLC in 2022

Erewhon Books
2 W. 29th Street, Suite 3S
New York, NY 10001
www.erewhonbooks.com

Erewhon books are available at special discounts when purchased in bulk for premiums and sales promotions as well as for fund-raising or educational use. For details, send an email to info@erewhonbooks.com.

Library of Congress Control Number: 2022942218

ISBN 978-1-64566-017-0 (hardcover)
ISBN 978-1-64566-022-4 (ebook)

Cover art by Anka Lavriv
Cover and interior design by Dana Li
Author photograph by Kaitlyn Dolores Spina

Printed in the United States of America

First US Edition: October 2022
10 9 8 7 6 5 4 3 2 1

for queers who live in towns like this. keep going! keep going! keep going!

"And the history of this, their expropriation, is written in the annals of history in letters of blood and fire." —Karl Marx

"Oh my god, they were right. I'm a homo." —But I'm a Cheerleader

STRIKE FOR PIKE

It was hot for December, hotter than Halloween had been, but I guess that's the Midwest for you. Saturday at nautical twilight. The sky fell around us in a fog. We wore street clothes under kitschy little jackets that read SCAPE-GRACERS, each a different color—bruisy lilac for Jing, baby blue for Yates, gunmetal for Daisy, and red 40 for me—to match the marble-sized witch organs that lived in our throats and processed our powers. Their throats, that is. Would be cute if I had my soul, too.

Anyway, dragging boys behind the bowling alley was easy as shit.

Daisy had him by his elbows. She blew a bubblegum bubble so huge it masked her as she lugged him down the alley side, around the corner to the back lot, then backwards up the abandoned school bus steps. Her bubble popped as she reached the top stair. It smelled like fake apples. She smacked her lips, adjusted her hold, and bounced him twice before she dragged him into the dank bus depths, seemingly unmoved by his carp-on-a-line-style thrashing. Usually I did the guy-hauling part, but she'd been in a mood and that energy had to go *somewhere*. Besides, for a girl as small as her, Daisy had a hell of a grip. We followed her at heel down the slick black school bus aisle. There was a hint of risk, what with us nabbing this guy and forcing him into a bowling-alley-anterior bus husk being theoretically illegal and all, maybe a smidgeon near kidnapping and assault, but we weren't too worried. This wasn't the first time we'd done this sort of thing. We hadn't gotten caught yet. Why would we now?

This was Alexis Nguyen's ex-boyfriend. Travis something. Beefy corn-faced prick in a letter jacket and expensive showy never-been-worked-in cowboy boots. Kind of an auxiliary friend to Austin Grass and the like, but more belonging to the pseudo-popular youth-group-cum-drug-dealer clique who genuinely thought that Jing and Yates and Daisy had signed their names in the devil's book by hanging around with me. Gotta love fundy assholes. One wonders how he dated the likes of Alexis in the first place, even as he was, in this instance, correct on technicality. We've done a lot of scribbling in and around our devil's book.

Daisy pushed Travis against the emergency door at the back of the bus. She shoved hard, then down. He skittered onto his tailbone and spat a long string of stupid that I didn't care to process. *What do you think you're what the fuck are you what is this what fuck.* Ugh. Whatever. With a flip of her skirt, Daisy slammed her knee into his solar plexus, pinning him in place, and Travis heaved a cough and kicked so hard one of his boots flew off, banging against a smudged window and clattering to the floor. Smelled like corn chips. Boys are gross.

Jing and Yates stalked ahead of me with Jing in the lead. She had a jumbo roll of duct tape like a bangle on her wrist that she hula hooped around as she strut, shoulders squared, chin out, whistling one of Yates' favorite pop songs. She stopped just before the kicking prick. Grabbed the end of the tape and pulled. It made a sound like a lightning strike. She got his mouth, then moved lower, taped him to the door in zigzags between FUCK BIO I HATE IT HERE and DONNA + SNAKE 5EVR in a Sharpied arrow heart. His wriggling popped the initial tape ribbons off, but Daisy kept him in place, and Jing made short work of the rest. In a blink, Travis something was affixed. He twitched, wide-eyed. Looked like a fly in a spiderweb. A fly whose primary idols were SoundCloud rappers.

"Travis." Yates looked at down at him, doe eyes heavy. She clasped her perfect hands together and tucked them against her perfect chest, gold-ringed knuckles sparkling just beneath her candy-charm necklace. Beatific. "You've been following Alexis around. You keep texting her and messaging her nonstop, and when she blocks you, you make new accounts and start again. You park outside the store where she works and wait for her shift to end so that you can follow her. Travis, Alexis isn't into you anymore. You're freaking her out. How could you lack the basic human decency to respect the dismissal of a girl you claim to care about, or *literally anybody* for that matter? She came to us scared for what might happen if she couldn't keep avoiding you. It makes me sick to my stomach. I'm sick, Travis. How could you do this?"

Travis made muffled sounds. His eyebrows jumped together.

Jing and Daisy looked at each other. Girl telepathy. Jing curled her bright red lip. Daisy's eye twitched. A host of microexpressions too fast to map that made their highlights shimmer, then they simultaneously came to their conclusion, and Daisy ripped off the tape along with a couple of whiskers from Travis' mouth.

"Ow! Jesus Christ." Travis kissed his teeth and coughed. "You're fucking crazy! What the shit, let me out of here, you little—"

"Time to gag him again?" Jing looked to Yates like, *Please say yes.*

Yates bit her bottom lip. Felt very *no.*

With a flicker of exasperation, Jing stayed her hand. Crossed her arms to holster her tape bangle.

Spotlight back on Yates, who patted her curls, then adjusted the ruffled hem of her little dress. Minty green, looked nice with her blue. Soothing and frosty. I liked the pearly buttons. "Do you know who we are?"

"Yes, I know who you are, Yates. Fucking, of course I know who you are, we've gone to school together since second grade." He opened his mouth to say more, but then recognition hit him, and his eyes flashed. "Jackets. The fucking jackets. This is Scapegracer shit, isn't it? *No.* No no no, count me out. I'm not fucking around, you better let me go, my dad's a pastor and—"

"Boys don't treat girls like that in our town," said Jing, dripping venom. "When they do, that's Scapegracer shit. You got it right."

"Don't kill me," Travis squeaked. Squeaked! Wasn't so big and bad in the face of supernatural retribution, now was he? "What do you want? What do you want from me? Don't kill me, please don't kill me, I didn't do it, I swear to god."

"Get a load of this guy," said Daisy. She sniffed, smiled mirthlessly. "Don't flatter yourself, ugly. You smell and nobody likes you. I only kill for love. Yates, got the Chett poppet?"

Yates produced the poppet from an inner jacket pocket. One-armed Ken doll. She held it by a buff-toned mono-toed foot and took a breath. "Ready, Sideways?"

Sideways. That was me. Talking to me.

I was here. My body was in this space with the rest of them. I was breathing, my lungs beat when I kept my mouth open like this, sucked air between my teeth and down my throat then out my stuffed-up nose. Blood moved inside my gut. Fingers hummed at the ends of my hands, throbbing numb but still attached. Fucked-up ratty boots below, fucked-up ratty hair above. Solve et coagula. Yuck. My body stood still aside from the occasional absent fidgeting, upright, alive, and I was present. I was on earth. I tasted ink. Our coven's unbooked devil swam languidly inside me, evidenced from the outside only in the jet stains pooling around my nail beds and the corners of my mouth, and if he had any opinions on the Chett-Travis situation, he didn't offer them. Around us the bus smelled like hot crayons and trash bags. Old sweat. Fruit snacks. Clammy, clingy scents that recalled being smaller and worse. Jing looked sweat-glossy under her bangs. Yates thumbed at the plastic dip of the poppet's ankle. A gnat zipped around the hollow bus cavity until it got too close to Daisy, who crushed it twitching with her elbow against a slashed-up vinyl bench. Chettboy whimpered something that sounded like *You're a buncha crazy bitches.*

"Ready to start?" Jing was looking at me. I *felt* her looking at me.

I was still something to see.

I rolled my hands into fists, stubby nails deep into my palm meat, and the dull pain was an anchor that proved to me that I was here. I was right here, right fucking here. I was standing here empty-handed, trying to make myself think about how I was standing here empty-handed.

I was also panting in the woods with a handle in my grip. Jackknife. I'd pilfered it from my ex. He'd used it to cut open little animals, so he told me, because it's easy to find witches if you dig around in their fresh wet insides. Lungs burning because I ran here, I ran here in kicks that weren't made for running in the woods and I haven't run drills in months. My hair hung in my eyes and stuck to my cheeks and my shoulders and dipped in between my lips. Straight hair, soft and heavy, blue-black, thick. I had the knife in one hand and had the other hand pushed up against a broad tree trunk. Rough bark, felt like her leather. Grip tightened on the handle, I crushed it as close to my bones as my skin would allow. I pressed down on the bark with the knife. My body thrummed all over, alive with a pulse like ants swarming on a dropped ice-cream cone. I was crawling with it, with the manic rush of magic. Bad-batch-ecstasy rancid-maggot magic. It felt like doing donuts in a stolen sports car. I felt sick and it wasn't mine. It couldn't be mine. It felt *good*. I drove the knife tip into the tree and sawed down. Sap oozed down the knife and gummed around my knuckles. I carved faster. Long lines, jaggedy, overexaggerated. Her handwriting is so tacky. It's too big and damn near illegible. So be it. I can see you. I can see everything you do now. Extra eyes to watch my back.

Her handwriting?

Right. My handwriting. Sideways' handwriting. I am Sideways. I'm on a bus.

Ten points of soft pressure on either side of my neck, five on each side. Gentle touch. Little shaking, just enough to rustle the curls. "Sideways. Hey. What's up?" I blinked, and there was Yates. She had me by the shoulders, dark fingers soft on the red satin, and she looked at me with a dimple between her eyebrows. She smelled like honey. "Are you okay? Talk to me."

"Some bitch ripped her soul out," Daisy sneered. "Duh, she's not okay."

"I'm talking to Sideways, Daze."

"I'm fine." My tongue felt weird in my mouth in a different way than it usually did whenever Yates was touching me. Like it wasn't attached. I couldn't remember how to make it move like I wanted. It was a big dumb clumsy slug that was super bad at language.

You're not fine. Mr. Scratch purred in the seams of my skull. His voice was overinflected, unctuous and slithery, unplaceably accented. Just left of mid-Atlantic. He stretched a tendril down the top knobs of my spine and coiled it under the flat bone of a shoulder blade, swished it to and fro in a bizarrely comforting gesture, like he was giving me a pat from the inside. It was a weird chilly, wet feeling. Kinda ticklish. *Does lying make it better?*

"Sure it does," I hissed under my breath with my eyes squeezed shut. My hands scrubbed up my face and over my head, skimmed the greasy tangles as they went. Cracked-up mucky nails snagged the edge of knots. Split split split. How long had it been since I'd had a proper shower? "They don't need to deal with it right now. Just help me do this, okay?"

Yates adjusted her hold on me. Whispered, "I don't know what he said, but we're not dealing with this. We're doing this. There's a difference."

Daisy sucked in her cheeks.

Jing grinned and mouthed, *Tell Scratchy I say hi.*

We were all getting used to my whole *I have a weird fucking roommate inside my brain who jacks up our magic and is keeping me alive, but the thing is, he is literally a chatty little wet boneless demon freak and being around me means overhearing half of our conversations on a semi-regular basis* thing in our own ways.

Mr. Scratch, who had access to my optic nerves so plainly saw Jing's lips move, went, *Hello to Jing! I love you.*

Okay. How about no. I jumped over Yates' kindness and mumbled, "He says hi yourself."

Yates looked genuinely worried but like she didn't want me to worry about her being worried. Offered me the curse doll.

I swayed out of her touch and palmed it.

Here we are. A hex for my girlies. Scratch gushed down my shoulders, down the gristle of my arms and into my wide wrists, where he split himself into ribbons and twined himself around my individual carpal bones. Full-body brain freeze. It felt like diving out of a mosh pit into fresh snow. Mr. Scratch made himself like a liquid magnet in my palm. He hummed in the poppet's direction, tugged me from the inside. I followed the pull and grabbed the Ken doll by its head. Its nose inverted under my trigger finger. Mr. Scratch soaked into my voice box, and together we said, "We the Scapegracers call upon our power to hex Travis forever."

"Us Scapegracers forever," went Jing and Yates and Daisy in unison.

We'd gotten pretty good at this.

"For the crimes this boy committed, we pronounce him Chett." I scowled down at the doll. Projected complete dominion upon it. The thrumming wormed in my breastbone. Magic rattled with a sound like old-TV static in my head, or maybe that was just Scratch's breathing, and at once my body ached and rang, which was how it should be, but I didn't feel it right. My body wasn't right. I was all hollow pieces and no joints. My skeleton was a series of cheap plastic pony beads on an elastic string. That string was Scratch. He kept me strung together, but if he went slack or snapped, I'd fall to pieces. I'd become a spill of beads for people to slip on. Magic kept my circulatory system going like coffee or nicotine in place of automatic vitality, but it wasn't *my* magic, and as much as I was obsessed with it, it also sucked. It *sucked.* I'd been having palpitations for a month. Shouldn't magic feel good? When it felt bad in the old way, that felt so good.

"Us Scapegracers forever, we deem him Chett," my girls said.

"*Chett,*" I said, and devil ink oozed through the cracks in my hands and wriggled in fronds across the doll's body, flowered around his throat into little hatch marks of my handwriting. I tongued my inky gums, then passed the doll to Yates.

"*Chett,*" said Yates, and her handwriting unfurled along the doll's body beside mine, her old THOU SHALT NOT in pretty cursive. She passed it on to Jing, who said her hex and passed it on to Daisy.

When Daisy's handwriting sprawled around the little plastic body, her handwriting latched onto Jing's, whose amalgamated half-Daisy handwriting latched on Yates', which then flowed upwards into mine. Styles smeared. Our own chimeric communal voice, janky and perfect, marked the doll forever. Daisy held the poppet out, and we all reached forward, pressed a finger somewhere against the organless body. I got around where his belly button should be. Daisy spat out her gum and with it, the incantation's end. "Travis Meijer is Chett forever, enforceable by us Scapegracers. No reprieve and no relent. So be it."

"So be it," said Yates and Jing.

"So be it," I said.

So be it.

The doll's joints snapped with a waft of burning plastic.

Travis let out a yelp. I let myself glance over, and sure as morning, a thick black stripe had bloomed around his throat. Literally permanent marker. It recalled the velvet choker Daisy had stolen from the Delacroix archives, the one that'd belonged to her dead mom.

Daisy tugged the doll out of our collective grip and turned to peer down at Travis like he was some kind of fucked-up bug. She waved the doll around as she spoke. Gesticulated with it. "So, here's how this works. You don't look at girls unless your thoughts are pure. That means no thinking about hurting girls or using them or deceiving them, any shit like that. You don't talk about girls with malice, you don't follow them around, you *so* don't touch them without permission, or else you're going to be in a world of pain that medicine won't fix! Nothing fixes it. You don't snitch on us. If you snitch, it gets worse. Lucky for you, if you're not a terrible person, if you stop and never do creepy predator bullshit again, you'll be fine. If you're bad, it'll get bad. That's easy math. Clear enough for you?"

Travis opened and shut his mouth a bunch, like a fish.

Daisy spoke slowly, sweetly, like she was explaining something to a snotty kid. "Do you get me, Travis?"

"You're the devil," he whispered.

"You're thinking of Sideways." Jing wagged her brows. "Daisy's just like that."

The devil adjusted his perch inside my jawbone, and he felt too wriggly, so I swatted at him and bade him hold still.

Daisy was done. She reached for the red emergency handle just above Travis' head, and with a yank and a heave, the door swung backwards. It took Travis with it. His torso swept out with the door, and his legs dragged behind him, slung their way off the bus. Then, gravity! The duct tape that'd held him in place gave way, and he dropped off the door, fell with cartoonish slowness into a heap on the dead grass below. Said *oof* and everything. Then came a moan, a string of cussy nothings, and the snap of brittle yellow weeds as Travis found his feet. I could hear him the whole time he hauled ass into the woods, long after he was out of sight. He breathed like a hot computer.

Now, it was just us in the bus. The magic hangovers I used to get didn't really happen anymore, not since Mr. Scratch set up shop inside me, but there was a release of tension, a turning down of the dials. I felt less. I hated feeling less. Jing thumbed through her phone and Yates zipped up her jacket, smoothed the fabric against her chest. Daisy stared at the hole Travis had left in his wake. I yearned for a migraine. I looked at my hands.

"Daze," said Yates. She walked down the aisle and stopped by Daisy's side, placed a hand between her shoulder blades. She rubbed in little diamond shapes. "Are you alright?"

Jing's attention snapped from her screen to the pair of them.

I remembered, vaguely, stories that'd gone around about some ex of Daisy's. That he was an asshole of note. That he and Daisy got into it after homecoming last year, and that she'd locked herself in the girls' locker room and cried for hours. Daisy crying over, or because of, a boy was hard to imagine. I didn't think I could fathom Daisy shedding actual human tears. Anyway, the guy doesn't go here anymore. He got into a really bad wreck a few days after the homecoming incident, fell a semester behind in the hospital, and moved away to live with some Indianan cousin or something so that he could retake junior year. As for the rumors, well. The rumor was that Jing poured canola oil on the guy's windshield. He'd turned the wipers on, and the whole windshield blurred over, and he drove blind into a telephone pole on Fourth Street.

But there were lots of rumors about Jing and Yates and Daisy that weren't true.

"I'm fine," Daisy snapped. Her voice brought me back into it. She didn't quite look it—she was smiling but her eyes were hard—but her tone didn't leave room for argument. She shot her eyes at me. "Are you?"

"Yeah."

"Liar." It wasn't an accusation. It was a statement of fact. She snorted and looked away from us, and after a pause, she patted her eyelids with her fingertips until she found the edge of one of her falsies. She peeled off the right strip, then the left, and I thought for a second about feathers being plucked. Her eyes looked smaller, older without them. She pressed the strips together, ran the edges against her bottom lip. Sounded hoarse. "I know that look. You were in *her* head again, weren't you? What's she doing? She daydreaming about sucking bruises on your hipbones again?"

That was once. Shouldn't have told her about that. I scuffed the toe of my boot against the floor, watched the shitty black leather scuff the shitty black aisle. I blended in. "She's hexing something," I said. I thought about the knife in my hand, my hand on the tree, my knife in the tree, my soul in my teeth. Thief. "I don't know why."

"The fucking nerve." She crossed her arms. The poppet jutted out from the crook of her left elbow like a broken bone. "I'm skinning her once we catch her. Make you a nice new jacket. Your old leather one is trash anyway. Let's get out of here. It smells like middle school. Yates, are we still good for your place?"

"Mhm. My dad is making dinner." She gently pulled the poppet out of Daisy's grip and tucked it back in her inside pocket. One little flipper foot stuck out. "We should get going."

"Don't have to tell me twice," Jing said. She stood up, stretched like a cat, and sauntered in my direction. She'd retoned her hair recently, and it was the palest shade of blond I'd ever seen on a person. Star-glow bright. She hooked an arm around my waist and whisked me down the aisle, and I let myself be brought along.

Feelings were harder without my specter inside of me. Emotions filtered like a song through another room. Hazier.

Seldom a high note, but a bulk of the low. Jing's arm on my waist still felt like something, though. Something for sure.

I didn't dwell. We were friends. *We were friends.*

"I got the dye in the car," she said. "Provided you're still up for it."

Dye. Right. God, I was bad at thinking.

We had thrown around the idea of dyeing my hair recently and I'd said yes without much thought. I mean, I would let Jing tattoo her name on my forehead if she asked in the right way. Hair? Hair grows back. Yeah. Yes. Up for anything.

I just nodded.

Jing released me in front of the bus stairs, leaped down them in one giant step. Flipped her hair back. It flashed in the air around her head. She turned to face me, locked eyes with me. She put one foot in front of the other, gave me a neat little grin, and bowed with a flourish that'd make Kit Marlowe jealous. Then one hand came up. An offer. "May I ease you to the chariot, handsome lady?"

Daisy snickered somewhere behind my head.

I tried to swallow. Input was failing. I looked over my shoulder at Yates, the angel to whom this clearly oughta be offered, but she smiled behind her baby-blue nails and shook her head. Curls bounced everywhere in slow motion with cartoon sparkles.

I really was a potoo in the company of flamingoes, huh.

I looked back down at Jing, still holding her pose with a mean little smirk, and gnawed my bottom lip. I took her hand, held it as I clomped down the steps and landed in the dry mud below. She didn't drop her smile, didn't drop the bow. She brought my hand to her mouth. My pulse sped up so fast that it shoved Mr. Scratch from his perch in my ribs, sent him spiraling around inside me. Jing's eyes burned. She wouldn't blink. She rubbed circles on my palm with her thumb, and her lips ghosted just above my knuckles. Almost a kiss. Then she jammed out her tongue and licked me.

I recoiled so fast that I lost balance, smacked against the side of the bus. My fingers glistened with spit. "What gives?"

Jing, who'd just stood up straight, bent over again with laughter. Her cackle spooked birds from the trees. Daisy joined in, sounding hollow, and Yates sighed something about Jing being nasty. They climbed down the steps and headed for Jing's cherry-colored convertible, and Jing lingered behind, still laughing, while I regathered my nerve and my chill.

"Hey." She crossed her arms over her chest, smile gone.

I rubbed my hand on my jeans and glanced her way in response.

"We're going to get your specter back. It's going to happen."

We'd been saying that for the past month.

My gross wet hand was dry, far away, wrapped tight around a knife. My skin was unbroken but somewhere else it was heavy with long splinters. Somewhere else I was doing magic. I cut and I wanted to sob and spit and smile until my cheeks split. I felt a thrill without any pleasure in it. It wasn't pleasure. I didn't like this, the carving. The rush wasn't in the destruction and the creation, it was in something else.

I made myself look at my hand, at the fact that there wasn't a knife in it, and then I made myself look at Jing. She'd stepped closer. A gust of wind caught her hair and streamed it by my cheek, stripes of moonlight. "I was just trying to wig you out. That's all. I wanted to make you smile. You hardly do that anymore. What's up, Sideways? What's happening in your head?"

"Nothing," I said. Jing was looking at me and I wanted her to *know*, I wanted her to know everything I'd ever thought about anything, but there weren't words that existed for that. Not the right ones. Not right now. I looked at her, and the weight of all my bullshit slammed down against my sternum so hard I thought it would rip me. Padlock dropped in a thin plastic bag. My mouth opened again, and I couldn't miraculously figure out how to say anything that would fish out words. I lied to her. Said, "Nothing at all. It's a void up here."

Jing looked at me for a second. Just looked. She wasn't like Daisy. She wouldn't call me on dishonesty where my crazy was concerned. But she said it without saying it, and when she hooked her arm around my shoulder and steered me toward her car, I wasn't sure if she was getting fed up with me. I imagined it was hard being friends with somebody whose soul is somewhere else, particularly when you hadn't been friends for long before that. She'd known me longer as a zombie than she had as a normal lez. My equivalent of normal. Jing's an angel, that's the point. She'd been more patient with me than I deserve. All of them have been.

"Jing," I said when we got closer to the car, where Daisy was reapplying her shimmery nude lipstick in the rearview mirror and Yates was paging through a meticulously organized and photo-op-ready notebook. One of them had turned on metallic citric acid pop, and it played just loud enough that I thought they maybe wouldn't hear me if I spoke low. "Can I ask you something?"

"Shoot," she said. "Anything you want."

"That guy Daisy used to date."

Jing made a sound in her throat. "You're gonna have to specify that further, Jesus Christ. There've been a lot. What do you want to know?"

"The football player." Lots of them were football players. I couldn't think of his name for the life of me. I could think of the shape of him, though. He and Daisy at the front of the gym in glitzy plastic crowns, wearing sashes, speckled by the disco ball strung in the rafters overhead. My lonely ass in an ill-fitting tux half-watching from the risers, feeling glum, drinking straight from a handle I'd snuck in my sleeve. "The linebacker. Last year's homecoming king."

Jing stopped walking. She straightened her back. Breathed through her teeth, moved her mouth as though she was smiling and said, "Don't talk about him." Then, she seized me above my elbow and yanked me close, breathed just under my ear: "What do you need to know? We can't Chett him, he moved to Indianapolis to live with his dad over the summer. He isn't worth the trip."

"I just." I chewed the words before I spoke them.

Bubblegum words. Daisy's bubble popping. Jing held me so hard it hurt. "Is the rumor true about what you did? People say all sorts of things about the three of you. I heard all sorts of stuff before we were close. I get it if it's fake, I mean, I—"

"I tried to kill him," she said. She released me and tore her hand over her skull, and I watched her knot her fingers in all that platinum blond. Her knuckles moved like she was strangling something. The green veins twitched in the back of her hand. "We tried the cops and took him to court and everything. Good lawyers, too, what with all Daze's money. Nothing. We got nothing. Not even a restraining order. No evidence and most of it wasn't strictly illegal. Her word against his and all that."

A baby-fist-sized lump lodged in my throat.

"Nobody fucks with my friends." Jing set her jaw. She seemed incredibly alive, more alive than she'd been before— power strobed through her and I felt with newfound surety that she'd been magic way before me, even if she hadn't known the language for it. She vibrated with a particular vigor, an intensity. She focused it all on me. Scalded me with it. Leaned against me and I could not think for a moment about anything else but her gravity, the intensity of her presence. "Believe me when I say this, Sideways Pike. We're going to get your soul back. We're going to get your soul back if it's the last thing I do. Get it?"

She was wonderful. Jing is wonderful and I did not believe her. My brain was knotted worms.

"Yeah," I managed. "Got it."

"Good." With that, she was gone from me. She booted

Daisy out of the front seat, changed tracks to something lower and slower, and gathered up all the hair on her head into a twist. She jammed a lavender pen through it. The novelty feathered end fluttered in the breeze. She revved her engine. "Pike," she said. "You getting in my car or is your ass walking from here to Castle Yates?"

"Please don't call it that," Yates said woefully.

Go on, dove. Go with your friends.

I climbed in the back seat and tried my best to preemptively mash down any car-related panic responses. Breathed on a count. Yates put her ankles in my lap, and I rested my hands on the ruffled edge of her socks. The convertible's top opened above us, shrank behind our heads, and Jing pulled out of the bowling alley parking lot and cut across the country road beyond. We bounced over potholes. The machinery throbbed with bass.

Madeline folded her knife somewhere else. She slipped it in her bra. The metal was cold, and it bit against my skin. Conjured gooseflesh. Madeline stood back, I stood back, and we admired our handiwork. We admired the sigils we'd drawn in her handwriting—in my handwriting, Sideways', mine—and felt nauseous. She clamped her hands around her skull. She pressed hard; I felt the ghost of nails kiss my scalp. She doubled over like her knife. She shoved hard against her temples, and alone in the woods with herself in a vise, she screamed.

HOME SWEET

Castle Yates was big. Like, no shit, we call it a castle for a reason, but *man*. I'd been there a few times already but hadn't acclimated to it at all, and every time Jing pulled into the drive, its ridiculous immensity overwhelmed me fresh. It was a cream-and-blue Victorian, all lacy and covered with scales, and just kept going. Frosted dragon house. It could've been the little sister of the Delacroix House, perhaps less gaudy and audacious, but the Delacroix was a business, and this was a private residence, so! Dr. and Dr. Yates had rhubarb plants right up against the house, and their big fan leaves managed to be a vivid bottle green despite the rest of the vegetation having gone sallow with winter. They looked like giant wings. We parked and I applauded myself for not having freaked the fuck out even slightly as we filed out of the cherry convertible, and Jing slapped a rhubarb palm as we passed it.

"You don't have to slap the plants," Yates said.

Jing furrowed her brow. "I got no choice."

Unseen wind chimes knocked low sweet sounds out of each other as we ascended the porch steps. Birds that oughta be migratory and elsewhere sang. Yates was a princess, not in the sense of a legalistic hierarchal state domination girl-boss or anything, but in that ultra-girly sense, in the way that provoked nature to mirror her poise and grace and kindness. Maybe the chime sounds were just an effect of being near her. Like ascending angel harp chords or whatever. Also, wealth. She was a princess in the sense that she was very fucking rich.

Daisy's rich and doesn't have bell sounds.

"Thank you for the commentary." I rubbed the corner of my mouth.

The whole month we'd been doing this, we hadn't quite hit a balance yet, Scratch and I. In the beginning it'd been bad—I'd been bad—and he'd thrown most of his energy into keeping me upright, and it'd exhausted him of his ability to hold elaborate conversations, and me of my ability to initiate them. It got easier after a while, not having my specter inside me, or I guess it got manageable, and I learned how to hold most of my own weight. Shared some of the burden of being. As I did, I gave Scratch more room to stretch out and settle, and now we were falling into a kind of buddy-buddy mentor-student cohabitation situation. It was a comfortable if kooky possession. I just still wasn't sure how to make small talk, that was all.

He was in my head.

He must've heard me.

Sideways, is it strange when I am chatty? Off-putting? Would it be more comfortable for you if I were silent instead? I imagined that shacking up in total silence might be unpleasant. Fashion me more like a voyeur and less like a participant companion, you know. Never mind that I have loads of observations and I am famously charming. I could totally hush. Anything for you. Thoughts?

I'm a lot of things but I won't be a shitty host. Ugh. Talk on, I guess.

Marvelous! I am a molten glob of language and shutting up is torture.

We took our shoes off at the door, and then Yates led us like a flock of ducklings across the reflective mahogany floors to the kitchen. Copper pots dangled over a butcher-block island, and Dr. and Dr. Yates bustled together, chatting and laughing while they minced peppers and greens. Garlic sizzled. Dr. Yates (the mom one) glanced up. She looked very much like our Yates, I thought, albeit with gray around her temples and a gap between her two front teeth. I liked that about her. Made me mind my own gap less. "Hello, Jing and Daisy and Eloise! It's good to see you. Do all of you eat chicken? I can sub out potatoes if one of you doesn't eat chicken."

"We're good with chicken," I said. "Thanks, Dr. Yates."

"Yeah, thanks, Dr. Yates," said Daisy.

Jing pressed herself close to my ear and not-so-quietly whispered, "For a girl who's not into meat you sure eat a lot of meat."

I stepped on her foot.

"Potatoes seem like an inadequate meat substitute. No

protein, and I have zero childhood scars from potatoes pecking me, so there isn't the same satisfaction in eating them. Apples and oranges." Dr. Yates (the dad one) coughed a laugh, and unsuccessfully dodged the rag with which Dr. Yates (the mom one) thwacked his hand.

Oh, the antics of parents in love. I wondered if they'd get on well with my dads.

"Can we go upstairs?" Yates asked.

"May we go upstairs?" Dr. Yates (the dad one) quirked a brow.

"Right. May we go upstairs?" Yates said, unflappable. Her ability not to sound exasperated was beyond me.

"I'll ask you to come down to set the table, but yes. Go have fun." Dr. Yates (the mom one) dismissed us with a wave, then got back to slicing.

Yates turned and we all followed close after her, around the corner and up a flight of carpeted stairs. Her dog, an amazingly fat and lazy Yorkie-poo who let us dress him up sometimes, licked our ankles and accepted rubs as we passed him on the stairs, but he did not follow after us. We passed the study, the master bedroom, the guest room, and a room whose door bore a sign that read HOME OF AKEEM'S PREMIUM MEME CREAM. Below the sign, an artistic rendering of a toothpaste tube labeled "fast-drying cement." It wasn't a printed photo collage. It was an oil painting. Someone had made a little internet Monet.

I hadn't ever met Yates' brother Akeem. He was off at college being a nerd major and so on. Engineering or something. STEM. Even without having ever witnessed him, I understood that he walked that line between being deeply cool and irredeemably corny, but Yates loved him. That was enough. We'd play Smash or something someday, I don't know.

The odyssey to Yates' room concluded. Daisy shut the door behind us. Inside felt frothy, light. Largely bare walls and a four-poster bed, butterfly fairy lights, powder-blue sheets. Valentine's Day–looking plush bears lounged on her ruffle-edged pillowcases. There was a pink desk upon which rested her neatly stacked bullet journals, textbooks, and nineties romance manga, along with a little rabbit figurine whose ears she used as a jewelry stand. Behind the stack lived the fancy microphone for the ASMR affirmations channel we all pretended that we didn't know she dutifully ran. It was a good channel. Lots of mouth sounds. I'd leaned on it a lot lately.

Yates flopped onto her bed, stomach down. She rested her chin on the backs of her hands. "So, we have to bleach her hair before we dye it, right?"

"Right," Jing said. She leaned against a wall, popped a hip. "She'll keep it in for a while, wash it out before dinner, then we dye it afterwards. Sound good, Eloise?"

Fucking "Eloise." "Sounds great."

Then why are you nervous?

I wasn't, not specifically about the hair dye. I was nervous about maintaining a solid happy mood for the duration of an entire sleepover. I was nervous about changing this body when it didn't even feel properly mine. I was nervous about having long hair at all for some reason; I wasn't sure why, I just knew that every time it touched my neck, I felt like I was crawling with spiders. Not that it was even all that long to begin with. I was in the gnarly no-man's-land between a curly shag and a mullet, it's not like I'm a shampoo model over here. I don't know. I don't know.

I wanted my specter back. I wanted to feel like a full person again, or at least a living one.

You don't have to do this or anything. We can focus on organ-finding.

"We don't have any leads," I mumbled, but not quite quietly enough to escape notice.

Yates frowned. "Are you having a conversation with Mr. Scratch?"

"Yeah, sorry. He wants us to find my specter, that's all. Antsy." I crossed my arms and shrank into my jacket. The fabric rubbed soft on my neck. That was something. "We can get to bleaching."

"I'll go through her socials again," Jing said. She knelt by a container of salon supplies and yanked forth an empty trash bag, which she stretched on the floor like a rug. She snapped on gloves, cracked her knuckles, and jabbed a finger at the ground. Indicated where I oughta plant my ass. "She's reactivated some of her accounts. I'll see if she was stupid enough to leave on her location or take a selfie somewhere incriminating."

"You could catfish her for information," Yates said, worrying her nails against her bottom lip. Yates was so pretty. "Shouldn't be hard."

"I've tried," said Daisy. "I nearly talked her into meeting up with me, but she weaseled out of it and blocked the account before we could. She hasn't been in school for a while, and hasn't stayed in one place, neither. Maybe she dropped out? Takes online classes or something. Didn't get anything further than that. None of her basketball teammates know where the fuck she is, I tried that route."

I opened my mouth, tried to suggest scrying again, but there was a slithering between the lobes of my brain that distracted me before I managed to make a sound.

We've tried scrying, remember? It's all thorns and static when we try. She's smart enough to cast veils around herself to fend off witchfinders. It isn't that your spell isn't working when you all cast it, love. It's that she's got the same kinds of cloaking charms protecting her that you and your scapegracers have protecting you. Save your energy.

My heart sank, but I thwacked the back of my neck where Scratch swam anyway. It was meant to be affectionate. A little thanks.

"We'll get her," Jing insisted. She rolled her shoulders. "Okay. I want to dye your hair in zigzags. One big zigzag part down your head, so that it slices your scalp into triangles, you know? Alternating colors with each triangle. How do you feel about that?"

Pretty.

I smiled. It was crooked but earnest in intention. "Whatever you want sounds good."

"Lila!" called a voice from downstairs.

"Yes, coming!" Yates sprang off her bed and bolted through the door, mouthed a *sorry* on her way out.

Jing sized up my skull. "Sit on our sexy luxury haute couture rug so that we don't murder Yates' carpet. We want to get it as light as we can so that the colors actually show up. Mids then ends then roots. I promise not to fuck up your hair, by the way. Daisy and I have done the bleaching part plenty of times. I've been blond for three years now and I flat-out refuse to pay legitimate prices for it." A phone buzzed on the desk. Buzz buzz buzz buzz. "Daisy, can you answer that or hang up? Jesus Christ."

"Not my phone," said Daisy, texting at breakneck speed.

"Seriously?" Jing scoffed and yanked off her gloves, snatched the phone off the desk, and swiped her thumb over the screen without checking the number. "What do you— oh, sorry, hello, how are you?" Her eyes got wider. She stuffed her free hand in a pocket, rocked back on her heels. "Yes," she said. "One moment." She tucked the phone into her neck and looked at us both, brows stabbing up past her hairline toward heaven. "It's the Delacroix House. Speak of the fucking devil, Jacques says he's got updates on Madeline. Sideways, do you want to take this?"

I tried to breathe. It wasn't going well.

Jing nodded minutely. "I'm gonna go outside, the reception is shit in here. Daisy, start on her hair, yeah? Be back soon."

Daisy looked up from her phone. She looked at me.

I counted backwards from ninety-nine.

Jing pressed the phone back to her cheek and ducked out. I heard her round the banister and trample down the stairs, heard her speaking too low and harsh for me to understand anything more than tone, and the spans of her long pauses. She hadn't shut the door behind her, and I hallucinated that I felt the gush of wind as she slammed the front door and stepped onto the stoop. At some point, Jing had become our networking contact with Delacroix. It was both because she loved social chess and because, early on in my Scratchmoded era, I'd cussed out a worker for telling me that Scratch was dangerous over the phone and nearly fucked up the only connections we had going for us.

Daisy made a *hm* sound.

I crossed my arms over my belly and stared at the ceiling. There were cracks but I couldn't focus enough to trace them. They blurred, got wider. I tried to feel for Madeline, for myself inside her far away, but I couldn't ever slip into it when I tried. She was out of my reach. But what if she wasn't? What if Jacques was telling Jing that I was imminently about to be okay?

My stomach went sour. Teeth chattered. Bad signs.

"Sit." Daisy tossed her phone aside. She stood at the end of the shiny black trash-bag tarp, expectant. "We should get started."

I sat. I crossed my legs.

She pulled the hair off my neck and ran a comb through

it. I hissed when it snagged and she slowed down, worked from the ends up, pulled the snaggles apart with expert quickness. Barely hurt. I shut my eyes. This kind of closeness still felt melty, too weird for me to fully parse. Friendship was sensitive. I still wasn't as good at receiving as I'd like.

"Have you ever been with a guy?"

I coughed. "Pardon?"

"Have you ever had sex with a boy?" Her tone was impassable.

"No," I said. "Never appealed."

"Are you a virgin?"

"No."

Does such a thing exist?

"And you've never any sexual anything with a boy? Not clumsy second base, nothing? Not even a kiss?"

"No," I said again. "Are kisses always sexual?"

She was silent for a moment. "How did you know, then?"

Classic. Nausea kicked in my gut and *bam*, my patience busted. "Are you asking me why I'm a lesbian, Daisy? Because I am so not in the fucking mood. What do you want, I turned gay because I watched *Sailor Moon* as a kid? My root was watching women's professional wrestling with one of my foster parents? I made my Bratz dolls scissor and felt some kind of way about it? What do you—"

"I've been with a lot of guys." She sectioned off a stripe of hair at the back of my neck, tied up the rest with a clip. "I always keep a lot of guys around me. I've needed them for selfish reasons, but I haven't liked many. I just like *it*. The look of it, I mean. I like the look of having a boyfriend. Things are easier when you have one. It's like carrying the best fake ID."

The string of nasty things I was about to say to her snagged between my tongue and teeth.

"You know, I've heard that the problem is that they're teenagers. That's what my dad's girlfriend keeps saying, or one of them, he's got three, it's whatever. The bitchy redhead one I like said that it's different when they're older. Boys don't know what they're doing but men will. Men take good care of you." She made a fluttery note in her throat like a laugh, but there wasn't a lick of humor present. Diaphragm spasm. She sounded something colder than angry. I didn't have the right words. "The poor baby's deluded! See, I've tried older guys and they are genuinely not any better. I thought maybe just any male-type person was an idiot for a while, that naturally men don't know what they're doing neither, or at least cis men I guess, but I've been thinking and I'm not so sure that's right. Maybe they do know what they're doing. I mean, I've been with guys who adore me, Sideways. Just absolutely idolize me. I've been with guys that despise me, likewise. Really fucking awful guys who demonstrate how much they hate me. I didn't like *any* of them. I like it when they like me, the good ones at least, and when we take pretty pictures together, and I like saying that oh, he's my boyfriend, he's an athlete, he's mine. It's just that I've never so much as had a crush on one of them. Even the ones who don't annoy me, the sweet ones. There's supposed to be butterflies. The movies say that there are butterflies but I don't feel like I'm full of butterflies when I'm around them, Sideways. I don't feel like I'm full of anything at all, apart from fear of being without some boy. I saw a video somebody took of me once and the look on my face—it's nothing. I felt nothing. Numbness is so blasé."

Her fingers were colder, now. The bleach smell struck my lungs.

I opened my mouth and shut it. I took a breath. I should've said things like, *You didn't deserve any of that shit that those guys did to you, nobody does, I fucking hate every man who's ever wronged you and not a lick of it was your fault* but saying all that felt selfish somehow. Like it was making it about me and how I hate people. I swallowed all of it. I took a slow breath, and the bleach smell made my skull hurt, and uselessly said, "Yeah?"

"Yeah." Her hands moved slower. "Your hair is really soft."

"Daisy." My lungs were going to pop. "Are you—"

"Don't tell Jing or Yates. Don't tell anybody. Don't even think about it too hard." She unclipped a section and globbed the bleach higher up my head. It was above my ears, now. The smell singed the air. "My dad's a prick. Seriously, Sideways, I don't need any rumors."

"I wouldn't tell a soul without permission." Wouldn't tell anybody what? There was a lot inside what she said to me—deep hurt and ache and *want*, the ringing absence of naming what she wanted. But I hadn't told her or Jing about Yates, now had I? "You have my word."

"I wonder—"

"Listen up, fuckers." The door swung open, and Jing stood in the light. Looked like a damn movie star. "Madeline's been sighted in the area. Just out of Sycamore Gorge township. They think she's staying at this murder motel. There's a chance she's still there. I think we should," she started, then stopped, and fixed her eyes on me. "You alright?"

"She's fine," said Daisy.

"Right. So. I think we should go tonight. We have to corner her while she's still at this motel. Jacques said the house can't go after her until later this week, that he thinks she's cloaked herself with something nasty, that we need more qualified people to pursue her for safety's sake, but you can think of a way around that, right, Mr. Scratch?"

May I?

This was weird. This felt so fucking weird. I nodded, and he crawled into my mouth.

"She's certainly cloaked herself, but that's not the whole matter of it." We spoke together. His voice fell a little higher in my register, a little breathier, and I couldn't help but shiver the whole way through. Brain freeze. He globbed in my throat like postnasal drip. "Her magic is volatile because it isn't hers. It could lash out unexpectedly. It could warp or deform. The withdrawal could rebound onto other people. Maurice and his crowd are curators. They aren't witches predisposed to pursuing a wayward spellcaster. Very few witches are. They're consequently overcautious, and they will not put themselves in an unpredictable situation. I know this because they were after me before I made a home in your precious hearts, and they didn't catch me because they were afraid of getting hurt."

"How hurt are we talking?" Jing lifted a brow.

"Oh, very, probably." He swirled under my tongue. "If they tried to scoop me back into an urn, I would have dissolved their bones."

Daisy twisted hair around her finger. Yates put her face in her hands.

Jing said, "Hot of you, molasses man. But like, what's the risk level for being near Sideways' magic in Madeline's hands?"

I didn't like hearing her say it like that. I did not like it one fucking bit. I wanted to hyperventilate. "Sometimes," Mr. Scratch said, gliding right over my peril, "unstable specters incinerate the host body and everything around."

"Spontaneous human combustion?" Daisy jolted like she'd been pricked. "Wait, is that why that happens? Holy shit, are you serious?"

"I do *not* know what that is," said Mr. Scratch with my tongue and teeth. "I *do* know that thieves and borrowers have been known to immolate, or to be crushed by open air, or to drown in nothing by overextending themselves. Magic unbodied is dangerous. That's why they were so frightened of me. I'm kneaded entropy stripped of my structure. I'm risky. They cannot guess what I might do."

I squeezed my wrist and hoped he felt it, understood that it was for him.

"Our Sideways' soul in her hands is without equilibrium. They're afraid of her lashing out, using a spell on instinct. Raw casting without sigils and forethought is already risky for young witches, but using someone else's soul to do so? Tough."

"We can't just not go. We can't hide and wait. We know where she is, we have to go after her," Jing hissed. I felt a twinge in my belly about her championing me. Or was that way too bold a read?

"We shall," Mr. Scratch insisted. "We'll mask ourselves. Make ourselves sneakier and draw a trap for her, snare her before she can move against us. We go to the motel, we cast outside her door, she steps into our spell unawares, she is bound from retaliation. Safety."

"We can't go tonight," said Yates. She'd appeared in the door behind us without my noticing, hand still plunged in an oven mitt. "My parents have caught me every time I've ever tried to sneak out in my life. And they'll call your parents. We'll leave first thing in the morning, how about that? Really early. Crack of dawn."

"That works," said Daisy. "Any chance Sideways can wash the bleach out of her hair before dinner?"

"Of course," said Yates. "Be down as soon as you can, okay?"

Dinner came and I felt deranged. Seemed to be a group sentiment, but I could've been projecting. We sat around a beautiful meal that I could hardly see because I fixated on potential sigils that we could draw later, and on incantations that might hold Madeline in place, and about whether Madeline would see me and fall to her knees and plead my forgiveness in instant recognition of the pain she'd caused me. *Sideways, Sideways, I'm sorry I ruined your life. Wanna kiss?* My appetite was jacked up. This was the closest we'd gotten to getting me back since it happened. It felt like years ago, it happening. November had been so fucking long. Good riddance. I rubbed the spot on my throat where Madeline had ripped my specter out and stared vacantly at my plate. Steam curled off my meal. You'd think something like that would leave a mark. You'd think I'd have a scar.

Due to my being crazy and Daisy's vibe being off and Jing being wound up about leaving for the motel and Yates being perfect for her parents, it was a mostly silent dinner, punctuated by Dr. and Dr. Yates asking each of us about college. They reminded us that the deadline for most places was the new year, provided that we hadn't applied with early decision options earlier on. They talked about important considerations and financial aid and scholarships and tutoring. I dodged the questions. I'd hardly thought about college, or anything that wasn't the Scapegracers and my far-off soul, since it happened. My future was impossible to comprehend. It was hard to imagine myself a week from now, feeling like this, much less imagining myself a year from now. Way too early to deal with the fact that none of us had applied for any of the same schools, and I hadn't applied to any yet at all. I was fine. It was fine.

"Mm, Eloise. I've got a non-college question for you."
Dr. Yates (the mom one) looked up from her plate and
smiled. It was a smile hooked up with question marks.

Here we go.

"Yes, ma'am?"

"Didn't you walk into my home as a brunette?"

❋

Jing rubbed on the last of the dye. The pattern we'd gone for
was red-purple-gray-blue, red-purple-gray-blue, because
that was the order we'd learned our specters and we were
cheesy and sentimental, I guess. The final triangular slice
was the one closest to my face, and once it was pinned in
place, I was finally allowed to move.

"Show me the sigils you've been sketching," Mr. Scratch
and I asked the air.

Yates helped me to my feet and waved a hand at her
desk, where she and Daisy had filled a page of loose-leaf
paper with different little sketched ideas. Daisy had that
round girly handwriting that everyone who'd been mean to
me in middle school wrote with, and it lent itself to circular
sigils, simple ones with short lines and open spaces. Yates'
sigils leaned symmetrical and delicate, intricately geometric,
lines so light you could hardly see them. Mr. Scratch gazed
at the marks they made. He felt, if I could get a sense of how
he felt, vaguely glum.

They're so lovely.

"And what's wrong with that?" I snorted. My head felt weird, what with all my hair slick and twisted and clipped. I wanted to smear it. Jing would kill me if I did. She'd been so attentive.

"What's wrong with what?" Yates and Daisy looked at each other, and then at the doodles they'd scrawled across the page.

Nothing is wrong with them at all. He still sounded swishy, but there was a distance in his voice that felt new. *In fact, I think they'd look beautiful written in me.*

Holy hell, I stung for him. It was so weird being inhabited by something that often felt really jealous of pens. I guess I could get it. Couldn't be easy, being an ink that couldn't write.

"These will work," he said through me. "I'll help with the trapping—it takes a certain finesse that you haven't perfected as of yet."

"Are you calling us amateurs?" Daisy pouted. "Squiggly prick."

"I'm calling you green," he said. Then, in my head: *Touch the sigils, if you please.*

I brushed a finger over the page.

A sliver of him ribboned down the length of my arm. It was visible if you watched for it, like an unfurling bruise. When it reached my outstretched fingertip, it bled through my nail, and a swirl of his ink swept through the paper pulp. *Oh, I miss the days of writing on skin. Skin is a good medium. Lasts so much longer, feels so much sweeter than crushed-up tree gunk.* He swept up two of the sigils, and in a whirl of black across the page, mixed them into a single shape.

Yates parted her lips and whistled.

A hybrid sigil soaked itself into the pulp. One of Yates' Qs collided with one of Daisy's Ts. Scribbles unwound and snaked into a circle. The game of hangman they'd played when they'd gotten distracted twisted into the notches of a seven-pointed star.

"Trap sigil," we said. "Mark a doorknob with this. Whoever twists it will drift a foot off the floor until you my daughters command otherwise." Inwards, he said, *Do you remember the shape of the sigil you drew for Madeline? The shape that drew the specter from your neck.*

I didn't think I'd ever forget.

Draw it on your hand and touch her throat once she's up there. Then we can find a proper book-shaped home for me.

I white-knuckled my free hand around the wrist he was occupying. I hoped it felt like confirmation. We trick the door, we corner Madeline, we yank the me out of her and everything would be right again. Easy, actionable. We could do this.

"Gold," said Jing, tapping a clip on the back of my head. She was usually intense about the spell writing component of this; I wasn't sure why she felt so distant. She pulled off her gloves and touched the nape of my neck. "Now let's wash Sideways' hair out and rest up. We're not doing this on two hours of sleep."

"Whatever," said Daisy in affirmation.

Yates yawned, as if proving a point, and smoothed her hands over the fabric of her silken pajama pants. "I'll get the face masks. Try not to get dye everywhere, okay?"

∗

We got dye everywhere.

Poor sheets. Poor walls. Whoopsy-daisy. Daisy everywhere. Yates gave war a try.

Hijinks exhausted us and I slept with my head on Jing's lap. Her hand stayed in my hair. I did not dream at all.

∗

In the morning, or maybe just before, the four of us put on rubber-soled shoes. We'd drawn our sneaky sigils across the bottoms with silver Sharpie, and we'd whispered over the lines until our tongues felt thick between our teeth. We pulled on our jackets, confident that the sneaking sigils would tamp down the conspicuousness of multicolored matching jackets. We tiptoed down the stairs.

The sigils were supposed to make us easy to overlook. Riffing off the simpler spell I'd stick-and-poked onto my arm a few weeks back, one that makes Scratch harder to notice in my mouth, on account of my dads thinking I had a dire case of gum disease and dragging me to two dentists about it. This was bigger, broader. Harder to execute. Daisy said that she'd imagined it like a chemistry textbook. There could be anything in a chemistry textbook, raunchy things, funny things, unforgivable things, but nobody would ever know because chemistry textbooks are repellently boring. Zero data input going on there.

Issue: Yates actually knew how to read a chemistry textbook. She was the singular smart Scapegracer and there could be more people like her out there. Observant people. Our tricks might not work on the likes of them, assuming the metaphor held.

We just needed this seedy motel to be staffed at this hour by people duller than Yates. The odds of that seemed good. Fingers crossed.

We set out. We brought very little with us and determined what few things we did bring we'd leave out in the car. We didn't wake Yates' precious little baby dog when we left, and her parents thought we were leaving to go pick up Boris, one of my fathers, from the airport. They thought it was extraneous and silly, if ultimately thoughtful, for all of us to pick him up together. We'd given them Boris' cell phone number in case they were curious, and they didn't ask additional questions.

On the off chance they really did call Dad, he'd play along like a champ so long as there was a good story in it for him later. I'd make up one on the way home.

I sat in the passenger's seat, a privilege rarely afforded me. We drove with the top up, but the windows down, and my newly Technicolor hair fluttered around my cheeks in a haze. It'd turned out well, I thought. The colors were antagonistically bold and bright, brindled where they mingled. Garish in a way that skewed masculine. A stoplight-red strand stuck to my chin.

Sycamore Gorge's pastel houses and scraggly lawns dissolved into forest. Forest was cut by the bone-husks of cornfields, low flat soybean expanses, wide machine-cut ditches filled with silk flowers and fast-food trash. Meaty turkey vultures flocked on telephone poles with such density that they looked like an evil eldritch cluster of grapes. Huge paint splashes on slanted barn roofs read BUY EGGS AND STRAWBERRIES or reported support of protofascist local politicians who hated women and farmers and factory workers. Broken-windowed double-wides shivered beside bright white bloated farmhouses. Then, a Gold Star. A Frisch's. Church, church, smaller church, shed everybody knows is a meth lab. A cat perched on a plastic mailbox licked a rodent's open ribs. Fast little rabbits. Occasional bent-up syringe. Herds of deer that sewed in and out of sight but mostly avoided the road. I looked too close and caught the tail of an unseasonably small one as it melted behind a skinny ash-bore-pocked tree, and I stupidly thought it looked like a specific deer, one I'd seen limp in a swimming pool and stretched over the hood of a car.

On somebody's lawn in lacquered plastic: RE-ELECT ELIAS CHANTRY AS SYCAMORE COUNTY SHERIFF FOR GOD COUNTRY AND OUR CHILDREN.

I covered my mouth with my wrist and mashed the terror down.

Jing turned the music down as we came close.

The motel cut itself right off the highway. Across the road was farmland, but around the motel itself there was just barren gray earth that sprawled featurelessly until trees gouged it up. Not even a bush before that. The asphalt was broken like a windshield in the middle and nearly ground to dust around the edges. Broken bottles lit up under Jing's headlights like eyes. Up on the building, which was pink where the paint was present, was a sign that read SEVEN VACANCIES. Two layers of rooms, probably twelve-some rooms total. The banister that supported the second-level walkway looked dubiously constructed and the shingles up above dribbled dingy lichen. There was a staple-pocked stairway that led up there. Only light on was downstairs.

"You ready?" Jing barely spoke above a whisper.

I nodded twice. I could barely feel my fingertips, car ride be thanked, but I had my sigil on my hand and the ones Yates and Daisy and Mr. Scratch made on a sticky note. I was ready as I was going to be.

"Let's go." Daisy slipped out of the car and prowled motelwards, and the three of us followed her up the wet crumble of drive, and I let myself feel hopeful.

THREE

FUCK BATES

The person behind the counter was watching a tiddy slasher on a huge, primordial-looking television box. They used to be so big. The nineties must've been something else. Stacks of foul-smelling VHS tapes had been stacked beside it, along with grimy crunched Styrofoam cups and crumpled up pages of the newspaper. The guy had a handlebar mustache and a flat-brimmed cap. His shirt, sleeves hacked free, was an American flag. He ate plain tortilla chips seasoned only by the dip pouch tucked against his bottom teeth, and when he looked up at us, he did not seem particularly thrown by our age, or the time, or the jackets. Maybe it was the sigils? On vibes alone, minus the flag, part of me wished I was him.

"Excuse me," said Jing. "We're looking for a school friend of ours. Her name is Madeline Kline. We were wondering—"

"Are you camgirls?"

Jing stopped. She blinked a few times. "Ask me again come January."

Daisy and I exchanged looks of nervous glee. Yates looked helplessly at the ceiling.

The guy wiggled his jaw back and forth. "Asking you now."

"No," said Jing. "We're not camgirls."

"You doing any other profitable sex stuff? Or drugs, are you here to sell or pack?" The guy crunched a chip. "I charge extra, and I don't care to get sued. Nobody's got that time."

"None of that," Jing assured him. "Just want to see her."

"We don't officially give out people's room numbers."

Daisy fished around in her wallet and withdrew a fresh hundred-dollar bill. She held it between her first and middle fingertips, like she was about to break a promise. The lavender security stripe glistened. She made real money feel girly.

"Huh." He thumbed a button on the ancient TV box and paused his show, rubbed the dimple in his chin, and pretended to flip through a sign-in book. Palimpsest handwriting flashed. Mr. Scratch coiled in the back of my head. "Didn't mention up front that you were her cosigners. You should do that next time. Save me the trouble. Room number six. It's on the balcony, all the way down. Don't got extra keys to give you, you'll have to deal with that on your own."

Daisy smoothed the bill on the countertop. I watched her knuckles move.

The guy snatched the dollar up and held it to the light, grunted to himself, and then it vanished. Gone. Like some kind of magician coin trick. He looked away from us and unpaused his tiddy slasher, and it was like we'd never existed. The killer adjusted his grip on his hatchet—the blood-speckled girl in a lilac bikini and elaborate eye makeup howled and retched—together they staggered through the woods. He crunched another chip. Eyes glazed over.

Why wasn't this my life?

Who needs college if this could be my life?

Maybe I'd have a future after all.

We stepped back out onto the curb, and I broke into the giggles that I'd barely managed to choke down that whole stretch. Jing clamped a hand over my mouth, but my diaphragm was busted. I was trembling all over, torn to the bone. I've always had a nervous laughter thing. Jing's rings dented my lower lip and I felt dizzy.

"Is it possible to get scabies without touching anything?" Yates rubbed her hands together and shivered. "That place wasn't evoking straight-As health code report card. Ick."

"If airborne scabies were a thing, we'd all be goners," Jing snorted. She released me, adjusted her high ponytail, and was suddenly all business. "Come on, camgirls. We've got a thief to catch."

Daisy mimed stabbing a ghost. Her eyes looked a little red, I thought. Funny. Didn't dwell. God, here it comes.

We made our way over to the stairs. The stairs looked— and upon putting my weight on the first step, *sounded*— deeply sketch. They heaved underfoot in a way stairs really shouldn't. Nothing should ever heave like that. This was a ghost of that same fear I'd felt at the Delacroix House, when I'd been so racked with paranoia and hope that I thought I'd fall down the spiral staircase and shatter my stupid gay head into stupid gay tesserae like a stupid gay Humpty Dumpty that I almost missed out on freeing Mr. Scratch. The steps bowed under my boots like arched backs. I squeezed splinters into the meat of my hands with how hard I choked either handrail, but while the steps squealed they didn't drop me, and I reached the top alive. My girls all lingered up there, the air taut and lively around their heads, electric. Jing mouthed something at me that I didn't catch. Her hair swished in a breeze that only existed for her. Yates kneaded her hands, Daisy bounced on her toes. I cracked my knuckles.

Sixth room was the last room.

Last room was Madeline.

Fuck. Here we go.

Down the hall, anticipatory magic crackling. Our sneakers made no sound. We clustered around her door in an arch. I slapped the sticky-note sigil on the door's handle, watched the paper twitch, expand, paste itself over the metal and *pulse*. I reached for Jing's hand to my right and Yates' to my left and clutched them. Clung to them. Yates grabbed Daisy's. Mr. Scratch dripped thick and cold down the ropes of my arms and oozed out from under my fingernails, wriggled in tendrils under theirs, linked us in a single current. I could see it hit them. Saw him squirm along their cuticles. All at once, I saw the whites of their eyes. Bottom lashes fluttering.

"Touch this and float 'til we set you back down." We spoke in unison six times on a rhythm; *bum*-ba-da *bum*-ba-da

bum-ba-da *bum*-ba-da *bum*-ba-da *bum*-ba-da *bum*-ba-da
bum-ba-da *bum*-ba-da *bum*-ba-da *bum*-ba-da *bum*-ba-da
bum-ba-da *bum*-ba-da *bum*-ba-da *bum*-ba-da *bum*-ba-da
bum-ba-da *bum*-ba-da *bum*-ba-da *bum*-ba-da *bum*-ba-da
bum-ba-da *bum*-ba-da *bum*-ba-da *bum*, and upon the sixth
evocation, the ink comprising the sigil wept to the sticky note's
surface, linework blacker than ballpoint, thicker, glossy with
inexplicable condensation. It dribbled off the knob, reversed
instantly upon hitting open air, oozed backwards into the
mark. I peeled my eyes as wide as I could, then I blinked, and
the sigil looked matte and dry and normal.

Mr. Scratch swam out of them and back into me.

We let go of each other. Daisy balled her hands into fists.
Yates rubbed her hands over her arms, whispered something
about feeling squirmy, like there were centipedes under her
sleeves. Jing cleared her throat. She scrunched up her sleeves,
scanned her arms like she was checking for Yates' phantom
bugs, and when she was convinced of their buglessness she
knocked on the door, and said: "Housekeeping."

The sigil I'd drawn on my hand, the one I'd drawn for
Madeline way back when, twinged. My jaw twinged, too. I
needed to stop clenching it. Palpitations, oh my fucking god.

The doorknob jimmied. After a moment, it swung
down, and the door opened ever so slowly. There was a
whoosh and a gasp. The door went motionless, barely ajar.

Whoever had touched the handle couldn't reach it
anymore.

My heartbeat boxed my ears. It was pounding, everything was pounding. The clouds pulsated in the sky. Heaven contorted. I seized the door handle and wrenched it back, tried to condense in my yanking all the energy required to grab Madeline Kline by the jaw and lift her off the floor and throw her past the moon. I could see it in my head. I could picture Madeline in my grip so vividly, could imagine the heat of my specter against my palms. Me in my hands.

The door swung open.

I gaped up at the body in midair before me.

It was a bony older white lady with big hair the color of banana peels. Her eyes were the size of baseballs, white and red like them, too, stitched through with lumpy, angry veins. She had on rubber gloves and an apron with skinny stripes. Her left hand, the one she presumably hadn't used to open the door, still strangled a bottle of ambiguous cleaning fluid. Her feet dangled limp at the ankles. She drifted a solid foot above the floor.

"Jesus Christ," Jing breathed. She seized Yates' hand and hissed, "We set you back down, we set you back down, *we set you back the fuck down.*"

The woman drifted gently to her feet. She dropped the cleaning fluid and shoved her palms against her temples, sucked in a breath. "Oh boy," she said. "Oh boy, oh baby Jesus. You've got to lay off the sauce, Cheryl."

We blinked at each other. We blinked up at her.

The woman, Cheryl, I guess, gathered herself. She blinked a few times. Bleary. "You four, what do you want? What do you think you're doing here?"

"Excuse me, miss. We wanted to play a joke on our friend. Her name is Madeline Kline." Daisy tried for a huge smile but used too many of her teeth and too much of the whites of her eyes and wound up looking utterly insane. She waved her fingers above her head. "About yea high, really leggy, has stringy black hair, kind of futch, dark eyebags. Is she here?"

"Not anymore. Took off at two in the morning," Cheryl said. She kept pressing at her face, kneading it, and the motion made her gloves make squeaky sounds.

Okay. Fuck.

She could've driven a crowbar through my guts, and I'd have felt the same. My throat pinched and I couldn't swallow all of a sudden. My chest hurt. My everything hurt. "The guy downstairs said—"

"Yeah, well, Pete's full of it." The woman turned away from us and wandered back inside the room, sat on the edge of the bed. I think she was trying to justify the whole floating thing. She was handling it better than I would've. "She's long gone."

My hope broke. The snapping drowned out what Jing and Yates said next, what they told the woman, what the woman told them in turn. It was so loud that it overwhelmed my other senses, and I couldn't feel my hands, I couldn't feel my feet as they turned, as they pounded across the walk and down the rotten stairs. I didn't feel the jarring in my knees when my boots struck smashed asphalt. I couldn't feel the wind that raked my cheeks and my bleach-tight scalp.

Long gone.

"Mr. Scratch," I spat. I was searching for something in the empty parking lot. Something midsize and damageable. I needed to ruin something immediately. "Do you think she feels what I feel? Do you think she has to suffer through my mood swings as much as I suffer through hers? If I scream, is it gonna tear her throat up, Mr. Scratch? Can I do that? Could I do that to her?"

Don't try. He poured around my head, pushed up my nose and my ears and my tear ducts. *Don't damage yourself in hopes of giving her a reflection of your hurt. Please?*

There was a tin trash can on its side. Empty, aside from a few glass bottles whose necks poked through its mouth. Midsize and damageable. Wouldn't you look at that.

I took a step, but ink sloshed from my head and whirlpooled between my shoulder blades like a spiral of syrup and tar and snot. There was something so weird about the feeling that I couldn't make myself step forward. This was disgusting, disarming. Distracting. He'd never done this before, not this insistently. It felt like someone had tipped guppies down the back of my shirt.

"What gives?" I slapped my back, but that did nothing besides ripple the writhing devil gelatin under my skin. Can't shake off something under your skin, now can you?

Please don't.

I opened my mouth to retort, but there were hands on my back all of a sudden. External, human hands. Lots of them.

"Sideways, listen." One set of hands spun me around. My hair went everywhere, purple and gray flipped in my eyes. I shook them aside and spat stray strands out of my mouth and there was Jing. I was in Jing's grip. She had me tight with her thumbs vised just above my elbows. "I'm sorry. I'm sorry we dragged you out here and it was a bust, but we're going to find her, alright? You've got my word. Look, she left something in the room. Does this mean anything to you?"

It was a necklace. Silvery letters hanging from a curb chain as thick as my pinky that spelled out A-D-D-I-E.

"No," I said. I took it out of her hand and put it in my pocket anyway.

"What do you want to do right now? Where do you want to go?"

Nowhere. I wanted to combust. "Home."

"We'll drive you home, then. Get some sleep. We're going to catch her, you hear me? You've got my word."

"You've said that." Harsher than I intended, but I didn't have the mental bandwidth to try at sounding any different. It took focus not to fly out of my skin right now. Snapping was the kindest I could do. I was reverting. None of my friends deserved this. Even with all Jing's toughness, I saw it hit her, saw her eye twitch, her bottom lip tense. A steeliness came over her. I breathed in slow through my nose, and said, "Just take me home, okay?"

Jing didn't say anything. She released me, turned away from me, went to start her car.

It was still dark. Wouldn't be light for another hour and a half.

"Let's get you home," said Yates. She stroked my hair, pulled different colors of curl together and twisted them. "Come on, honey."

I didn't say anything. I didn't believe in hell, because I didn't believe in anything that was said on billboards as a rule, but I did think that being mean to Yates was a supernaturally punishable offense. Kept my molars meshed together. Let her lead me toward Jing's car.

Daisy had already occupied the front seat. She was smiling for some reason.

I sat in the back with Yates, shut my eyes, and seethed 'til we got home.

A little sliver of mercy: I didn't dissociate once the whole entire ride.

✳

"Lamby," Julian said. He sat on the foot of my bed. He was like an owl in tweed, my dad—all big eyes and hooked nose and soft, downy gawkiness. He had been coming upstairs every two hours or so, checking my forehead, refilling the glass of water beside my bed. I was glad we stayed open on Sundays. If the shop closed, he wouldn't have left at all without stubbornness beyond my current faculties. "Are you sure you can't tell me why you're glum?"

"I'm not," I lied.

"Oh, dear." He took off his glasses and rubbed his nose. "Okay. Well, I want us to work on your common app tonight. The plan is sending it to three schools, right?"

The thought made my chest feel gluey and my throat clapped like I'd swallowed cough medicine. That weird grape flavor always makes my gag reflex flip. It was flipping now. I shrugged and hoped it'd stave off further provocations.

"Please? We just have to do one tonight."

He looked sad.

I hated that.

"Sure, whatever," I said. "Can I get some rest?"

"Okay," he said again. He kissed my forehead and drew himself up. He misbuttoned his blazer. "I like your hair like this, by the way. It's very festive. Boris will be duly impressed."

"Thanks." I wanted to cry for some reason. Wanting to cry made me want to become completely boneless and maybe corrosive. Be a sludge monster for a while. An angry Technicolor sludge monster who still loves her dad a lot even though everything else makes her want to eviscerate the earth itself. Apocalypse right now this very moment please. Come on, meteor.

He nodded a few dozen times and swept out of my room, leaving the door open behind him. I heard him walk down the stairs. A few steps down, I heard an *ah!*

Must've noticed the buttons on his jacket, then.

I got back to work. After my four-hour depression nap, I was determined to find a way to find Madeline, some way we hadn't thought of yet. There had to be one.

I dragged both of the *Vade Mecvm Magici* out of my closet where they'd been sent in exile for having betrayed me and ripped out my heart in October and heaved them onto my bed. I hadn't looked at them much since the later volumes rejected me. Call me bitter. I opened both and riffled through the pages, searched for tracking spells, scrying spells we hadn't tried yet, predictive spells, anything.

Mr. Scratch kept making little *hmph* sounds. If I had to hazard a guess, he wasn't exactly cool with other spell books. I did my best not to think about him trapped in an urn a few aisles down from the *Vade Mecvm* book set. Did they, like . . . talk?

He slunk behind my occipital bone, and it felt like impossible phlegm dislodgement.

"Yeah, yeah, I know," I breathed. "But I've got to try it, alright? Ease up."

Second volume, toward the beginning. There was a bit of history there that struck my eye. I leaned down so close that my nose nearly touched the page. It was the bit about Abner Grier torturing his little sister in 1472. The story of the first real witchfinder, Chantry family ground zero and all that. I'd read it before, but I pored over it now.

Abner fucking Grier.

Reading about this made my sternum prickle. I made myself skip the details about how he found her and was an unforgivable and heinous asshole to her, et cetera, et cetera, skimmed over Grier gathering up his protestant bros and herding them into the church where he had his naked sister chained up like some sort of terrible Hammer horror flick made real and much, much worse. The information I wanted came after that—it was what he had supposedly tortured out of her that I was interested in. The spells whose contents she'd narked.

So said the book, *Fortune supposedly taught them two spells during her confession. First, she taught them how to make a spectral mimic, and second, she taught them how to extract and destroy a witch's specter. After she taught them the second, they enacted said spell upon her. She died within the hour.*

This was the genesis of several witchfinding families, many of which are still active today. They're predominantly in the Western world, particularly in England, where Grier's village was, and America, where many of them migrated in hopes of breeding witchless colonies. Their success has largely been hinging on their use of minor magics, most of which they steal from their victims via confession. In the winter of 1892, New York, they discovered a sizable coven in Manhattan. It was a massacre. Not a single witch survived. The deaths were listed as having been a result of smoke inhalation, as the coven's mansion was burned to the ground. Whatever the witch hunters stole from the Manhattan coven, it made them massively successful. We stopped being able to scry for them. They became magically invisible, and this has led to countless deaths, more than we could ever know. They can find witches before we do. They destroy witches before those witches even know who they are.

Yadda, yadda. So, scry-proofing and mimic making. If the Pythoness Society couldn't scry for witchfinding assholes after they do whatever it is they do, I couldn't imagine that I'd have better luck on my own. Just confirmed what I already knew. That stung, but not for long; my wheels were turning. *Mimics.* I'd forgotten about mimics. I recalled standing at Jing's poolside, bloody and shaken, compelled by unseen forces to walk directly into the Chantry boys' clutches. I remembered all of them standing around in blazers with their baby-blond hair and their baby-blue eyes, looking like overgrown Victorian ghost orphans. I remembered them. I remember.

"Scratch," I whispered. "How the fuck do you make a mimic? We could make a mimic and then we'd have her, right?"

He was silent. He wasn't even squirming. Couldn't pinpoint where in my body he was currently lurking, as a matter of fact.

"Mr. Scratch?" I screwed my brows together. "Are you listening?"

Absolutely not. His voice cracked over me like a pitcher of water. Gooseflesh everywhere. *You will absolutely not be making a mimic. It'd just reflect my magic, you fool. Don't you dare suggest I teach you witchfinding methods. Don't you dare.*

"Hey," I said. I shoved the book away from me and sat upright, tossed my hands over the back of my neck, prodded at the thrashing glob from whence that voice was coming. As though poking him would calm him down. "Hey now. What's wrong?"

He slopped down past my nape, thinned, and jutted outwards, shot down through the pulp of my arms and my hands and crammed in my fingertips so thickly that I could *see* him bunch up under my skin, slug-sized and purplish and viscous. Second-day-clot type shit. He tugged my fingertips downward. I followed his motion, put him and my fingers on the outstretched page.

A daub of him bled onto the parchment.

The *Vade Mecvm Magici* devil—who existed, I realized with a start, and must've been some level of sentient the whole time I'd had the book—leaped back when he approached. The words undulated over the parchment, letters distorting, flowing together. Mr. Scratch eddied around the other devil, his ink shade darker and glossier than the stuff originally on the page, and I blinked, tried to keep the motion straight in my head. Were they arguing? Fighting?

Whatever it was resolved quickly.

The paragraphs became legible as such again. One of

them rearranged itself—rewrote itself. Clauses melted. Letters drew themselves into being.

In the winter of 1892, New York, witchfinders ambushed the illustrious Honeyeaters coven in their performance hall in Manhattan. Witchfinders pillaged, then burned the Honeyeater theater. Sixty witches were murdered. Those Honeyeaters who escaped the flames were captured and tortured until they gave forth spells, then were stripped of their specters and turned into the cold, all dying soon thereafter. Witchfinders have been impossible to catch ever since.

I opened my mouth and shut it.

Please close the book, Mr. Scratch said. He recoiled from the *Vade Mecvm* and retreated up the backs of my hands, sounding *exhausted,* if he could be such a thing. *Go downstairs. Your fathers have been calling. It's time for you to eat.*

✳

Instead of Madeline's trauma or mine that night, I dreamed about my bookshelf wearing fire. I dreamed I lived inside of it like some kind of organ, like a bookspleen or something stupid like that. I dreamed about fire licking between my pages and melting my banded spine and giving off electric colors, sparkling white and blue. I dreamed about embers made of me raining down on my bed like fireworks and the books around me spasming, shrieking, squealing like dogs on a too-tight line. All of us undone together. Our leather charring. My ceiling warping above me. My guts and all my poetry sizzling to dust.

Mr. Scratch must've soaked the grooves of my brain with his ink tonight. I don't think he meant to do it. I watched his horror ripple back and forth and I recalled briefly the feeling of the footage of that train blowing my mother's car to fucking smithereens, that kind of compulsive documentarian attention to irreversible violence. Awful. Sticky. I felt phantom fingertips pried off my—his—stomach—cover—and at once I was naked of hands. My shoulders were thrust backwards into the fire. Books don't have nerves in the octopus sense people do, but they've got every word we've given them about how pain works, and where my mind was my body, Mr. Scratch's body was his mind. His mind went up like s'mores. All those syllables liquefying, boiling into foamy slosh unhoused of his unifying structure. Pulpy pages scorched to nothing without muscle to resist. He couldn't crawl off the fire. He couldn't move. No control. He had, we had, no mouth to enunciate our agonies, our vitriol, his magic, his daughters' names— and annunciation was our only talent. Holding and giving language was all we had, and we did not have it. His daughters were dead. He couldn't do a damn thing about it.

Then the air stilled, and the smoke turned back to vapor.

It was quiet. The coals went cold and gritty.

We just laid there. We couldn't do anything else.

At some point, he swallowed grit. Or it contaminated him, polluted my wounds by contact. His wounds. Our wounds. Whatever, we were a wound that could not scar and a mouth without a stomach and however we particularly conceptualized our destroyed lack of body and its method of taking in debris didn't matter. The point is, we had no edges. We absorbed the tools of our destruction and the dirt and floating flecks of dead skin. We barely existed, but our metabolism stayed, and we never once slept. We became inextricable from the scene of the crime. We stayed alert. We waited.

We waited for a very long time.

Somebody else's daughters found us. They sifted us from the rubble and scraped us into an urn and put the urn in an attic. They grieved us abstractly, but they didn't recognize us for what we were, because we looked different after the violence. Fundamentally, we were. We were a substance, not an object, and we were mad. We were not the first instance of a magic clot rewilded. They were afraid of what we might do. They feared any and all reminders that the violence occurred in the first place. They feared the fact that with all their pretty magic they still couldn't stop violence of this or any kind. It could've been their witch-siblings, their lovers, their peers with their organs out. It could even have been them! It could have been them so easily. Dumb fucking luck that it'd been the Honeyeaters instead. They locked us away alive, awake, limbless inside a funerary shell.

Then we stayed in blue darkness for decades.

And then you, said Mr. Scratch when he noticed. He said it in a funny way. He was embarrassed, I think, that I'd been seeing all of this.

I sat up in bed and tried to decide where to look. It was weird, trying to find a spot for my eyes when I was talking to somebody I couldn't see. Something? Whatever. I looked at my bookcase but that felt weird, so I looked in the mirror instead. My new hair made me look like a parrot. "I'm sorry," I said. It tasted inadequate. "I'm really fucking sorry."

Mr. Scratch didn't say anything, but I felt him ripple. Recollection, more pain, stuff I shouldn't be privy to, but we had no privacy from one another, and his pain was mine. I felt a flash of something I didn't understand. Felt a memory of some prior place, the edgeless flowering every-colored whirlpool of jellied darkness and ultimate sound that fluxes forever through itself, the stuff that was not awake but was alive in a way older than life and dreamed in every language. The movement that was potential, that ossified into power, that flowed into magic. That would be coaxed into matter and kneaded into watchfulness, taught to recognize a name. The stuff before Scratch. The stuff that was all books that have been and will be. I felt him recall being that stuff, felt myself writhe in its afterimage. He would never return to that place. He could never be possibility itself again. He was individuated, angry, vigilant. He *was*. He loved and he could not be killed. Witchcraft had brought him here and he would stay here until the oceans turned to glass.

I blinked. Dizzy. I rubbed my nose and the memory was already indistinct. I was mortal and normal again. I cleared my throat. My voice was slime. "Would you have picked me if I hadn't fucked up your vase?"

You're the right kind of person for a burned book, Sideways.

Sideways in the mirror looked splotch-faced. Fuck. I hadn't noticed. I scrubbed my eyes with the sleeves of the hoodie I'd slept in, and the fabric came away salt-wet. I shoved my knees up against my chest. "I'm glad I knocked you over."

As am I.

"Mr. Scratch," I said. My throat felt funny. "Are you a boy?"

Sideways, my gruntling, I am a glob. My last daughters thought I sounded like a fop, though. Therefore, Mr. Scratch.

Despite myself, I snickered. It made a rattling sound in my chest. My lungs were like maracas. I curled my toes in the fold of a flannel blanket and said, "Do you want us to call you something else?"

A sweet question, but no. Mr. Scratch will do. I've grown fond of it. Do keep calling me mister.

I picked a scab on my shin, which instantly rescabbed with a gross, inky crust. Mr. Scratch wasn't into me bleeding. I did not deserve him—I would work to deserve him. To take care of him like he took care of me.

Did you know that it's 6:30? You've got to be getting dressed. You've got to go to school.

Wait.

No.

Mr. Scratch made a noise I've heard from devious cats. He slithered down my spine and splashed along the citrus-pulp-y tendons of my arms, and in one luxurious motion, hurled me by the elbows over the edge of the bed.

The world did a cartwheel.

My chin slammed into the cup of a Takis-dust-encrusted bra. Wrists, knees, then heaving stomach, I hoisted myself upright and braced an arm around my bedpost. My clothes swam around my feet. Like fish. I wasn't sure which articles of debris were clean and which weren't. My room was a nuclear wasteland.

Wear something interesting! I want to look interesting.

I mashed my forehead against a mostly flat portion of wall. "I don't recall asking you your opinion about what I should wear."

We were bonding. Why are you being grumpy? You are speaking with a grumpy tone of voice. Stop it.

"I am so not being grumpy." I toed a mysteriously damp T-shirt. "I think cool lesbians wear Hawaiian shirts now."

You have none of those. Are you not a cool lesbian?

"Chill." I cleared my throat and then yawned, as loud as I could manage, the name Boris.

There was a thump, then a shudder. My door heaved in a motion that would've been dramatic if it hadn't been for all of the clothes in the way. Around the lip came a nose and a slick of dark hair. Boris manifest. "Are you dying?" His eyes flashed like beetle shells. They were lined with an allergic pink. Definitely not awake yet.

"Do you have a Hawaiian shirt?"

He wiped a hand over his mouth. "Are you serious? God, no. No. Why would you ask me something like that?"

"The cool lesbians are wearing them."

"You're already a cool lesbian. Nice hair, by the by."

I told you so.

"Dad." The jeans I stood upon felt weird. Clammy underfoot. Eely between my toes. "Come on."

Boris waved a ring-spangled hand (perhaps he'd slept in them?) and staggered away from my bedroom, not shutting the door behind. He trudged down the hall, slipped into the darkness of his room, and emerged again after a moment of clattering with something slung over his shoulder. When he reached me, he pulled it off and rolled it like a towel and flicked me with its edge accordingly.

I snatched it from the air, coughed a smile, and shook it out. Black graphic tee.

"Broke my nose at this concert before you were born. There's a little stain on it still for proof. Never suggest I own barbecue-dad shit again, yeah? I'm going back to bed." He turned on his heel.

"Thank you," I hollered after him.

He waved a hand then slipped back into the dark.

I pulled off the hoodie and on Boris' shirt, then hooked

my arms through my Scapegracers jacket with a shiver. "I'm going to get you a new book, Mr. Scratch." One pant leg, then the other. Felt chill on the back of my knees. "When I have my specter back, I'm going to get you the coolest fucking book in the whole wide world. You will no longer be an unshelled hermit crab."

Thank you. I appreciate you. I know and trust you will.

"You know what? You know fucking what, Mr. Scratch? You're going to have your pick of books. I'm gonna take you to a damn stationery shop and you can pick your favorite and I'll get whatever you want, savings be damned." I shoved my hands into my jacket pockets and froze. The fingertips on my left hand brushed something hard and cold. I wrapped my fist around the something and pulled it out, rolled it around on my palm.

Madeline's necklace. A-D-D-I-E. Only Levi Chantry called her that.

She's been thinking about him, then. Didn't she want revenge? Isn't that why she has your soul in her mouth in the first place?

I thought about the woods she'd been carving up. Woods like the ones outside of the Chantry house.

"Tell me this is a stupid idea," I said.

And why would I tell you that?

✳ F O U R ✳

OVER THE MEADOW AND THROUGH THE WOODS

"Ladies." I slapped both hands on the lunch table so hard that Daisy's pudding rippled. "I've got an idea of how we're going to get my specter back."

Jing and Yates looked up from their respective lunches with interest. Partly, that might have been because they had both bought the square pizza today only to discover that it remained unthawed in the center. Visible ice crystals. Even so, they put their eyes on me, and not in a *shut up and sit down, Sideways, you absolute buffoon* kind of way. I perched on the bench's edge, head buzzing, and did not shut up. I'd not paid attention to a single stitch of the information I was given in class today and absolutely did not try my best on the history test I had taken—but trying to make myself remember absolutely anything about the the revisionist history of the US government's genocidal foundations with thoughts of getting my soul back sizzling around my brain was impossible. I had to out this stuff. If I didn't, I'd explode into a cloud of dust.

"Sideways," said Alexis, who was sitting on the other side of Daisy. I hadn't noticed her, because I am the most bullheaded person alive, but it suddenly occurred to me that Alexis and two other girls, Monique and Sheridan, were crowded around the end of our lunch table. Alexis wore a screaming fuchsia sweatshirt with a rhinestoned cherub riding a leopard emblazoned across the chest. She squeezed her hands together. Looked at me with her eyes alight. "I just wanted to say thanks. I mean, to all of you, but you're witch prime. Scapegracers coven stuff is because of what you did for Yates, right?"

It dawned on me. Chetting Travis. I'd nearly forgotten in the commotion of everything else. "Yeah, no problem," I said. I awkwardly sat myself down. It'd been all of us—all four of us made the Chett hex, and I shouldn't take all the credit, and I chewed on an explanation uselessly before I gave up and said, "Anytime."

"Do you know Mo and Sheridan?"

I looked between them. Monique had an enormous, glittered cheer bow perched atop her blond box-braid ponytail and Sheridan wore earrings shaped like razor blades. Cute strangers. Like, I knew them in an abstract way but could initially cite zero facts about them. I tried to deduce fast. Obviously, they were in the faction of people who thought that Jing and Daisy and Yates were still cool, if not cooler, after the three of them took prominence as magic-doers in the school consciousness. If they weren't, they wouldn't be here. I think they went to the big scare party in October, the one where it happened. Might have been at the scare party Jing threw earlier that month, too. I recalled the image of them dancing together and sharing a Solo cup that they'd filled with gummy worms and triple sec. Biographical details evaded me, though. Monique maybe worked at the animal shelter?

"You took a huge weight off my back, dealing with Travis. Monique and Sheridan are good friends of mine. They'd be in good hands if you helped them." Alexis chewed on the edge of a lime-green nail. "I want them to feel safe."

Details finally clicked in my head about them. I cleared my throat, pulled my hair out of my eyes and fisted the curly knot in place at the base of my skull. "Right. Of course. I think we were in Health together last year, no?"

We'd all burned our purity pledges together behind the locker rooms. Made s'mores.

"Yeah," said Sheridan, nodding fervently. It made her little razor blades look like, were they not cast acrylic, they might slice off the pigtails at either side of her jaw. "Do you take on hex requests that aren't just boyfriends?"

"Uh." I blinked a few times and glanced at Yates and Jing and Daisy, all of whom nodded ever so slightly like, *Yeah, go on.* "I don't see why not. What's up? Are you okay?"

"My dad is a prick, and I . . ." Sheridan opened her mouth and shut it. She reached for something under the table. I realized, with a start, that she had taken Monique's hand. "We don't want him dead or anything. But you know. Getting him to stop screaming at us would be nice."

Fuck. Okay.

"It would have to be long distance. No way we'd get away with cornering him, not like we do with teenagers. But that's fine, we've done distance hexing before. We only have to see him for the actual casting, and that will only take a second, just long enough for me to point and name him." That's how it worked when we finally Chett-hexed Levi at that party, anyway. Mr. Scratch was living magic concentrate and he had better range than we did. Could Nerf scumbags at twenty paces back. "Look, text me exactly what you want it to do, and I'll work on it. Do you have my number?"

Both of them shook their heads like, *No, obviously not.*

I pulled out my phone, opened a new contact and handed it to the girl who sat nearest. Weird that this was my life now. "I'll text you."

While Sheridan thumbed away, Monique leaned a little closer. "Can you not spread this around? We're not telling people about us, you know, not until college."

"No problem." Monique was the other flyer on the varsity cheer team, if memory served. Were she and Daisy close? Maybe they should be.

"Thank you," Monique said. She stood up, and Sheridan stood with her.

"Anytime," Daisy said. "Pro bono."

Pro homo, I mentally emended. When had we ever charged anybody for this, anyway?

"This means the world to me, I won't forget it," Sheridan said. She cleared her throat. "Also. Sorry for telling everybody you kept a dead squirrel in your locker in eighth grade, Sideways, and for telling everybody that you literally worshiped Britney Spears with candles and Latin chants and everything. That wasn't cool of me to do."

"Yeah," said Monique. "I'm sorry about that, too, and for putting a lollipop in your hair on that field trip in middle school. It was fucked up and super not okay."

So that's where those rumors came from. Genuinely couldn't remember the lollipop. Repression!

They left before I could say something like *Don't worry about it.* I stared in their hazy sapphic wake and felt shapes of feelings that I could not parse at all. My brain was a blue-raspberry slushie. It was a slushie that somebody, me, was pouring on the floor.

"So," said Yates. "Your specter. What's the new plan?"

"Oh fuck, yeah." I took a breath, withdrew, and opened my lunch thermos. I plunged a spoon down into its darkness and popped whatever I'd scooped between my teeth without inspection. Chewy. Savory. Gnocchi? Julian had been on an Italian kick lately. "We scope out the Chantry house. She was carrying around a necklace Levi must've given her. He was her ex—he maimed her like she maimed me, and she wants revenge on him, so that's where she'll be headed. At least, there's gotta be a lead inside. We could go through Levi's shit. It's the best we got. I say we all go and—"

"You're shitting me," Jing said.

"I'm not!" I looked between the three of them, searched for even a lick of validation on their faces. "I think it's a good idea. It's better than anything else we've come up with lately."

"The Chantrys are witchfinders. Not to mention literal cops." Jing crossed her arms over her chest. "There's no way that'd go well, babe. Not a single fucking way."

"Mr. Scratch thinks it's a good idea!"

"He's also kind of the devil," Yates said quietly.

"He's keeping me alive," I spat back, suddenly irretrievably and disproportionately pissed. I kept getting louder, I knew that, but I couldn't make myself stop. Inhabitants of other tables were glancing over. The eyes made me bristle. "You've been using his magic, so clearly you can't mind that much. We need him and he's right. They've hurt him as much as us, more so, and he says we ought to go stake them out! It's a good idea. I trust him. Can't you just fucking trust me?"

"Shut up." Daisy raised her spoon. There was a look on her face that I didn't have the patience to understand—it was sharp, mean, but not mean at me. I don't fucking know. She tossed back her head and sneered and pieced out, "We are *not* going to the Chantry house. As much as I'd love torching the place, sneaking into the sheriff's house when he wants nothing more than to rip our magic organs out and play Ping-Pong with them is stupid. You're being stupid."

"Don't tell me to shut up."

"Sideways. Daisy. Chill the fuck out." Jing crossed her arms. "Yates, are you okay?"

Yates sniffed and shrugged and examined her nails.

Jing turned to me. She inclined her head. "Look, we just

took on a new hex request. We're responsible for these girls now. Let's take care of them, and then we recalibrate, come up with something that won't get you hurt. Daisy is right. I would love for everybody in that family to choke, but setting aside the fact that they are literally The Man, their whole shtick is eviscerating our brand of girl. They're experts at being evil. If we get caught snooping, all of us might be in your situation, and there won't be enough friendly devil to go around. And like, stand your ground laws. Think about it."

"I can't believe this." I wanted to crush the table like a shitty foam lunch tray. I shoved my hands over my mouth and said, as quietly as I could, "Why don't they believe us?"

Fear makes for caution. A very justified caution at that.

"I need this." Wasn't like I wasn't afraid! For fuck's sake, I still get antsy in cars sometimes, and that's after we successfully hexed Levi Chantry beyond being a threat and tripled down on protective stalk-not charms against the Chantrys. I pressed down harder against my lips. It was hard to breathe with my sleeve over my mouth. My lungs just weren't working right. I was scared, but this was my specter. What happened to anything? "We need this."

And we shall have it. Perhaps it's a matter best pursued alone for now, Sideways. It is your specter, after all. Your choice.

Alone. That'd mean I wouldn't have to worry about the Chantry family nabbing my friends, at least. I'd escaped their place once. I could probably do it again. So what if it re-upped my itchiness with woods and cars and Radiohead? Besides, if they caught me, it's not like they could take out my soul again.

I chose not to dwell on the jail possibility.

I slouched a little, made myself eat a few gnocchi.

Everybody was quiet for a moment.

After a beat, Yates reached across the table and brushed her fingertips over mine. "I had to write a few poems for class," she said. "Would you mind skimming them before next period?"

I nodded and Jing and Daisy both sank in their seats. They went back to eating (or picking) at the disgusting frigid limp cheese on even colder more disgusting soggy bread, and we went on in mostly unbroken silence, Yates' poetic quandaries aside. I ate my gnocchi. I complimented Yates' poetry, which was, as one would expect, meticulously metered and jarringly adorable.

Have you done all your homework?

"What's it to you?" I said it under my breath, and while I'm sure that Jing and Daisy heard me, they were good enough to mostly ignore it. Daisy still made a face down at her cold pizza. Brows up, eyes stretched, mouth in a tight little line. She'd painted little hearts at the far edges of her eyes, today. She looked like a doll come to life.

Homework completion matters for next year, doesn't it? That is also important.

A laugh cut through me, one dry, punctuated *ha*. Next year. "Who are you, Julian?"

You didn't do any of it last week. Take it out, please? Just let me see it.

Nothing was worse than fighting the magic voice in your head. I groaned, but I shoved my hand in my bag obediently, clawed around then slapped my crinkled homework on the table and half-heartedly rubbed it flat. I'd written nothing on the worksheet apart from my name. Not even Eloise Pike, either. Just a jaggedy, kid's-fist-shaky SIDE-WAYS. "Happy?"

A stringy glob of him oozed from my nail and injected itself into my homework. The swirl of ink wrapped its liquidy limbs around the letters of my name and dismantled them, and quickly, with spidery scurrying motions, took my broken name and shaped sentences with it across the page. My handwriting. Raggedy, pointy at the edges, completely inconsistent in terms of size and spacing. I watched with horror and a surge of admiration that made my throat tight.

It isn't perfect, mind you. I'm rambling. I don't know anything about this. You've got too much to worry about without a failing grade, though, Sideways.

"Thanks." I sucked the edge of my sleeve. The fabric had a weird texture when I pulled it between the gap in my teeth. Hypnotically scratchy, like sawdust breakfast cereal. "I owe you one."

"Damn," said Jing. She leaned forward, the edges of her hair brushing her shitty misery pizza. "Can he do mine next?"

✳

Night fell.

I planned for once. I packed. Backpack, complete with flashlight, matches, switchblade, notebook, chalk, candles,

ADDIE necklace, and bag of Julian's homemade pretzels-cranberries-hazelnuts-white chocolate trail mix. Shoes, re-marked with the sneaking sigil that Yates and Daisy'd made for the motel. Black hoodie under my leather jacket, just for sake of being less conspicuous than the Scapegracers red at night. Phone at full battery. Devil well-rested. I had a helmet that I'd found in a closet to go with the bike I'd stolen from the Chantry boys in October, which miracu-lously hadn't since been stolen by anybody else since.

It was 2:00 a.m. Julian was asleep, but Boris had his ringer on, knew so much as to be vaguely aware that he might receive an SOS text with rescue details. It meant he could hop in his car and save me.

Doubted he'd have the need.

I climbed down the stairs that divided our apartment from the shop. Rothschild & Pike looked like a fairytale museum at night, all leather-gloved statuary and eldritch curios and jewel-ried taxidermy. I slipped between racks, ducked under low-hanging chandelier crystal points, dodged the outstretched hands of dummies in corsets and broad, feathered hats. Adjusted my backpack straps. Pulled my hood down over my Technicolor curls. I opened the shop door, stiffened against the gust of wind it breathed out, and locked it shut behind me.

Clear night, crisp night. The black-aspic sky looked stuffed with extra stars. My bike leaned against an empty flowerbox, and I pulled it upright with a metallic squeak. I rolled it onto the road. The street was abandoned at this hour, without any non-vacant cars. Raccoons feasted on trash across the way and didn't scatter when I got close. Loved those little bastards.

I'd googled Elias Chantry and his home phone number (which I'd added as a contact in my phone for record-keeping's sake), and the address took all of five minutes to find. He held receptions there sometimes, apparently. Wild what was online these days, huh? Digital white pages were just mercilessly doxing everybody.

The map beamed on my screen, but I didn't think I'd need it, not when push came to shove. I might not have remembered the path I'd taken when I fled the Chantry house back in October, but it felt all too familiar now. It'd stick in my head for the rest of my fucking life in an ugly singed impression that spanned my whole entire parietal bone. Just a few turns. Nothing tricky.

A laugh creaked out of me. I clapped one hand over my mouth and mashed it down. Was this stupid? Was Daisy right? I didn't know. I did know that Jing was *always* right. I'd barely gotten out of this place the last time I'd gone. It was hubristic, going back willingly. It was foolishness. I was a fucking clown.

Focus, little one. Climb on your bike with your big clown shoes. Breathe.

I got on. I pulled air in through my incisors. It whistled in the gap.

Focus.

"Aren't you scared for me? Didn't these people kill your old kids?"

I'm always scared. They won't kill you, I wouldn't have it. Now go.

I kicked off, cranked the pedals around a few times until momentum caught us. I rode in the middle of the street, tires on the dashed line, in the heart of the harsh yellow streetlamp spill. The buildings around me, posh little businesses and shifty lawyer's offices and dentists and cavernous rooms left vacant by rocketing rent, melted into little pastel houses that became progressively dingier the farther I biked.

Only a few lights on. Two of them flipped off as I went by. Somebody slept on the couch on their porch and the bottle in their slack hand winked at me as I passed. A tire swing on the left spun unattended. Rotten leaves looked like tar in the dark. The trees held stock-still, and as the residential chunks of town broke into expanses of ruddy fields and brittle half-dead crops, there wasn't a hint of parallel movement. The world was motionless. No bugs, it was too late in the year for any of those to be alive. No birds I could hear, or baying dogs. No distant moaning cattle.

It was like time had been switched off.

Then came the woods.

All this weird prelude suddenly made sense. The ground immediately surrounding the Chantry property was devoid of life. They were a hunting family. They shot the things that moved, dragged them home, beheaded and dried and bleached them. Made them into extravagant wall art. The trees felt petrified, long dead. No undergrowth. Nothing scurrying in the dark.

I had been living in Sycamore Gorge for a long time. Since my miraculous adoption, there were only a few periods of my life when I'd been out of it, and those had been brief, no matter how long they'd felt at the time. At no point of time, and in no region of space, had I ever felt so overwhelmingly inhuman as I did when I got nearer to the Chantry family mansion. I didn't feel like a witch with power all my own, off to reclaim the stolen chunk of my body. I didn't feel like the shitty little public menace who leers at people from alleyways and gets in tussles behind corner stores. I didn't feel like a stupid kid. I felt like a deer with a nice rack of antlers.

I turned down the driveway and tried to remember how to swallow.

The dirt broke under my tires, ground to gravel. It jittered my teeth around inside my head. My hoodie felt paper-thin all of a sudden, my leather jacket insubstantial, and for the first time all month, I saw my breath thicken around my face like a rain cloud. The air cut at the back of my throat. It wasn't clean. It had a hard edge going down, like soot or cheap, bad whiskey.

Oh, how I hate the witchfinders, Mr. Scratch said. It was like an incantation. Like prayer. He chanted it over and over again in my skull, quiet but persistent. *Oh, how I hate the witchfinders. Oh, how I hate the witchfinders.*

"Is that iambic?" I curled my lip, which was the closest facsimile I could conjure to smiling. If I actually smiled, I'd fall apart into giddy laughter, crash, and kill us.

The road wound around like a river. Wide curves. Erratic. It didn't make any sense, seeing as the road didn't pull off into different driveways or anything. It wasn't conforming to the natural shapes of the landscape's ridges and hills. It just snaked around for the hell of it, and I had to keep my eyes focused dead ahead just to keep myself on the road. It seemed to get narrower. The gravel got sandier. The lack of animal life, as convincing as my theory was, seemed plausibly false all of a sudden. I couldn't hear coyotes. That didn't mean there weren't coyotes. They didn't have coyote trophies, after all. Coyotes wouldn't attack a person, but the ones in these parts had been known to maul dogs and goats from time to time. Was I really all that different from a goat? I felt like I could be mistaken for a goat.

The Chantry boys would maul me first.

All but Levi. He was probably still clawing at the stripe on his neck our Chett hex left him, horrified by his own inability to hate women without overwhelming physical pain. That was one down out of four. Three against one. Could I take them? If there wasn't magic foul play or like, guns on their end, totally yes. I bench whatever the oldest Chantry is. I could break their faces. I get rough.

Focus! Focus!

I rounded another corner, eyes peeled wide.

It was like the universe cracked a lamp over my head. All the colors went bright, then white-hot, then rushed me. The lines that comprised everything, every tree shape and road shape and flash of horizon line, became razors that flew at my eyes. The trees lunged for my neck and shoulders, their leafless fingers stabbed down toward my scalp. My focus tore. My body throbbed hard, not from normal spell casting or the awful luring drain of a mimic, but something else, something different and lugging and familiar. The world was too crisp. I took in too many details; I could see every blade of grass and every bristle on the veiny poison oak, every suede fold in the tree bark around me, every nodule of broken twiglets and each bloody amber drip of sap. I gagged on a sweet smell. There was a whirring in my guts. Gashes. I was seeing gashes in the trees all around me. Fresh, heavy gashes whittled like how you'd deface a park bench with a penknife when you loved somebody very much. The gashes shaped sigils. A metric fuckton of sigils, all excruciatingly graphic and jammed against my brain. Sigils tucked at odd angles, just out of my line of sight, peeking behind weird branches and gill-shaped shelf mushrooms. A person in a car would have terrible vantage of them, wouldn't notice them, but me? I could see everything. My brain was cleaving itself into mincemeat. Beholding them was going to burst my eyes.

It dawned and I wanted to scream.

This was my handwriting. This was my magic. This is what she'd been carving the other day when I'd been hexing Travis Meijer on that bus.

"Turn it off," I panted. I swerved the handles, tried to keep on the road, but the road was covered with ten billion sand prisms. There were infinite planes on every little crag of stone. Gravel was like stars in the universe. Every sliver was different, and I could see their every luminous face. I could see myself refracted off bits of dust, could see my own shoulders reflected back at me, could see my face splintered across every surface that broke the night. I couldn't blink.

"Mr. Scratch, do something!"

I'm trying, Sideways be careful, you've got to turn—

A tree trunk reared up in front of me. Its torso was the size of a pencil, then the size of a python, then the size of the iceberg that killed the *Titanic*. I yanked my handlebars to the left, and the tires rasped and howled and veered right. The gears jolted and I sped up. There was an incline. Everything went faster, my lungs went faster, they flew up and slammed against my hard palate, ballooned out my nose and my ears. Huge forking trees jumped up everywhere and swung at me with twigs like bayonets.

The front tire caught a rock and abruptly stopped.

I did not stop.

My body was suspended in air. My body was flung through space, hurtling forward toward certain death, except it was taking an awfully long time to die like physics said I should. Cold tendrils shot out, twined around my extremities, bound me like ribbons on ballet shoes. The cold buoyed me upwards. It smelled inky-tart. My body slowed, floated forward at a nonlethal pace, still compelled by the motion of the crash but buffeted, controlled. I felt myself arranged upright in midair. My heart slammed against my breastbone and my brain flipped and my whole body ached like it was being wrung, but there was not any pain. The further I was carried from the road, the less I saw. I didn't feel like my head was in genuine jeopardy of getting split and scrambled in the dirt.

My shoes were placed on grass.

Mr. Scratch fell slack inside me.

Breathe, Sideways. He sounded worn. If a flag in a storm could speak, it'd have a voice like his. *We're alright.*

"What was that?" I wrapped an arm around my stomach. There was a second where I thought I'd retch, but it didn't happen. I just swayed instead. Even without the agony, I was still swimming with the feeling, the trippy noxious hypervigilance. "Those were mine. How were those mine?"

You know how. Madeline put them there.

"But why?" I took a few steps forward, just to prove to myself that I could. They were my sigils. I didn't think of them, but it was my soul that brought them into being. I ought to know what they were. I ought to be able to just *read* them. Or—a hunch knotted up in me. "Are those for spying on the Chantry house? Jesus, I get it, but why are they *like* that?"

Could be the unstable casting. Mr. Scratch took a long pause. His words felt windy. *It might be a reaction that your body is having to your specter, as well. I think it's more likely that. You and your misplaced organ aren't designed to be separate. It's not good for you, being confronted with your own segmentation. It could be a psychic rejection of sorts.*

Your body being shocked by its lack of agency over its soul and having an allergic reaction to the exposure. The sigils are to keep eyes on the Chantry family. You don't need extra eyes.

I hacked a laugh. I wanted to scream. "I can't go back up there," I said. "I can't look at them. We'll have to loop around when I catch my breath." I still had my backpack, and still had my phone safe inside it. If there was even a single star in heaven that had my back, there would be enough signal for me to GPS my way out of here. I had to count on it.

We know that Madeline has been here, without a doubt. That's something, is it not?

"You sound like I feel." I rubbed the edge of my sleeve over my nose and took a breath. He'd carried me deeper into the woods than I'd realized. How steep had that incline been? I hadn't noticed one at all from up on the road. I looked over my shoulder and couldn't see the bike, and that prickled more laughter out of me. My guts ached. I was so fucked. "You okay in there?"

I am ragged. Give me leave awhile, dear. I'll mend soon.

I felt a twinge of guilt and a rush of something warm. If my soul was in my neck where it belonged, I might call the feeling love. I wrapped my arms around my belly, a gesture of care as much for him as for me, then took another stumble forward, rounded a particularly obstructive tree. "You must've saved my life back there." I bit my tongue. "Thank you."

I am undying but as much as life is worth, you saved mine breaking that urn. Reciprocity is good. Besides, you're my daughter now. I wouldn't let you smash your head on rocks.

I took a breath, but before I could offer him something by way of appreciation, I shut myself up. Something looked, felt, different. Out of place in the rest of the blackness. Ahead of me was a hard broad swath of darkness, not a long, vertical stripe like the trees that surrounded it. Wide as a trailer was long.

I reached behind me, fumbled around my backpack for its zipper, and yanked it open just wide enough for my wrist. I plunged my hand between its teeth and pawed around for something cylindrical. *There.* I pulled the flashlight out, twisted it on, and pointed its eye toward the weird dark shape.

As soon as light struck it, the whole thing went powder blue. Building. Or, physical structure, in any event. It was mostly painted, but leprous looking. Ribbons of the stuff peeled off around the little angel stained-glass windows. Up above was a steeple that leaned at a funny angle. Christ on his cross held the whole thing up with his left wrist, which was propped against the broken shingled roof. There was a little driveway that led up to the crumbling concrete steps. The sign to the left was mossy past the point of readability.

"I'll be fucked. Of course, it's a fucking chapel. Fuck my life." I rubbed my hands over my face. It wasn't too weird to find abandoned structures around this area. The rotten place we'd thrown that party in October, that place wasn't unique by any stretch. We were just close enough to Appalachia for that sort of thing to happen semiregularly, particularly outside the Sycamore Gorge incorporated limits. Things crumble around here and return to earth. Banks don't fight to get them back. People forget them. Structures unfold. The knowledge of that, however, did not make me hate this chapel business any less. Fuck this place. Nope.

If you sat, Mr. Scratch said, *I could rest for a moment. Just a moment. I want to be helpful on the way back, Sideways. I just can't right now. Not like this.*

"So, I go in the creepy church, you mean." I shoved my hands in my hoodie's tube-shaped mono-pocket. Choked my own hands out. "Just hang out in there for a little while. Casually."

Please?

✳ FIVE ✳

PRAYER OF THANKSGIVING

The doors weren't locked. They outright repelled themselves from my fingertips and left my skin flecked with chips of paint. Lead? Lead. To complement my robust biocollection of microplastics. Alrighty. I was all for exploring during the day, even for it at night provided there were better circumstances. Like having friends with a video camera. Having friends around, generally. If my girls were here, Jing and Daisy and I would be so caught up in riling each other up and freaking the fuck out of Yates that I'd have no space to be scared. At present, though? As it stood?

Maybe this hadn't been my best idea, this whole thing.

It was warmer inside the church.

The worship space was maybe as big as a gas station's interior. I brought my flashlight around slow, tried to catch the whole shape of the place. The chapel had twelve rows of pews, chalky with cobwebs but still mostly upright. Trash on the floor. Empty bottles mostly, and moth-colored pages torn from prayer books. Also, dry rice. Maybe from a wedding? I pulled the flashlight higher. Its beam struck pupils. The walls had eyes, and I nearly bit my tongue off before I saw that I'd illuminated a stretch of framed cherub paintings that hung between each dirty window. The cherubs were all white babies, red-cheeked and blue-eyed, plump little hands folded in dimpled prayer. It was not people or monsters standing around the perimeter of the room watching me. Just cherubs. Okay. They were caked with mold. That's good. That's great. There were statues that matched at the front of the room, surrounding the vacant altar. They faced the absent audience. I thought one had a bizarrely long set of eyelashes, until the lashes shivered its little thorax and crawled away. Daddy longlegs. A little surprise from entropy to me.

I love it in here. Having a blast.

I like it in here, too! It seems there is a bench behind the altar; you could rest there a while. You wouldn't have your back to the doors that way. Would that be a balm to you?

I tried to think of something mean and pithy to say about Mr. Scratch liking it for real, because what the fuck, but the lingering guilt/gratitude amalgam in my gut left over from him saving my life stopped me from saying anything out loud.

Could he read my thoughts?

Only sometimes.

"Rest up," I growled. I made my way down the aisle, unduly conscious of every creak and rustle of my boots across the rotten carpet. I think it'd been red, once. It was brown now. The bench Mr. Scratch had wanted was right underneath an enormous crucifix. Moldy white Jesus' eyes were clouded glass marbles. They looked like mimics. There was a vague thought in the back of my head about the crooked steeple, and by extension the state of the structural integrity of this chapel after fuck knows how long it'd sat without tending, and the thought was bad. Every step I took was a chance that I'd startle the building and make it fall on my head.

It's not going to fall on your head.

I tried to ignore him. His commentary wasn't helping. I swept the flashlight's beam back and forth over the ground, let it sway with my stride. The longer I walked, the farther back the altar seemed. The chapel accordioned. Felt like a bad high. Rice crunched beneath my boots. I held the light up again, illuminated the dangling Jesus' chest. Somebody had written something around where his top surgery scars might be. I squinted, craned my neck.

Pugnantes Deum Amamus.

Something crinkled underfoot. Louder than a leaf, that was for sure. I jerked the light down and took my foot off the unopened bag of chips I'd just crushed. It wasn't dusty or grimy. It looked new. Salt and vinegar, freshly smudged with mud. It was tucked against the corner of the last pew, lay beside two empty cans of garbanzo beans and an empty water jug.

I opened my mouth to say something to Mr. Scratch. Something like, *Huh, that's weird and not something that would normally just hang out in a church.*

One of the pews creaked behind me. I heard breathing.

My knife was in my bag, it was in the pocket of my bag, the pocket that was nowhere near where my hand rested now. Why'd I put it so far out of reach? I seized a bible off the floor and whirled around, wound it back. My non-bible hand fumbled until it aimed my flashlight in the breathing's direction.

It caught a human face.

I couldn't make out the features at first. Pale hair and pale skin, a pale hand thrown over pale eyes, a scowl twisting over pale lips. The flashlight bleached whatever color existed there, if there even was color there, left this person looking ghostly. Then the person shifted. They rose to their feet. The sheet they'd been lying beneath tumbled off their body, and they wore a white shirt underneath, light wash jeans.

Chantry boy.

Reflex took over. I hurled the bible at his face.

He caught it one-handed, gingerly dropped it on the pew he'd been lying on. "Don't," he said. His voice was thick, raw sounding. Like he'd been screaming or was sick. "Just don't."

"Which Chantry are you?" I slapped around my bag pocket until I found a handle. I yanked it out, switched it open. The knife blade looked blue in this light. "Answer me!"

"I'm not." The boy coughed a laugh, eased himself back down into a pew. He put his skull in his hands. I saw his shoulders move under his shirt. He was breathing funny. "Caleb. To answer your question." He looked up after a moment. Peered at me from between his fingers. Rat-poison-blue eyes. "You're that girl we found by the pool. What are you doing here?"

"You evil fuck," I hissed. I heaved myself forward, slammed the sole of my boot square in the middle of his ribs. The force shoved him back, pinned him against the pew. I remembered him. This was the fucker who'd carried me up the Chantry stairs and oh-so-gently arranged me for the removal of my fucking soul. I felt the air clap out of his mouth. His eyes shot wide, and he seized the leather around my ankle, but his leverage was shit and I was leaning all of my weight into my heel. He gasped. His eyes fixed on the tip of my knife. They followed it back and forth as I waved it about. Rancid-candy blue. Adderall blue. Antifreeze blue. "Were you waiting for me? Did you come looking for me?" He wasn't supposed to be able to do that. The stalk-not spell the Scapegracers had put up against the Chantrys, I hadn't felt it break. What if I can't feel when spells break? Fuck! I curled my lip over my teeth. "Speak up. What are you doing here?"

He panted, struggled to pull a breath down his throat. I saw the whites of his eyes. When the words wouldn't come, he shook his head, curled his mouth—a grimace? a sneer? an ugly, dismal smile?—and released my ankle. Held his splayed fingers by either side of his head like, *Don't cut me, I'm unarmed.*

Hair hung in his eyes. It was stringy, looked almost wet. Was that grease?

I sniffed. There was something sour about this situation, something itching at me. I looked down at the cans by my ankles, the water jug, the chips I'd ruined. I looked at the pew he'd been sleeping on, the sheet he'd been wrapped in, the suitcase that I now noticed had been propped between the pew and the wall. "Well, I'll be damned," I said. Slowly, in a move that made my heart hurt a little, I took my boot off his ribs.

He lurched forward, folded his spine into a candy-cane shape, and sputtered a breath. He wrapped his arms around his stomach. Rubbed his mouth with his wrist. "Obviously, witch."

"Witch with a knife. Watch your fucking tone." I curled my lip, but given the context, I decided not to kick him again. Not yet. "They threw you out, huh?" It felt obvious enough, but it didn't make any sense. I knelt, picked the chip bag up. Crinkled it between my fists. "Why?"

Caleb didn't say anything for a moment. Set his jaw in a hard line. Venomous, stoic.

I shook myself. Even without my soul in my teeth, I felt a phantom rush of anger. I wanted to break my hands on his face. I could make that jaw move. The anger passed as quick as it came, though, looking at the chip bag.

Fucking empathy, come to ruin my life.

I felt cotton-stuffed and strange.

"How'd you escape?" He fixed his eyes on me. "When we caught you, you vanished. Was it the window?"

I snorted affirmatively.

"That was a steep drop. You could have broken your neck." He said this matter-of-factly. His monotone was resonant, hard-edged enough to push through all the grit in his voice. "Why would you come back this way, witch?"

"Why are you sleeping in a death trap, bootlicker?"

He blinked. "I was thrown out. Like you said."

"Why?"

Why do you care, Sideways? Don't talk to him. He's a Chantry boy. His blood and his bones are evil. He was bred to break my daughters. I want him not to be alive. Let me eat him. Please let me eat him. I could never be too tired not to eat him.

I had no idea how that would work and didn't presently care to find out.

Caleb just looked at me.

Against all my screaming instincts, I sat down on the pew beside him. Not next to him, not close enough to touch, but still. We were at eye level, now. I kept my knife out but tucked it against my thigh, out of sight. "Question for a question?"

He scissored his fingers shut, hid his eyes. Didn't negate me, though. He said, "What did you do to Levi?"

"Cursed him that he'd be in pain every time he thought about hurting women. He had it coming."

Caleb didn't negate that either. He leaned back a little, pulled his hands off his face, and closed his eyes. He was waiting, I realized. It was my turn.

I chewed my tongue. "How long have you been here?"

"Four days." He closed his eyes. "How did you find this place?"

"Accident." Literally. "Where the fuck are we?"

"It was a Baptist chapel a few decades ago, I think. That or some copycat denomination." He opened one eye, fixed it on the graffitied, glass-eyed Jesus. "My brothers and I played in here as kids."

Spectacular how much I hated that, wow.

He said, "Did my brother hurt you?"

"I mean, you all fucking *kidnapped* me." I rubbed my teeth on the inside of my collar, tried to free myself of the memory's taste. It smelled like mildew in here. "But no. He hurt somebody I know." Lila Yates, namely. There was an impulse that fired in my head, and I followed it. I fished around my backpack for the chain and pulled it out.

Caleb's look sharpened. Something flickered behind his eyes. He leaned toward me, and a few lank locks of hair fell across his nose, and he didn't move to shove them aside. I thought his face might twitch, make a human expression, but it didn't. Unreadable. "How do you know Madeline Kline?"

"It's my turn." My pulse sped up a little.

He knew things about Madeline.

He might know how to find her.

I needed to know that I could trust him, though. I needed assurance that he wouldn't be leading me into his family's jaws, regardless of whether or not they were close at the moment. I licked my gums, clenched my fists tighter. I said, "Why did your parents throw you out?"

Caleb's shoulders tensed. His whole body did. The veins in his arms stood out like blue worms. He stared at the floor, and after a moment, he opened his mouth. "I write journals every night," he said. "My brother David read them. Showed my father something he knew he wouldn't like." He opened his mouth, but only a thin, watery sound escaped it. His brows came together. They peaked upwards, and he shut his eyes, pushed his mouth into a line. Color bloomed in the peaks of his cheeks, around his eye sockets, in the meat of his pursed lips. The splotches flushed a deep pink. He pressed his hands over his face, prodded like he could get the blood to flow backwards, could nudge the mushrooming tears back in their ducts. "Why would you care, anyway?"

Oh.

So, he's gay, huh.

The thought fell from my brain into my stomach like an anchor. It ripped up everything it collided with, and all at once, I couldn't breathe properly. My ribs felt tight. My vision sparkled with bright white lights. Oh fuck. Oh no. "Why would I care?" I whistled a breath between my tooth gap and shoved my hood back, knotted my hands in my quad-colored hair. He was a witchfinder. He was an evil fucking witchfinder. He'd helped kidnap me. I owed him *nothing*. But still, there was a deeper loyalty that ran through me, the nebulous, seething draw of potential community. I couldn't leave him here. I couldn't leave him in this death trap when it was gonna freeze this weekend. I couldn't leave him with just a sheet. I cared when I asked the

question because I cared whether or not he was lying. Now?
"I'm a fucking dyke, Caleb. I can't not care." Even soulless.
Even when you loudly don't deserve it.

His expression flickered, and he looked genuinely
surprised for a moment, gooey blue eyes wide and strung
with question marks. He looked like a rabbit. He was
panting like one, too. "You are?"

"Fucking obviously." I screwed my brows together and
crossed my arms over my ribs. "Hair not enough for you?"

"I thought you were just alternative." His voice was
monotone again, and I thought he might've been making an
attempt toward being impassive again, but his splotches gave
him away. Too blotched to be emotionless.

"Yeah. Alternative to heterosexuality." I rocked my head
back, rested it against the pew behind me. I stared at the
ceiling. It was green with mold. Mr. Scratch was seething
inside me, whirling around in my rib cage like he'd been put
on spin cycle. "Not a Chantry. You still a witchfinder?"

He blinked. "Goes with being a Chantry."

*Don't believe him. He might love like you, but he's not
one of you, he's one of them. What if he turns on you? What
if he gives you up as evidence of his loyalty, his resolve? You
can't forgive him, Sideways. You can't redeem him.*

"Madeline Kline ripped my specter out." I squeezed my
fingers in the ruts of my rib cage, tried to compress the
howling devil that kept spasming around inside me. He
didn't want me to tell him. A lot of me didn't want to, either.
"I've been trying to find her."

"Oh, Addie. If that's the case, I might be able to help you." He folded his hands together. Shut his eyes again. "I've got some idea of what she might be planning."

"Yeah?" I rubbed a hand over my mouth. My pulse was a little faster. There was hope. Real, glittering hope. Even if it smelled like a mildewed church. "And what might that be?"

He swayed forward, rested his forehead on the pew in front of him. It looked like he might crumble. Now that I looked for it, I could see the exhaustion in his shoulders, hear it in the chalky timbre of his voice. It should've occurred to me earlier, but I was too keyed up to think about it. I'd woken him up when I stepped on those chips. He might not have woken at all if I hadn't crushed them, what with my sneaking runes burning holes in the soles of my shoes. I wanted more information out of him, wanted to wring every drop of knowledge he had out of his body, but I wasn't sure how much he could give right now, even if I tried. "She's intending to kill us," he finally said. "We earned it."

Yes, you did.

"Got that right." My agreeing with Mr. Scratch didn't seem to make him feel any better. I considered pointing out that pinballing around my guts wasn't going to give him any rest, but he'd saved my life, so I spared him sass. Besides. He was owed his fury.

My hand slipped into my bag. I fished around, half-confused at myself the whole while, and pulled out two things: the trail mix and my phone. I thrust the trail mix at him. It hit him in the back of the neck, but the bag didn't split. "Eat," I said. Then my screen was alight, and I was thumbing through my contacts, scrolling until I found the face that some animal instinct said I needed.

Reception. So luck hadn't completely fucked me over, huh?

I hit call, held the phone to my ear.

"You alive?" Boris sounded fully awake, which wasn't surprising. He stayed up later than I did some nights, fiddling away with the antiques, reading sleazy novels, video chatting his intensely cool queer performer friends who lived on the other side of the world. "You're calling me for a ride, yes?"

"Yes. I'll turn my location on." I took a hard breath. It felt like I'd swallowed a hunk of glue stick. "Dad, is it cool if somebody stays the night? Or a couple of nights?"

"It's cool with me if it's cool with you. Who and why?"

"Caleb. Don't know him well, you haven't met him before." I couldn't fucking believe myself. I couldn't believe the words that came out of my mouth but they kept happening, one after another, marching off the tip of my tongue and into the open air. "Homeless homo, Dad. He needs a couch and a shower."

There was a pause.

Caleb was looking at me with his mouth open. His eyes were enormous. Took up his whole entire stupid face. Gathered his hands into fists that he squeezed so tightly I thought his knuckles might pop like buttons.

"I'll be there in ten," he said. The phone clicked.

Mr. Scratch seethed inside me, but he didn't contradict me. Instead, he said, just loud enough for me to hear him, *I hope your gamble is worth it. You know I can't protect you right now, Sideways. If he attacks you, there's nothing I can do.*

I stroked my hands up and down my sides, tried to soothe him like I would a shaking dog. He was right, after all. This could go so spectacularly wrong.

I stood up again, scowled down at Caleb. "Gather your shit. He'll be here soon."

Caleb looked stricken. He held the trail mix in its bag delicately, reverently. His fingertips didn't even warp the plastic. "What's your name?"

I stared.

Did he really not know?

"Sideways Pike." I cracked my knuckles. "Gathering your shit involves moving, you know."

"Sideways," he said. There wasn't the upward bend at the end of the word that people usually gave it when they heard it the first time. He didn't sneer or condescend. His eyes were still big, still glassy like the Jesus on the wall. "Why are you doing this?"

"Because I'm a halfway decent human being? Who wouldn't?" I kicked one of his empty cans. It flew through the air, knocked over a googly-eyed angel statue, and hit the ground in a plume of dust. "I need your help." That sounded less feelings-y. Maybe his toxic masculine ass could comprehend that better.

"I won't forget it." He pressed the trail mix against his stomach. "Believe that."

"You can express your gratitude by not dragging me back to your ex-folks' house as a peace offering." I shoved my hands in my pockets. "No funny business. I will be so, so fucking pissed if you try to pull anything, do you understand me?"

"Loud and clear." He rose to his feet. "I wouldn't double-cross your hospitality like that."

A laugh crawled up my throat and I didn't choke it back down. "Good to know that you've got standards. Witch-snatching is fine, being rude to your host isn't. Alright. Sick."

He didn't say anything back, which was smart. Just gathered up his suitcase, a backpack I hadn't noticed, a grocery bag that looked filled with seemingly random things—a photo album, a bottle of Advil, a pair of dress shoes, some Moleskines. Must not have had much time to pack.

I felt a little sick to my stomach. Distracted myself with zigzagging my flashlight over the angel statues. Ugly little fuckers. Why were angels in churches like this, always uncanny terrible big-headed kids? Like, horror-movie-looking brats with wings that couldn't feasibly be big enough to lift their shiny little ceramic bodies? Weren't angels supposed to be eldritch badasses? I wasn't sure. Julian obliquely referred to himself as a recovering Catholic and Boris was nonpracticing conservative Jewish, but both were atheists and neither had ever done much by my religious education one way or the other. I knew what I knew thanks to movies and the internet.

Had my mother been religious? For the life of me, I couldn't say.

"I've got everything," Caleb said. He'd arranged it neatly on the bench, organized it like we were about to go through an airport security check. He had his elbows clamped to his sides. "Does your father know where we are?"

"He'll find us." I wasn't worried about that. Boris had picked me up from weirder places than this without questions. If it was Julian, it'd be a different story, but Julian was probably sleeping and blissfully unaware that I was even out of bed. I eyed Caleb, the unnatural way he was standing. "Are you shivering?"

"It's December," he said flatly.

I grabbed the sheet off the pew—it didn't look like he'd been planning on bringing it—and cast it over his shoulders like a net. I threw one corner around his neck an extra time, tied it with another corner. "Sheet toga," I said. "Now stop twitching. It's making me nervous."

The corner of his mouth jerked. I thought it might've been the ghost of a smile.

My phone buzzed in my pocket. I swiped, cradled it against my ear.

"Are you in the creepy chapel?"

"I'm in the creepy chapel," I confirmed. "Want a souvenir?"

"Yeah," said Boris. I thought I heard the edge of his music through the speakers. Heavy guitars and distorted synths. "You know I do."

I glanced around, then made my way to the front of the chapel, toward the altar and bench Mr. Scratch had originally wanted me to rest on. There were so many angel statues. So fucking many of them. Surely one of them wasn't so heavy and disgusting that I couldn't take it with me? I rooted around until I found a viable ugly at the outer edge. The upper half of its head had been clipped off somehow, just above the rosebud lips. Its hands were clasped in prayer, wrapped with rosary beads that didn't really belong in a protestant church, but maybe whoever had bought it hadn't quite thought that part through. Its wings were gilded. It wore a lavender dress. I wrapped my hand around its body, thick as a roll of wrapping paper, and found that it was lighter than I thought it'd be. I mean, it'd probably kill somebody if you beaned them on the head with it, but it wasn't a billion tons and by extension completely immovable.

"Got you something you'll like," I said into my phone. "We're heading out."

"Copy," he said, then promptly hung up.

I carried my angel back toward Caleb, jerked my head in the door's direction and waited only long enough for him to sling his bags over his shoulder. The bags and the sheet in combination looked bizarre. Like a Roman senator going camping. When he had his stuff in hand, I hauled myself toward the door, flashlight tucked in the crook of my arm. I opened the door with a kick.

Night air gusted in around us, threw my curls around.

Boris' car purred on the church's overgrown drive. He

had his windows down, and one of his arms jutted into the night. Patent leather jacket. It caught the beam of my flashlight and threw it back. His music played loud. Its bass was steadying, easy for my heartbeat to match itself against. He opened his door when he saw us, popped the trunk, and stepped out. He must not have even gotten into bed. His hair was still teased into a pompadour and the black he'd tightlined his eyes with had yet to be washed off. Mismatched earrings. He walked past me. Stopped in front of Caleb, who had frozen midmotion on the steps.

"May I?" Boris waved a hand at Caleb's bags.

Caleb didn't move. I didn't think he was breathing. He didn't so much as blink. He obediently dropped the suitcase by his feet, though. It hit the ground with a thud.

Boris picked it up without remarking on Caleb's squirreliness. "We've got a pullout bed in our study. It's cluttered but there's enough space for your bags. I'll work on getting drawers for you tomorrow. You'll be using Sideways' bathroom. Beware. Kitchen is always open, graze as you like, wash your own dishes. My husband is always stress cooking. If you've got dietary restrictions, he's the one you should tell. How old are you?"

Caleb hitched a breath. "Eighteen," he said. It was barely above a whisper.

"Good. If you weren't, I'd be half-inclined to swing you by a shelter. Lucky you, you're a legal adult. You can stay as long as you need." He turned, carried the bag toward his car. "House rules," he said as he thunked the bag in the trunk.

"No smoking inside, Julian has asthma. Don't take things out of the shop. If you need one, we can give you a job working the desk. It's not much, but we pay above what minimum wage ought to be. We'll make work if you need extra hours. There isn't a curfew and I'm not going to tell you what to do with your body but know that if you bring police into my shop or my home, I won't be pleased. Dinner is at six every night. Julian's punctual. I'm going to expect you to do your own laundry and tidy after yourself, but that's going to be honor system. No overnight guests without a heads-up, but I am amenable provided that said heads-up occurs. No narking, no bad music, no reality TV that I have to hear. Are you a conservative?"

Caleb blinked. "Libertarian."

Boris made a yacking sound in his throat. "We'll work on that."

I hid my grin under my fist.

"I'm not expecting you to pay rent on a room." Boris hardly believed that rent should be a legal thing to charge, anyway. I'd gotten the landlord lecture more than once. "Staying at our place has no expectations on your end but know that I'll expect you to learn a thing or two about your history when you're in our space. Are you in school?"

"St. Joseph's," he said in affirmation. "I'm a senior."

That tracked. St. Joseph's was a little private school for rich boys who thought East High was below them. It was Catholic, technically, but so far as I knew the boys were mostly wealthy protestants, Lutherans or whatever the fuck.

Daisy had been complaining about them just last week. Said she had a hard time telling them apart, what with their uniforms and all, and it meant she kept accidentally flirting with the same boy twice.

Or maybe that was more to do with her whole *not being really into boys* thing.

Man.

"You'll need a ride, then." Boris gave him a little nod. "Give me a timetable and I'll make sure you have one. Do you have scheduled extracurriculars I should know about?"

"No," he said. He ghosted down the steps and joined Boris at the back of the car, gingerly placed his backpack and his grocery sack beside his suitcase. "Thank you."

Boris waved a hand. He turned his attention to me. "So, what'd you get me?"

I strode over, pressed my forehead against his shoulder for a moment, then offered him my split-faced angel statue. I was smiling a little. I wasn't sure why. I love my dad a lot.

Boris clapped a hand on my shoulder, beheld my awful offering with his eyebrows raised. He must've penciled them this morning. They looked more arched than normal. "Wow," he said. He released me, took the angel in hand and slapped it against his opposing palm. "This is hideous. Is this the only one?"

"Only one I thought you'd like." I shrugged.

"Shame." He kissed my forehead, then turned around, made his way back to the driver's seat. "If I can hollow out the head somehow, I bet I could use it as a candle-holder.

How gross would that be? It'd be unforgivable. It'd look haunted. Nobody would buy it. It could be mine and live in the shop forever."

I cracked a laugh, climbed in the passenger's seat. As soon as I made contact with the leather upholstery, I felt like my bones went soft. Exhaustion fell over me. I matched Scratch. This was the only car that didn't induce hyperventilation, not ever, and I relaxed enough to turn to butter. I looked over my shoulder and stared vaguely at Caleb as he climbed in the back seat. "You alive back there?"

"Yes," said Caleb. He still had his arms wrapped around the trail mix bag I'd thrown him. He clutched it like a bear. "I'm alive."

✳ SIX ✳

TOUGHEST CROWD IN TOWN

In the morning, Monique and Sheridan texted me their requests. I sent them along to the group chat. I'd only had three hours of sleep. I felt like a walking rock. A rock that walked. A lesbian-shaped stone formation. Stone butch? Not quite. Geological dyke? I brushed my teeth, applied and quickly fucked up my black lipstick, resorted to feathering the edges until my mouth looked like a void space, and successfully forced a comb through my rat's-nest hair, all without making eye contact with the evil untrustworthy Sideways in the mirror. Muscle shirt. Barbed-wire necklace. I pulled on a flannel inside out, shoved the sleeves up over my elbows. Clean underwear (I hoped, oof) and stiff wide jeans. I put on socks and then boots. I slung my bag over my shoulders and heaved under the weight. I lumbered into the kitchen and ate an omelet Julian had made without tasting it. My head pounded. I poured myself a mug of coffee and drank it still scalding in one gulp. I moved to pour more but I stopped myself. That wasn't polite. Even brain-dead, I knew that much. I'd be nice. Left some in the pot in case our ex-witchfinder wanted some.

Is it normal for sleeplessness to make you feel kinda nauseous? Is it normal for me to share coffee with dubious others? Could I pick normal out of a lineup?

"I'm taking you. Boris is taking Caleb to the mall once he's awake. He's going to buy him pajamas, and other assorted necessities, I think," said Julian faintly as he gnawed on the edge of a stale bran muffin. He'd run out of eggs before he could make an omelet of his own. Boris finished before he realized and looked guilty as a dog. He looked like how I felt. Boris must not have taken the time to wash himself off last night. His hair was still coiffed but dented miserably. Liner looser, but present. I wondered vaguely if he'd even gone to bed at all.

I hadn't been present for the Caleb conversation. I wasn't sure how it'd gone. Julian was cool, and he was the biggest empath I'd ever met, but I hadn't ever sprung this kind of thing on him before. If he had concerns, he didn't voice them.

Caleb wasn't going to school this morning. He'd communicated obliquely that he'd managed to go three of the four days he'd been homeless, but he'd skipped yesterday, and Boris and Julian thought it best he skip today as well.

I got it. I totally did. I was just jealous as death, that's all.

Julian herded me into his car, and I woke up in front of school. He gave my curls a good shake and exiled me to walk the cold stretch of pavement that led, inevitably, to the will-crushing halls of Sycamore Gorge West High.

I'd find some way to tell my friends about Caleb. I'd find

some casual place in conversation to admit that, after the group at large vetoed my idea, I'd gone and done it myself, nearly died falling off the road, wandered into a crumbling chapel, and stumbled upon an excommunicated witchfinder who I brought home with me like a mangy puppy. I'd tell them and I would articulate it well, sprinkle the moments of suspense with humorous release, balance the sadness with gestures of hope. I'd let them know that I had a lead. A real lead, something we could grab onto and ride to victory.

I'd tell them as soon as I saw them.

Everybody around me shut their lockers and I was suddenly in class.

The fluorescent lighting made that buzzing noise, the one that makes me feel absolutely rabid with irritation. This must have been English, because we were reading "The Yellow Wallpaper." A kid to the left of me said, "Why is this bitch so nervous? It's a wall. Somebody get her a blunt."

Somebody else said, "Blunts weren't invented yet, idiot."

Somebody else said, "I wish I was a wall. You know?"

Different class. The lighting was still loud but a slightly different color, bluish rather than dingy-dishwater looking. It was cold in here. There was a plastic plant in the corner that somebody tried to water. The teacher attempted to turn on his projector for a solid fifteen minutes. He didn't have a smart board because the school board loved him the least. He called somebody next door. They didn't know how to turn it on either. He gave up at that point and handwrote the questions for our pop quiz on the board. His handwriting looked like cuneiform. I wrote my name backwards and forwards as the answer to every question.

Yet another class! There are so many and every day, they last longer and shorter at the same time. I watched the clock with an almost religious intensity. A student beside me was crying because she'd just gotten her ACT scores back and she hadn't improved at all, not by much, and she was convinced that her parents were going to kill her. Somebody sold somebody else brownies and a bag full of pills. A different student, unrelated to those two, was sent to the principal's office for her third offense of chewing gum.

Lunch happened. I saw my friends and thought about telling them, but when I got to them, they were already embroiled in conversation. Jing had her phone out, and Yates, Daisy, and a myriad of girls who didn't usually sit with us all crowded around her. I shoved my way between plaids and pastels and peered down, only to find, with a lick of surprise, that our school was trending on a bad social media site. Somebody had apparently climbed on the roof and painted a giant phallus-goose monster that spanned nearly a third of the total surface area. It was well done, too. Clearly half-goose, half-phallus. I hadn't thought such a thing was possible. The guerrilla mural was discovered by a police heli-copter, apparently, one of the ones that spends all its time flying over cornfields in search of hidden weed crops. There was a quote from the cop who'd found it. He said, "We'll catch that gooser. He was a sneaky son of a gun, probably thinks he's very clever, but we'll get him. We always do."

Gooser! 12 said gooser! "Gooser" cropped up all over social media. What an amazing title. I wished I was the gooser.

Needless to say, I didn't tell them at lunch. I nearly forgot.

More class.

Endless class.

The teacher tried to teach but it was no use. All we wanted to talk about was the gooser, and who we thought it could possibly be. Somebody kept floating the idea that it was Austin Grass, but that suggestion made me want to crush something, and I shot it down as venomously as I could. Austin Grass didn't have a creative bone in his body. He's a spineless shitty nothing boy. Asking for extra creativity bones is a bit much, don't you think? Somebody tried to tell me about his bone right around then, and I regretted having spoken in the first place.

Every second I spent in class was like peeling a layer of skin off my toes with a spoon. It sucked. It really sucked. It made me feel itchy all over, achy and raw and like my skull was full of pillow fluff. I was bored and feeling bored made me feel stupid. I couldn't bring myself to flash my teeth at the fistful of boys walking around school with post-hex Sharpie chokers. I couldn't focus on bullshit on my phone. I was hungry and my back hurt inexplicably. I was tired. I was so fucking tired.

Somebody had a seizure in the hallway during my last class. An ambulance came and everything. It would've been exciting if the schoolness of it all hadn't eroded my ability to connect human emotion to any and all material stimuli. The kid writhed for a whole five minutes.

Focus. I had to focus.

I had to tell my friends about Caleb.

I had to tell my friends.

*

The cheer girls threw Daisy way up in the air. She flipped head over heels, higher and higher until she just missed skimming the gymnasium rafters. I wondered if people who didn't know her noticed how she hung in the air just a second longer than she should have. I wondered if they noticed how she floated down just a hair slower than gravity dictated she should, how she slipped through empty space as easy as swimming underwater. She landed in her team-mates' cradled arms with a vicious little smile. They bounced her to the mats on the floor.

Competition was in two months, apparently. I didn't really know what that meant but they were rehearsing really hard for it. Jing and Yates and I waited around in the high rafters, out of earshot, eating Oreos and passing Jing's Juul around.

The coach called it, and the cheerleaders dispersed. Most of them headed to the locker rooms, chatting and swigging their water bottles. Monique was greeted by Sheridan at the door, which made my heart fuzzy. Daisy climbed the stairs, bounded in our direction. Her ponytail swished back and forth with every step. There was barely a sheen of sweat across her brow, but her cheekbones shimmered with her crushed glitter highlighter, the tip of her button nose, too. When she finally reached us, she laid herself down across a bench, arranged her head in Jing's lap and her ankles in my own.

What was it with my friends and putting their feet in my lap?

I passed Jing her Juul and gave Daisy's shin an awkward pat.

"So, here's what I'm thinking," said Yates before I could awkwardly segue into the whole Caleb situation. "We should do a Secret Santa. Quick turnaround, but that means we have to be creative! It'd be cute. I want to get you guys cute things."

Jing gave Yates a smile. "I do love any excuse to pull names from a hat. I'm game."

"I vote yes. I want to spend my dad's money." Daisy closed her eyes and basked. "Did you see how high I got? I nearly kicked the roof down."

"You're a star, Daze," Jing said. She licked the creamy guts out of an Oreo and I pretended like I felt normally about that, then she shoved the carton away from herself, focused on the girl in her lap.

"I was afraid you'd knock your head on the rafters," said Yates. "You went so high!"

"You're a bird person," I said. It did not receive a laugh.

"If you draw your own name, we've got to do it over. So

don't do that." Yates tore up a sheet of notebook paper. Her tearing paper was very different from my tearing paper. When she did it, everything looked nearly cut apart from the softer edges. When I did it, it looked chewed. Yates wrote a name on each slip in her lovely, perfect handwriting, and without having to ask, was offered the beanie Jing was illegally wearing inside. She crumpled the names up and dropped them in the hat. She reached it out.

I leaned forward to take one. Everybody did.

Mine said SIDEWAYS.

"Sorry," I said. I folded the paper in half again. "Can we redo it? Drew myself." I waited for the wave of groans to pass, and as I tossed my name back in the cap, I made myself open my mouth and talk again. Just a little more. "Also, I've got an update."

"Is the update that you suck at Secret Santa?" Jing cracked a grin.

"It's about Madeline, actually. I have a lead."

The Santa-ing halted. Everybody looked at me. Daisy craned her neck in Jing's lap. Yates' lips popped into a little *oh*. Jing whipped her head around so fast her hair got in her face.

Okay. I cleared my throat. "So, I went to the Chantry house. Or I tried. I—"

"You did what?" Daisy hoisted herself onto her elbows to look at me properly. Her smile inverted. She stared hard enough to chap my skin. Whatever little quiver of weirdness had been going on with her didn't seem so little, suddenly.

Her whole body tensed when livid, and she arched her back like a rearing cobra. She stretched her lips over her teeth. "I must not have heard you correctly because holy fucking shit, Sideways. Excuse me! Excuse me, but did you say you went to the Chantry house? What the fuck? When did this happen?"

"Last night, and, see, I didn't actually get there. When I went—"

"Last night?" Jing this time. She looked stricken, drew her brows in a tight little V. "You didn't text us anything. You said you went to bed early. You snuck out to the Chantry house? Alone? Holy shit, why would you do that? I'm glad you're alive, first of all, and second of all, I am about to kill you right now."

"I didn't actually get there!" I threw my hands up, half in defense and half in utter exasperation. Why did they keep cutting me off? "When I biked over, there were all these sigils in the trees that Madeline must've carved. It turns out that magic freaks the fuck out when it's cast with a disconnected specter, so it over- and underreacts or something, I don't really know. I guess it overreacted or I had an allergic reaction or something. So, I was biking through and I accidently ran off the road, and I got kind of lost and wandered around and—"

"You got in an accident?" Yates' eyes went big.

"Are you fucking okay?" Jing dragged her bangs out of her face. "Jesus Christ, did you know that? About her sigils? Did you know that they could be weird like that? That could be bad news, Sideways."

"I mean, vaguely! I didn't know I'd crash my bike!" I shook my head. I felt myself talking fast and I couldn't slow down. "Look, the crash isn't the part of the story that matters. What matters is that I wound up in this shady little church and I ran across Caleb Chantry."

Everybody went silent. Cold, metallic silent. *Could've heard a hair tie hit the floor* silent. Evoking the Chantry boys by name was no small thing.

Daisy Brink was vibrating. Her ankles on my lap were live dynamite. Slowly, with a deliberateness that made my gut drop, she withdrew from Jing and me, and she stepped onto the riser behind us. Her shadow fell over my shoulders. She clapped her fists to her chest. Without the pompoms, the pose looked almost pious. Daisy smiled with all her teeth. She said, "Did you Chett-hex Caleb Chantry last night?"

Jing and Yates leaned forward, equal parts wary and interested.

My face roasted. Everything was hot and smushed too close against me. I couldn't breathe right. I couldn't think. My mind was flipping around like Daisy on a pyramid, head-over-heels-over-heels-over-head. I didn't like her standing like this. I didn't like that I hadn't. I wouldn't have liked it if I had. "I didn't hex him. No."

"Did you hurt him? Do him some good old-fashioned bodily harm? Did you kill him with your hands? Did something good come out of you breaking a covenant with us?" Daisy wasn't blinking. She stared the meat off my bones.

She stared the marrow right out of me. I thought her eyes might pop. "What did you do last night, Sideways?"

"Why am I on trial right now?" I stood up, rolled a kink out of my left shoulder. With her on the bench, she and I were on eye level. "I didn't jump him. I thought I could extort some information, and I did."

"Information out of a witchfinder? Information like how to get you and all of us fucking eviscerated, that kind of information?" Daisy beamed. "Do you often seek out curse-worthy boys for civil little chats?"

Jing rubbed her temples. She curled her lip, mouthed numbers backwards from ten, and said, "Both of you need to chill the fuck out. Take a pill, Daze. Sideways, he and his brothers attacked you. People who kidnap people aren't exactly reliable witnesses, and I swear to fuck, you cannot just go do this sort of thing alone. We're a fucking team. You have to think about all of us, too."

"I was thinking about you!" I scraped my tongue with my teeth and spat on the honey-blond bleacher beside me. Oreo dust speckled my spit. "We aren't moving fast enough. I need to be useful to you. He's a way for me to be useful to you."

"I am not friends with you because you're *useful*," Yates breathed. "Please sit down."

Neither of us sat down.

"Trusting a witchfinder is 'Scorpion and the Frog' shit," said Daisy. She bounced on her toes. Wiggled her fingers like she was going to drive her nails through the meat of my belly and skewer my heart, yank it out, and slam dunk it.

"Say you trust him. Say you're stupid enough to trust him. I wanna hear you say that. Come on, Sideways, show me how fucking stupid you are. Don't you wanna?"

"Daisy," Jing snapped.

"You don't know what the fuck you're talking about."

Like hell if I knew! She was right, I was stupid and I was risking everything and I didn't *know* if I trusted him, but right now if I didn't, he'd be dangerous, and I'd be losing. I refused to lose. "He's not here to fuck us over. He's not even a Chantry anymore, so he's technically not even a witchfinder, and—"

"Duh, he's trying to fuck you over." The particular smile Daisy flashed at me used to make me hate myself. Things I hadn't thought about—little citric-acid flashes of middle school meanness—twinged at the edges of my focus. "Are you joking? Is this all an elaborate bit? Cannot stress how quickly I'll delete your number from my phone if this is a bit."

"I'm not messing with you," I hissed. "I don't fucking mess with you unless you ask me to mess with you, you *know* that."

"You two are going to give me an aneurism. Jesus Christ. Okay, just—fucking, Chantry boys are dangerous, point blank." Jing also came to her feet, much to Yates' dismay. She put her arms behind her head. She was thinking fast, and I'd gotten pretty good at guessing, but right now I couldn't read her for the life of me. She hated me. Let's call it early. I wanted to eat my fist. "Did you tell him about us?"

"I didn't tell him a damn thing about the Scapegracers," I said. "The only person who could get hurt out of this is me."

"You can't know that," said Jing.

"You make it sound like it wouldn't be awful if *you* got hurt," said Yates.

Daisy smacked her lips. "What *did* you tell him, then?"

"Madeline!" My hands balled up on either side of me. "I talked to him about Madeline! It might be easy for you to forget, but she *ripped* out my *soul*. I'd do anything for it back. I have to do anything to get it back."

"Literally, us too," said Jing. "I get that you're frustrated, I truly do, but this isn't—"

"Don't talk to me like we haven't been there for you. We've done stupid shit for you and your specter, Sideways. All we've done the past few weeks is look for it. Ungrateful!" Daisy was a blur of motion. I thought she was going to explode. "All this work and you'd rather collaborate with the enemy! You're the CIA!"

"Can you stop and listen to me? Actually listen to me? I need my specter. I need it. I can't do anything without it. I don't feel half the time. I'm numb all over, I can't remember the last time I've really tasted food, really felt anything, I'm not always in my own body and I can't do anything to stop it. I need control over myself. I need this. You can't understand."

Jing breathed out through her teeth. "My Wellbutrin prescription begs to differ."

"I didn't mean," I started, but I stopped myself. My

words were all jumbling around in my brain. They were coming out too fast. I didn't have the time or mental faculties to iron them out before I spat them. "I didn't mean to say that you're not hurting or whatever else. I know I'm not special, I know that other people, that you three, feel similar ways to this, and I know you're doing this in solidarity with me and because you care about me for some godforsaken reason, but I feel like I'm losing my mind and we keep doing other shit, we keep going on with our lives like I'm not in actual pieces, and you wouldn't do this with me. It needed to be done. But you know, it's fine, I'm *glad* you didn't come, because if you came I might not have crashed and—"

"Did you really just say that?" Daisy's smile warped into a snarl. "Listen to yourself, Sideways, you pathetic little—"

"Little what?" I smiled at her. It felt awful. I leaned in. "Dyke? Were you gonna call me a dyke? Hm? Used to like the word 'dyke,' didn't you, Daisy? Don't you remember when you used to call me a hairy mannish ugly little dyke?"

She stiffened like I'd slapped her.

Jing looked between the two of us, aghast.

Yates kept her head in her hands. She'd been like that for a while, now.

"You still hang out with guys who were horrible to me, you know that? Like unspeakably, violently awful to me." It was true, but it wasn't something I'd ever dwelled on. I was in a corner, though. My mind was conjuring whatever it could that was sharp-shaped to fling at her. I refused to lose. I had to slug back harder. "They throw around the word 'dyke' damn near constantly. They invent their own slurs, too! They're real artists about it. You're still friends with them, even though you're friends with me, because it's hard being friends with me. Dripping off the arm of some Homophobe of the Week is a good reputational Band-Aid, right?"

A darkness came over the gym. Not real, but palpable. My hair prickled at the nape of my neck. Curls slithered of their own accord. I was bristling. The place in my throat where my specter should have been throbbed like I'd slammed it in a car door.

"Easy now," Jing warned. "Chose your next words very carefully."

The look Daisy gave me made my knees lock.

I thought she was going to cry.

A sliver of clarity in the worm knot of my head: I was not going to out Daisy. I wasn't even sure if she was gay, but I wasn't going to risk it. I wouldn't say the easy thing. I would not out Caleb, either.

"Caleb's going to be staying at my place for a while." I shifted around like a boxer and felt so heavy that I could crack the bleachers and tear tectonic plates. "He thinks he can help me find Madeline."

"Madeline is doing all of this for revenge," Yates said. Her voice was so low that I barely heard her. "That means they probably yanked her soul out, Sideways. If he helps you find her, that could be a really bad thing. Maybe he shouldn't be near her. His motives might be really, really bad."

Daisy spoke like she hadn't heard her. "Staying at your place? You invited him into your place?" Her eye twitched, and she repeated, "Staying with you? The witchfinder is staying with you? With you? With you?"

"You have to Chett him," Jing insisted.

I curled my lip. "I don't think that's necessary."

"For fuck's sake, Sideways!" Jing spread her hands. "Why is he even at your place?"

"I can't tell you," I said before I could think of an excuse. "Not without his permission."

Daisy broke into a laugh. It sliced me down the middle. "You're sick."

"Please stop," said Yates. "We were doing other work. Important work. Helping girls is important work. We cannot afford to get distracted from that, and we are doing Secret Santa, please just—"

"This is the closest lead I have," I said.

"Not everything is about you." Daisy seemed to fill the entire room with her body. The whole gymnasium thrummed with nothing but her. "Tell me, how's Levi? Did you talk about him at all?"

I opened my mouth and shut it. Had we talked about him? Briefly, but not like that.

It was like she could pluck the thoughts out of my ears. Daisy flashed her canines at me. "If you talked about him, don't talk to me."

My skull buzzed. The whole of my stomach went rotten soft, like the walls of that dinky little church. Like if I was touched, I'd cave in on myself. Why did I want somebody to touch me?

"Lookie here." Daisy, eyes enormous and red and flashing, pulled one of her fists from her chest and opened her palm. She gestured beside her. "You made Lila cry."

She was crying?

I looked down and felt faint.

Yates rose, and she fluttered down the bleachers away from us. She cut across the gym floor. She spun on her heels and walked backwards, sleeve paws shoved against her face, daubing the tears so thick I could count from this distance. She locked eyes with me. She turned back around and ran.

No. No no no no no.

Jing split. She seized all of Yates' abandoned bags in one hand and her own in the other, and she sprinted down the bleachers after Yates, barked her name after her, *Lila, Lila.* Jing didn't look back at us. She disappeared between the blue double doors after Yates.

I moved to follow them.

Daisy clotheslined me.

I gasped a breath and scowled down at her, opened my mouth to cross a line, but I couldn't speak. I was fresh out of language. I looked at the girl seething beneath me, at the pain on her face, the undeniable veins of real unadulterated anguish under all the nastiness, and it seemed that of all the Scapegracers, she and I were the most alike.

"Don't go after her. You did this," Daisy said.

"We did this," I said. My lip kept twitching. "We should make amends."

"Fuck you. That's not how this works."

"What about Monique and Sheridan?" It was a weak excuse, a flimsy one, but swirling in my rage I felt fear's chilly undercurrent. I was about to drown in it. They were leaving. "Yatesy's right. This work matters. Are we just not going to help them out?"

Daisy breathed hard. "We're going to help them out. Jing and Lila and I. We've all still got our specters. We can do it ourselves. You're useless like this. We don't need your help."

My lungs slammed flat.

Daisy's hands flew. She seized my collar, jerked me down, pressed her forehead against mine. Her eyelashes tangled with mine. All I could see were her eyes. She had eyes like a lab rabbit. "Don't text me, Sideways. I'm confused enough as-is."

Then, she released me, and she was gone.

I was alone in the gym with my mouth open.

How was I going to get home?

ALL THE SHADES OF BLUE

At some point during the storm, I put my hand through the drywall. I thought I'd outgrown this sort of thing. When I was a kid, I'd rage like that for hours and utterly demolish whatever shitty little shared closet my foster parents had stowed me in, just obliterated dressers and nightstands and ugly papered walls. Maybe I was still a kid. The tide subsided. Thoughts slugged back. I lay across the foot of my bed with my hand in the air, and I watched blood dribble up along my split knuckle skin, wondered about nothing in particular. If I would be alone forever. If that was for the best. Fuck, crying sucked. My face felt tight. My sinuses slimed down my throat. There was no catharsis at the end. There wasn't some grand exorcism of all my grief. After it all I felt kind of disgusting. I put the edge of my sleeve in my mouth and sucked it.

Mr. Scratch didn't say anything. He hadn't, either out of exhaustion or an understandable desire to keep the fuck out of this. Now, he stretched his tendrils down, oozed out of my pores and slime-hooked the edge of my comforter. He pulled it over my shoulders, then collapsed back in my chest. Made a low thrumming sound like purring.

The last time I'd gotten into a fight—two weeks ago I'd hit the boy we hexed, fucking fuck that guy—Jing wanted to bandage my knuckles immediately, but she didn't have a first aid kit in her car, so Daisy coughed up some gel stickers and Jing and Yatesy triaged me by stickering the split skin shut. Made Jing laugh, made Daisy laugh, too. *Probably not sterile,* Yates had said the whole time, *but cute's got to count for something, right?* I didn't feel cute. I hid my hand under the pillow and pretended like that made the ache go away. "I fucked everything up, didn't I?"

You made a decision. I hope the benefits outweigh the consequences.

How very fucking diplomatic. My stomach went tart.

There was a rapping on my door.

I didn't want it to be Julian. Boris, maybe, but Julian would hug me and fuss and worry, and I'd crack into tears again and this whole thing would repeat. If I moved one of my sleazy slasher pinup posters over the hole I made, would either of them ever know?

"What do you want?" I sounded rough.

"To talk." Was that Boris? Definitely not Julian.

"It's open," I said. I wormed myself around, shrouded myself in a fleecy blanket. My lipstick smudged on one of the corners. It was definitely going to stain, but that was fine, I guess. Wouldn't be the first time.

The door cracked, and shoulders slipped through it.

They shrugged the door shut behind them and went still for a moment, hardly breathing. The blond hair was the same, if less stringy, but the bible-camp-J.Crew-model look had been swapped for busted jeans and one of Boris' beaten-looking concert shirts.

"Didn't take you as a fan of the Cramps, Caleb."

Mr. Scratch stopped purring.

Caleb took a long look around my room. I think he was less examining the mess and more examining the textures; I watched him trace my stacks of books, the spell-casting circle on my floor, the candles, the pulp-horror prints, the shitty Halloween decorations, the days-old apple pipe I'd hollowed out still browning on my bedside table with a lighter. Finally, he looked at me, all swaddled in my own sticky grossness. "I'm not familiar," he said. "Are you alright?"

"Peachy fucking keen."

"Can I sit?"

"Touch me and you lose a hand. But fine. Whatever."

He positioned himself on the edge of my bed. Eyes downcast. It wasn't like I had much of a metric for what he'd looked like before now, but seeing Caleb dressed like Boris was bizarre. So much of the Chantry look was about uniformity. This was just a sad-sack queer.

"I'm sorry."

"Pardon?" I blinked. "You're sorry?"

He stretched his hands over his knees and shuttered his eyes, worried a line between his brows. He chewed on something then swallowed it. "I've got a lot to be sorry for."

"Yeah." I sat up, pulled one thigh to my chest, and looped my arms around it. "You do."

"You don't have to listen to this." He opened his eyes and looked at me. At my fucked-up hand, rather. "I've been thinking about the kindness you and family have shown me. About what me and mine nearly did to you." He breathed in sharply. "Say the word and I'm gone."

"You know my friends and I are fighting because I'm letting you stay here?" I smiled so I didn't start screaming. Daisy trick.

"The fact you'd let me under your roof even after the damage I've done to you—that I'm still doing to you—is hard to get my head around. People aren't *compassionate* in real life. They aren't just *neighborly*. People are awful, they're selfish and myopic and cruel. People don't open their lives to the people who've wronged them for nothing in return."

There was that libertarianism. Batter up. "You're helping me get my specter back."

"That's not why I'm here. You wouldn't have taken me into your home just for information. Your father spent the whole day making sure I had everything I could need to do well here for a while, among other things." He made a sound in his throat. "Your hand. Did you get in a fight?"

"Not this time." I pulled my blankets closer around me. "What other things?"

He whistled through his teeth and looked, dare I say it, a little bashful. "We had a talk."

"A talk." The man loved a lecture. "Christo-fascism talk? Rent is evil talk? ACAB talk?"

"Bar raids and ACT UP talk." He inclined his head a touch. "Said I should know my history. Are you alright?"

Before he and Julian fell quickly and desperately in U-Haul love, Boris had a dedicated delinquent activist period of his life. Specifically, it was his early twenties in the late nineties, early aughts. Direct-action angel era. I only knew about portions of it. Boris and Julian can both be shy about their lives before me, I think for different reasons. Anyway, he'd surfed couches and rabble-roused and defended clinics and was arrested three or four times, depending on who was telling the story, and during that time had a veritable pantheon of mentors, the most venerated being Dennis and Antonio, a leather couple who floated in the periphery of my familial imaginary like lost grandparents. There was a framed picture of their memorial quilts in the dining room. Boris talked to the picture sometimes when he felt low, or else when he was really excited about something. I squeezed my eyes shut then opened them way too wide and imagined I could shoot beams out of my pupils that would project the word "UGH" into Caleb's mind. "You already asked me that."

"Your hand. You're bleeding."

I chewed on the seams of my cheeks.

"One second." He slid off my bed, left the room, and for a moment I thought he'd up and ditched me, but I blinked and he was back, this time with a gauze roll in his hands. "It's one of the only things I thought to take with me.

Heaven knows why." He unwound the gauze with intense attention. Like he was counting the threads as they passed over his knuckle or something. "My brothers and I fought a lot when we were smaller. I was always the one who patched up the aftermath. Made everyone feel better, myself included. I always thought so, anyway." Larynx bobbed. "May I?"

I thought seriously about saying no. Telling him to buzz off.

My hand moved before my head did. I plopped it in his lap. It felt numb immediately, not attached to me, and when he took it and smoothed the gauze's end against my palm, it was like watching a field dressing on TV. Caleb's eyelashes were translucent. I watched them abstractly.

He said, "Does your father know?"

"That I'm a witch?" I leaned my head back. "Yeah. I think witchcraft means something occult 101 to him, like my parents think I'm some kind of neopagan, but they're down with that. Plus, they love my coven. Boris told me once that he thinks the presence of a ruthless girl gang engenders stronger community. Doesn't know about witchfinders. Doesn't know what you've done to me, or else I doubt he would've let you under his roof."

He looped gauze around my biggest knuckle. Something was going on with his face, and I was in no mood to decipher it. "How much do you know about the Brethren?"

"The fuck do you mean, *the Brethren?*"

"Okay." He worked the second knuckle. "I was raised in the Soldiers of Purity Holiness Church, Ministry of the

Witchfinder Brethren. Until ninth grade, I knew exclusively other Brethren faithfuls, and attended a sort of home-schooling group with other children of the Church. Our families assume they've been anointed by Christ under the teachings of Reverend General Grier to eradicate all specters from the world. Most witchfinders in the States are Brethren."

"Jesus fucking Christ," I said.

He flashed his eyes at me and looked palpably insane. Smiled at me. I saw his gums. He held that expression, unblinking, and then slumped, jaw slack, and resumed wrapping my hand. "Yes, baby," he said. "Very much so."

Whoa! *Baby?* Suddenly I could feel my hand again. It hurt. I balked at him. "You had the vibe, I mean your brothers in that pool were basically a boymode Christian Girl Autumn cult brigade, but your Christian mission is explicitly to mask-off *rip out people's souls?*"

"Hm." He chewed his bottom lip. "Specters aren't souls. They're accessory organs born of experience, and in the eyes of the Church, their presence in the body is pollution. They aren't reflected in the body of God and are therefore irre-deemable and must be wrenched forth. Specters are moral tumors, and they're contagious. They sow the pollution of disorder on the world. Even a witch who doesn't practice her craft is a threat to the larger spiritual balance. Some Witchfinder Brethren understand having a specter as— hermaphrodizing, they'd say. A kind of third gonad. That's what my father thinks. It's against the grand design.

"If Brethren salvation comes at the washing of every hex-stained hand, taking specters is the means and the method. The Church says that a miracle allows witchfinders to pull power from extracted specters without the fallout degradation of our souls. So, it goes as you might expect. Some witchfinders use extracted specters for damn near everything, particularly witchfinders who hunt often. The Church believes it uses evil to make good." Caleb finished wrapping my hand. He tucked the gauze's corner and smoothed the edges flat. "Or espouses such."

I looked at my hand in his. I looked up at his face. I chewed, then spat, "Vile. That's vile." The image of Levi *using* Madeline's specter flickered between my eyes, and it jolted a rage through me so sudden and consuming that it almost overwrote the horror of everything else he'd said. I shook my head. Flexed my mummy-knuckled fingers, focused on the sting. "How about you, Caleb. Have you used any organs you've robbed for magic tricks lately? If your dad yanked mine out of me, what would you have done with it?"

"You were the third witch I'd ever been out after. " He rubbed a hand over his face. His eyes got bigger, wetter, harder. "I've never used a specter. I wouldn't have used yours. I wouldn't have touched it."

"Too dirty for you? Or did the miracle just skip you?"

"I was discouraged from being near them when I was little. I was *too feminine*. My family thought they'd influence me further in that direction." He smiled again, wider. "I don't believe in this, Sideways. I think it's barbarous. I've been an atheist for years. I guess for a long time I believed that witches were harmful. Specters are observable, my belief in magic is empirical, and I thought that witches holding enormous stores of auto-generated unchecked power was dangerous. Teenagers spawning nuclear reactors inside their throats. I thought our work was like a charity hospital. Pompous and condescending, hysterically corrupt, but ultimately of good and without a more ethical alternative."

"You think it's good?"

"Not anymore."

"You attacked me literally less than two months ago. Your heart wasn't in it? Is that supposed to be good enough?"

"It's not good enough," he said curtly. "I did what I was raised to do, and I did so of my own volition."

I wanted to push him off the bed. I rolled my shoulders, shrugged off the blanket. I lunged forward and pushed him off the bed.

He pitched, caught himself on my footboard. "Should I go?"

"What would they have done to you if you'd refused?" I huffed. I wouldn't forgive him. I would remember forever and I'd savor my fits of rage over it. But I wanted to get it. I wanted to wrap my head around it. I don't know what I wanted. Me and him were the same age. How old had he been the first time?

"It would not have gone unpunished. I don't know." He held the footboard tighter. "Doesn't change anything."

I rocked forward into a crouch. My bedsprings squealed. "If you ever go on an organ hunt again, I am going to kill you myself. Not joking."

He inclined his head a touch. "That'd be warranted."

"This is so fucked."

"Yes."

Inside me, my devil foamed. He whipped himself into sharp edges, and something older and uglier than language pieced out, *EAT THEM EAT THEM EAT THEM.*

"What happened to you is anomalous. Old-fashioned hunts are mostly"—he breathed in sharply—"social. My ancestors set up shop in Jamestown. Accruing specters under the pretense of saving people meant that they used magic to terraform the colonies to their liking. They used extracted specters to pull improbable luck. For surveillance, call it divine prophecy, and enforcement. I know Brethren in Congress. I know Brethren all over corporate, Brethren in the financial sector, Brethren in medicine. My father's the sheriff. Law enforcement is a hugely popular career path for us, litigation too. Every time my father books somebody, he inspects them for spectral radiation and extracts anything he finds. I'd put down good money that my father's used specters to pad every election he's won. He's on the school board, and he certainly used one for that. A cousin of mine wanted to buy land from a farmer who wouldn't cough up his field, so he cursed it, and all his crops rotted alive, and the bank foreclosed his farm, and my cousin built a five-car garage there."

He curled his lip. "Making anything happen requires theft first. Fuel first. Brethren have systematized witchfinding, and the power that systematized witchfinding has produced has made everyone in the Church filthy rich, and being filthy rich expands power, which means more insidious, broader-reaching methods of witchfinding. It just grows and grows."

"Specters are like calluses." Scratch fizzled behind my sinuses. He beat in my ears. "They develop when ossified power chafes on you. You don't fit with power, you get your little liver, you can process power in a watery weird way that doesn't fit structure. Building systems to capture people," I said, "literally makes more witches."

"Profit." He made a thin sound in his throat. "I never was good enough at running away. They caught me all the times I tried. I should've been better. I'll be making up for it forever."

"When did you start running away?"

"Oh. Abel had just started going to high school, so I guess Levi and I were thirteen? Something like that." He rolled his mouth. "Levi always caught me. Him and Abel both."

My brain hurt, and my tongue, on account of how hard I'd been biting it. "I cannot remember how fucking many of you there are. You all blur together in my head. Fuck Levi, though."

He closed his eyes. "There's four of us. Abel, my older brother, wants to be a televangelist. David is my little brother. He's a dumb kid. I could've been better with him. Levi is my twin."

"Twins are freaky."

"I don't think we're a fair representation." He pressed his palms together suddenly, then shoved the base of his thumbs against the bridge of his nose. "They aren't my brothers anymore. I don't have any brothers."

"Like, good. Sucks that you were homeless, glad you're not, but fuck 'em. Say *fuck 'em*, Caleb."

Third smile. I thought he might cry. "Fuck 'em is right." He tucked his hands between his knees. "I'm sorry, Sideways. I'm going to be proving that for a long time."

I sniffed. "Talk about Madeline."

In the back of my head, Mr. Scratch thrummed and said, *What happened to the two witches that came before you? All of my daughters are dead.*

I squeezed my own wrist.

"Right." His smile scooped downwards. "Mom was her tutor. I don't know how they met. Always suspected that my father picked Madeline up somewhere and offered his wife as a personal finishing school as an alternative to juvie. Anyway. Starting last fall, Madeline came over twice a week, and she and Mom would arrange themselves in the parlor and look over Madeline's AP homework and ACT prep and so on. Voice lessons. Etiquette, sometimes. Madeline paid by helping in the garden and making dinner. Levi was completely obsessed with her. It's beyond me how she ever reciprocated. She's a cool girl and he earnestly wishes that he could've been a character in *Dead Poets Society*. She's out of his league.

"It got intense fast. Levi doesn't understand the meaning of the word 'casual,' and Madeline seemed interested in being interesting. You couldn't have pried them apart with a crowbar. It was revolting. I'd turn corners and they'd jump-scare me. Enthusiastically obsoleted Levi's purity ring. Kill me. But I liked Madeline, and she spent more and more time at our house, and my father gets it in his head that Madeline and Levi might get married after graduation. Everybody was thrilled about the idea, Madeline aside. I think it was just a relief that Levi was extravagantly and menacingly monogamous after the staggering disappointment of Abel being a total pervert. Then, eventually, Levi takes her to service. She runs out halfway through the sermon. At the time, I thought it was a healthy reaction to watching my little brother speak in tongues for an hour, but everyone else suspects that she objected to the sermon's contents. The proverbial sweating sinner in church, come to roost.

"So, she starts skipping tutoring sessions. She comes around less often, and when she does, things are different. Tense. She and Levi have this blowout fight. It was right around Christmas, so about a year ago on the dot. They threw things at each other. Destroyed a sitting room. She wouldn't tell me what happened, but the way Levi said it, she'd wanted to run away with him. She wanted Levi to shrug off his name, the family, the Brethren, and just be a stupid kid with her. Catch an overnight bus and go west. She told him that she thought Abel wanted to kill her, that he'd threatened her. Levi wouldn't ever abandon his legacy. He loves the story of being a Witchfinder, he loves feeling grand and like he matters, like he's on a special mission, and he rebuked her for saying otherwise. Told her that they could be happy in the Brethren. That he loved her. That he'd take care of her and that Abel wouldn't lay a finger on her. She was dead set. Immovable. So he told her that he caved, he'd run away with her, and they should go upstairs and pack before the Christmas party so that they could leave that night, steal away from the party and vanish.

"They go upstairs. We're all waiting around in the foyer, all kind of impatient. Then Levi comes downstairs. Just Levi. He looked awful, white-lipped and boiling with sweat. There was a rip in his sleeve that hadn't been there before. He was panting. He said he felt poorly, that he should take a separate car. My father—Elias—explodes, as he does, and instead of immediately showing belly Levi's getting progressively weirder and weirder, and then there's a crash upstairs. Mom goes up to investigate. When she comes down, she asks Levi where Madeline had gone.

"Levi panics. He bolts upstairs, busts into a screaming fit, then flutters back downstairs sobbing. We pressed him about it. He said that they'd broken up and she'd left. I guess she left out that window, the same way you did. I didn't know what Levi had done to her. Not for the next month or two. Right around Valentine's Day, a bunch of family friends came over, and we went out hunting." He looked green. "We talked about witchfinding while we were out. These family friends have really high numbers, much higher than my dad's, even. They were talking about how they faked people's deaths after they sawed their specter out. They kept joking about how you have to hope for convenient cardiac arrest so that you don't have to deal with bribing medical examiners. Levi bugged out. He *fixated* on finding Madeline again. I think he needed to make sure she was alive. He did nothing but drive around the places where they used to hang out for months. He didn't have any luck until that party in early October. It's only around then that he told me what he did to her. He should thank his stars that Abel got between us. He was so heartbroken that his mimic caught you, Sideways. Last conversation we had, he kept muttering her name."

I balled my fists so tightly that I thought the gauze might split.

"I don't know where Madeline is now. I make it my business not to know." He smoothed the denim on his thighs and exhaled. It sounded jagged. "I think I know what might help."

"Say it, then."

"Levi's neurotic, and sentimental, and territorial. He absolutely kept her specter. I'd bet you anything he's got it locked in his room."

Wait. Shit. Fuck!

"If we got it, we could return it. Trade it for mine." I felt a throbbing in my throat. I dug my fingers into the meat above my rib cage. I wanted to cry.

We sat in silence for a moment.

"I bet he showed her how to do that. How to rob you of yours, that is." Caleb shuddered. Actually shuddered, trembled all over. He shook his head. "I know she did something unforgivable to you, Sideways, but you can't blame her. Not all the way. Levi did that to you. My whole family did. I did." His eyes got bigger. They filled up his entire face. Big bright blue. "Why am I here?"

"Existentially?" I smiled, not kindly, but with the wryness of being unable to scream like I oughta. "That's your problem to work out, fucko."

"In your home. In your room." He turned to face me fully, crisscrossed his legs, shoved his hands in his lap. "I know we've been over this. I know. You're a good person and you don't like people sleeping on benches and so on. Listen, I thought I was going to *freeze to death* this weekend, Sideways. I thought I was going to die in that chapel and that *nobody would miss me.* My only friends are family friends, which means they aren't my friends at all. Good. I mean they shouldn't be my friends because they're awful, *everybody I've ever fucking met is awful,* and the only person who's been kind to me is somebody who I've irrevocably wronged. Look, after this, I'm never going to bring up my witchfinding damage with you, because you shouldn't have to deal with it. But I want you to know that I am going to be better. I refuse not to be better. I might fuck up and falter and say the wrong things because I haven't figured out how not to be wrong yet, not all the way, but I'm going to *try*. Anything you need, it's yours. Anything. If that means"—he hitched his breath—"if that means I go back in that house, I will. I'll go back to help you look. Anything you want."

I breathed through my open mouth. His face turned an odd, iridescent pink.

Think he's earnest?

I nodded. Didn't have a reason not to. But then, it'd take a hot fucking second to deal with the whole *two other witches* thing. I wasn't ready to ask about that yet because I wasn't ready to think about it. I sucked my cheeks in. "Would you be willing to tell all of what you just said to my friends? They might not be so kind." Understatement of the century.

Assuming they were still my friends, that is.

Everything sucks!

I fucking hate everything.

His cheeks went red, but he shut his mouth and swallowed. "Yes. Anything you want."

"Okay," I said. "Okay, I believe you. Please breathe."

He rubbed the back of his hand over his mouth. When he moved that way, his sleeve shifted back, and I thought the skin by his shoulder might've been tinged black and green.

The crows outside were really going wild.

I needed something to do with my hands. I scanned the

cacophony of my room and my brain plucked the box of nail polish I kept beneath my bedside table, deemed it handworthy. I reached off the bed, fished for the box's handle, pulled it into my lap.

Caleb's eyes fell on the box. He blinked a few times.

"Movie's starting in fifteen!" Boris' voice ricocheted through the air vents.

"Movie?" I hadn't been informed we'd be watching a movie. I opened the box, shifted through the mass of little bottles. I'd tried to drink nail polish once. Wouldn't recommend. Sucked hard. "What movie?"

"He thinks I should watch"—he blinked—"*The Fires of Paris.*"

"*Paris Is Burning.*" Boris education session continues, then. Figures. "Should be enough time to paint my nails, then. They can dry while we're watching."

He nodded. He hadn't looked away from the box.

"Want some?" I licked my gums. They tasted inky. Oh, Mr. Scratch. "The orange would look good on you. I never wear it, anyway."

He froze.

"You don't have—"

He thrust out his hands and nodded yes.

✳ EIGHT ✳

SCRUMDIDDLYUMPTIOUS

I hadn't guessed exactly how shitty the feeling of sitting alone again at lunch would be, but holy mother of fuck, it wasn't great. I hadn't been formally excommunicated from the table (and the friend group under whose dominion the table fell), but Daisy had reverse pick-pocketed me a slip of notebook paper in first period that read IN EXILIUM BITCH. I thought I was the weird one. Plus, Yates wasn't here today, which was unlike her. Everything about Yates screamed Perfect Attendance Sticker Prize. I worried about it, felt certain that because I'd made her cry—send my ass right to hell—that I'd also gotten her sick. Somehow. I fished my phone out of my pocket, nearly texted her *Im sorry about the fight* and *I miss us* and *Are u doing ok,* but all of those felt excruciating, and sending a meme felt gauche, so I landed clumsily on, **Are you sick should i bring you soup?**

> **not sick, just sad. eating in the library. ugh!**
> **please say you still love everybody**

> **Yeah. I do**

**Do you want me to come eat in there with
you**

**no i kind of want the quiet. said no to jing
too. talk soon**

That was that. I do still love everybody. Squirmy to have
questioned and squirmier still to acknowledge, but it was
Yates, and she was upset. Vulnerability and space would
have to work. I wanted neither. I had to keep my head in the
game.

Keeping one's head in the game is an essential part of
winning said game, and I wasn't being near as good at doing
shit today as I needed to be. I needed to be thinking up
sigils. Needed to be thinking of an action plan, of a way to
get me through Madeline's barbed-wire mess of hex marks
without spiraling off the road and snapping my neck. I
needed to consider how to work with Caleb without getting
skewered by him, because I guess I believed that he was a
cult survivor or whatever and that he'd been programmed to
do evil and it wasn't *entirely* his fault, though some of it
absolutely was, and I bought his grief and shame, but I
didn't believe that he wouldn't fuck me over in a corner. I
didn't know him like that. He could Judas my ass immediately. I couldn't afford to get paranoid about that. I had so
many things to do. Why was it so hard to concentrate on
even a single thing?

Somewhere else, Madeline was feeling good. First time I

could feel her feeling good in weeks. In the back of my throat, there was a greasy shimmer of oil. She was eating something fried and bathed in salt. It clung to my—to her— fingertips and made the grooves on each pad slick. I kept rubbing my hands on my jeans, kept trying to get the feeling off me, but it was no use. Wasn't my hands that were grimy. I kept inspecting my nail beds for shine.

My thumbnail felt wet. Had she licked it?

"Eloise." A little cough by my desk.

I blinked. Looked up slowly, button by button, at my biology teacher. He had a name, but he looked enough like a toad that everybody called him Toady, poor fuck. Toady looked extra-toady today, flat-eyed, flat-mouthed and crinkled like a plastic bag, perpetually inexplicably moist. He had pale fingers clasped like he was pleading.

"Eloise," he said again. "Care to explain the structural difference between a fish's eye and a sheep's?"

I fought the urge to slam my head through my desk. I imagined it vividly. Little explosion of smoking sawdust and old dried bubblegum. My forehead busted. The whole classroom like, *Ooh shit. She really is crazy.* "One's in a fish."

"Please listen to the conversation in the room. It makes it less awkward for everyone when you're called on." He turned his back, went like he was going to write something on the whiteboard, and I shoved my face in my hands.

"Yeah, yeah," I breathed. "Ribbit-ribbit, I'll keep that in mind."

Toady froze.

I froze, too.

Toady pursed his lips. "Stay for a moment after class, Eloise."

Cool! I was going to die.

He took a box off his desk and turned to face the class again, made his way along the first row of shitty blond desks. Toady had a stately vibe. Like a Roman senator. "We're diagramming the parts of a sheep's eye today. Dissection procedures are not different this time than last time— wear gloves, don't cut yourself, and take care when you're making incisions. If you cut your specimen into shredded cheese, you can't use it successfully as a diagramming tool, and you won't learn anything from it. It'd be a waste. I'll write PETA myself. We don't have enough eyes for everybody, so I'll be pairing you up."

My fingertips tingled down to the marrow. Damp and buzzing. Madeline had licked them all by this point. Goose bumps bloomed up and down me. I felt deranged.

Through the pulsating numbness of my horror, a woozy, almost drunk-sounding Mr. Scratch said, *Not enough eyes for everybody? Don't you all already have eyes of your own? Do you need extras? Do you have a spare, perchance?*

"Dissection," I hissed under my breath. Mr. Scratch hadn't been talkative much today, and he'd spent most of his time pooled in my elbows, slogging around and refusing to circulate. Made it look like I'd tried to crack my arms in half with a car door. He was so bruisy looking under the skin. "Are you still feeling bad from saving my ass?" Not mentioned, but implied: *and from having saintly restraint what with the ex-witchfinder in my house?*

I've felt better.

Toady passed out little kits—punch-red Tupperware-looking boxes filled with studs, scalpels, and scissors, I'd guess, torture devices, and gloves, and the eyes. He made his rounds around the classroom, setting down the plastic boxes on every other desk, naming pairs of students as he went. In seconds he'd descended on me. He avoided eye contact and pressed one edge of the box against my desk, let the other edge fall with a decisive *click.* "Eloise and Michael," he said.

Michael?

Mickey-Dick.

Mickey-Dick had been a friend of mine, vaguely, since the start of high school. He was the only other crew person in drama club, and we'd been the only out queer kids freshman year. We'd never really hung out outside of school. He was into the farm parties where you packed as many kids into the back of a truck as possible, drove out into the fields, blasted rap music, got stupid high, and caught something on fire. Sounds fun, but the only one I'd ever been to nearly killed me. Somebody had put a can of peaches on the pyre in the name of stoner science, and when it'd exploded into fruity shrapnel, two kids had to go to the ER. One of those kids was me. Four stitches in my arm. Still have the scar. Point is, Mickey-Dick and I aren't that kind of tight. Also, he hasn't really talked to me much since I slept with his ex-girlfriend last summer, and really-really hasn't after the advent of the Scapegracers. Thought my illustrious cofounders were stupid conniving sluts, etc. etc.

One would think that straight boys would be more into girls. I don't know. He was an edgelord. I hate it here.

Mickey-Dick dragged his desk over to mine. He pressed them nose to nose, blatantly ignoring the foot he stepped on in the process, and flipped the ill-dyed hair out of his eyes with a toss of his head. "Sideways," he said. "My favorite dyke."

"Mickey-Dick," I said. Weird. This wasn't banter that I thought we were allowed to have, now that I was estranged from the drama club lunch table on account of my being an alleged normie-loving traitor. Shaming me for having hot friends when you unironically own a waifu body pillow? Pretty rich. I felt so tired. Besides, I wasn't even sure he was my favorite transmasc. "Boy that's here."

"Okay, touchy. I'll be delicate and shit."

Mr. Scratch said, *Where are the eyes, Sideways?*

"Jesus, chill the fuck out," I said to both of them. I pulled the box closer, mostly so that he wouldn't have the chance to look at it properly, and surveyed the contents. Aluminum tin, sharp things, lilac latex, and the eye.

The eye looked like fresh mozzarella. Fresh mozzarella with a raisin emblazoned in the center like a badge, a horrible, no-good badge. And the eyelashes! It still had fucking eyelashes!

"No. Nope. Fuck that," said Mickey-Dick. "I can't look at that. I'll yack up everywhere."

"Wuss." I pulled on the latex gloves with a satisfactory snap. "You do the paperwork and I'll do the cutting, sound good?"

He nodded vigorously.

Oh, Sideways. Oh, my daughter. Mr. Scratch had a watery, reverent tone. *What a beautiful eye that is. What is on it? Is that formaldehyde on it?*

"Formalin," I said. "Why do you care?"

"I do *not* care," Mickey-Dick hissed. "This is awful. I'm vegan. Can I be exempt?"

"Vegans don't eat Slim Jims." I licked my teeth and tasted ink. A lot of ink, enough to cut the grease of Madeline's meal. Why was he in my mouth? He was *prominently* in my mouth, more than he usually was. It felt like when a clot falls on your tongue after a nosebleed. If I tried to speak right now I'd run the risk of him gushing between my teeth.

Sideways, Mr. Scratch cooed. *Oh, that looks delicious.*

I balked so hard I nearly spat him on the scalpels.

You wouldn't eat it! You wouldn't even have to swallow. I'd do that. You would just have to put it in your mouth until I was done eating it. I'd feel so much better if I ate something, dear heart. I am so sluggish. I feel useless to you this way. And it's such a beautiful eye! I would love to eat it. Please let me eat it. Please oh please.

I shook my head. Hair flew everywhere, nearly scourged Mickey-Dick across the face.

"You having a seizure?" Mickey-Dick squinted at me.

I shoved a hand over my mouth to hide the devil ink and

said, "Just not thrilled about eye-chopping. Just. Give me a second." I took up the scalpel. Gave it a squeaky, latex squeeze. My reflection in the blade looked greenish.

Please oh please oh please.

He filled my whole mouth now. Took effort not to chipmunk my cheeks just to hold him.

He saved your life, I told myself. He is continually saving your lesbian ass. You are alive because you are the shell to his devilish hermit crab. Oughtn't you repay him?

Dear conscience: mind your own business.

I picked up the eyeball. We were supposed to thumb over it, said the instructions I'd somehow internalized, to find the optic nerve where it jutted out of the back of the eye like a stupid springy erect finger. I flashed it at Mickey-Dick, who scratched it off our list, and then I went for scissors. Cut the lashes, peeled the fatty eyelids back.

Yes, yes, like that. Oh, just like that. It's the underneath that I want the most.

"Sclera, cornea," he breathed. "It looks like a little ghost. Oh god."

I punctured the white and juices dripped on the tray.

"Oh my god. Oh my god." Mickey-Dick sweated like a dog in a locked car. "Oh my god oh my god. I don't want to see. Don't let me see. Can I just not see? Look I'm just going to fill out the rest of this from the textbook and not look at this oh my god, Sideways."

Don't keep cutting. You'll let the lovely chewy bits loose. It's much better with the lovely chewy bits, Sideways. It's so delicious. It's very good for me. I will feel so much better if I eat it with the chewy middle bits and all. Sideways, my darling dearest dear. My noble daughter. My courageous, goodly child. Please put this eye in your mouth.

My pulse jackhammered in my temples.

Under my breath, ground between my teeth, I said, "You sure I won't have to swallow?"

Yes!

"Mickey-Dick, don't look," I said.

Mickey-Dick nodded enthusiastically.

I palmed the eye. Nobody seemed to notice. I held it under the desk for a moment, thrumming all over, and when I thought that nobody was looking, I slammed my palm against my open mouth. Popped the eye between my teeth like a kumquat.

Miraculous how quick Formalin makes your whole face burn!

The chemical taste curdled my blood.

There are not words to describe the texture of preserved eye. It was weighty on my tongue but was yielding in a way that confirmed it was delicate, membranous, like a bursting bubble in bubble tea. A little rubbery. Briny, vaguely pork-like. I drank Windex once as a kid, and until now I thought without a doubt that that was the worst taste a human can weather, but a Formalin-soaked sheep's eye hits different. It burned all the way down my throat and stung up in my nasal cavities. My toes curled in my boots. My throat clapped and my gut screwed.

Mr. Scratch purred. Then he started to move. He slithered circles around my mouth, orbited the eye at rapid speed. His ink enveloped it. He whirled faster, and faster still, like self-gargling mouthwash if mouthwash was thicker and tasted like a busted pen. With each rotation, the eye was stripped away. His spinning peeled back all the squelching hard and soft of it, the outside layers dissolving, the lens wearing to dust. Felt fucking bizarre on my soft palate. Unmentionable on my tongue. When the bulk was gone, tendrils of Mr. Scratch slipped down the lining of my throat and up my nose, and he lapped up the chemical smell with happy, catlike sounds. It felt like I was being brain-sucked by a jellyfish.

What I'd do for that french-fry Madeline taste again.

I put my face in my latex-y hands and moaned.

"You okay?" Mickey-Dick sounded croaky. "You look kinda rough, Sideways."

The thought of opening my mouth right now to speak was hilariously bad. What if eye gunk fell out? I didn't think Mr. Scratch was quite finished yet, seeing as he hadn't stopped lacing between my teeth. I just shrugged. Hoped my shrug was convincing.

"Hey, uh." He must've shifted around because his desk kept squeaking. "It's not the same without you eating lunch with us on the stage, you know? Just saying. You're the closest thing to another guy we've got."

I felt a little twinge in my stomach. It might not be a twinge that could've existed if I hadn't fought with my

Scapegracers, because I wasn't generally twingy about fucking Mickey-Dick, but now? Maybe it was a gender thing. I was doing my best not to dwell on gender things right now, and the fact that maybe I was a spicier kind of lezzie than I'd automatically assumed. You know, like a lezzie whose gender is just lezzie. Butch exclusively. One of those. Man oh man. I glanced at him between cracks in my fingers. He wasn't looking at me, he was looking at his crusty thumbs.

"They aren't your crowd, you know." He scraped the dirt from under his nail with a pencil tip. "Since when have you ever been comfortable around skinny cishets? Huh? Do they really understand anything about you? I know they're playing along with all your occult shit, but that doesn't mean they *get* you. Besides, don't you think it's kind of fucked up that people were terrible to you when you were doing that stuff on your own, but now they're suddenly super into it once the pretties got involved? It isn't fair. They're upcycling your bit. I'm just saying that we're where you make sense, is all. We've had our spats or whatever, but at least we understand each other."

Not a single damn Scapegracer was het. Anyway. That's no tone to take when talking about girls, goddamn it.

Mr. Scratch was slowing down. He hummed a little tune that sounded vaguely ragtime-ish and settled, warm and content, in the hollow of my collarbone. My mouth was empty again, and mercifully tasteless. It felt like I'd had a weeklong gnarly head cold in the span of five minutes.

"Don't talk about them." I coughed. "You thought my occult shit was freaky, didn't you?"

"Well, sure," he said. "It is."

"Didn't much feel like you were understanding me then." I tongued my gums. What the fuck would I do if I found left-over eye globs? Just expire? Combust? I bumped my bad hand's knuckles and focused on the grounding hurt. "Did you fill out our worksheet stuff? Are we good?"

"Yeah, we're good." He didn't say anything about not getting it, didn't defend himself. He looked vaguely bored, actually. He offered his bitten-up pencil to me and jabbed a finger at the name line, where he'd already chicken-scratched MICHAELRICHARDSON in Linear B. "Want gum?"

"I've never wanted gum more in my fucking life." I accepted the pencil and wrote my name, the legal one, under his scribbling. He hadn't really left space on the line proper because manspreading is conceptual as well, evidently. "Yeah, please."

He passed me a slice under the table with the serious-ness of a drug deal.

How anybody took him seriously with his actual drug deals was beyond me.

I took the gum, crumpled the foil, and relished the fake clean of mint. Mint makes your bones feel new and my teeth are my favorite bones. This undid the tarnish of pressing a fucking formaldehyde-pickled sheep's eye between them, at least in gesture.

Bell rang.

Everybody got up before Toady told them all to clean. A couple of well-intentioned kiss-asses straggled behind, desperately trying to clean up all the eyeball debris, and I nearly lunged for the door toward freedom before Toady gave me a *look*.

I sat back down and waited.

Everybody filed out of the classroom, and I was left with him and the mostly tidied kits. If I was in a better mood, I maybe would've helped. Or maybe I wouldn't have because I'm a shitty, selfish kid. Who knows.

Toady came up me. He sat in the spot where Mickey-Dick had been, propped up one elbow on the desk. "Eloise," he said. "I'm going to be real with you for a moment, okay?"

Goody.

"I think it'd be a good idea if you went to visit the school guidance counselor. She has group sessions that would get you out of class, you know? How's that sound? I've been teaching for a long time. You're a bright student. I've seen bright students absolutely deflate before, and it has never once been just because they're lazy or entitled. I don't think this is senoritis, that doesn't usually hit until second semester. Are you alright? Anything, erm, going on?"

I hated him and this and suddenly wanted to sob my lungs up.

"You're straddling that D line right now. You could pull it up to a high C, low B if you do *really* well on the final next week and turn in all the assignments you skipped. I'll take them late. I want you to succeed, I really do. I don't particularly enjoy watching kids crash and burn. If you don't turn in everything you owe by, say, Friday? I'm going to call your parents. I should've called them a while ago, but I kept expecting you to pick yourself up on your own. I'm going to give you a few days' catch-up, though, before I do that. It's the end of the semester, there isn't a whole lot I can do, but I think you can manage this. Turning in something is better than turning in nothing."

Telling Boris and Julian about this would not be good. Boris would give me a lecture about how grades don't matter but the system is broken and values numbers over kids, etc. etc. etc., and Julian would think he'd personally failed and was a terrible father and I'd feel so guilty that I'd have to run away into the woods and never come back.

"Which is why I'm giving you detention for the rest of the week." He folded his hands politely. "It'll be time for you to do the work. Designated time without any distractions, no phone, no TV, no boys, no nothing."

Fascism! What! I screwed my mouth open and through my fury, all I could manage was, "No boys?"

"It'll be good for you," he said. "Just get it over with. You'll want to be in the library after last bell. It's an hour. You'll survive. I'll send you with fresh copies of all the assignments and let you borrow the book. Just crank out as many as possible. It'll drag your grade up. Understand me?"

The gum in my mouth was losing flavor. I shook all over and somewhere in there, I nodded. The motion made my neck hurt. Mr. Scratch stirred in his fed happiness, listlessly billowed little bits of himself around my sternum.

"Yeah," I said. "I understand."

"Good." He knocked on the desk and smiled. "I'll write you a slip for your next class. You're already late."

✳

Caleb texted like Daisy. Who'd have thunk it.

back from school where r u

Detention, fuck off

srsly wait y??

What's it to you

when will u b home i have news

Just tell me now

"No phones in detention," snapped the detention teacher who seemed to be under the impression that she'd been employed as a correctional officer. She slammed her tyrant hand over my phone screen and knocked it against the desk. "Turn it off and keep it out of sight . . . Pike."

Was that a little tongue-against-the-hard-palate action she'd tried before the P? Did I catch a half-formed pansy attempt at a D before her flimsy conscience—or her career-instability bone—jerked into place? Maybe so. Lots of dyke talk going around! None of the fun kind.

Or maybe I was being hypervigilant for no reason.

Between me and Madeline and Mr. Scratch, I really must have triple-deluxe bespoke PTSD. I was a psychoanalytic nightmare. I was a nightmare in general.

I turned off my phone and chucked it into the depths of my backpack. The library smelled wet and mildewed, which I didn't quite mind, but it mixed in a funny awful way with how hungry I felt.

I am sorry I didn't share the eye.

It was spectacular how much I didn't mind his lack of generosity.

I spread out all the assignments I'd neglected and stared at them. There were so many of them, just fistfuls and fistfuls, more than should have fit in my bag. A whole ream of paper. Had I really forgotten so much since Madeline ripped the me out of me?

Some part of me ached like I slept on it wrong. That part wanted me to be able to focus and write down answers because it should be easy, or it should at least be doable. It was reading and writing things down. Same stuff I'd been doing since I was little. It wasn't new, it wasn't hard, it certainly wasn't worth fucking up my grades for, but honestly?

How was I supposed to care about grades? Really care, care enough to supersede my hunger for being me again? I couldn't picture myself without myself, not in college, not at a job, not rotting away in my dads' antique shop behind the skin mag fridge. Why would it matter about the grades? Seriously, why? What future was I meant to be defending, here?

Would you like me to help?

I needed help. In a lot of fucking ways, I needed help.

I put one hand on the textbook and the other on my homework stack, and I felt Mr. Scratch bleed through the palms of my hand. He seeped through the textbook, then zoomed up the length of my arm, looped around my chest and popped out the other arm in a bloom of my scratchy handwriting. Answers swam around the pages and settled neatly below each question.

Cheating, sure. Sue me. Wasn't like we weren't allowed to use the book.

Something knocked against my ankle and twined around the leg of my rickety desk chair. A solid something. Like the size of a chestnut. Kinda stung. I jerked on impact, then blinked down at my boots in bewilderment.

There was a yo-yo wrapped around my ankle. A plastic, coin-operated-vending-machine-style yo-yo, whose string looked bizarrely like dental floss. There was something taped to either face of it. I bent my head and picked it up, flipped it in my palm.

One side read, MEET ME BEHIND THE LOCKER ROOMS AFTER DETENTION IS UP BITCH.

The other side read, XOXOX JING.

NINE

THE DOGHOUSE

Jing waited as promised. She wore her hair up in two buns with straggler locks escaping here and there, blond burning where the sunlight glanced off her. Red sunglasses, cheetah-print parka, jeans cuffed up above the ankles. Ruffly sweetheart-pink gingham crop top that somehow didn't get her killed by firing squad for dress code violation. Arms crossed. Chin jerked downwards. Shoulders shoved up against the sallow locker room bricks. She had a toothpick hanging out of the corner of her mouth, or maybe it was the stem of a Dum Dum. Her music was playing loud enough that I could hear it from a few paces out. It was her BIG DUMB LOUD ANGRY playlist. I recognized it. I'd made it for her.

I shoved my hands in my pockets to keep them from fluttering around and scuffed my toe across the pavement. It was chillier today than it'd been earlier this week, crisp in the bridge of my nose. Breathing was crunchy. My guts all thrummed together.

Her music clicked off before she looked at me. She didn't look at me when she took a step forward, neither. Her hands flew out and seized my collar, and she yanked me forward, spun me around so that my back shoved up against where she'd just been, pushed hard. My head spun and I blinked like it'd actually help me adjust. Lungs reinflated with effort.

Jing looked at me now that she had me. She sized up something, read something on my face, then slackened up her grip, slid her touch down my lapels and off, put her hands on her hips. I opened my mouth to say something. She spat the stick—definitely a former lollipop, candy carnage still clinging to the paper—squarely at my nose.

It glanced off but hit my hair and stuck there. Time is a crushed Coke can.

"What do you want, Jing?" I didn't bother plucking the stick out. I just got comfortable against the wall, tried at least, and looked at her neutrally. Jaw set, cold and casual. No crying. Wasn't going to happen. "I thought you three were mad at me."

"First off. We're not a fucking hive mind," she said.

I gnawed on my tongue.

"Second off"—she shoved her sunglasses up on her forehead, rumbled her swoopy bangs—"I'm mad in general." She bounced on the balls of her feet like a boxer. "Listen. Lila is beside herself, she's so upset. She hates conflict, she's all kinds of stressed about applications, and before you texted her she kept wondering if she should text you, but she was afraid that if she did, Daisy would be mad. Which, for the record, she was. Then I get furious because Daisy shouldn't be the arbiter of who Yates texts, and anybody that makes Yates upset deserves the goddamn guillotine. So I'm mad at you for making Yates sad and for shoving already wigged-out Daisy deeper into whatever spiral of entitled bitchy ridiculousness is preoccupying her precious evil mind right now, and I'm mad at Daisy, because she's clearly in crisis and refuses to open up about it, and if I could stand to be mad at Yates, I'd be mad at her, too. It's deeply and profoundly stupid. I hate all of it. And that's not even broaching the big thing, huh." She pushed the flats of her palms behind her ears, which knocked her glasses askew, not that she noticed. "We got to talk about your Chantry, Sideways."

My jaws flapped open and I nearly said something like, *He's not my Chantry*, but I caught it before it fell out. A throbbing section of my stomach said that it'd be a super stupid idea. "Okay," I said instead. "Let's talk, then."

"He still in your house?"

"Yeah. He is."

"Well, fuck me sideways."

"What?" Blood buzzed in my skull.

"Not you. It's an expression." She massaged little circles on her scalp. "I'm not going to pretend like I'm cool with this. I'm not. I think it's dangerous and stupid and I don't want you getting hurt. You're my friend. You fucking matter to me. I'm not thrilled about the idea of leaving you high and dry with this guy, either."

Wow. Felt that somewhere.

I held my hand up like, *pause*. Fished out my phone, ignored whatever text Caleb had most recently sent me and asked, **can I tell a witch in my coven why tf I let you stay over?**

Jing clucked her tongue.

yes. pls just don't post anything

I confirmed and stowed the phone in my pocket again. Rubbed my fingertips on my coat. "Okay, so. Caleb's queer. Sheriff Chantry and their weird evangelical girl-killer cult disowned him. He'd been sleeping in a shitty abandoned building for days when I found him, and I didn't have the heart to turn away a homeless queer kid, Jing, I just can't do that. Boris has been giving him a queer politics smackdown, and he's taking it really well. I believe him when he says he's been thinking about it. About how he was wrong before, I mean. About witches and the rest. Maybe it's stupid to believe him, but I do."

Jing looked at me for a moment. She sucked in her cheeks.

"I know he's—"

"Fuck. I knew that's a thing. Like I knew it's a thing that parents throw their kids out, I've seen the statistics or what-ever. I did a lot of nervous googling a while back about being bisexual, being in the community and so on. I've tried to bring it up, but I think my parents are just like, nervous weird liberals who loudly accept gays but don't know anything about gays and don't really believe me, it's what-ever, but they wouldn't ever do something like that. Holy shit. I intellectually understand. Just."

"Yeah," I said. Whistled out a breath through my gap teeth. "Like, double-fuck Sheriff Chantry, man."

"For sure," she said. "Alright, I get it. I still hate it, but I get it. I get it and I adore you being so generous. Here's the thing though, Sideways—you should still Chett him."

"That's a little—"

"Hear me out. Discuss it with him. If you Chett him, it shouldn't actually punish him so long as he does nothing wrong. He'll have a pretty little tattoo choker without any of the symptoms, and if he so much as muses over the idea of dragging you to his parents, the hex will let us know and keep you safe. If he wants to change, he'll agree to it." Jing, fidgety—she was nervous—pulled the glasses off her head and popped one end between her teeth, spoke in muffled tones around it. "It's safer. So, so much safer."

I nearly retorted for pride's sake, but something flickered in the back of my head.

I was the third. Caleb had assisted in the soul-ripping of two witches before me.

"Yeah," I said. Giving up tasted bitter on the tongue, so I scraped it with my buck front teeth like it was that fuzz that clings to your mouth when you just wake up. "Yeah, that's a good idea." Would he let me? He'd been willing to let me paint his nails and lecture him about music and capitalism, sat still and receptive the whole time. But a former witchfinder just allowing me to hex him? We'll see. At least, Mr. Scratch was vibrating at the idea.

"It might take Daisy a little longer to warm up to the

idea." Jing chewed thoughtfully. "Yates loves a sad story, she's a big bleeding heart and I think she'd do a lot just to get us all to stop fighting. She's languishing, Sideways. It's bad. It's just Daisy that I'm worried about. She gets so stubborn about these things. Loyalty, stuff like that. I totally get that she's got fun trauma around it, but she lets it spill into things it shouldn't, and she gets her feelings invested. Plus, whatever is going on with her is making her very nearly literally impossible to be around. I don't think Caleb's situation would warm her up very much. Or maybe it would. I don't know." She paused for a moment, stared at me dead-on. She didn't blink, didn't break eye contact for a good few seconds. "Can I confide in you, Sideways?"

"Does confiding mean you still like me?"

"Look at you and your silly little brain. Dummy. The Scapegracers might be in a fucking grind right now, but I never once said I stopped liking you, now did I? Don't be stupid. Firm reminder for the thousandth time: I like you, we all like you, even Daisy likes you, she's just having a nervous breakdown diva moment right now." She snorted. "Look, that's what I wanted to tell you. About Daisy, I mean. She made a pass at me last night."

Oh. Huh. A memory of her hands in my hair flickered around the back of my skull, of her telling me how soft it was, that she wasn't much fond of boys. So, picking up on details hadn't been me being pigheaded. I wasn't sure how to feel about Daisy liking Jing. I wasn't sure if that made me happy or weirdly cagey. Jealous, but of whom? I chewed on my cheeks and fought the bizarre, inexplicable urge to cry, really cry. Had I been a dick? "Were you into it?"

"I don't know." The glasses in her mouth went still. "She kept bringing you up."

"Bringing me up?"

"How she was mad at you, yeah. Other things that I'll spare you." One of her hands flew to her throat, and she unbuttoned the first three buttons of her cheetah coat and yanked it crooked, flashed a string of hickeys at me. They looked like smashed raspberries. My gut dropped. "It didn't go anywhere, but. I don't know. I don't even know why I'm telling you."

I breathed hard and fought for something helpful to say. "I just want us to be normal again." Biffed it. We'd been friends for not even three months. What was normal about us? What the fuck was normalcy? "Like we were, I mean."

"Yeah, well." She took a breath and put her glasses back on. "Daisy's going to be mad until she isn't. I've gotten her and Yates in the same space, and I'm going to work on her so that all of us can coexist without violence. She's not going to want us to help you, and she's not going to let you help us. Or she'll claim as much."

"Help you?" I gnawed my bottom lip, lost for a moment. My neurons clanged together after a moment, sparked just enough to give me words. "Is this about Monique and Sheridan?"

"Yes." Jing inclined her head. "I don't relish saying this, but I'm not sure that the three of us can do it without you. Not in a way that sticks. We need Mr. Scratch, and you as well, or else the two of them might be in serious trouble. There are consequences if we fuck this up. I wouldn't do that to them. They want to go to prom together, as an item, and if they get caught by an unhexed dad? Yeah. No."

There was a moment where something hung in the air between our faces. Caleb's name in squiggly invisible letters, maybe. Something like that.

I shook my nausea. "Alright, well. If Daisy won't let me help, how exactly am I supposed to do this?"

"That's what I've been thinking about." She made a little huff sound. "The plan was, we were going to do it tonight. Sheridan's dad is going to an ATM to get himself cigarette cash—Sheridan says he goes every other day at seven exactly, because that's when he gets off of work. It's the one in the alley between the movie theater and the abandoned Wendy's, you know the one. We were going to do something like we were planning for Madeline. Trap him in place with a sigil, cast while he can't get away. We were thinking, if we set it up properly beforehand, that we could stay in one of our cars. He wouldn't even see us coming, and he wouldn't be able to report us or anything."

"That checks out." I jerked out my chin. "So what's the problem, exactly?"

"I want you to be there to actually name him Chett. I feel like we always have you do the naming part for a reason. It feels right. That, and you have Mr. Scratch inside you, which means that you'll be able to amp it up and make it permanent, right? Besides"—she curled her lip—"planning magic shit without you has proven to be super fucking diffi-cult. Yates keeps looking sad because you're not around, so the Scapegracers don't feel whole, and Daisy is being difficult and gets easily distracted"—she touched her neck—"and I'm using most of my energy just to corral them both into being chill, which doesn't leave much left for this sort of thing. I wanted to run the sigils we had by you and Scratch, and I wanted to see if you'd be willing to do something potentially really stupid just to make sure that Monique and Sheridan are okay."

"Right," I said. "How stupid are we talking?"

"Deeply." She fished around in her pocket and pulled out a balled-up wad of paper. She mostly unwadded it. Handed it to me. "First, does this look fine?"

The sigil wasn't all that different from the ones we'd made for Madeline. The only real change I could see was the direction of two of the lines. Instead of branching upwards and outwards, they doubled in on each other, converged like an anchor.

It's very pretty, Mr. Scratch hummed. *This will do if you pair it with good words. Heavy words with long, open, yawny vowels. I missed Jing. Tell her that I missed her. She is a star.*

I scrunched my nose up a little. "Yeah, this is good. He's giving it a pass." He let out a whining sound, and I slapped my right elbow, tried to bop him into submission a little. "And he misses you."

"Yeah, I miss his inky ass, too." She scrunched her brows. "Does he have an ass?"

"Nah," I said. "Now, the stupid thing?"

"You can say no."

God. My bones quaked under the skin, I wanted them back so much. I was angry and I wasn't sure that I was thrilled with them, or myself, but I needed attention. More than attention. I needed them, the way I felt when I was with them, the way their unique brands of chaos calibrated my life. Yeah, it'd been like a day. A shitty day. I needed my girls back. "I don't care how profoundly stupid it is, Jing, I want in. I want to help out Monique and Sheridan." Holy hell, I want you back. Neither of us are wearing our Scapegracer jackets. Wild how quickly it feels like we've abandoned our shared skin, no?

"You said it." She finally looked away, stared in the direction of the parking lot. Her falsies cast fluttery shadows on her cheekbones. "Follow me, I'll show you." She took off faster than I expected, cutting across the brown, scratchy grass away from me.

I fell off the wall and stumbled after her.

"You can back out," she repeated. Walking the way she was, her two buns framed the sun. "Last time I'm saying it."

"I won't." I stuck my hands in my pockets for safe-keeping. "So, why were you in detention? And why the hell did you throw a yo-yo at me instead of a paper airplane or something?"

"Someone was talking shit. I tripped her and she broke a tooth. Nobody caught me, but I was snickering, so Mr. New sent me to detention. Circumstantial evidence, I tell you."

"You did it, though."

Jing rolled her shoulders.

I tried to keep pace and scrounged for more questions, anything to keep her talking to me. "What sort of stuff was she saying?"

"Blah blah blah. You know that this town is conservative as fuck, right? That's occurred to you?" Jing didn't wait for an answer. "Not everybody is thrilled that me and Yates and Daze are into magic now. The robes and stuff, and the abandoned house party, the levitation—shit, I mean people around these parts don't even let their kids read millennial transphobic British colonial magic boarding school trash. Some people I used to be on halfway decent terms with, they're scared of us. I'm cool with just the fear piece, but people hate being afraid, so they metabolize it into disgust and loathing. I mean, that's one of the big reasons people used to hate you." She didn't say that in a way that left room for doubt. "Being scared of you gives you the power. Way easier on the simple psyche to get squicked instead. That means they're the ones with power, and you're the object that triggers that and not the subject who's causing it. Nobody wants to be scared of teenage girls. Everybody wants to hate them, teenage girls included. You're an easier target than we were, but it's not like we're hard. So yeah, people were talking shit. It's boring and predictable and very kitschy-campy. *Vampyros Lesbos*, you know. We're evil pulp witches who spend all our time killing little animals and scissoring each other."

There was a lump in my throat. It might've been Mr. Scratch. "You alright?"

"Always. It's really hard to get to me. Born with a preternaturally thick skin. It's Yates and Daze I worry about."

Yates, I understood. She's an empath or whatever. But Daisy?

She must've read my silence. "Sideways, if Daisy wasn't sensitive as a rotten tooth, why the fuck would she bother being so mean? Or drinking so much, let alone all the stuff she messes around with? Or playing up exactly how little she cares about everybody's opinion while practically running a smack talk archive? She could probably recite every mean thing anybody's ever said about her alphabetically and by date. She's been taking her Scapegracer popularity adjustment pretty well, all things considered."

"I thought you were still pretty popular."

"You wouldn't know popular if it slugged you upside the head with a bat." She jerked her head to the left and popped a few vertebrae. The sound was like a gunshot. It echoed in my ears. "Tell me, Sideways. Why were you in detention?"

"I'm close to flunking Bio," I said. "Also, I accidentally said 'ribbit-ribbit' to Toady's face, which was my own carelessness or whatever."

"Bailout detentions," she whistled, "are the *worst*. That was me all sophomore year with my damn geology class. I don't know anything about any fucking shapes. Also, I was ceaselessly fried that whole semester, so." She glanced at me. "That isn't what I heard."

"And what did you hear?" She didn't answer the yo-yo question, but maybe the mystery was better than knowledge in this circumstance. "Did I sacrifice a deer on school grounds or something, in Beelzebub's name?"

"Too soon," Jing said.

I nearly said something about it always being Beelzebub season, but I remembered the pool situation. Scare party fawn. Trauma! "Right."

She wrinkled her nose. "Somebody told me that you got detention for eating a sheep's eye. Like, one of the pickled ones for dissection."

Hell is real and all around us. I broke into a laugh. It was a jaggedy laugh and it lasted too long. I could not breathe. "Wouldn't that be something?"

Thanks again!

Jing cast me a glance, but she didn't say anything.

We stopped in front of her car.

"Here's what's up. You need to be with us. Daisy and Yates can't know you're here, because Daisy would turn into a werewolf and Yates would be furious at me, and that's just not conducive to a productive evening of hex-reforming shitty men. This work matters. I am willing to do some objectively silly shit to execute it." She dug around in her jeans pocket. I watched her elbow move. "That means you have to keep quiet. If you're suffocating or something, I'll let the fury happen, but unless you think you'll die? I'd appreciate you not detonating our social bomb. It would *so* impress and thrill me if you pull this off. I'll owe you."

"So, am I hiding?" I wondered abstractly if she was flirting with me. My brain was on fire. Immolation station. The fact that I was angry did not square with the fact that I would take a bullet for her on request. I worked my jaw and said, "I'm not conspicuous. I'm a big masc lesbian with a screaming fruity dye job and a studded leather jacket, Jing."

She stopped digging in her pocket and revealed what she'd been looking for. It dangled by the ring off her finger, glittered in the burnished light. Car keys on an oversized ring, strung with a fairy keychain and a cussy friendship bracelet. SLUT KING. She popped the trunk.

There wasn't anything in the trunk. No magic supplies or something like that. Not even snacks or jumper cables. Nothing. I failed to see how an empty trunk would help us out.

Then, lightning strike. Understanding walloped me. Haha. Nuh-uh.

"Jing," I sounded out, "I am too fucking big to fit in your trunk."

"You're not." She flashed her teeth. "I've fit two checked bags in here. Also, a linebacker. You can fit with room to spare. I'll text you when we see him. I'll even sneak a picture if you need a visual. We'll do the incantation, and when the time comes, you'll cast the Chett hex. Sound good?"

"You want me to be in your trunk," I said. "This is not fucking *Jawbreaker*."

"Duh. You're alive. You'll just be in my trunk for the casting," said Jing. "Seems foolproof."

"It's foolproof to put me in the trunk of your car?"

"Yeah," she repeated, a little less patiently this time. She glanced over my shoulder and then looked back at me, bounced on the balls of her feet. "Look, Daisy's going to be out of cheer any minute now, and Yates will be coming with her, because yours truly is the best diplomat alive. I can't let them see you either way. Are you in this or not?"

I opened and shut my mouth. It was a very dark trunk. Very snug. "I don't know if trunk spelunking is my style."

"Think about the queers, Sideways. Think about the queers who need you." Jing's eyes glittered. "Monique and Sheridan"—she blinked—"and me. Will you help me?"

Well, fuck.

I looked at that trunk, and I felt myself succumb to the allure of being decent, and far more important, the unbreakable and unquenchable desire to affirm that people needed and wanted me. Jing needed me. Maybe she wanted me, too. *Wanted me.* This was so stupid. I was so stupid.

"If I die in there," I said, "mellify me and bury my honey body in a peat bog. I will Mr. Scratch and my record collection to you."

"How sweet." She slapped the side of the car. "In you go."

One foot and then the other, I flung myself into the depths.

It felt like a giant felted mouth. Like a Muppet's guts.

Jing blew me a kiss and slammed the trunk door shut.

I'd fucking outdone myself.

Welcome to my musty darkness. Pearl in a clamshell era.

Fuck my life. The air felt a tad thin for comfort, but there was a hole that punctured the trunk/seat area and filtered in a steady trickle of oxygen, and I shoved my big nose up against it. Maybe this is what it's like to be a rabbit in those ventilated cardboard boxes? I supposed in a perverse kinda way that it might be superior to the person-half of a car, aka panic city. Car trips still made me extravagantly unwell sometimes. Thing is, when the Chantry witchfinders kidnapped me, they had buckled me into the back seat of their car, not stuffed me unceremoniously into the bowels in the back. I had zero trunk-related trauma. Could be that this shaped up like my easiest ride in months. I felt like a 4H pig. I'd be such a shitty show pig.

On the other side of the car, the bourgeois side with windows and person-shaped seats, I heard talking.

The talking set my teeth on edge.

"You need to dress well for it." There was something else said, but the syllables were too muddled through the walls of the trunk for me to make them out distinctly. Something something *later*, something something *awful*, something something *fine*. Daisy's vocal fry. I knew that much.

A big fuzzy palimpsest of murmurs, then something crisp.

"Not a crop-top nice, or knee-length-dress nice?" Yates' voice. Trepidation in her tone, but nevertheless, she sounded sweet. Measured. "Please say knee-length, I want to wear my little polka-dot dress. Unless you think it's not seasonable?"

"Slap a Santa hat on it and it's perfect." Jing's voice. "This party's gonna fucking suck."

Party?

I rubbed the corner of my mouth and stared at the part of the darkness where the door should be. They'd fought with me all of one day ago, and already they'd planned something without me. I grinned, or grimaced, something awful between the two. Hurt spoils like milk, turns to envy and anger quick. What was that Jing had said about fear?

The walls around me started convulsing, which meant that the engine had started. Previously unseen things moved around in the dark, a little bottle of pills, loose change, a box of condoms, and I wondered abstractly about what might happen in the event that somebody rear-ended Jing. Dying soulless in the trunk of a convertible for girls who'd planned a secret party without me sounded so, so trash.

But Jing needed me. Monique and Sheridan, too. They needed me.

It's just that them wanting me felt like a stretch.

TEN

STRANGE WEATHER

Over the caramelized bass grind of Daisy's music, I was positive that nobody seat-side would be able to hear me if I started talking to myself. That is, if I started talking to the devil in my gut. No light, appealing rubber smell. I felt like I was riding a jackhammer like a pogo stick, but I was starting to acclimate. I cleared my throat. Had to fucking distract myself. "Hey, Mr. Scratch," I said. "Do you want to sneak through the upholstery and spy on them, huh? Be a good little snitch for me? I want to hear about this party."

I could do that, theoretically, but it is very bright out there. You know I don't care for harsh lights. They're garish and they hurt. Besides—would you really want to know? Would it make you happier, safer, or wiser to know?

"I'm rarely any of those things." I blinked at nothing. "Trunks suck."

I like it. It is dark and snug in here.

"You're like a cat," I groaned. I sort of had a cat. It was Julian's cat, and he never talked to me or let me pet him. His name was Schnitzel. He lived in the shop unless he decided to commandeer the bathroom sink. Bit me sometimes. I let him.

I like cats. I was a cat once, for some years, actually. I was loved and doted upon by many brilliant women. Cats make for excellent familiars, because I like them and they are very comfortable.

"Goals. Wait, there was a lot in that. First, familiars? That shit's real? Like, *I saw Goody Proctor sic a dope half-invisible dog on me,* that sort of thing is legit?" I screwed my brows up, not that he could see in all this dark. But then, he also was inside me, so. "Can I get one? Can I make Schnitzel be my familiar? Also—you dwelling inside of a cat for years is an insane thing to drop on somebody, even if you're an ink-based immortal non-human entity."

Familiars in practice are animals with something like me inside of them. We are far better suited to being inside of books, but there are circumstances in which we find ourselves keen to live inside a breathing host. You are a familiar. Your body is the box that holds me.

"Familiar," in my head, just meant pet. Cool pet.

Was I the Scapegracer pet?

You don't put your pet in the fucking trunk, huh.

The car took a sharp turn, then halted. The music cut. Everything still buzzed, but I felt like Jing had put it in park. Weird how sensitive you get to that sort of thing when you lack a cushion between you and the wheels.

All the doors besides mine opened up and shut. I heard sneakers thump pavement, the flutter of fabric on fabric.

"Are they doing magic out there?"

Yes. It smells like them. Scapegracer sugary. They're drawing the sigil, now.

Sugary. That felt right. Pop Rocks angels, my girls.

I wondered if they were having fun making an itch without me.

Might I remind you that they are performing a public service, not preparing for some sort of activity? It's not exactly Bacchic, drawing sigils with chalk on the ground.

"Thanks for the editorial," I snapped.

My phone buzzed.

Jing's contact lit up with an image attachment. Her contact read CURSE DADDY because I made the choice to let her update herself last month when we'd been crossfaded and weirdly touchy on her couch during that *Ginger Snaps* and *All Cheerleaders Die* double feature after Yates and Daze had fallen asleep. I remember her hand on my sternum. Shimmery nail polish hypnotic in the flickering screen light. Her saying in my ear, *Would you do anything for me?* and me saying against the top of her hair, *You'd like that.* CURSE DADDY had sent me a picture of the sigil and a text that read, **feedback?**

A grainy shot of an ATM with scratchy sidewalk-chalk sigils beneath it was magic enough as-is. Would've fit right in on one of the uncanny image forums I lurk around all the time, the place where I sought validation for my talents before I had this coven. Mr. Scratch hummed a note of approval, and I couldn't see anything technically wrong, and

I wasn't sure if it'd matter if it were wrong so long as all of them thought otherwise. It was all in the incantation, anyway. Sigils are gestural.

Yeah, looks good.

A second later, the doors around the car all opened and shut again. The Scapegracers crawled on the seats, knees squeaking the leather, whispering between each other.

CURSE DADDY sent me another picture, this time of a Ken doll.

The Ken doll was off-brand and wildly, hysterically jacked up. Tan, blond, hideous. Like Rocky Horror had a face like a toe.

Doll factory fumbled that one woof

will it work.

Don't see why not

"There he is," said Daisy. She must be in the back seat, which was weird for her. Her voice seemed close. "What an ugly mug."

"He looks like an evil miner," said Yates.

Daisy scoffed. "The fuck does that even mean? What does an evil miner look like, exactly?"

"Like him! If there was a movie about coal miners and one of them was evil, that guy would look exactly like him. Like a corrupt gold prospector. A union scab. I don't know, leave me be. Can you be nice for like five minutes?" Yates' voice carried a little louder than it should've, apparently, because as she said this Jing and Daisy hushed her in tandem.

I got the quiet bit, but I hated them shushing her. Yates gets to do whatever the fuck she wants, including get us caught. She was right, besides. Some questions demand answers.

My phone buzzed again, and the screen beamed in the darkness. It attracted little moths who were apparently trapped in here with me. The notification read *video chat: CURSE DADDY.* I thumbed over my screen and sucked my teeth.

Jing's face flashed on the other side for just a moment. Below angle, showed the extremes of her cheekbones and her false lashes. Her bangs blurred. Then she was gone, replaced via camera switch with a shot of the window. There was a man outside—it was hard to see him clearly, but I caught his silhouette, his shoulders in a heavy work coat— and he hunched over the ATM and punched away with a rigor completely unnecessary for the task at hand. It was like he was playing chicken. What'd crack first, the buttons or his fingertips?

The incantation started. The video delayed a split second, so the words played in a round, first muffled through the seat, then filtered through the speaker. Felt like an accelerant. The air went taut and crackly. Chafed against my arm hair, scraped the follicles on my scalp and inside my nose. The atmosphere foamed thicker around the car. Light imperceptibly crystalized. Mr. Scratch threaded himself around my knucklebones. My physical discomfort morphed from low-level misery into layered anticipation, and it flaked with every breath. This felt like dancing. I missed dancing.

The man on the screen froze. He jerked in place, but his feet were rooted, or else so heavy that he couldn't pry them off the concrete. I couldn't hear him, but everything about the curve of his spine screamed theater on fire. He braced a hand against the ATM and yanked himself, grabbed his pant leg with his spare hand and jerked, but his foot wouldn't budge. Fucker was glued.

The other Scapegracers switched chants. These vowels were shorter, the fricatives spit. The shape of the hex was more specific than it usually was, but it felt the same on the skin: taut, like a dental dam stretched across the knuckles. My hair stood on edge. My teeth hurt from the lack of chanting. Language wriggled under my tongue. Keeping quiet was like holding my breath. It was like trying not to blink.

I wasn't sure if there was meant to be a signal. If I was supposed to wait for a sign, a thumbs-up from Jing, a text, anything. I saw Sheridan's father writhing before the machine, and a jolt of pain leaped down the length of my arm. The pain coiled from my wrist to my first finger. I needed to point. I needed to snap my jaws.

The chant rose to a boiling point.

I jerked my fingertip against the screen, Mr. Scratch in my nail. Through clenched teeth, I named: "Chett."

The man on the screen went stock still.

The chanting inside the car fell silent.

Sheridan's father swatted the side of his neck. He held his hand there, felt for something—maybe a break in skin, a bug bite, a lymph node. Something to prove that he wasn't hallucinating.

Sorry, motherfucker. What he needed was a mirror.

"Let's get out of here," Yates said.

Jing ended the video call. The engine revved.

New text from CURSE DADDY: **thank you bb. i get that this is insane. i really appreciate it**

Yeah? I had no idea how to read this. Should I be generous? I oughta be, but they were planning a party without me. Being hurt about it was stupid and I was stupid. I wanted to say something back that wasn't kind. Something that I would've said freely (even relished) before I knew them. I didn't text that.

Instead: **Let me out**

> **i'll pop the trunk in a second! just gotta get away first. is the gas station good?**

> **Couldn't you drop me off at Rothschild&Pike ??**

> **we're going to daisy's place for a bit...you'd have to be in there a long time**

I was an inch from tearing my bones out of my skin. Less than an inch.

look i kno this is shitty. i stg i will make it up to u soon

pls, sideways?

i won't forget this

i rlly rlly appreciate it youre the best ok ilu

Fine. Drop me off wherever tf you want.

Jing didn't read the text. The car was vibrating, which meant it was moving. My stomach flipped up in my teeth. I'd never been one to get carsick, but I felt nauseous all at once, like I might lose all constitution if things didn't get still real quick.

Things didn't get still. They got bumpier.

"You guys," said Yates. "This feels wrong."

"What does?" Daisy was decidedly flippant, like she was making a point of it.

"It just being the three of us. This isn't our thing."

"Sure, it is." That was the tone Daisy took with prey. It was the perfect cocktail of snide, sweet, bored, and hungry. I recalled her using it to tell me her observations about the thumb holes cut in my hoodie sleeves, about how for a fashion trend meant to conceal self-harm, it did such a good job of whoring attention about it. Not the words she used. How long ago was that? Five years, now? Funny how that shit sticks in your head. Thing was, though, at the time I was an awkward early alternative kid, and she was a middle-school cheerleader who kept her Dior lip gloss in a Coach purse. The dynamic was preestablished.

It was not a tone one took with Lila Yates.

The music cut with an accompanying thump. Jing must've slammed her hand on the knob, shut the whole system off. The car rolled to a halt, then the vibrations stopped.

"What'd you kill the music for?" Daisy's voice went nasal. "It was my turn with the—"

"This isn't fucking cute, Daze." Jing spoke slowly. "The whole bratty indifference thing is starting to get on my fucking nerves. You wanna be mad? Be my fucking guest. In fact, with open arms I welcome you having a full conniption! Have your nervous breakdown. Express yourself. But don't pretend like this is our thing outside of Sideways. It isn't. We need her. I want her. She's a part of us."

"You think we need that little—"

"Daisy," Yates said. "Stop."

"Stop what? Just asking questions!" I heard her mouth curl. "I don't *need* anything, but if you *want* to tell me about how much you *want* Sideways, be my guest. Tell me, is it her big leather shoulders, or is it her long calloused hands?"

"I love you, Daisy. You're making that hard."

Raspy quiet. The muffled sounds of other cars.

"I want to steal some gum," Jing snapped. She opened the car door, slammed it shut. "You're both coming with me."

There wasn't any complaining. The back doors opened, sneakers hit the pavement, and then the shutting sound echoed around the car. I heard them walk until I couldn't.

The door popped, and a crack of light spilled over me.

I oozed out onto the pavement. Rolled onto my back on the oil-slick rainbows with a thud. Everything seized and cramped, either from the magic or the trunk-compression, and it took me a second to locate my feet and drag them under my belly. When I stood, my knees clicked. My jeans would smell like gasoline for weeks. Wasn't like I'd wash them after this.

My ears were ringing. What the fuck did I think?

"Should I hate them?" Refreshingly acidic, saying it out loud. "It might feel great to hate them." To hate Daisy, that is. Could I hate Daisy? My gut rebelled against the thought. I hugged my belly and squeezed fistfuls of myself. I was a stress ball and Mr. Scratch my microbead filling.

You love your friends. You love giving and receiving love. I don't condemn the children I've had who pick the quick medicines for things; the world is a very sharp place for daughters, particularly and especially mine. I've watched them wither over it, though. I hate to watch it. I want you all to bloom.

"Being pissed isn't shooting up, Scratch."

Being pissed isn't hating, sweetums.

"Whatever." I considered, for a moment, hanging around the back of the car and letting them see me, revealing that I'd been the one pulling the magic trigger, that I'd been helping the whole time, yours truly, you're welcome. But there was a rotten taste in my mouth and I felt like it'd just get worse, staying here.

It was only a few blocks to Rothschild & Pike. I could

walk it. Might shave off a bit of bitter, too. I fished around in my pockets for headphones, found them tangled, and couldn't be bothered to unwind them. I stuck one in my left ear and left the right dangling.

"I think I'll hit up the corner store on the way home," I said as I trudged down the walk toward the intersection. "You want anything, or do you only eat the worst possible things?"

It is hard to know what will make me hungry until I see it. I will let you know.

"Fuck, you and me both."

The wind picked up, cut through my coat. It was sharper than I'd gotten used to, cold like it'd been in October, colder. Dingy paper skies up above, completely sunless but light in a fuzzy sense. It looked like it might snow.

I picked up my pace. Walking fast meant warming up and putting distance between myself and the girls, and the thought of being too close was sparking stupid ideas. I needed to eat something bad for me and lock myself in my room, scribble out new sigils while bingeing trash TV. I'd drink, but Mr. Scratch liked the alcohol and always stole it, leaving boring virgin juice in my mouth. I'd given up trying.

Maybe when I got my soul out of Madeline, I'd make some well-earned mistakes.

Sycamore Gorge township wasn't a proper city, but it was slightly more of a town than most places around here. Multiple stoplights. There was a fistful of businesses open currently, filled with lights and drinking people, and stragglers on benches, flowers in boxes. Sports cars cozied up beside pickup trucks. Syringes under lumpy hedges. I avoided looking in stores where the owners knew me, because they'd want to talk and I wasn't in the mood, and if I didn't talk to them they'd complain to Julian, and Julian would make a fuss about my rudeness. I didn't look in the new businesses either, the ones who didn't know my dads yet, not that there were many of those around here. Lots of empty storefronts. Those were sometimes useful. On the left, there was a pizza place that was always out of pizza on account of them being a drug front. On the right, there was a dry-cleaning place that once made a petition to get my dads' shop removed on the grounds of "incidents of indecency," the incident in question being my fathers slow dancing around the shop when Ella Fitzgerald's "Dream a Little Dream of Me" came on the radio.

I kept moving. The day had been so long that it stopped feeling like a day. Time was muddy. All of it, all of time, today and all the days before it. It'd been twelve million years that I'd been soulless, but also five minutes. I could have had my own personal Cambrian explosion during the duration of my soullessness. I was creating brand-new germs.

Shame about the pizza place. I really could've gone for a slice.

Around this next corner was an easy shortcut to my dads' shop. It was an alley, or at least a gulch between two buildings, both of which were made of dirty bricks. No hard edges. Each line was crumbly like graham crackers. It shaved a good four minutes off the walk, and I was eager to get home, rip off my jeans, crawl into the shower and howl into the steam for an hour or four. I headed down, ignored the string of notification buzzes that shook against my thigh, nearly grumbled something to Mr. Scratch when I stopped.

There were boys at the other end of the alleyway.

There was enough distance between them that I had a hard time distinguishing who they were. Four big white boys, round-faced with teenage newness. They wouldn't carve into anything distinct until their twenties. Their jackets were unusual, though, and they gave me pause from this distance. Camo on two boys, expensive fleece activewear on the others. Sycamore Gorge had nasty gashes of class segregation that were seldom erased. It was unusual for boys in hunting gear to mingle with the Future Fratboys of America.

One of the boys in hunting gear said something with a chuckle.

Everybody sneered.

They didn't seem to notice me. I snuck closer, strained my neck. Hearing their voices, it occurred to me that some of them might have had a class with me. Last year's PE, maybe? It'd explain why I couldn't remember names; I was a gold medalist in the PE trauma repression department. Weight training and dissociation, that's my game. Closer still, I made out words.

"They really scared the shit out of Travis. I've never seen him flip out like that."

"It's some *Crucible* shit."

"Did you actually read that shit, man? Jesus fucking Christ, you're such a faggot."

"Whatever! Point is, somebody needs to teach these sluts some manners."

"You wanna wind up like Travis? Is that what you want?"

"Who the fuck said I was going after them? That's so much fucking work. I'll just upload that clip of Daisy Brink—keep them busy for a while. What are they gonna do, hex everybody in the entire school who sees? The entire internet? If you ask me, that's balance."

"What clip?"

"Wait, you haven't seen the video? Jesus Christ, it's from last year, back before Brandon transferred. He was dating her, remember? He filmed her at this house party, let me show you—"

Fight or flight. Fight fight fight.

I had to crush them into pill powder and scatter them to the four winds.

"Scratch," I spat, "what do I do? What can I do?" I couldn't thrash all of them at once, and I didn't have any spare curse poppets laying around. My hands twitched. I was already moving down the alley. I became a murderer in my mind.

Do you have a pen in your pocket?

Bless the broken pavement, I did. I seized it from a pocket and squeezed it like a weapon.

There's a spell I've been taught that might help you. Scribble on your hand and say something, anything. Think about twisters. Quickly.

I carved the pen's head against my thumb knuckle, hacked away at my upper layer of skin until the ink tube flowed, electric blue with a smear of Scratch-gloss black. I stared at the boys and my stomach dropped. My hair prickled across my scalp, bristled with static. Joints went jittery. Organs wrung. I looked at the four of them, who hadn't noticed me yet, and I opened my mouth and screamed.

They jumped, swore, looked around in shock.

"You're disgusting, you're absolutely disgusting, I'd turn you into pigs, but I don't hate pigs, you insidious, evil little fucks, I hope this ruins your life, I hope you spiral out of control and crash and burn, I hope nothing helps, I hope everything hurts, especially looking at me!" My voice keyed out of me. I must be open from jaw to guts. Ribbons of angry pink rift, gushing noise like pus from a wound. "I hate you, I fucking hate you, I hate everybody like you, twisters, twisters, I wish the sky would come down and rob the earth of you, I wish the sky would hurl you into outer space! I wish your spines looked like bedsprings! You hideous little boys, do you not have even a shred of fucking empathy? Why doesn't anybody in this town have fucking empathy? I hate you! I fucking hate you!"

The air went thin around us. My hair blew straight up, danced away from my neck and toward the purpling sky. My eyes pinched, so did my sinuses. My face felt like a snail's stomach. I twisted my fists against my scalp and screamed, wailed until the words weren't words, until there was nothing but animal noise from inside me. My vision swam. The colors pinwheeled.

The boys all turned on their heels.

It was slow at first, horrifyingly synchronized. Their left

feet extended, pulled away from their bodies, hovered just above the dirty ground. Like marionette strings had been pulled. They spaced themselves out, somehow, drifted apart. Then they all turned backwards. They twirled. They spun on their right foot, left foot trailing like the hand on a clock. Music box ballerina circles. Stunned silence cracked and went loud, broke into cussing and shivering shouts, but I didn't care to listen. They spun faster. Their bodies blurred like tops. All at once, they whirled up into the air, propelled by their own oscillation and the sheer force of me sobbing on the pavement. Their trailing sneakers clanged against streetlamps. Their arms lifted above their heads, wrists together, fingers outstretched. The whirlwind held them there, twirling suspended over the alleyway like synchronized swimmers, and I felt like my lungs might pop.

Breathe, Sideways, please breathe.

If you fucking insist.

What do you want to do?

Chett them into oblivion.

Then do so. I'll help you.

I don't have any dolls.

Improvise.

I blinked through the stickiness, scanned the alleyway for anything that struck me. There were withered weeds and dirty papers. Cigarette butts. Empty bottles of beer. Those would do, I decided. I squeezed my pen, squeezed my stomach, and went after the shiny green glass.

ELEVEN

SOMETIMES MOTHERS USE TOO MUCH FORCE

There was a letter waiting for me when I got home. It'd been stuck in the hinge seam between my door and the wall and jutted out like a skin tag or a splinter. I yanked it. My lack of care crunched the envelope's corners.

It was heavy, milky paper. Tacky to the touch like whipping cream. Clung to the grooves in my fingerprints. My legal name had been written in handwriting I could barely read across the upper corner, the address underneath in neat, blocky caps. There was a seal on the front of the paper. A wreath of snakes in depthless ink. A crown.

I stood snot-faced in my hallway, holding the piece of paper in my fists, and found myself unable to cry anymore, or scream, or even facially respond. My arms and legs felt heavy. My tongue was a lump in my mouth.

I unceremoniously tore the paper with the edge of a nail.

To Ms. Eloise Pike,
We congratulate you on your coming of age and

the affirmation of your specter. We have been informed by our archival volumes that it is a deep red, like your mother's before you. Of this we are especially proud. We will be in touch with details concerning the returning of our loaned volumes and your initiation to our fold.

—PS

I looked at it for a long time.

My brain stopped registering the script as words. They weren't symbols on paper, they weren't even lines. They were little inky shapes on the page.

I tucked the letter in my shirt so that it rested against my stomach.

I went to the kitchen in search of Julian.

Julian was singing "La Vie en rose," sort of. He knew maybe half of the words and substituted the rest with cheery multisyllabic nonsense that mostly fit the rhythm. *Quand il me pray la-di-da, la-day parle tout bas, li-da la vie en rose.* He was crushing away with a pestle in his mortar, smashing herbs and peppercorns, his glasses dipping so dangerously low on his nose that they threatened to dive floorwards. Julian looked more like a witch than me, most days. Maybe he was.

"Dad," I said. My voice was raw from all the screaming. "Do you have a second?"

"Always for my lovely lamb." His amazing, nasal monotone was the only stability in my life. No inflection, no exceptions. Smooth waters. "I am making mushroom toast. A couple at Dorothy's trivia night hunts mushrooms and gave me these beautiful morels, and we've got to use the bread before it gets fuzzy. Boris wanted something with poached eggs on top, so there will be eggs. I can leave yours eggless if you would rather. What's the matter?"

"Eggs are fine." I gnawed my tongue. "Can we talk about Mom?"

Julian stopped mashing. His Adam's apple bobbed in his throat. Slowly, he resumed. "We can talk about Lenora if you'd like."

"I know it stings, but I have some questions. It feels important." I clapped a hand around the back of my neck, wrapped the other around the letter through my shirt. "You're the only person I know who really knew her."

He tapped the pestle on the mortar's lip and stared at it. "Alright."

"Was she into witchcraft at my age? Collect occult books or divination tools or trinkets or anything?" I wet my lips. "Did she like witches, at least? Movies and books about them? Or urban legends, or—"

"I talked her into reading one of the Discworld books, once." He spooned his crushed herbs into a pan with olive oil and garlic. "I don't think she cared for it."

I blinked a few times. Shifted on my feet. "Did she have many female friends around?"

"She wasn't home often. I presume she had friends and some of them were women, seeing as she had to be going somewhere in her leaves of absence, and I find it unlikely that she was always alone." The pan sizzled thoughtfully. "She liked an audience."

"Was she popular, then?"

"Not in the traditional sense of the word, no. People always seemed to know who she was whenever we were together. Servers and random people on the bus would say hello. She was"—he took a breath—"a theatrical person."

I liked theater. That was something. But it wasn't the something I was looking for.

"Did you ever see a wreath of snakes on any of her things?" I fished the envelope out of my shirt and showed him the design on its middle. "This symbol, was it branded anywhere?"

He looked at it, but only briefly, not with that keen-eyed antique-appraisal raptor vision that I was hoping he'd use. He looked at it like it was a piece of paper. "I don't believe so."

"Why are you being so avoidant?" I sounded a little more childish than I meant to, but I didn't have it in me to sound mature, whatever that means. My bottom lip felt swollen. Maybe I bit it on the way home. "I really need to know."

He stopped again. He braced his hands against the counter and took a breath, then he cranked a dial timer and turned to me, looked at me full-on. His eyes looked more deeply rooted in his skull, somehow. The lids drooped and caught the light. "What do you really need to know, Sideways?"

"I need to know if Mom was like me." It was a hard string

of words to pull out of my mouth. Each beaded syllable had ridges. "Was she like me? Did she have a soul like mine?"

Julian's brows shot together. They steepled upwards, drew the lines on his forehead like curtains. He gripped the counter a little tighter. "Maybe we should sit."

I yanked a chair away from the table and shoved it in his direction. Pulled out a second for myself, spun it around, straddled it. I braced the meat of my upper arms against the back of the chair, propped my chin on the folds of my arms.

He sat carefully. Spidered his fingertips over his knobby kneecap. "I wouldn't ever lie to you, nor would I want to paint a picture of events that was not accurate or fair. But Lenora was your mother. You weren't afforded any control over what happened when you were little. I wanted to give you control of the image you held of her. She wasn't here. She could be whatever you liked." He took his glasses off, held them in one hand and rubbed his face with the other. "You're eighteen, now. You've become such an amazing human being. You're courageous and creative and intuitive and resolute."

"Yeah?" I didn't blink.

"If you want to know about Lenora, I can tell you." He put his glasses back on. They were crooked. He looked at me without noticing. "I need you to understand that it might change the way you think about her. The way you think about yourself."

I nodded. It was barely a motion, my head propped like it was. My teeth buzzed inside my head like bees in comb. It was maybe the feeling of a nascent nervous giggle. My body was obedient enough, at least at the moment, to snuff it before it started.

"Lenora liked knowing things," he said. He fixed his eyes on some indeterminate speck on the floor, something I couldn't see and that maybe didn't exist. "She liked winning. She was brilliant, but she was never school-wise. I don't think she could stomach anything she didn't find interesting for long. She started smoking to spite our father when she was fifteen. She stole his pipe and smoked it at a church party, wearing the tiniest shorts you've ever seen, just for dominance's sake. I think she took the punishment as a proof of purchase. Besides that, she was an accomplished climber. She could scale rock walls and streetlamps and sea cliffs without gear or evident strain. She'd just mosey her way out of the bedroom window and go out despite her confinement, and our parents were none the wiser. Our parents—the ones I was born to, anyway—were very traditional, very conservative, I guess you could say. They had horribly old-fashioned ideas about women and dating. She'd do just about anything to rile them up, just as a reminder that they didn't have power over her. She'd bring home men who she knew they'd hate. Lots of them. I don't think she particularly cared about them one way or the other. She'd flaunt them for reputation's sake. She pinned a condom wrapper to her lapel for Easter services one year. My mother nearly had a stroke." He smiled a little. "She brought up politics just for a fight. She loved arguments over dinner. I think she thought of herself as a kind of conversational matador.

"In that way, she had a tendency to proclaim weighty truths just for a reaction. She very loudly announced that her good friend had recently had an abortion on a family call, for instance. She told my father that my mother had slept with their accountant during a family road trip. She told our aunt that our cousin was in the hospital again. Her parrhesia knew no bounds and was without mercy. Or perception." His jaw moved. "If there was anything about the Lenora I knew that I'd call witchcraft, it was her propensity to use her words as tools. There weren't any empty speech acts with her. If she was talking to you, there was always some other layer, some concealed trick to the conversation that you weren't privy to. She was good at pulling information out of people without rousing their suspicions. She was good at making you confess everything to her, your whole heart and soul, and then she'd remember parts of it that you hadn't even intended to tell her, or anyone. Then she'd bring it up coyly over coffee with your least favorite people in earshot. I don't think it was sadism. She wasn't a vindictive person. She just liked the power of knowing, and she wielded it indiscriminately. She said that she was like God in that way. It was about the only time she mentioned God at all.

"I was so obviously queer when I was young. I was, and am, a limp-wristed hyper-academic effete. I might as well be communist Robbie Ross. My parents tried desperately to butch me up. They signed me up for sports that I refused to play, they dragged me on fishing trips that horrified me for their inhumanity, they tried to curve my suspiciously flowery reading habit toward Westerns and military stories, all of it. They'd shear off my curls and have me do push-ups. My body resisted any such efforts. I never got bigger. There was a time when my father decided that I needed masculine company for inspiration, and he signed me up for Boy Scouts and shipped me off to camp." The corner of Julian's mouth twitched up. "Needless to say, I lasted a week and a half before the counselors shipped me home."

"Why?" Julian never talked about his childhood. I strained in my chair.

"Too many boys wanted to kiss me." He shrugged his shoulders. "I never formally came out to my parents, and they never asked. Much mutual not asking and not telling in the Pike house. They made offhanded comments about how at least I was focused on school, even if it troubled their red-scare American sensibilities to have a flimsy manicured son around the neighbors. I went to university on a full-ride scholarship and majored in Art History. They were horrified, but I collected fellowships like stray dogs collect fleas and there wasn't much they could do. I was accepted into a prestigious doctoral program directly out of undergrad. I was making well for myself. I took good care of myself, had the financial privilege and good timing to be able to do so. So, the holidays roll around, and out of some perverse sense of familial obligation I returned to the ancestral Pike home. Our grandmother was doing poorly. There wasn't any way to avoid it, really." Julian shoved his glasses up his nose with the knuckle of his middle finger.

My tongue felt thick in my neck.

"I don't know how she knew. I certainly hadn't told her. Maybe she found some of the pill bottles in my luggage? There were more capsules to be had, in those days. Things are so much more convenient now, more streamlined. Less packaging waste, surely." His expression was inscrutable, but I felt its meaning in some prelinguistic way. His tension burned the air around him. Singed air crackled and chafed against skin. "We were sitting around the table on Christmas Eve. There was this ridiculous, obscenely enormous turkey as a centerpiece, four bowls of cranberry sauce, inedible casseroles, and all these pine-scented candles. It was like we could prove that we were the most enthusiastic denizens of worldwide suburbia if we outdid the catalogues. It was abject, the whole thing. Everybody was gathered around, three generations of blood family, a few family friends, wayward neighbors, lonely fellow parishioners whom my mother pitied, everybody. The entire world was crammed in our dining room, huddled in nice clothes around this Goliath bird carcass and bowls of wet red slush. The Elvis Christmas album was playing. The dogs were howling like sinners at rapture. It could've been a perverse Lynch cum Hallmark piece. You would've hated it.

"Lenora asked to say grace. Everybody was astounded, because Lenora was a proud atheist, or was she a Buddhist at this point? I can't recall, it was different every time you asked her. She certainly was not a devout Catholic, is the point. Not one for rosy holiday sentiments, broadly. But she seemed adamant, and our sick grandmother was so touched that she finally wanted to lead the family prayer, so my parents acquiesced and made all of us hold hands. We shut our eyes and bowed our heads. I kept trying not to cough, but the air smelled so sharply of artificial pine that I thought I might have an asthma attack and die right there, collapse in solidarity with the avian elephant my mother had so diligently crammed with vegetables earlier. It took all my concentration to seem neutral and prayerful rather than dead bored, agnostic, and vaguely repulsed.

"Lenora says, 'Dear God and Mary and their tiny bastard son, thank you for giving us this fat dead bird, and thank you for freezing our pipes. Thank you for forbidding divorce, it's the only thing holding this family together. Thank you for keeping things fresh by making Father an alcoholic. Thank you for Mother's relatively inexpensive hotel room visits. Thank you for televisions so that we can rewatch *Miracle on 34th Street* again and avoid discussing Nathan's suicide attempts. Thank you for the weather that's made leaving this house as intolerable as staying inside it. Most of all, thank you for making medicine for my dear brother Julian, who has AIDS and will die without it, because if our family didn't have a sick homosexual, we'd be so boring that I'd have to burn down the house. Merry Christmas, kumbaya, ho ho ho, amen.'"

The timer behind Julian dinged.

Julian stood up, swayed on his feet, then poured a bowl of wine-soaked mushrooms into the pan. He reduced the heat and covered it, reset the timer, poured himself a cup of water, and then sat down again. He drank the entire glass in one go. His hand tremored. He set the glass on the counter with a clink.

"What happened?" The varnish on the chair felt thick under my nails. My voice was little. I couldn't inflate it, didn't have the thought to. "After that, what happened?"

"I called Boris. We'd only been dating for two months at that point, but he drove six hours to come and rescue me. Never saw my birth parents in person again. I wasn't invited to my grandmother's funeral, though I did get some calls about whether I'd be willing to relinquish my bit of the will. They didn't call me after that until I'd dropped out of my doctoral program ABD, had moved two states over with Boris to take over his uncle's antique shop, and was planning my commitment ceremony, because they wanted to know if I had any idea where Lenora was, seeing as she'd completely dropped off the radar, and they hadn't the slightest idea how to find her. I didn't know. That was that. I mean, I didn't even know she'd had you, lamby. We didn't speak a single time after that night. I didn't even receive the funeral announcements."

I stared at a spot on the floor. I kept waiting for it to crack and melt. For the whole foundation to slush into nothing, for our chairs to dissolve beneath us, for our bodies to hurtle through the air and the shop and the mantle of the earth. I expected my body to produce sparks of anger, anger that fueled my survival like coal in a freight train. It was noxious. It was essential. I had none of it. I just had the feeling that nothing would feel solid underfoot again. Cartoon character walks off the cliff, looks down. Whistle.

I stood up and my knees were soft.

I tossed my arms around his neck.

We stayed close like that for a moment, me standing bent over him, him patting my elbow with the flat of his palm. He hummed to me like he had when I was little and terrified of sleeping. Some Indigo Girls song, not that I'd known back then. I kissed him on the forehead, and I felt the thinnest edge of it come on. The anger.

God, how I'd worshipped my mother.

We must've stayed like this for a while. The timer dinged again, and Julian made a little *ah* sound, and I released him so that he could check his mushrooms. For agents of decay, they smelled amazing. My hunger ripped at me. I'd forgotten about it in all of this. The letter in my shirt felt too slick. Our souls were just alike, it said. Made me almost not want mine back.

"I hadn't seen Lenora in such a long time, and being a parent can change people. I have no doubt that she was an amazing mother to you. She probably adored you with all her heart. You're allowed to feel about her however you'd like." He cracked eggs into a pot of water. "Do you think Caleb would like an egg?"

I'd forgotten about Caleb for a second. Couldn't find it in me to pull out my phone and text him.

He made one just in case.

I felt the edge of the letter through my shirt. For the

time being, fuck the Pythoness Society. I'd deal with it after I had all my specter bullshit sorted out. Had I thought about my mother when I Chett hexed those boys in the alley? It used to be that I thought about her, about the loss of her, every time I was angry. I'd always thought the pain of losing her had been the kindling for my magic. Survival mechanism, just like Mr. Scratch said.

I like your father, said Mr. Scratch.

That's because he is the best human person that exists, I thought clearly enough that Mr. Scratch must've caught it. He felt content, looped little shapes around my ankles. My phone buzzed and I didn't check it. I collapsed in a chair by the table, and after a moment, a plate was set in front of me. Julian rang a little bell, because he was adorable, and I heard the unmistakable rustling of Boris emerging from another room. Normal footsteps, too. Caleb.

Caleb must've changed out of his uniform already. He wore one of Julian's big sweaters, long enough on him that the sleeves hit his knuckles, and a pair of corduroy pants. With the painted nails, you would've thought he'd announced himself as a member of the club two years ago. He made for a stylish gay. He gave me a weird, curt nod.

It occurred to me that I looked like a rag, what with how much I'd been sobbing outside. I'd tightlined my eyes today. For sure, it'd smudged everywhere. I was a grime ball. Oscar the Grouch doesn't have shit on me.

I flashed all my teeth at him and bit the air.

"It smells awesome." Boris slunk into the room, all

glossy pompadour and rose-print button-down, and gave Julian a quick kiss. "Thank you for dinner, baby."

"Mmm. Mhm." Julian pecked him back, then ushered him toward the stove. "Caleb. Egg?"

Caleb blinked. "Yes." His expression flickered. "Mm. Sure."

Julian scooped an egg onto his toast and put it before him.

Caleb peered down at the plate with wonder. He reached out his hands like he was expecting Boris and me to take them, and when we didn't, he turtled them into his sleeves. Turned grayish.

"You alright?" Boris put a pitcher of lemonade on the table. I wasn't sure if he was addressing me or Caleb.

I wanted to cry.

"I'm used to saying grace before a meal." Caleb furrowed his brow. "Weird reflex."

I poured us all some lemonade, then raised my glass. I felt insane. "To Julian," I said. "Love and perseverance."

Boris gave a hearty *hear, hear*, clinked glasses with me.

Caleb flushed. He knocked back his whole glass in one gulp.

Julian finally sat. He motioned for us to eat, and we did with enthusiasm. We left clean plates. My devil hooked a few mushrooms out of my throat, ate with us. He liked mushrooms, he told me. He thought rot flowers tasted prettiest. I wondered what Caleb's prayer would've been.

TWELVE

RAPUNZEL LET ME DOWN

Caleb sat at the foot of my bed. He listened without comment, didn't so much as nod between story events. He sat and listened to me talk about meeting up with Jing, about Sheridan's father, about the boys in the alleyway. The only thing about him that moved were his toesies in his socks. They had a flamingo pattern.

I rubbed my nose with my wrist when I was finished. Nudged him with my foot.

He glanced at me.

"Speak, jackass."

Caleb took a breath. "About what?"

"Whatever you're thinking. Process out loud."

"Your coven mate is right." Caleb pulled a knee to his chest. "Hex me."

"Yeah?" I hugged my arms over my chest.

"I was texting you earlier today to tell you that my parents will be out of the house this Friday night. We could look for Madeline's specter there without having to worry about running into them. We could give Addie her soul back, and then you could get yours, too." He swallowed. "I bet the ones I've helped get are in there, too. The witches I helped hunt. Maybe they could be returned. Amends made."

That's assuming they survived your violence, Mr. Scratch sneered inside me.

"I want you to trust me." He traced the edge of his flamingoes with a nail. "The hex only attacks you if you've got bad intentions, yes? I want to prove that I've got good ones, and if I fuck up and think something disgusting, I don't mind a little shock collar action. I welcome it."

I breathed in hard through my nose, out through my teeth. "Sixth Chett hex today," I said. "Okay."

Caleb flopped backwards. He covered his eyes with his hands and lay there like a vampire.

"What are you doing?" I cocked a brow.

"Succumbing."

"I need a poppet first. Chill." I leaned back on my pillows and stared at my ceiling, tried not to focus on the pinup poster I'd taped up there at some point. Model looked awfully nice in that tiny little string bikini. "How many souls are just in your fucking house?"

"I don't know. It's not like we have a display case," he said. He didn't move his hands. "I don't think there are all that many. My dad works too much to take us hunting. It's our cousins, mostly. Other witchfinder families, who might as well be cousins. The Brethren network."

"I want to butcher all your cousins."

He nodded.

I snatched up a shitty Halloween store witch figurine—I collect them, fucking sue me—off my bedside table, along with a Sharpie I used to deface various stolen magazines. I popped the cap. The smell sizzled through the room.

Caleb held still.

I scrawled on the figure's back, where most of the flat space happened to be. *Thou shalt not plot harm against witches and girls, not speak/spread evil about witches and girls, inflict no damage, and profit not from witches and girls. Thou shalt not be a bystander. Thou shalt not be an accomplice.* I was running out of room. *Harm ye none, slut.* I drew a star at the base of the figurine's spine, or where a vivified version's base of the spine would be, and a thin line around the figurine's throat. I wasn't confident I could do it evenly, so I let the line wave up and down like sound.

Scratch jumped down and added a touch of himself, for good measure.

"Buckle up," I said.

Caleb clamped tighter.

I sucked in a breath, magic wormed around my skull like leeches on steak, and I spoke. "I name you Chett. You'll be Chett forever. May the chains of your perpetual Chettdom never untangle from your body. Speak evil and your tongue will bleed. Seek fantasies of evil and migraines will split you. Benefit from evil and your skin will shrink, you'll never sleep, you'll never eat. If you know of evil and do not prevent it, you are an accomplice to it, and if you are an accomplice to it, it'll sound in you like a spinal tap. Your agony will be triple what you inflict. I name you Chett. You'll be Chett forever, enforceable by us Scapegracers. The Scapegracers deem it so. So be it."

A shiver wrenched through Caleb, and a thin, squiggly line roped its way around his throat. It zipped itself into existence, black as a fresh tattoo. He didn't touch it, but I heard his breath rattle in his mouth.

The invisible electrical storm around my head subsided, and my jaw ached like I'd hit it. It was so rare these days to get post-magic aches, and I relished it, decided not to suss out what pain was from where or how it could be happening, given my spectral circumstances. All of it was dull and livable. I almost wished it was sharper. Sharpness brings clarity, dullness calls on the numb. Numbness is a facsimile of death. I flopped back beside him, hurled the figurine into the bowels of my closet, and put my hands behind my head. "How you feeling?"

"Weird." Caleb's voice was watery, faint. "I feel like I swallowed an ice cube."

Wow. Cool. Never done an exit interview before.

"Can I confess something?"

I didn't negate.

He didn't move, but his posture changed. It felt smaller. "My father didn't throw me out because I like boys." He spoke carefully, like every syllable was made of glass and might cut him if he wasn't careful. "We weren't allowed allegedly unsupervised internet access before high school, and Elias ritualistically read all my texts. Content consumption had to fall within certain *moral parameters*. God is surveillance. Of course, I hate that. Enter: VPNs. Naturally, I immediately started researching all my familial taboos. It should be easy to chalk things up to curiosity. To say I was just curious. I made up names and joined forums because I wanted to see what it was like. I'm not prone to self-delusion. I craved certain interactions because I needed them. I had a language to account for the particular kind of despair I've been wrestling with forever, certainly since adolescence, and I've got the path forward. I've got examples of success. I've got great grades, I'm a shoo-in for robust academic scholarships, if I got cut off, it'd be eminently workable. It's not too long until college. I figured I'd experiment once I was away from my brothers. Nobody would know me. I could do whatever I wanted. Abel buys drugs off the dark web all the time. I might as well buy medicine."

I sat up and chomped on my tongue. Forbid myself from interruptions. "Medicine?"

"Mhm. To try it, I guess. Maybe I should've gone to a doctor, but my GP is friends with my father, and I don't trust anyone friends with my father not to overstep ethical lines if my father asks it of them." Tone got softer. "It was a list of names. That's what my little brother found."

"Okay." I rubbed the corner of my mouth. "Did you pick one?"

"Shiloh."

"Shiloh's a pretty name. What pronouns should I use for you, Shiloh?"

"They and them. For now. We'll see." They spliced their fingers and shot me a glance. I recognized that look—it was a dare. *Say something condescending and ignorant and heartless. Do it. Make my day.*

I whistled a breath through my teeth, put my arms behind my head. My brain was fizzing and not just because I felt a sudden overwhelming retrospective fear and fury on their behalf, but because I was thinking about those two syllables. They and them. Singular plurality. Multiplicity. Negation. The glide of teeth over tongue. "Glad I didn't use your deadname in the hex, in that case. Shit wouldn't have worked." I knew this instinctually, somehow. Deadnames wouldn't be magically conducive. If somebody hexed me as Eloise over Sideways, that shit would roll off my back. "Which name and pronouns should I use around my dads?"

"I told Boris earlier today." They pulled their hands off their face, rubbed them together. "Boris is really cool, Sideways. He's helped me a lot. He phoned a bunch of his genderqueer friends and let me chat with them. Adult people, people with careers and families who've been nonconforming for decades." They curled their lip a little. "Feel free to hit me for this, but I feel like the hunting I did, the glee I sometimes got from it? It was triumph over *me*. If I was good at squelching the strange in others, I'd be good at stamping it out of myself."

"Gross. Evil phase, glad we're moving forward. Proud of you for poking around queer chat boards behind your ex-parents' back, I mean that." I jerked a fist through my hair.

There were a billion gallons of emotion inside me, fermenting, pickling, putrefying. Pain by the ladleful. Do you feel this, Madeline? "Doesn't really answer the name and pronoun question."

"I've been disowned. Not to mention excommunicated." Shiloh's eyes fluttered back in their head. Something residing in smirk territory floated around their mouth. Made them look pointier. "I can't imagine further consequences cropping up. I am who I am. I don't quite know what that means, but whatever. You can call me Shiloh. I'd really like that, actually."

"Shiloh it is."

Should I ask them to try different pronouns for me?

Not now. I felt weird about it now. This was their moment.

They sat up, looked at the mirror on my wall. They pressed a fingertip to the hex line on their neck, twisted their jaw this way and that for a full view. There was a touch of color in their cheeks. "It looks like a nineties choker."

"You're welcome." I rubbed my hands up and down my knees. Scraped the ingrown hair bumps. Should I hug them? Profoundly weird urge. Pushed it down ASAP. "Do you want to take a second? Or should I proceed with the game plan?"

"Proceed." They took a breath, rubbed one palm with their opposing thumb.

"So. We're breaking into your house and liberating stolen specters. Here's what's up, I'm apparently allergic to the sigils that Madeline's been putting around your house—"

"She's been putting up what?"

"Sigils. Focus. She's using my magic, and my body fucking hates that and freaks out when I see the sigils she casts. So that's going to be a problem. We've gotta plan for—"

My phone buzzed like crazy. Buzzed like somebody was calling it. Who the fuck calls anymore? When are scammers going to learn that I don't have a car for which I could have an expired warranty? I wasn't even really sure what an expired warranty entailed. I snatched it up, fully prepared to turn it off, but the contact that lit up the screen read CURSE DADDY.

I swiped and shoved it against my ear.

"Hey, can you come outside? You left your backpack in my car." Jing's voice crackled through the speaker. "It'll just be a second. I'm parked illegally, so."

"Yeah," I breathed. Was Jing dying? Was I dying? She had never called me before all the weirdness. I slid off my bed, bounced my weight on my heels, waggled fingers in Shiloh's direction that didn't mean much other than *one-second pause*. Jing didn't elaborate. Her connection sounded weird. I wandered out of my room with a huff, oozed into the hallway. Shiloh might've gotten up to follow me, but I didn't look back to check. Across the creaky floor, neither dad in sight, unblinking art pieces watching with serene pastel happiness as I shoved the apartment door open with my foot. Weird crackle sounds on the phone. I tramped down the creaky stairs and trudged out into the shop. It was dark, but that hardly mattered; I knew the shop's anatomy like the inside of my mouth. I stepped around baskets of vintage Barbies and jutting yellowed stacks of books, ducked under an outstretched statue arm strung thick with Mardi Gras beads. Either I was being haunted or Shiloh was following me. I heard a soft shuffling sound of footsteps over the plush red rugs, but I didn't glance around to verify. Was willing enough to bet it was Shiloh and not a murderer or something. There wasn't any speaking between Jing and me, but I knew she was still there, because even through the frizzy static sounds there was a faint pounding of her music. Or was it my music? It didn't seem like her genre, but it was something I listened to religiously while walking between class periods. I was into sludge metal these days. Had I gotten Jing Gao into sludge metal?

I shouldered open the shop door and stepped into the night. It was cold; I hadn't thought about that beforehand. Icy air ripped across my scalp. I hugged my arms around my stomach and swore, blinked around, scanned for a flash of Jing's hot rod in the blackness. I saw it. Candy-red in the night. A moment later and there she was. She opened the door when she saw me and stepped out, white sneakers on the wet pavement, then leaned one hip against the hood. She was wearing her SCAPEGRACERS jacket. She had my backpack strap dangling from one hand and a twelve-pack of pop dangling from the other. That lemon Squirt brand we all found so hilarious. She pulled her bottom lip between her teeth when I got closer, scrunched her brows in a V. She looked over my shoulder at Shiloh. "Who's—"

"Jing, this is Shiloh, former witchfinder, current jackass

housemate. Tell them their Chett hex looks pretty. They took it like a champ. Shiloh"—I turned to them for a split second, waved a hand—"this is my coven mate, Jing. She's cooler than you, but that's a given."

Shiloh slipped their hands in their pockets and nodded, a quick downward jerk of their chin. Their sugar-blond fringe flopped in their face.

"Right," said Jing. Something passed over her—waves of old distrust and new understanding, maybe. She opened her mouth and I braced myself for something, but it didn't come. She looked between us, tucked a lock of her even blonder hair behind her ear. "Does Mr. Scratch approve?"

"Ish." Generous read of him, maybe.

Generous is right.

"Look, I needed to talk to you. Face to face. Just— thanks for today," Jing said. The car lights haloed her, caught the gloss of her jacket, the fine lavender glitter of the highlight on her cheekbones, the starlight of her hair. She took a step toward me, swung out the bag and the drinks. The cans clinked together. She sucked in her cheeks and rocked back on her heels, glanced over my shoulder again. These were new false lashes, or at least ones I didn't remember her wearing before. Plush, full of little Xs. They cast saw-blade shadows underneath her eyes. "Can we be alone for a second?"

I nodded and turned to tell Shiloh to scram, but their retreat was already in motion. They slipped themself into the alcove under the shop's sign, presumably slinked behind the door and back into the dark safety of the shop. Hoped they waited inside for me. It was easy to get lost on the floor after hours. I turned back to Jing, got ready to say something harder than the situation called for.

Jing was all I could see all of a sudden.

She'd stepped closer. We could've knocked our knees together if we moved, that's how close we were. I could count every wisp of her hair on her cheek in the breeze. I just looked at her for a moment, lost, brain emptied of whatever I'd expected a moment previous. Something glinted in her eyes. Gravity. I thought for a second that she was going to hit me, or maybe gut me with the shimmery knife she keeps with her car keys.

Jing reached out her hands. I'd forgotten that she'd been holding things somehow, and as her knuckles pressed against mine, offering things to me, a phantom fist shut around my throat. My backpack. Just giving me my backpack, and a compensatory sweet little something to help me along in my quest to rot all my teeth out. Normal. I forgot that there were feet underneath me that held my body upright, and that there were lungs inside me moving, moving. A grand circuit of blood under my skin. Jing Gao was shorter than me but it felt like she was towering above me, looking down at me, filling the sky. She was a pillar. I felt like I'd huffed paint.

I took the backpack and the drinks. They were heavy, which was good. Kept me tethered to earth. The downside was that their heaviness rendered me immobile in the arm department, and I had this feeling like I might want my full range of motion, might want both of my hands free.

"Are you mad at me?" Her bangs floated just above her eyelashes like a line of vampire teeth. I focused on the way they fell instead of making proper eye contact, which would've incinerated me. The shop beside Rothschild & Pike had a red neon sign in the window, still lit despite the hour, and it cast a weird cherry shine over her. Bluish head-lights and red neon in opposition felt like 3D glasses, and in my dizziness, it struck me that Jing was so lovely. There it was. Lovely. "To be honest, I think you should be."

"I am," I said. "I'm mad at you." My tongue was all gristle. I chewed it to get the words out. Ought I mention knowing about the party? No. That'd be weak. I was already so desperate to get my specter back. I couldn't afford extra layers of neediness. I wanted to seem sturdy. I wanted her to want to lean on me. "If you care for me, you'll make sure I'm seen. You'll make sure I got a place next to you. You won't fucking hide me."

She held perfectly still. Something shifted behind her blackboard irises. Her hair fluttered again on a breeze I couldn't feel. "I'll talk to Daisy," she finally said. She didn't blink. "You're being a better person than I might've been."

I pressed the tip of my tongue against my tooth gap.

"This is bullshit. I want us together again." Jing dragged the fringe off her face, and I watched her wrist bones move against her skin, watched her knuckles stir, watched her shimmery nails traipse along her scalp. Her dark roots were mesmerizing whenever I got a flash of them. I wanted to put my sleeve in my mouth and sob hard, like a kid, which made me want to break a window. I wanted—something else. I wasn't sure what I wanted. My guts felt like jelly. She said, "This feels so fucked, Sideways."

I said, "Then unfuck it."

"Goddamn it," she said. "I want to go back to Dorothy's with you, I mean, I—"

"I caught a couple of guys talking smack about Daisy." I cut her off before my lungs popped. My head was spinning. I worried vaguely about blood flow. My kneecaps were dissolving and all I could do was finish my thought before my spine unthreaded and spilled vertebrae pony beads down my pant leg. Was she asking to go to the gay bar with me again? Was she —Jesus Christ, *of course she wasn't*, don't be fucking ridiculous, Sideways. In what world would Jing have any interest in the likes of you? "They won't bother any of you anymore. Can't post what they were threatening to post, that's for sure. I think Daisy knows about—about whatever they were talking about, and I don't know how to hex that off the cloud, but the four of them can't look at it, or anything stolen like that, again." Meaner iteration of the hex than normal. This one would glue their eyes shut. There was no unglue clause.

Jing breathed in sharply. Eyes widened, brows lifted.

My fingers were threatening to give out on me. I visualized the Squirt cans crashing to the pavement and bursting between our feet and somehow flooding the whole of Sycamore Gorge with citrusy corn syrup. Sweeping us away. Drowning could be nice, right now.

"When?"

"Earlier tonight, after I rolled out of your trunk."

"Where?"

"In an alley. Shortcut from the gas station to Rothschild & Pike."

"Did you know them?"

"I don't know. Average Sycamore Gorge boys. Probably."

"Are you okay?"

"Like, existentially?"

"Sideways," Jing said. She bounced once on her toes, an athletic, excess-of-energy habit that I associated more with Daisy. Maybe she was cold. Tension pulsed off her and the air around her head was dense and faintly luminous. She furrowed her brows. "How many guys were there, exactly?"

"Four." I don't think I'd forget that, even if I was already losing the concrete details of their faces and the tones of their voices. All four of them spinning would stay in me forever. They'd clicked off like cardinal directions in my brain.

"You hexed four guys without us? You're sure it took?"

"Mr. Scratch helped." Credit where credit is due. "I'm confident."

Imagine if you'd had your specter in you. They'd be weeds in the pavement, now.

"And they say chivalry is dead. You're magic."

I blinked, a little taken aback. "Well, yeah, you knew—"

"No. You're miraculous, Sideways." She swayed closer. "Knowing you feels like magic."

My breath caught. I couldn't breathe.

Somewhere else—*no no no no no*—Madeline hurled a

glass bottle against a wall. It shattered into a million eye-shaped flecks. The sound clapped in the back of my head, and the spray slapped the tops of my feet through my boots. Little baby needles. Madeline wanted to howl. *Idiot.* You did it on purpose. Why are you shocked when it hurt? She had none of my goose bumps. She was hot. She was burning up. She made me sweat through my shirt, she was so scalding hot. Hot like Joan of Arc. She clawed the tank top off her shoulders. She was suffocating in her skin, she was roasting, her meat cooking to softness on her bones. She was wrung out with borrowed magic. Practicing. Her chest filled to bursting. She opened her mouth. My jaw, our jaw, clicked.

Not now. I needed to be me right now. I needed to be with her.

Jing looked at me and I fought to look back.

Fucking Madeline. Stop crying. Stop feeling so much, stop slicing my focus in half. Be a catastrophe later, for the love of sweet gay Jesus. Stop doing magic when I'm with people, stop stealing me away from myself when I need to be present, need to be grounded, want to be around.

"Sideways," Jing said.

Madeline wasn't satisfied with what she'd done. What an elaborate and costly fuckup. The whole thing was sloppy. It was a bomb where she wanted a bullet. The thing was, Madeline was an exceptionally gifted witch. She'd been gifted enough to keep herself alive after she'd been hollowed of her hex gland, she'd made this specter work for her, even if she couldn't metabolize Sideways. Sideways did not want to be inside of her. You betrayed me. Why would I want to be inside of you? Doesn't fucking matter, I can muscle through this. Failure was Sideways' fault. Maybe her magic was no good, maybe she had a dud specter. Maybe I should have robbed somebody better than her. More competent, more magically potent. But how do you talk a smart girl into giving up her own soul? I was an echo inside my own head. My head was someone else's. My finger joints screamed for me to readjust my grip. My bag and the cans were slipping.

"Sideways," Jing said again, softer this time.

I looked at her and nothing else. I forced myself to look at her.

"Will you forgive me, you think?"

"Yes," I said.

"Do you miss me any?" I couldn't read her expression, couldn't tell if she was being coy, if she was making fun of me. "Has this been hard on you, too?"

I couldn't think of something clever, or even something stupid. It took all my energy just to move my lips around my teeth and speak. "Yes," I said.

She swayed closer. Her thighs brushed mine.

Madeline's screaming echoed off the walls around us. My skull was going to split open, her tantrum was going to split my skull open Lizzie Borden style. Mr. Scratch was going to fall out of me and splash the pavement and get swept away in carbonated sugar.

"Can I kiss you?"

The bag and the bottles slipped out of my hands. They

smacked the ground. Neither of us moved to catch them. They dented but somehow, I wasn't drowning in sugar. No flood. No rupture. I throbbed in two bodies and wanted to scream.

"Not like this," fell out. Not with her in my head.

Jing flinched. She looked down, at the bottles maybe, and then over her shoulder at the car. "I should be headed back," she said.

I worked my jaw. I should say something. I should clarify. I didn't.

"I'll see you soon, Sideways." She followed her gaze, turned head and shoulders toward the car and left. The door slammed, the engine revved and woke neighboring dogs, her music blared louder than local ordinances would ever permit. Her car pulled out of the alley and sped down a road so dark it looked like water. It vanished around a corner. The sound of it disappeared a gasp later. It happened in an instant. Jing was gone.

I stood with my bag and a heap of cans.

I seized fistfuls of my belly and hyperventilated.

Someone stepped behind me. Silently, swish of moving fabric aside, they dropped to their knees and started plucking cans off the pavement, tucked them under their arms one by one. Their blond hair looked colorless in this light, the same shade as littered papers or the moon reflected in oil-slicked puddles. Shiloh didn't speak, and their face in profile didn't give any emotions away, but there was a distinct stiffness around their shoulders.

"What are you doing?" I said when I was down enough to speak. I wanted it to sound mean. I wanted to be mean to someone. It barely sounded like anything at all.

"The door is locked," they said. They gathered up the last of the cans and held them in their arms, gently, like they were carrying a bushel of kittens. They stood upright again. "So."

So, they saw the whole thing. Wow! Wow.

Madeline Kline kicked a wall.

"It's cold." It occurred to me that they hadn't been wearing shoes when they'd followed me out here. They stood on the asphalt with nothing but flamingo socks between them and the slick pavement. It was easier to think about this than the thin, pinkish glow across their cheekbones. "Ready to go back inside?"

I grabbed my backpack and slung it over one shoulder in response.

The two of us walked back up to the shop's awning.

The silence made me want to eat dirt and wormify. I felt too big for my skin.

"May I please have a can?"

I snapped back and blinked at them. "You think you get apology Squirt as recompense for being forced to witness dyke drama?"

The cans jostled a bit in their arms. Pink got pinker. "I was more thinking that I—"

"Yeah," I said. "You can have a damn Squirt."

We stopped in front of the door.

Would you look at that. Totally locked. It auto-locks after a certain hour. Time was, there was an emergency backup key in the flower box, but I had the distinct memory of digging up the key after Shiloh and their family kidnapped me earlier this year. I'd jangled it around in the knob, gone upstairs, and forgotten completely about the existence of the key. Threw it on the floor of my bedroom somewhere. It hadn't been replaced.

"You can unlock it," Shiloh said. "Yes?"

"Well." I licked my teeth. "What was your prayer gonna be earlier? Before dinner?"

They cleared their throat. "Gratitude. Praise for your family's hospitality, their generosity. Forgiveness. Redemption. That sort of thing. My relationship with divinity is contentious and I don't want to impose my traditions on you, particularly when I'm not so sure I even want them. But it felt right. I didn't mean to make things weird."

"Everything's weird." I shrugged. "Cute idea. Do you miss that sort of thing?"

"I miss knowing my part." They shivered. "I'll leave the rest."

Sideways, I've got an idea. Mr. Scratch sounded unusually citric, oblivious to the appropriate tone. Not that any tone would feel right. He whirled around my sternum, like his idea would stay better if he wove it into cobwebs. *Sideways, I should have thought of this earlier, oh Sideways my darling dear—*

"Does this idea involve unlocking the door," I scowled, "my darling dear?"

Shiloh looked at me like I'd licked the knob. I hadn't ever told them about Mr. Scratch, had I? Definitely just sounded like I was talking to myself.

Imagine, a Mr. Scratch conversation with Shiloh not-Chantry. What a doozy that'd be.

No, Mr. Scratch said cheerfully. *It has nothing to do with the door.*

"Great," I breathed. "That's awesome."

"Sideways."

"I'm talking to my devil. Not to you. Nose out of it, Shiloh."

Shiloh dropped a can. It rolled toward the ditch. "Come again?"

I didn't feel like explaining. I opened my mouth extra wide, stuck my tongue out, let them see the whirling ink-glob spider across the roof of my mouth. I shut again. "His name is Mr. Scratch."

Shiloh jolted backwards, clowned over the cans, barely kept a hold on them. They looked like I'd shown them a box full of bugs. Their ears burned screaming pink.

I felt smug about that. Wigging people out brought such a particular pleasure. I could call Boris at this juncture, but the issue was, I felt insane, and needed to bloodlet some excess energy. I wanted to vandalize a building with Daisy. Fucking Daisy. I eyeballed a trellis on the side of the building. "Hey Shiloh," I said. God, what was my fucking life. "Think you could give me a lift?"

THIRTEEN

BLOODY MARY CANDY MAN

We didn't die climbing inside, somehow.

Anyway, I drank pop then slept and then school came. Half the day was spent in a lockdown, so I spent three hours with my back shoved up under the chalkboard. The lights were off and all of us were breathing, three kids slept, someone else passed around pills concealed by a mint box. I might've taken one. I didn't get my come up, though, because Mr. Scratch stole it from under my tongue. Probably for the best. None of my friends were in class with me, but Sheridan was there, and she spent the whole period with her head in my lap. We didn't talk much. She texted Monique.

So, my idea is this, said Mr. Scratch, who didn't know what was going on. *I think there are sigils you could use to help you through the woods, and maybe even something that'd let you see inside of Madeline, so you've got some idea of where she is and what she's planning. I should've thought of it sooner, but I was trying so hard not to think about it, Sideways. They're sigils I already know, because they were my daughters' sigils. My daughters before you. They put so much love in my pages. They were so brilliant, and they had so many sharp ideas, ideas you could use as tools. I thought about it because the twister spell, that was one of theirs. It was Laverne's spell, specifically. She was my daughter. She was born in Oklahoma and she found her magic because she and her lover survived a storm by sheer force of will. They climbed on top of her family's barn and held each other and screamed, and the twister split down the middle, passed around either side of the barn, spared them. All her magic was in gusts of wind after that. She'd call them down to protect her. It was Laverne's spell. You saved yourself from those boys by Laverne's hand.*

I had a daughter named Iris, and another named Priya, and they made spells for walking through pain without laceration to the heart and soul. They made it so that they could walk outside at night together without hearing people's shouting. They wouldn't see the things written on walls around them and they wouldn't feel the force of ire. They wouldn't feel the force of loathing, which is itself a vestige of ill-conceived magic, and would traverse paths undisturbed. It offered the courage of euphoria in the face of despair. It wasn't intended to help with the pain of seeing your own magic cast by something outside of your body, and I don't know if it would alleviate the disorientation. It guided the two of them through many a barbed path, though, Sideways. Priya and Iris would wear trousers and kiss each other in full daylight with this sigil. I think it could help. If Shiloh is good as you think they are, they will be willing to guide you through the woods, and the sigil will stave off the agony. I think it could work.

There's another. It would be harder. I think it may give you a glimpse inside her without the scrying methods she's already blocked off, assuming we can make it work.

"Why's it harder?" I spoke just loudly enough that I could hear myself, but it didn't make Sheridan move. She was checking the news, now. I told myself not to look. There should maybe be fear, or at least apprehension, but I was wrung out past the point of that. I just felt the ghost fingers of dead lesbians on my shoulders. Scratch's daughters. My pulse throbbed in my teeth.

It was toward the end. The flow of his voice, which'd been quick and velvety before, slowed and went chalky. *The weaving caught a snag. That's why I hadn't thought about it.*

"Toward the end of what, Scratch?"

Me. Us. The Honeyeaters.

"Are you ready to talk about that?"

Whether or not he was didn't seem to matter. Another room unfurled around me like a rug. It covered the students, the desks, the blue-tinged walls. I was somewhere else. It wasn't like getting lost in Madeline's panic, it was fuzzier, like plunging into an old photograph. No hard edges. No harsh lines.

A woman hurled herself onto the ground before me.

She howled her eyes out. She resisted comfort, lashed out her limbs whenever hands were offered. The makeup swam down her face, curved the hollows of her cheeks, splattered the hem of her dress. Her hairpins had fallen. Her curls were wet and clung to her skull, or else jutted out at odd angles. They burst from her head like stuffing bursts from a slashed-up pillow. Her dress just hung off her. It looked thin as paper, like it'd crumble if you touched it. It was wet. Buttons of water speckled her arms. She threw herself to the ground in front of us, and everybody held their breath.

I could not reach for the woman.

The woman and I were in a place where brocade tapestries hung from the walls, long swaths of cream and gold. Tasseled ropes that bound curtains. Roses bound with sigil-inscribed ribbons hung uvula-like from the mirrored ceiling. There were plush chairs everywhere. The chairs were filled with women. The women looked like Beardsley drawings come to life, all heavy eye makeup and thick, animated brows. They gathered together, wearing all sorts of things— some in clothes that I could only approximate as "standard boymode vintage," trousers and vests and gloves and so on, but others in what must've been costumery, beaded bodices and elaborate headpieces, enormous ostrich fans—some of them surrounded the howling woman and some held back, looked not at me, but just in front of me. Why the fuck wouldn't anyone meet my eyes?

I didn't have eyes. I was in a book. I *was* a book. We rested on a silky pedestal sprinkled with flower petals and bits of flinty confetti.

The howling woman touched the pages of our book. We reached up, twined little tendrils of ourselves around her knobby elbows and higher, lapped the dripping coal off her eyelids. We tried to make her feel clean. We stretched our voice across the page in long, elegant lines: *Why are you crying, Elaina my child?*

Her voice rattled from somewhere deeper than her throat.

I, Sideways, recognized that voice. I'd had it once myself.

"They followed me from the market," she said. "I was buying peaches, they followed me back. I was down by the water. It was daylight, broad and blinding. I walked by the waterside, and they were in front of me, they were behind me. They overwhelmed me. I bit their hands. They threw me in the water. All the peaches floated." Her eyes filled up the entire room. She was smiling. Her teeth were long as fingers. Everyone wanted to cry, but Elaina didn't. She couldn't do that anymore. "They pulled me out of the water, and they asked me to draw them up a spell. I said no. They took my hair and shoved me low, they held me underwater. My skirt tangled in my ankles. They pulled me up and asked me to draw them a spell. I said no. I said no. I couldn't see, I couldn't breathe, my head was filled with sparks. They pulled me out of the water. They put a pen in my hand. They pressed until I coughed the water up."

Someone across the room stood up. "Did you write?"

"She's alive," said someone else. "Of course she wrote."

We felt along her pulse. It was missing notes. All bass,

all thrumming, none of the resonant ringing we knew and loved. There wasn't the lick of green. Elaina was the deepest, loveliest green. She was verdant like midsummer. It was a color of venom and pride.

She was empty of herself.

Nobody moved.

"Did you tell them where we live?"

"How many were there?"

"What did you say?"

"Let her breathe, stop yelling at her, oh Hell, oh Scratch, oh how—"

Our seething shook the letters throughout us. We wanted to bleed through the pages and stain our lovely plush altar cloth and become a liquid monster, stream into the night and smother men alive. We wanted to strangle. To devour. We couldn't do that. Instead, we brought ourselves up, wrote across our face for her, that we might ease her pain. We said, *You are my child. You are forever my child. What do you ask of us?*

"I want to see inside it." She shivered all over. "I want to see inside of my specter. If I see it, I'll know what they're doing with it. What they're planning. I'll know . . ."

My vision furred over, and everything swam orange. I was sitting in the classroom again. I was a big dumb dyke named Sideways Pike and the world was ending and I wanted to scream.

Sheridan was editing a selfie, which was a decent sign that she hadn't seen any juicy not-so-good updates about the news. It was still dark in there. Our teacher was hyperventilating while reading a book. I contracted and expanded my hands.

"What happened? Did it work?" I swiped my tongue over my gums. I tasted Scratch there.

Yes. He sounded distant. *I think it did.*

I imagined it without his helping. Imagined watching a group of witchfinders march to murder all my friends and found family, imagined the realization spread that the holy soldiers would arrive imminently, that no defense could be taken, that no adequate offense could be planned, no goodbyes made. Watching them surround the Honeyeaters' theater and being helpless to do a damn thing about it. Trying, still trying. Then, cold.

I felt nauseous, which Sheridan must've sensed because she passed me a stick of contraband gum. I popped it between my teeth and tried to focus on how the spearmint made my throat feel.

I can't remember what the sigil looked like, Mr. Scratch said. *I can't remember much of anything after that. I remember the burning, but the burning spread and it ate things that came before it. I can't remember what Elaina said to me. I can't—*

"It's okay," I breathed. I rubbed the bone down the middle of my chest, behind which he was trembling. I felt him through my shirt. Felt like squishing berries under my skin. "It's okay."

"It's okay," Sheridan repeated.

"Did you stay inside her like a familiar? Like you did with me?" I said this quieter, and Sheridan didn't seem to hear me.

She wouldn't let me. I remember that I asked her. She thought everybody needed me as I was, as a book to be read by all my daughters.

I hated knowing what happened next. I hated memory. I never wanted to forget.

"What do you think we should do?" I closed my eyes, tried to imagine that Mr. Scratch was somebody sitting across from me. It was easier to have a conversation that way. I could've grabbed his limbs and squeezed them that way, could've held him against my chest and slapped his back and stared at the wall for an hour. I needed to find her. My method died with a long-dead girl. What was I supposed to do with that? Not like I could slide into her DMs about it. Next thought, initially stupid: Were ghosts real? I'm a witch, I've got no grounds to say any given Halloween monster existing is stupid. If they're real, could I commune with Scratch's daughters? I mulled contact styles that didn't feel ridiculous, even for me. Would something like a Ouija board be disrespectful? Despite being the way that I am, I didn't own a real Ouija board. They gave Julian the heebies and the jeebies. I was spiraling. I was going nowhere fast.

That might work.

It hadn't been a serious thought. Forgot that he could hear. I felt like I'd swallowed ice.

Ghosts don't exist like you're anticipating, Sideways. Parts of her live inside me, because her magic has moved through me and her language constitutes part of what I am. I have an imprint of her, of all my girls. You can pull that imprint out of me. Project it, be with it.

Mechanical bell chime overhead.

"Alrighty," said the teacher, gulping water or something from a metal canister with abandon. "It's officially not lockdown any longer! We're going to fourth period, I think. Or maybe lunch. I've got to make a call."

"Looks like they arrested somebody," Sheridan said.

"Yeah?" I stood up after she crawled off. My knees made a gross clicking sound.

"Yeah," she said, scrolling fast.

I left before she told me who.

✳

I made my spirit board out of a cereal box with foam letter stickers that I found in a box of miscellaneous craft supplies I keep in my closet for witchcraft's sake. I have no memory of starting the box or replenishing its contents, but it was always full, and it always contained the shit I required. The spirit board was deeply ugly, but it had a full alphabet. I didn't bother with suns and moons and formal greetings. We could spell that shit out.

I locked myself in my bathroom. I put the board on the counter beside the sink. I carved holes in an apple and jammed birthday candles in the punctures, lit them and a few sticks of frankincense. I shut off the lights. Bit my lip, smeared a daub of blood mixed with powdered sugar on the yielding skin under my ears. I threaded a mood ring through a curb chain, latched it. I dangled the chain off my trigger finger like a pendulum. I'd do this right for Mr. Scratch's sake. I would make this feel right.

He billowed in the darkness. Pulsed under my skin.

"Elaina," I said. I focused on nothing in particular. "I'd like a word with you."

Nothing happened. The candles drizzled pink wax on glossy green skin.

This is magic, Sideways. You have to believe it. Compel me to believe you.

"This is fucking important. I don't want it to feel stupid."

You feel stupid all the time and it seldom stops you.

"Okay. Just—will this hurt you?"

It will hurt me more if you need it and don't.

Well then. Specter be damned—I knew my craft. I could put on a good show. I pulled air through my teeth, shut my eyes, lifted my head. Made my spine as long as it could be. My breath felt louder. The sound pushed at me. I heard the wind comb the naked branches outside and the pipes slosh and the distant twinkling of synthesized music, the sound of someone dragging furniture downstairs. Water dripped periodically from the faucet, and from the shower-head behind me. I matched my breath to the drip-dropping.

It became the only thing in the world; the drip inhale, the drop exhale, the burn of smoke over my head, the mean bright twinge of cut sour apple. The noise became a part of me. I became a part of it. The blood in my body and the water in the pipes moved together, gushing, moving, flowing, all drip-dropping. Tension left me. My jaw loosened up. My neck got longer. I opened my mouth. I kneaded my need into something syllabic. Language eased out with my breath.

"My name is Sideways, Scapegracer, a child of Scratch. I am speaking to Elaina, Honeyeater, my sister through Scratch. Come to me. I call you. Show me that you're here."

Drip-drop.

A slow metal screech rolled behind me. It was the sound of rings scraping rail. Plastic crinkled. Wet heavy slap on the floor. Another, closer.

I opened my eyes.

I saw myself in the mirror. Just my profile in the candle-light, thick black Scratch veins heavy in my forehead, and the reflective bellies of shower tiles over my shoulder. I thought I was playing hypnotist. I thought it must've been in my head.

The shower curtain had been drawn. Something had drawn the curtain.

My heart hurled up my throat so fast I thought I'd choked on it. Hoarfrost. I felt plucked, I was sweating. What an honor it was—whatever this was. No comprehension, no inquiry into the mechanics, just a deeply felt knot of comradery. History. Being haunted was witnessing history.

"I need you, Elaina," I breathed. "Someone stole my specter from me. I want to see inside of it. I think it'd help me find it if I could."

My ring pendulum pulled taut, then swung so fast I nearly broke my hold. The ring zigzagged. It yanked like a dog on a lead. I swallowed sour and threaded the pinballing letters together, mouthed them as they were marked.

L-O-V-E-Y-O-U-S-O-R-R-Y-F-O-R-E-V-E-R

"Elaina," I said. The chain rubbed the crook of my finger raw. "Elaina, how did you see inside your specter?"

S-I-D-E-W-A-Y-S-L-O-O-K-A-T-M-E

"What spell did you use?"

C-O-L-D-I-N-S-I-D-E-Y-O-U-R-B-A-T-H-T-U-B

"Elaina." My knees locked up.

I-K-E-E-P-T-R-Y-I-N-G-T-O-R-O-T

I saw spots. I felt my finger bloat, my hand, my wrist. Mr. Scratch gummed around my carpals and contracted, expanded, made all the little muscle fingers twinge. My hand jerked, strained to hold him. It looked broken. I thought about the girl in *Willy Wonka and the Chocolate Factory*, the one who stole bubblegum and blew up into a blueberry. My hand looked ripe. My skin throbbed where it stretched. He'd never been like this. He'd never felt like this in me. I wasn't sure if I could hold him.

L-O-O-K-I-N-T-H-E-M-I-R-R-O-R

My chin wobbled. I didn't raise it, but I flicked up my eyes.

Breath that wasn't mine fogged the glass.

A shape traced itself. Then lines, two short and one long like a backwards 3. Its tail cut up through the hook-curve. It looked like a broken ampersand. I could see myself through the lines.

Mr. Scratch wailed in my wrist, then chanted something, chanted with more fervor than any of the Scapegracers or I ever had. Brutal, slimy syllables, clicking and twisting and chafing between my knucklebones. It wasn't in English. It might not have been any human language at all. It was jaggedy cosmic noise and it hurt my ears.

Wet fingers seized the back of my neck.

My forehead struck the glass.

✳

Madeline stood with her feet shoulder's width apart. Knees bent, strong foot forward. Both her coach and her choir teacher agreed that holding yourself like this kept you from passing out. Fighter's stance. She should never ever leave it.

Her grandmother's trailer wasn't nice, but it was free. That being said, she had no idea where her grandmother was. She'd worked really hard on a story that would justify her absence, had printed out scores from her online classes, had produced elaborate alibis and false references.

If her grandmother came back to the trailer, she'd tell her all about it. Sorry I keep vanishing. Sorry that I don't answer calls or tell anybody, you particularly, where I am. I didn't fight with Mom and I haven't been in touch with Dad or Lewis, I just left this time, and that sucks. It sucks that I won't have a senior night. It sucks that I won't walk this spring. Believe me, I know. I know it's hard on you, but listen, listen, everything's been hell lately and I've got so much to do. I love you. Thanks for the couch.

But Grammy didn't come home. She kept thinking she'd come outside and she'd be there, sitting on the stoop shooting squirrels who bit her tulips, but the tulips were dead anyway, and she hadn't grown them for years. Weird memories. She must be staying with Lewis or something. That was better than her stuck alone in the trailer park, anyway.

She told herself that.

She'd thrown out all the rotten food and dumped the maggots from the fruit bowl outside. Called the power company, turned on the lights with a credit card she found in the knife drawer. Fed the mangy stray cats.

Now, she dumped her shit across the glossy linoleum counter. Her tools: lighter, jackknife, compact, tape. She'd written out incantations on two spools of athletic tape, charged them each by twining them around her throat and pulling until her vision flickered and the tape zinged against the grooves of her hands, livid and live-wire electric. All her magic was from the throat. Sideways Pike's specter hadn't passed any lower. It stayed jammed in the spoons of her collarbone, screaming hot and ridged like a peach pit. It made eating hard. She could hardly breathe sometimes, considered ripping it out, stowing it under her mattress.

She never did that. She wouldn't open herself up like that. Refused to be empty again, even for a moment.

She opened her compact. Nothing across the glass but herself and a smudge from her powderpuff, which meant there wasn't any traffic to or from the Chantry house. If she could've gotten closer, she might have carved sigils into their walls, or the hoods of their cars. She couldn't manage it. She'd been repelled when she got close, as though by an unseen force. She didn't think it was magic. She chalked it up to grief.

This was happening. Vengeance glimmered low on the horizon like a storm. Not a damn thing could stop her. She didn't believe in making overly elaborate plans. That was asking for irony. She had the requisite junk and Sideways' mad red specter. She wouldn't need anything else.

After this Friday night, there wouldn't be any more witchfinders in this town. No more Levi Chantry. Him or the boys like him. Maybe if it worked well, she'd go find other families. Direct fucking action. If they didn't loathe her, her ex-coven would be proud.

It was so fucking hard, being patient. The Chantry family, for a bunch of Family First evangelical freaks, never did anything together out of the house besides church. They hated each other too much for that. Going after them one by one wasn't an option; the others would surely find her and kill her if she tried. They'd string her by her ankles from their porch and Abel would beat her with a nine iron or something. He used to joke about things like that. She tried and failed to repress a thought about the time she'd drunkenly made out with Abel under the pretense that he was Levi, how she hit him when she realized but she'd wanted to keep going, the fact that *they* found her and him together, and didn't tell Levi about it, but didn't save her from Levi either. Those nine-iron jokes were about *them*. About how Abel was suspicious about *them*. They'd always thought it was funny, they'd told her. They thought it was funny that Abel thought he stood a chance. Whatever. *They hadn't saved her.* They were Brethren and they weren't getting out of this alive. None of them spared, all of them at once.

Madeline breathed in shrimp Cup Noodles fumes and tried to focus. The sour MSG smell was grounding. Maybe this timing was a blessing. If they'd gone for a family outing a month ago, she would've fucked it up, so it was a good thing that they'd forced her to bide time. Sideways' specter wasn't easy to navigate. It didn't work for her all of the time, and when it did, it worked too much. She'd fucked up a motel's whole electrical grid once trying to cheat the Wi-Fi. She'd been so good at that shit with her own specter. She'd been spectacular.

Maybe it was Sideways. She wanted to blame Sideways.

She thought about her. She thought about her hands working when she scribbled magic. The intensity of her focus, her big villain brows drawn, bottom lip sucked between her blocky kid teeth. Eyes on fire. Blushy. She thought about her broad shoulders in her black leather, the strength of her arms, the way her ratty shirts clung to her chest. Long legs in cargo pants and tall boots. How her face scrunched when she smiled. It made that scar across her nose bridge wavy like sound.

Sideways had been so fucking sweet to her.

Madeline felt nauseous. She poured herself a glass of water. It tasted like mildew. There were calcium flecks on the rim of the cup. She looked at herself in the little compact mirror. What a wreck. Her eyes were red, there was fluid in her pores. Her gums hurt. Maybe she should brush her teeth. She'd singed hunks of her hair with a practice spell earlier, and the blackened clumps clustered under her chin.

She used to be so proud of all her long hair.

Fuck, Levi had loved her hair. The few weird times he'd written her poetry, all of them had waxed about how wonderful it was, how long and lustrously black. Like a raven's wing on the midnight sky. Rancid. Madeline thought all discount-bin Ovids should be shot. He loved her hair so much, looking back, because it was one of the only identifiably feminine things about her. Madeline didn't believe anything was really feminine or masculine, much less hair, unless the person who wore it endowed it with such, but Levi thought he was a knight in a Marie de France poem or some shit. He had all these romantic ideas about love and fate and the inherent properties of things. Womanly restraint was meant to be the answer to his tortured-soldier ways. Womanly meant long hair, clean nails, neutral makeup, slim figure, words like "soft" and "supple." She remembered when she used to think it was perversely charming, or even interesting. She remembered when his student-prince shtick didn't feel violent. Or at least, not violent in a way that scared her.

She opened a drawer and fished around. She found a pair of scissors. She took them out and examined them. They were dull, probably. There were flecks of rust along the lips. They squealed like a piglet when she snapped them.

Her hair was fried enough to flake against her skin when she took a fistful. She adjusted her grip. She cut.

✳

I fell back into myself. My candles were all snuffed. I sputtered like I was spitting up water. Equilibrium evaded me. Mr. Scratch throbbed in my fingertips, thick but less concentrated than before. He didn't speak. Sloshed under my skin when I made for the light switch.

I flipped it.

Light scalded. I swooned against the door and swore, heaved myself upright, fought the urge to puke. I couldn't see. My pupils wouldn't adjust. Trailer park. I knew where the Sycamore Gorge trailer park was. I could find that, no problem. The individual trailer might be tricky, but I'd find a fucking way. Something about tulips. I had some lingering taste of a memory, a yellow mailbox, a baby cherub statue that Madeline used to smear lipstick on as a kid.

She was going to kill the Chantry family with my specter, huh?

Sifting through someone else's thoughts felt like drinking lemon juice. I squeezed my eyes shut. Current plan: I let her do that. She does whatever she's gonna do, and then she comes back to the trailer park, and we trade specters. If she was waiting for Shiloh's family to leave the house together, I imagined that meant that she was going where they were headed. I'd have to get the specter from the Chantry house and head to the trailer park as fast as humanly possible.

Narrow window of time. We'd make it work. It would just be Shiloh and me, which would mean Shiloh lives, check, and my girls had independent plans, didn't they? Girls live, check. Maybe it was best that it was just the two of us. This plan was dangerous as shit and it was easier to think about me going without them to keep them safe than it was to think about them partying without me. Focus.

I imagined Madeline coming back to the trailer, covered in the blood of Shiloh's parents.

I should tell them. Should I tell them?

Their family disowned them. Their family was awful, they admitted it themself. I wasn't sure if that meant they would approve of Madeline slaughtering them, but you know. The Chantry family had it coming. It wasn't even their family anymore.

I'd tell them later. Palpitations.

Wrenched my eyes open. Boiling oil light. I white-knuckled through it and my pupils bent to my will and functioned right, and the world hurt only the normal, manageable amount. I swayed and caught myself on the counter. I'd dropped the ring-chain pendulum at some point; it lay still across the spirit board. The chain had laid itself in a loopy little heart shape, ring at the center. I had the thought to splash water on my face. It was then that I noticed the open drawer beside me and the scissors on the ledge.

In the sink, like an exploded parrot in a porcelain nest, was the bulk of my shorn hair.

FOURTEEN

LEVITICUS YOU OUT

Boris fixed it in the kitchen. Julian was somehow stress-mending clothes that didn't really need mending while simultaneously glancing over Shiloh's immaculate English homework. Shiloh kept their thoughts to themself, but their eyes seared little cigarette burns on the side of my neck. I sat on a stool. Boris whistled as he buzzed. "Your friends did a hell of a job dyeing your hair," he said as he thumbed the clippers off. "This looks sick."

"I feel sick," I said.

"You've got one more absence to burn this semester," he said. He rubbed a hand over my scalp. It was buzzed short, twenty-one millimeters, and the heat of his palm beamed directly into my brain. It felt good. "I will falsify a family death if you want to bail tomorrow morning."

"Why'd you let me do that?" I was hysterically happy and directionlessly terrified. I sounded like a kicked raccoon.

Julian made a little note in the back of his throat.

"Because you're eighteen, and you should be allowed to skip when you're not feeling well. I love this haircut on you, but I know what spontaneous chops mean." He gave my noggin a pat. "You can go to school, or you can sit behind the counter downstairs with us and do your homework. All of it, without any heartless bullshit teachers breathing down your neck. We'll listen to music, you'll get snack breaks, and you can come with me to an auction around lunch time. You go to school on Friday and turn everything in. How's that sound?"

Julian made a louder note in the back of his throat.

"Speak up, kiddo."

I gulped and said, "Yes, please."

For a moment, I thought Julian was going to protest. Instead, he looked up from the trousers he was sort of hemming and peered over at Shiloh. "Well. You still have to go to school."

"Yes, sir," said Shiloh.

Julian balked.

Shiloh balked when Julian balked.

Julian scraped his tongue with his teeth and said, "*Sir?*"

✳

I did my homework. Rather, I did maybe a third of it and then Scratch did the rest. My mind wandered. I was so close to having all my organs back in my body. Repair was in arm's reach. I ate an entire bag of licorice candy. I helped around the shop, couldn't bear customer-facing and just moved stock instead. I kept touching my head. My scalp felt amazing. It felt—different, energetically different. Without my curls my head was lighter. I felt alive in a way I usually didn't. Dizzy like I'd done magic. Good crazy. Still crazy. I realphabetized the records, polished sets of silver, waxed the floor, cleared cobwebs off the chandeliers, freshened up a display. Everything would be fine. I caught a mouse and carried it outside, washed my hands, scrubbed them dry on my Carhartts. I felt a draft on my scalp. Everything was abrasive and terribly romantic. I kept moving. I went back to my backpack and riffled through it, looked for more homework to barely do, and came across a book that wasn't mine.

It wasn't magic, or at least it wasn't a grimoire. It was a beaten paperback. I thumbed through it to find that it'd been annotated to hell and back, and that a little note had been tucked under the cover page.

The note read: *this book makes me think of you. i love it. if you love it too, i'd love to talk about it, or show you the fic i've written for it. (if u tell yates and daisy i write fanfiction i will unalive you.) thanks for suffering for me a little. i'll make it up. you're one of my favorite people alive and i'm so glad i know you. please let me still know you. yours forever, curse daddy*

I looked at the note for a very long time. I slipped it in my breast pocket, then slipped the book back in my backpack. Treat for when I traded my specter back. When I was whole again, I'd talk to her about it. About this.

I thought of her scowling in the dark. *Can I kiss you?*

I chased my hand over my head. Marveled at the velour

scrape of my buzz cut on the meat of my palms. I wanted to say yes. I wanted to say yes, and I wanted her to fold her hands over the back of my head and say, *You're so handsome, Sideways. You're such a handsome butch. I tell everybody, that's Sideways, they're my butch.*

I got myself a glass of water. I drank it too fast and gave myself brain freeze.

About an hour later, when Boris asked again if I wanted to go to the auction, I jumped on it. My head was foaming. I threw all my focus at being a good kid and good apprentice and being good, for once. Boris was into this lot, bid and won a set of chairs and a coffee table. It looked well made, authentic—I wasn't an expert, but I knew what looked right, had learned enough by osmosis to have good instincts—and I had an adrenaline rush like I'd been working out, despite how sitting in a silent auction hall ought to be boring as shit and mid-century modern doesn't generally do it for me. I felt like I was flying. Toward the end of the showing, the auctioneer brought up a brick-red bike with broad titanium handles, some 1970s model that looked like it'd been pilfered from a slasher set. I wanted it. I slapped down three hundred of my own dollars for it immediately, knew that if I had pointed it out to Boris, he would've gotten it for the shop, but I needed it to be mine. It was the right color. I'd trashed Shiloh's bike and this one reminded me of the goal. Victory steed.

It looked hilarious strapped to the top of Dad's car, and I didn't dissociate at all the whole ride home.

Back in the shop, as soon as I pulled my new bike down, I had half a mind to stomp upstairs and blast the hype playlist Daisy had made for me mid-November as loudly as possible, just psych myself up for Shiloh to get home from school so that we could prep for battle. I wanted to be with it, I wanted to be ready. I strode inside with a crate of new Boris acquisitions balanced on one shoulder and nearly had a heart attack and died.

Lila Yates sat at the counter in a white wicker chair. She wore a floral sweater and had her Mac open on her lap, and she spoke softly to Julian, who occasionally glanced at her screen as he polished a silver kettle I had already polished. She was, I realized after a moment of not being able to hold any thoughts in my head at all, discussing her K-pop boys. Yates had a thing about a few groups.

"He's a good dancer," Julian murmured, frowning.

"Oh, that's sweet of you to say," Yates said glumly. "Nobody thinks so."

I'd forgotten that she worked today.

My brain was a cicada husk. A distant memory bobbed at the edge of my consciousness—her discussing a reduction of hours with Julian because she was focusing on polishing her admissions essays, Julian being very flexible with their schedule, Julian openly pondering whether they ought to convert the shop into a member-owned establishment (which it had been, he'd supposed, prior to Yates' hiring), whether Yates would be interested in shares, how she felt about her statement of purpose, yadda yadda.

Yates looked up from her K-pop boys.

Her eyes locked on mine.

"Mr. Pike, may I have a moment away from the desk to help Sideways carry in new products?" Yates didn't look at Dad. Her big brown eyes stuck on me, liquidy and sparkling, and without a downward glance she closed her laptop and slipped it gently into her mock teddy-bear bag.

"Of course," said Julian, transfixed by the ghost shapes in the tarnish.

"In that case." Boris clapped his hands behind me. "I've got some calls to make. Sideways, you can be off shift when everything's out of the car."

Usually, I would've whined or been play-snide, but I suddenly couldn't make any sound or move at all. I wasn't convinced of my grip on this box on my shoulder. It was filled with glass ornaments. I couldn't afford to drop it.

Yates stood up. She murmured something else to Julian, a little *thank you*, and came my way. She wore candy-cane earrings, glittery pink and white, that danced with her every step. Her hands fluttered in space. She clasped them together, held them over her heart, and all at once we stood toe to toe, her ballet flats brushing my steel-toed boots.

"Sideways. Care to come with me?"

"Hi." I blinked at her. Lila Yates looked sad. Did I make her sad? In all of this, she'd never said ill against me, not once. The billboards oughta be right. Hell should be real. I made her sad. Let's go, cosmic carceration. I adjusted the crate on my shoulder. "Can I put this down first?"

She nodded. Candy canes whirled.

I carried the crate into a side room, gingerly brought it down, too aware of how my joints moved, of my utter lack of grace. I labeled it. She watched me the whole time with her hands tucked under her chin. I stood upright again, jerked my head at the door. Hoped she'd follow me.

She did. We walked out of the shop together, headed for Dad's car.

It was nice, being beside her. She made silence feel easy. I wasn't sure what to tell her, if anything at all. She'd be at whatever party they'd be having without me during the plan. A miserable reassurance. I didn't want her anywhere near the Chantry house. She was so stressed as-is! Yates was the only one of us with actionable plans for the future, plans she cared about. Daisy felt wildly ambivalent about her pre-law idea and Jing always changed the subject. I couldn't think past tomorrow. Yates deserved to give her applications her full attention. I'd hoarded too much of the stuff already.

"Sideways?" Yates hovered by the trunk. She didn't reach for a crate. Made sense, I guess. Yates lifting heavy objects wasn't really a done thing.

I went for one, widened my stance to accommodate its weight, took its heft in my hands and put it up on my shoulder where the last one had been. I rubbed my cheek against it. My face felt hot. "Yeah?"

"Can you hold still?"

I swallowed. I held still.

Yates threw her arms around my waist. She tucked

herself against my sternum, put her nose in my collarbone, squeezed me for a second that blossomed into minutes. She was warm, her perfume floated in the air, her lashes fluttered against the hole in my throat. "I keep fighting with Daisy about you," she half-said, muffled by her nearness. "I'm sorry this is happening. It's hectic for no reason. None of us are being our most kind. I miss you. I want our coven back."

"Lila," I managed. I shifted, wrapped my free arm around her shoulders. "It's alright. I can handle Daisy." That was a thing to say, holy shit. Wildly unsure if I could handle Daisy. I pushed the thought aside. I made my voice firm. "I'm not mad at you."

"Jing said you Chetted—her?"

"What?"

"The person living with you."

"Oh." I smiled, I almost laughed. "I thought you meant Jing for a second. I Chetted Shiloh. Them, they use they and them right now." Was I going to cry?

She frowned up at me. "You should've been there the other day with Monique and Sheridan."

Well, I mean.

"It wasn't right." She shook her head. "I should've reached out to you. I've been eating myself alive over these essays and studying and I love Daisy, but she requires a particular patience right now, and my well is running dry." She paused. Her brows kissed her hairline. "You cut your hair."

I must've made a face.

"I like it." She took a breath. "You look sharp. Just know we still love you, okay?"

She smiled then, and she looked so tired I thought she might blow apart in the wind like a dandelion. My grip felt slippery. Strength thawed. I nearly dropped the crate I was holding, damn all the vintage glasses inside. They could smash into glitter, they could be taken out of my wage, it didn't matter. I brought my chin down. Ghosted a kiss to her forehead.

"I know," I said. "Don't worry about it."

"Thank you," she said as she released me. There was a stripe down my front where she'd been that still felt warm. Yates sighed. "My mom picks me up in like, a half an hour. Would you mind staying down here a while? It's fine if—"

"I'm working," I assured her, then shook my head. "Even if I wasn't, I'd stay. Do you want to help me carry things?"

"No," she said sweetly. "But I can walk next to you while you carry them."

I choked a laugh. It felt good. "Alright," I said. "So be it."

✳

After dinner, Shiloh and I sat in my room. They had shucked off their uniform and were, with my permission, going through the tangles of my closet in pursuit of something more femme to wear. I wasn't sure if I had many things that fit those parameters, and Shiloh was slightly taller (and more than a fair bit skinnier) than me, but they seemed optimistic. Or at least, they seemed resolved. They were too cool to be properly hype and hopeful. Had I ever had anything femme-y in my life?

"This is lovely," Shiloh said, scrutinizing a sweater I didn't realize I had. They traced the edge of the woven pattern with their fingertips. They stuck their tongue tip between their teeth. Batted their lashes at the stitches. "Pretty."

"Yours now." I sat with a notebook in my lap. My mood was still frothy from earlier. I felt ever so slightly unhinged. "Wish I'd had a girly phase for the sake of sharing more old shit."

"What does your masculinity mean to you, Sideways?"

I glanced at them. "Pardon?"

"Your gender nonconformity, if you'd rather. What does it mean to you? What do you value about it?" They straightened the sweater on the hanger. "I've known plenty of people for whom masculinity is the be all and the end all of social existence, but theirs and yours feel nothing alike. Yours and your fathers'. I'd like to hear you talk about it."

"I've never thought about it in quite so certain terms." My gender nonconformity. I sniffed. My heart jackrabbited around my chest like crazy, and for what? Why was my head spinning? I stuck my pen behind my ear. "I'm not sure. What feels different about me?" It was an indulgent question, particularly considering that the men Shiloh knew were maniacal cartoon villains. I was a dyke who tried to be kind to them. Like, of course there's a difference.

"Your loyalty. Your compassion, your generosity, your

hospitality. Your pride. The tone you take with your people." Shiloh looked at me. Their spooky blue eyes looked luminous. They'd glow in the dark. "Taking me into your home and breaking bread with me, being steadfast and sure for me, and critical, and kind—you had no obligation to be so kind—that's what I admire about your masculinity. You're tough, but you're tough in a way that makes you a rock for people. I've known and seen people attempt masculinity by crushing everyone around them. You don't need to crush people to be the most masculine person in the room. You're solid, and grounded, and true."

Mr. Scratch wriggled around the grooves of my brain, bickering with himself about how to best manage Priya and Iris' sigil, along with the sneaking sigils the Scapegracers had made for the raid on Madeline's hotel room. He debated about whether the twister sigils would be a good idea, just in case we needed offense. The concern was, it's really hard to actively maintain three different enchantments at once, and the twister spell apparently only worked outside. Trying it indoors was an actively terrible idea, because it takes a lot of air to whirl a person off their feet and quenching all the oxygen by mistake was deeply fucking possible. Bug in a jar with no holes.

"We'll find the right balance," I breathed. "You'll be out of me soon. I want you to be excited about that."

"Do you make a habit of talking to yourself?" Shiloh examined the sweater's label. They seemed little impressed with what they found. Mouthed the words *polyester blend.*

I curled my lip and glowered over my notebook. "I'm talking to Mr. Scratch. Not my fault you can't hear him."

Shiloh gave me a look. "Mr. Scratch."

"Yeah."

"That's the demon."

"No, jackass." Here we fucking go, off to the races, la-di-da. I rolled my eyes. "He's my *book devil*. Every witch coven has a book devil. He's just inside of me instead of a book, to keep me living without a soul and all. Because your twin brother's ex-girlfriend ripped it out of me. Because your twin brother ripped hers out of her. Are you caught up?"

Mr. Scratch flushed around my teeth and over my eyes for a moment. He smelled obnoxiously inky, but the moment of black teeth and black irises had its desired effect. Shiloh's face shocked paler than their hair. They stared at me with unabashed horror. Satisfied, Mr. Scratch swam back down into my torso, and I snickered, tossed my arms behind my head.

Shiloh didn't look away. Their expression stayed frozen in place, and they watched me unblinking, glassy-eyed with their mouth in a thin, tight line. Their hands wandered up to their throat. They prodded around the Chett choker, fingertips searching for ridges of it that weren't there. The sweater they'd been holding fell to the floor. They stared at me. I didn't think they took an inward breath.

"It's not that freaky," I said after a beat. "Mr. Scratch is really nice."

"He's keeping you alive?"

I blinked. "I mean. Yeah."

"If he wasn't inside you, you'd be dead? Is that what you mean?" Shiloh's voice had an odd, fluttering waver around its edges. They always sounded sure of themself, usually. Perfectly measured. Their voice kept hitching half-steps higher with each successive syllable.

You might be. Mr. Scratch coaxed a tendril around my ear. A protective impulse, maybe. *It takes a hit on the mind and the immune system alike, losing your specter. Willpower healing vanishes. Good luck runs out all around. That, and the circumstances for which a witch developed her magic usually still exist, and seldom are they kind. You were alive when I came for you, Sideways. You might've made it, for a little while.* He paused for a moment. *For Elaina, it was two days.*

Madeline had stayed alive for months without her specter, or anything else inside her. She'd managed to look mostly normal at a party. I hadn't suspected a damn thing about her.

Miraculous, the might of spite alone.

"Yeah," I said again. "We've been over this. You're the one who told me that witchfinders bribe medical examiners and shit."

Shiloh clamped on their neck a little tighter. "I hadn't really thought about it."

"Okay, cognitive dissonance. What the fuck are you talking about, exactly?"

"I killed two people." Shiloh looked at the ceiling fan the

way a rabbit in a bear trap looks up at the moon. "Two people are dead because of me."

"Do you know that they're dead?" It seemed very fucking possible for them to be dead. "Do you know their names?"

Shiloh didn't say anything. Their eyes bulged out of their head.

"Words, Shiloh."

"Yes." Shiloh's voice was thin, breathless. I don't think they'd taken a real breath since the panic started. I wasn't sure how to deal with murderer panic. I grabbed a pillow from beside me and hurled it at them as hard as I could.

The pillow struck their stomach. They gasped an *oof*, released their neck to grab it. Their fingers spidered around the pillow's belly, and they pressed it against themself, crushed the life out of it for a moment. They opened their mouth and shut it.

"Have you looked them up? Their obituaries would be online, you know." I got my knees underneath me and knelt. "Check before you have a heart attack on my floor."

They whipped out their phone, somehow not dropping the pillow in the process.

I went back to thinking about sigils.

Could we combine them, maybe?

"One of them is dead," they said after a moment. "Cancer."

I grimaced.

"I didn't give anybody cancer."

"Maybe. You royally fucked up their ability to care about treating their cancer, I'd wager."

Shiloh rocked back against the wall.

"Look, eyes on the fucking prize. We do this right, and you can return specters to your living victim. Was the dead witch in a coven? If so, we can send the specter to their coven, maybe. It's not fucking good enough, but none of this is. It's just the best you've got."

Shiloh nodded.

I jammed my tongue against my teeth. An odd idea crept into my head, and I couldn't snuff it out. It was too yummy-smelling to kill. "Hey, Shiloh."

They shot me a glance.

"You ever gotten a stick and poke?"

"A what?"

An evil, gremlin part of me sprung to life. I flopped onto my stomach, tucked my hands under my chin, and smiled with all my teeth. "It's a DIY tattoo. You take a sterile needle, you dip it in ink, and you jab the skin with it. You do it over and over again, with all the little pricks close enough together that the ink forms a line. It's how they do it in a shop, really, it's just that they use a machine that does the pricking for them."

"That's interesting," they obviously lied.

"Isn't it true that witchfinders used to strip witches naked and prick them all over their bodies with long, sharp needles? That when they found a spot that didn't bleed, they took that as evidence that a devil had touched them and rendered them witchlike? Devil's spot?"

They narrowed their eyes a bit. "Why do you ask?"

"I've been thinking about safety." That was true. "I want to make sure that the two of us are protected tomorrow night, and that we're not in any danger from Madeline, neither. It'd be a good idea for me to put some sigils on you. You're not a witch, so I doubt you'd be able to cast on command." I knew in the back of my head that they probably knew some spells. My *VMM* had said as much, and there was the trauma-inducing mimic spell that Levi had done in October. The one where he killed the deer? Still, that didn't mean that Shiloh would be equipped to throw their brother in a twister at the drop of a hat.

"Sideways."

"Yes, Shiloh?"

"What are you insinuating?"

"That you should let me give you tattoos," I grinned.

Shiloh gave the pillow another squeeze. They looked at the sweater on the ground. They looked up at me. They looked at the ceiling above them again, and it offered no counsel. They took a deep breath in through their nose and out through their teeth. "Somewhere I can cover with clothes?"

"Sure thing."

"And a clean needle? Good ink that isn't going to poison me or something?"

"The best ink in the world."

Mr. Scratch, aware of his being evoked, swam figure eights around my stomach.

"Okay," they said.

I'd primed something stupid and taunting to say. I stumbled over it. I blinked. "Really?"

"Yeah," Shiloh said. "Just sigils. Don't ink a dick on me."

"Scout's honor," I whistled.

A little smile rippled the sides of their mouth. "You know what?"

"What?"

"My parents would hate this so much."

✳

We sat in the bathroom together, which was cleaner than my bedroom by a mile. The candles jammed in the irradiated apple stayed on the counter. I'd stuffed all my cut-off curls in a bag. I'd use them for something. I wasn't sure what.

"It suits you, by the way. Shows off your bone structure."

"Thanks." I put the bag of hair under the sink. "Impulse."

"Sideways?"

I washed my hands and felt gentlemanly, so I soaked my cuticles in rubbing alcohol. Went the extra mile. "Yeah?"

"What pronouns should I use for you?" They put their hands in their pockets. "We've never talked about it."

"Christ. I don't know." It'd been ages since I'd shaved anything, but there'd been a brief phase at the dawn of puberty, and the pink razors hadn't ever found their way out of my cabinet. Maybe I'd stowed them there on purpose, a gift from past Sideways to current Sideways. *Thanks, Sideways. You're so welcome, baby.* "Give me your arm."

They gave me their arm.

I gave their arm a little shave.

"How long have you been magic?" Small talk. I thought they were nervous. They watched their arm like they expected it to change on its own.

"My mom got run over by a train when I was a kid. I spectered up in foster care. Used it to pull Julian and Boris to me." Or at least, I'd always assumed that much. "When was your first witchhunt?"

"That's awful. I'm so sorry." They closed their eyes. "When Levi and I turned thirteen. Rite of passage. When did you join your coven?"

"Like five minutes before you kidnapped me. You took me out of Jing's pool." I swabbed their shaved patch down with alcohol. I liked the way it smelled, like the way they squirmed. Liked giving this much attention to something. "I would die for any of them. They're the best girls in the world."

"Tell me about them." Shi frowned. "Will this hurt?"

"Some. Are you going to be a baby about it?" I pulled on latex gloves and snapped them by their ear.

Shiloh made a thin sound like, *Yes, proceed.*

"There are four of us. Before that, it was the three of them. Jing and Yates and Daisy. They ran West High. Clique for the ages, professional mythmakers, they scared everybody to death, and everybody was in love with them. Yates is an angel. She's the single most compassionate person I've ever met. Brilliant, meticulous, kind. She's a dedicated bullet-journal keeper and stationery enthusiast, I know you're into that shit, there could be overlap. I had a panic attack once and she called me and made mouth sounds into the phone speaker until I was laughing so hard I couldn't be terrified anymore. Great head for logistics. Obscene amounts of grace. Daisy is a star. She's the flyer for the varsity cheer team and she reminds me of myself. She's angry like me. Hilarious, mean-spirited, wonderful. She's pint-sized and probably as strong as me. We roughhouse sometimes, mosh together. Stole a car together one time, drove it into a field and abandoned it there. Trust that the guy had it coming. Liveliness just rolls off her. She loves being a girl. I love that about her. I've learned a lot from her. Jing"—I took a breath—"is the heart of this. She's the heart of everything. The world turns because she keeps beating. Jing *cares*. She's devoted to this work because she's devoted to girls, she wants girls to be able to do whatever the fuck they want, unfettered by fear of violence. She's going to change the world. I fucking mean it. Our coven came together because your brother scared Yates, and we needed to make sure that wouldn't happen again. It was Jing's idea to expand that service outside of ourselves. Our reputation is the weight of Jing's desire. She's the most intense person I've ever met. She's resolute. She's a miracle."

Shiloh blinked slow. They smiled a little, a twitch at the right edge of their mouth. Their ears looked pinkish. "Jing's the one who came by with your things."

"Yeah." I took a breath. "That's her."

They smiled in earnest. Like they knew something.

I kneaded my latex fingers and tried to bring myself back.

"So." They let me off the hook. "How's this work, exactly?"

"The magic or the tattooing?"

"Yes." Shiloh kept wearing that face. They looked down at the needle I'd jammed in a pencil's end, watched me burn the needle's point with a kind of bemusement. Scientist looking down at a new kind of nuclear fission like, *Oh, isn't that something, perhaps it will go wrong.* "This doesn't look official."

"DIY or bust." I shivered and wasn't sure why. "I did these loads of times at improv camp." Gave myself a few, too. There's a snake on my left ankle, which was supposed to be a kinda Garden of Eden Satan thing, but he looks more like a worm with a fork tongue. Either way, cool. Worms are sick.

"Improv camp?"

I squinted at them. "You really making fun of the bastard who's about to poke you?"

"No," they said. Their tone was unconvincing. "And you're not a bastard."

"I literally am." I sniffed. "That's what I thought."

Shiloh leaned their head against the mirror. Their neck stretched long.

I put on music. Doom metal, all for me, not particularly Shiloh-friendly, but that's that. I sketched the sigils on in marker. The sneaking sigil that Yates and Daisy made demanded concentration; I took care to make it symmetrical, fluid as they'd drawn it. Below, I drew Priya and Iris' sigil. Mr. Scratch bloomed the image of it across the back of my eyes. It looked like damask, rich with intricacies that wouldn't have occurred to me. It was pretty, if elaborate. It was evident that it had been crafted as a romantic gesture. Protection for lovers.

"You ready?" I glanced up at them.

They nodded. "I'm ready."

Mr. Scratch swam down the length of my arm, twined branches out of my fingertips and around the pencil wood, then up through the tip of the needle. I brought the needle down. I guided it through the first layer of Shiloh's skin.

They hissed through their teeth, but they kept still.

A normal stick and poke takes a long time, and several rounds of outlining before you have a decent black line. This one felt fast. Mr. Scratch, unlike most ink, ached and yearned for shape-taking. He bloomed where I placed him, clung to the contours of the sigil sketch without extra encouragement. It was like a high-stakes game of connect the dots, where I, the dot-placer, could barely outpace the eager, oncoming line.

Permanent lines, permanent spells. This magic would stick. Skin's just parchment.

Despite the flicker of unease they'd expressed earlier, Shiloh sat like a stone. They stared straight ahead. Didn't so much as blink. When they'd wrapped my hand up the other day, they'd said how they and their brothers used to physically fight. I wondered how much pain they racked up in their *Lord of the Flies* childhood. I wondered how this compared.

I recited the chants under my breath as I finished the first sigil, followed Mr. Scratch's lead for the second. I didn't have any doubts about the spell's potency, but I worried a little about Shiloh being able to cast. It was Levi who'd killed the deer, after all. I gnawed the corner of my lip. "Do you know how to activate these?"

"Not quite," they admitted. "There's an incantation, isn't there?"

"Yeah." I traced the edge of a curlicue, said the first thing off the top of my head. Usually was the best thing, so far as magic was concerned. "See no evil, be seen by no evil."

"If I can't see evil, will my parents' house look like a hole?" They spoke flatly enough that I couldn't tell whether they were serious or not.

"More like a forcefield from homophobic and trans-phobic bullshit," I said. That and hostile autoimmune sigil rejection bullshit, but they didn't need to worry about that.

"Oh." They softened a touch, then resumed their dry composure. "Question stands."

"I'd thwack you if I wasn't busy."

"You're already stabbing me. Doesn't that suffice?"

We sat in silence for a moment as my phone speakers struggled to accommodate harsh edges of this song. Behind us, the shower dripped off-beat. I thought about Elaina. I felt vaguely faint.

"The buzz cut really does look good," Shiloh said as I finished inking the second sigil. I pulled the needle back, glanced over my handiwork with a critical eye I'd inherited from Julian. All those doodles in my notebook were paying off. This looked sharp and clean. Shiloh shut their eyes and rocked their head back, stretched out their neck to the fullest. "You look polished."

"You say that like it's new." I made a sound in my throat. "My head feels lighter."

"Air and bone alone," they said. They peered at their arm and all its new adornments. Their eyes bugged out, and a weird pinkish cloud coalesced across their cheeks and the bridge of their nose.

"You like?" Hoo, boy. If they didn't, I'd feel bad nasty.

They leaned toward their reflection, mostly with their eyes, because there was a part of Shiloh that desperately wanted to be a submarine, or some little winged creature with eyestalks. They gazed at their arm with their lips apart. Their breath misted up the glass.

"With words, Shi."

"I like Shi," they said. They flicked their eyes up at me. "May I hug you?"

Not what I thought they were going to say.

I offered one arm, angled myself away from that controlled lesion I'd just given them.

They swayed against me for a moment, breathed in sharply, then swayed back, returned their focus to the mirror. They twisted their arm back and forth, looked at it from competing angles, stretched it and posed it. "I love them," they said.

Well, shucks.

"Think you're ready for tomorrow night?"

"Yes. We should leave here at nineish if we're biking. They should be out of the house by then." Shiloh rolled their shoulder. "Sideways?"

"Yeah?"

"Could you add little hearts underneath?"

FIFTEEN

SEIZE THOSE MEANS

Revelation: showing up to school the Friday before finals week with your hair chopped off and your knuckles bruising like a pride flag in a too-little shirt and too-big jeans does not go unnoticed by one's peers. I hadn't really anticipated this degree of attention. Got wolf-whistled by Mickey-Dick (nice? gross? who's to say) and found myself, to my chagrin, the subject of open ogling. Eyes stuck to me and followed me as I slammed shut my locker and didn't leave when I made my way down the hall and sank onto a low, grimy cafeteria bench. Class started; the staring continued. Getting gawked at during study hall is exactly what every young lesbian desires. Great. Good. That's so good. *Old Yeller* me.

A few tables away, Austin Grass was not shutting the fuck up. A couple of his friends sported gnarly Sharpied Chett chokers, and Chett-hexed people seemed to keep to themselves for a while post-curse, but Austin had somehow gone hex-free and made up the douchebag volume difference by being individually louder than every other person alive on earth. We hexed on request. Nobody had asked about him, yet. Maybe I should. I don't know. He and a few unhexed boys yowled over their table with the fistful of JV cheerleaders they let sit with them for strictly creepy reasons, and I really wanted to sympathize with them, except for the fact that they were snickering and *eww*ing about me, which made my compassion kind of difficult.

I kept my back to them and let Mr. Scratch cheat my homework for me. It was hard to focus enough as-is without this shit. I wish I'd tattooed that sigil on me, too.

I'd have my specter for finals.

Wait, shit. Would that mean I'd need to do them myself?

Time ticked by. It was fucking miraculous how long a group of determined dickheads could stay on one subject. A few anecdotal deviations notwithstanding, Austin Grass and company managed to remain fixated on my haircut for forty-five fucking minutes. You'd think the staff watching study hall would do more, literally anything, to maintain a sense of quietude. My nerves skittered out my ears like ticker tape.

A sharp, nasal drawl cut the boy-voice din. "Um like seriously, shut the fuck up? Literally shut the fuck up. I don't even know why you still go to this school. Nobody wants you here. If I have to hear your voice for even a second longer I'm going to puke, and it'll mess up my lipstick, and if you mess up my lipstick, you are going to trip down the stairs! It's going to be so sad when you mysteriously fall down all those concrete stairs behind the bleachers, like *so* sad. I'm choking up just thinking about it. I can't wait to sign your neck brace!"

Daisy Brink.

My heart leaped in my throat.

Austin sounded a little taken aback, but he kept a jovial nonchalance to his tone. "Daisy, baby, what are you meowing about? Listen—"

"I'm not your baby." I could hear her smiling. She oozed sugar. "You're such an idiot. Tell me, Austin. Don't you like your friends' little neck tats?"

"I—"

"Hasn't it occurred to you," Daisy sniped, "that you might be next?"

"What's your damage? Jesus Christ—"

"Leave Sideways alone."

"What?" Austin's voice spiked. He sounded prematurely triumphant. "Daisy, you're a beautiful girl. I know that Satan's in style right now, but you can't really want to associate with *that*. Don't you know what they're saying about you? What, are you gonna buzz your empty little head for finals, too? Is that what you're gonna do?"

I, along with everybody else, swiveled in our seats to watch. My blood slammed in my temples. Austin looked Daisy in the eye. He grinned with big shark teeth.

"Don't be an idiot. I wouldn't chop all my hair off." Daisy rocked up on tiptoe, smacked her lips. "I'm femme."

Austin blinked. He didn't seem to get it.

I got it.

I wanted to fucking cry.

The bell rang and everybody stood up, crushed the moment under the weight of their gum-spot sneakers. I tried to find Daisy's eyes through the crowd, but by the time there was a gap in churning, she'd vanished. Austin was gone, too, evaporated with the bulk of his boys. The cafeteria was quickly emptied of teen bodies.

I felt myself get whisked along.

Classes blurred. Alexis and Monique both complimented my hair, which was nice, but I was so winded from the morning that it was hard to absorb any feedback, good and bad alike. Should I text her? What the fuck would I say? I tried to make myself focus on this evening, on getting my soul back, on how close I was for this fucking nightmare to be over. I was so fucking close. Daisy Brink is a lesbian. Daisy's a fucking lesbian.

"Sideways, can you solve for *x* on the board?"

What? No, actually.

And fucking yet.

After the bloodshed, I sent zero texts to Daisy and several to Shiloh. Tactical details interspersed with a bushel of memes to distract from the fact that they'd evidently run into Levi at school. It'd barely been an encounter, no words spoken, but it'd rattled Shi, so I talked them down with shitty copypastas and communist cowboys, forum threads,

Charli XCX. I sent them pictures of my teachers. They complained about being surrounded by boys, and I complained about the existence of Austin.

knife. insane that u havent hexed him

Ikr? Soon

first curse w your soul back

Then Shiloh vanished, presumably to do class things, and I was alone.

Their family would die tonight if Madeline had her way.

What was the right set of feelings to have?

A wave of masochism overtook me. Call it avoidance. It manipulated my thumbs and made me open my contacts, search until I found a now-defunct phone number. I opened up Madeline's old messages. I scrolled to the top and read down.

I'd had such a huge crush on her.

I got it. In the back of my head, I got why she did it, why she pried the specter out of my neck. I was a vehicle for righteous revenge. I could totally fuck with righteous revenge. That was why I kind of wanted to throw her off a bridge, after all. It was a sentiment we shared.

There was a pathetic bit at the end. After she'd mugged me of my soul, I spent a few days boneless on Jing's rug, during which time I'd sent some regrettable things. Miserable, *fuck you for taking my soul i feel awful how could you do this to me* things. *I trusted you*–type things. Most excruciating, *I thought you liked me*–type things, too. There weren't any read receipts.

New message broke up my pain binge.

Yates' contact.

I opened it, and the wall of text consumed me.

> **hey cutie!! it was so good to see you yesterday, once again am so so so sorry for all of the bullshit of the past few days, as discussed it's like really childish and it isn't fair. i think you did the right thing even though the right thing was scary, and i really admire that about you. i hope that i'm as strong as you are in making those sorts of decisions. we had a huge intervention with daisy last night. her idea actually? she's working through her shit i think. more updates to come i am really hoping we can hang out again soon?? i want us to all on my floor watching Bambi or something ok!! also daisy came out to us and i like kind of came out too (i mean i wasn't like in the closet but you and Akeem were the only people who i ever told explicitly) it was a whole thing. it definitely wouldn't have happened if you weren't in our life being so amazingly you. also again your haircut is super dreamy and it really suits you**

ilysm more soon!!

Angel. So, the whole coven was out now.

It was one thing to be out to your closest friends and another to be out to Austin Grass.

I felt melty in my throat.

After I got my specter back tonight, I'd be completely on board for forgiving and forgetting. I would be the best version of myself, the best friend they could have, and the bullshit since our failed Secret Santa would dissolve into nothing. I owed it to myself to get it back. I owed it to Scratch, who was eminently going to get a shiny new book body, one he deserved. I owed it to Elaina and Priya and Iris and all my dead sisters.

The bell rang, everybody switched classes, and my chest was filled with light.

*

Shi and I put on our boots. I repainted their nails and they rewrapped my knuckles. I'd drawn the Priya/Iris sigil on the back of my left hand, an emergency twister sigil on my right, then the sneaking sigil and my Madeline-commissioned specter extraction sigil on either palm. They were snug under the gauze, safe from wear, out of sight until I needed them. We'd eaten and lied without elaboration to Boris and Julian, who both understood us to be going out partying and wanted us to have fun and be careful, etc. We listened to my pump-up music (Jing's sleazy pop princesses) and Shiloh's (glossy *Pitchfork* alt girls). Adrenaline sizzled. I felt like a cut wire. I felt good.

The temperature dropped for the first time in weeks. It was snowing; the blacktop was powdered when we left. We'd both stolen coats from my fathers. I don't think Shiloh knew that we hadn't asked permission. They'd picked one of Julian's rosy tweed ones. I'd gone with one of Boris' big punk jackets that he hadn't worn since the nineties. It was covered in political patches—KILL THE COP IN YOUR HEAD, QUEERS BASH BACK, STOMP YOUR LOCAL FASCIST, NUCLEAR NEVER, ABORTION FOR ALL, NO PRISONS NO BORDERS, SILENCE EQUALS DEATH, etc. etc.—and endless knobby spikes.

I climbed up on the handlebars.

Shiloh pushed off.

The town unfurled around us. The park trees assumed their yearly fairy-light bondage. Sycamore Gorge tradition come holidays. The bulbs flickered like sequins in the dark. It was beautiful. Sycamore Gorge could be beautiful. I always forgot.

We turned a few corners. Shiloh's route wasn't the same as mine. Seemed shorter, weirder. They whistled along to a tune we couldn't hear anymore.

"You a big fan of Nat King Cole?" The tires hit an icy patch. I nearly fell to my death. I caught myself and we kept going and I didn't scream or anything, totally cool. I repositioned myself and Shiloh picked up some speed. "No judgment."

"I love Christmas. I love the pageantry. It's the best day of the year."

What!

I laughed like a cartoon villain, had to clap a hand over my mouth just to muzzle me. The gauze tasted funny and sweet. "Merry fucking Christmas to you, then, Shi."

"You must be insufferable high."

"Oh, you betcha."

I never find you insufferable, Sideways my plum.

It was nice of Scratch to think that. I patted myself on the thigh.

We left the town part of town. Businesses vanished, then the rows of atrophied pastel houses. We rode past stilted trailers and deer-murder treehouses. There weren't crumbling barns. There weren't churches or pawn shops. The trees hardly felt like trees, and the metal guardrail, pocked from vehicular abuse, felt more like a gate than a guide.

Shi stopped whistling. My diaphragm stuttered.

We'd reached Chantry land. You'd think that there would be mailboxes or something to mark the way. A shitty VOTE ELIAS CHANTRY FOR SHERIFF sign. Anything. The snow had thickened fast and erased the dirt road, and without Shi, I wouldn't have caught it. We held our breath and turned down the drive.

Winter made this forest worse. It was a *Dr. Caligari* nightmare of exaggerated angles and colliding lines. Tree limbs bore down with their raspy naked fingers, and I hated them. The snow muffled our bike sounds. The night wasn't over top of us, but around us like a smoke. It felt textured in my mouth. It hurt my teeth. "How didn't you go crazy in these woods?"

Shiloh was quiet. I hallucinated for a moment that I hadn't spoken. That when I'd moved my mouth, nothing came out. That the forest could swab up sound. "I'm not so sure I didn't," they said. They clucked their tongue. "If I understood you right, the sigils will be up here."

"Okay," I said. I flexed my hand into a fist, felt the buildup of enchantment itchiness gather around our bike. "Are you alright?"

"Fine," said Shi. "Yourself?"

"I will be."

I hate it out here, dripped Mr. Scratch. *Please don't fall.*

Shiloh pulled a necktie from their pocket and blindfolded me with it, tied off a half-Windsor near the base of my skull. Everything went dark. My eyelashes bent against sateen. I counted my exhales, two, four. The bike carried me forward. Every yard crossed was jitterier than the last.

Even blindfolded, sigil blazing, I felt when we hit my malformed magic. I couldn't see, couldn't be overwhelmed by it, but even still I felt it slip under my jacket and clip my soft spots. I was acutely aware of how many of them there were—fourteen—and how close they physically were to me, felt their proximity press on me.

The back of my hand buzzed. Distracting. So that's how it works. Priya and Iris' spell was *demanding.* I fed it attention, and it took double what I gave. I could only think about the sigil. I devoted my focus to it. Suddenly supernatural anguish seemed inconsequential. The damask billowed under my skin. I traced its edges in my head. Counted its petals.

"You're sure that there are spells in these trees?"

"Positive," I breathed. "Big, ugly, stolen sigils. They're carved in the bark. Can't you see them?"

"No," Shiloh said.

Okay, perhaps I was insane. Maybe they were small. Maybe my dread was disproportionate.

They're tucked at funny angles. Hard to see from the road. Maybe Chantry eyes can't see them at all, Mr. Scratch said. *They're big. Rest assured.*

"You fucked up some of the brush when you crashed," said Shi. Their breath warmed my ear. "It's a miracle you didn't snap your neck."

"Miracle," I repeated. The sigil made me almost dangerously loose. In service of dead lesbian filigree, all my muscles had completely relaxed. You could've pulled me apart like cotton candy. I wrapped my arms around myself to keep myself together.

"That's right." The bike slowed to a halt. "I hope you've got extras."

They tugged the blindfold down. It fell around my neck, and I pawed at it until the tie aligned with my breastbone. I hopped off the handlebars. Eyed the house that loomed ahead of us like an antebellum tumor.

Shiloh swung off the bike. "I feel like we should walk it from here," they said. "I don't want to ride too near the house."

I couldn't fathom questioning Shiloh about this. It wasn't like the Delacroix House, whose imposing opulence felt born of flamboyance and pride. This house was dead. It was empty in a way that couldn't be filled.

We walked up the last stretch of drive. There were cars in the lot, but they didn't seem to concern Shiloh much. For all the Chantrys' wealth, they lacked a garage, and their extraneous cars gathered snow. It was thick as my thumb on the hoods. Stuff was piling fast.

The endless porch looked ricketier without lights on inside. Like rot painted over. We passed their brothers' bikes and kept going around the house's edge. I followed them without question. This was their ex-home we were breaking and entering. They could call the shots.

I glanced over my shoulder.

Two sets of footprints in the snow.

I said a little prayer to some god, any god, entropy, the tooth fairy, the whirling primordial anti-space glob from which all book devils and language itself can be coaxed, that the snow would keep falling all night. If it kept falling, it'd swallow our tracks and it'd be like we'd never come. Nothing to tip off Sheriff Chantry. Tonight was going to be the night I fixed everything. I couldn't afford to tangle with the fucking sheriff now or ever. No.

We walked around the perimeter of the house. The

dead grass under the snow was disconcertingly spongy. My boots squelched. I muzzled my hands in my pockets. The further along we went, the higher the veranda rail soared above our heads. The house must've been built on a hill or something. Walking alongside felt like making some great descent.

We reached the back of the house. Looked like an Arctic cliff.

There was a door at the base of the cliff. Shabby. The window's mesh edges hadn't been smoothed, and the webbing left a tetanus-flavored fringe where it kissed the door. Bad vibes.

Shiloh rested the bike against the wall. They knelt, shook the snow off a welcome mat, and pawed the ground beneath it. Found a key in the cracked mud. You'd think witchfinders would put more effort into hiding their spares.

"Back door doesn't really match the undead Southern belle vibe you have out front," I said. I wasn't sure if I was trying to be funny, or if the quiet was just freaking me out. "Did your architect just give up back here?"

"This used to be the servants' entrance." Shiloh jostled the key in the lock, and it clicked. "We use it for hunting now. Turned the back room into a freezer. Mom hates it when we track blood in the house."

What a fucking thing to say! I opened my mouth and shut it. Pictured their brothers carrying mimic-immobilized me over their shoulder or dragging me through the brittle blond winter grass. Their old Hollywood mother heart-

broken over the carpet I ruined with the blood coming out
of my mouth. Crying daintily. Levi Chantry dabbing her
tears with a lace doily. Laugh track.

Mr. Scratch sizzled in my chest.

Shiloh didn't look behind them. "Game hunting, not
witchfinding," they clarified. Maybe my silence had taken a
tone. "The only bodies we drag through here are deer.
Maybe an unlucky coyote or two. We went on a boar-
hunting trip once when I was fourteen. Nearly killed Abel.
Are you coming?"

"Smart pig." I spat at the ground between my boots and
trudged after them, warring with my instincts every inch of
the way. "What an awful place to spend eternity. Why do
you even bother? I mean, does anybody *eat* coyote?"

"It's all sport," Shiloh said. "We keep trophies. Once in a
blue moon Dad sells venison to his friends on the force, but
he isn't doing it to feed us. It's just a witchfinder thing." They
inclined their head. "Ever heard of haruspicy?"

Scrying with the entrails of animals. I'm a witch and
dedicated occult forum crawler, I doubted there were many
documented European divination methods I hadn't read
about incessantly. It was a Roman thing. I sank deeper into
my leather, curled my lip. "Why?"

"It's how witchfinders found witches, back before we
stalked people on social media. It's still how we find witches
now and again. It's more reliable than making assumptions
off of someone's geotagging." Shiloh glanced at me for a
moment. "If it's any consolation, we just hunt locally for this.

There's this other Brethren family, the Jenkinses? They don't sift for witches in anything less than the guts of critically endangered megafauna. They have a biannual hunting trip to Zimbabwe. Their house is like a taxidermy fair." They snorted, dead-eyed. "Be happy we're satisfied with bucks, Pike."

A wave of physical revulsion rocked me, and for a moment I thought I might be sick on the Chantry family floor. Maybe I should've been. They would've deserved it. "Total opposite of consoling, holy shit. Everything in my entire life is worse for knowing that. Witchfinders are disgusting."

"You're not getting a rebuttal out of me. That's about right." Shiloh cocked their head to the side. "If Brethren families feel fine with hunting humans, would you expect them to draw the line at lions? Hm?"

"Jesus fucking Christ, Shi."

Inside was colder than outside. Shiloh flipped a switch and a dangling bulb coughed up moldy light. Surprise, there were little sunflowers on the wallpaper. A gas-station ice cooler was tucked against the far wall under a rack of hanging bladed instruments. Steel table in the room's dead center. There was an open, empty deer on the table. Its torso was slack like a mouth. I saw its ribs inside of it. Its crown of antlers scraped the floor.

"Fuck," Shiloh said.

I braced my hand against the wall. My knees threatened to give.

"Well," they drawled, disregarding the carcass with a flick of the wrist, "Abel's home. He never cleans up his messes. I don't care how cold it is. It'll go rancid left out like this."

"Abel's home," I repeated.

There was something cloudy in their expression and I didn't have the stamina to parse it. "He isn't *here*. No doubt he's at the party with my family. Annual tradition. You'd think being a college student would free him of his pathological need to wow his parents, and that he'd have better things to do, like preaching the gospels to tied-up sorority girls who made the mistake of thinking they'd get a fucking out of bondage, or whatever it is he's doing these days. Dogfighting or tennis. Tsk." Shiloh stalked across the room and opened a door I hadn't noticed kitty-corner to the cooler. "Come on."

I didn't scream or hurl. My throat felt too tight to let anything out. I made myself move. I brushed my fingertips along the stag's stiff chin as I passed it. It felt like a pit bull. I thought I saw it blink.

SIXTEEN

LIFESTYLES OF THE RICH AND FAMOUS

The Chantry foyer was burned into me. I remembered the fire-place, the family crest, the jutting trophies and loveless family portraits between electric candle sconces, the whole flaming phantasmagoria of horror and tackiness without trying to remember it. Jump-scared me at the damndest times. The point is, I had a solid sense for what the foyer materially entailed. The front of the house felt like a showroom, not a home. Sterile.

Back here, behind the foyer, felt like an actual dwelling.

I did not prefer this half.

Aside from the refrigerator-sized gun safe, it was like a costume drama movie set. A set that'd been occupied by marauding *Lord of the Flies*-ed frat boys for several months. Initially nice, appealing to the evil part of my brain that cared about antique furniture acquisition. Broad mahogany cabinets, well-upholstered wingback armchairs Julian would've sold for upwards of seven hundred apiece, a sturdy if scuffed-up table on a bluish Turkish rug. There was a chaise, little ottomans. Two bookshelves that framed a comi-cally big flat-screen. Books all leatherbound, pristine, dusty;

I suspected they'd been bought as a decorative set. Further down, there was a bloody-purple billiards table with something poisonous green threaded through a hole. Lacy poisonous green. I thought it might've been a thong.

Every surface was crammed with trash. A pizza box with gnawed-up crusts gathered flies the size of thumbs. Chicken bones went fuzzy on bone-china saucers. Beer bottles flashed between cushions and glinted on the floor. Posters of women with their heads cropped out of frame had been taped beside an oil-painted portrait of Jesus. A wire briar pit snaggled between this door and the next, attaching somehow to a gaming console tucked under the flat-screen. The bongs were inconsequential, but the smudged-up hand mirror—ornate, something I imagined could've been sold in Dads' shop for a fistful of bills—gave me pause. Was it the fucking eighties? Coke mirror just left on the couch? In the sheriff's house?

"This is the game room." Shiloh made a sound in the back of their throat. "Touch nothing."

"Wasn't planning on it," I said.

I locked eyes with a trophy stag mounted on the wall across from me. It looked smaller than the one I'd just seen in that cold room. This one's antlers were the size of my hands. There was a dartboard beside it that nobody had used; the darts instead jutted from the trophy stag's face. Easter colors, mint and peach, lilac and sky, spring-chick yellow. Darts swarmed along its nose and cheeks.

Shiloh snapped between my eyes. Their thumb was everywhere. "Are you alright?"

I unclenched my jaw. "Let's keep going."

"This way." They edged around the pool table, acknowledged the thong (two thongs, actually, tied in a knot) with a *fucking Abel*, and ducked behind a door.

Abel had seemed a very knock-on-your-door-and-refuse-to-leave-until-you've-been-converted, uber-goody kind of guy when we met. I wasn't sure how to mash that together with the deer body and the panty littering. All I knew was this: Abel was fucking weird. Bad weird. Hip to be a square weird. Normal, smiley, churchgoing-serial-killer weird. Podcasts will love him one day.

Boring, comparatively tolerable hallway. It had more stupid sconces but a lesser concentration of filth per square inch. My boots didn't make a squashing sound when I stepped onto this carpet. There was a suspicious brown stain down the middle that stretched from one side room to another, but it was crusty and dry, looked old. Paint? Mud? It was a smear more than a splatter, like a bag of something heavy had been lugged along the floor.

Shiloh turned on their heel, threw their hands up. "Alright. Levi's room is upstairs. That's probably where Madeline's specter is because Levi's possessive and he'd want it close to him. The ones I need to find, they're probably in this next room."

"Okay." I bounced on my toes. "Let's go."

"Sideways," they said. There was a look on their face I couldn't figure. Long and watery.

"Shiloh," I said. "What the fuck are you waiting around

for? We should get them and go. I want to be out of this damn house."

"You're not going to like it in there."

"Not a fan of a single room of this nightmare house. Not one."

"I hear you." Shiloh closed their eyes. Their brows crunched together and down, then steepled. "I just need you to brace yourself. Could you do that for me? We'll get through here faster if we're being systematic."

"Check all the surfaces and the drawers, I know how to find things."

Shiloh swallowed. I watched their throat move. They opened their eyes, eyelashes unzipping, and turned toward an unremarkable door. They opened it. They stepped into the darkness that waited inside, and it consumed them head and shoulders.

I shook myself off and strode in after.

The door hinged shut behind us.

Shiloh hit a switch.

A scream tore out of my body. It wasn't mine. It came from Mr. Scratch.

The room was strung with clothesline. Dense like beaded curtains. A filing cabinet flayed for display. There were photographs clamped to each string, candids with attached annotations that detailed names, ages, addresses, phone numbers, workplaces, criminal records, insurance providers, blood types, random acronyms. I staggered. I seized a random string and pulled it taut. The acronym was

"SC." I grabbed another. All "PS." PS, that's Pythoness Society. These were lists of witches. They were organized by coven.

A shrine dominated the back wall. Crucifix above, altar below. The altar was three stuffed swans, necks braided, heads bent backwards to shape a tabletop—it was the best taxidermy I'd ever seen and I kept waiting for the birds to squirm and croak. A book rested on their beaks. It was hedged with little angel statues, cleaner but no less cringey than the ones in the nearby abandoned chapel, and long white candles. There were cabinets all around the room, worktables, dental instruments, carpentry tools, stolen athames. The overhead lights were harsh and fluorescent. Surgical feeling.

Shiloh yanked open the first cabinet they came across and started riffling. They sank their elbows into the top drawer, rustled through the contents, then withdrew and slammed it shut. They dropped to their knees, pulled open the next one. "They're probably in here somewhere," they breathed, "so if you—"

"The people in these pictures." I couldn't make my knees bend. "Are they people your family's gone after?"

"No," Shiloh said. "They're suspected witches. Dad likes to keep an eye on them. Likes to know where they are."

"This is serial-killer shit," I breathed. I took a lap around the room, looked over all the faces and felt my nerve dissolve. I was numb. I was buzzing. There were so fucking many of us. I never thought there'd be so many of us. I spent so much time feeling alone, but here we were, all the witches of the godforsaken Midwest, trapped in a basement together. "This is so deeply, profoundly fucked up, Shiloh."

They didn't say anything. They yanked open another drawer.

There was a string toward the back. I'd caught on that these strings, maybe half of them, contained the details of "loners." Solitary practitioners and suspected witches that couldn't be paired up with a coven, that is.

On one such string, I found my face. The picture, a yearbook clipping, was labeled ELOISE MARIE PIKE in a blocky hand. It listed Sycamore Gorge West High, Rothschild & Pike, my date of birth, that I was AB positive, the date of that time I'd been in a cop car for five seconds after a party sophomore year, the time I'd been suspended, the time I was caught but not charged for shoplifting, fights I thought had gone unnoticed. I stared for a long time. I didn't even know my blood type. Any relief I would've felt that the Chantry family hadn't officially labeled the Scapegracers as an entity yet snuffed itself out before it formed, because Boris' and Julian's pictures hung underneath mine.

"Boris and Julian aren't witches," I said.

Shiloh jerked their head up. They were on their fifth drawer, and they'd nearly crawled inside of it, how fervently they scoured its contents. They stared at the string in my hands without really seeing it. "Yank those."

I closed my fists around the cord and pulled. It snapped from the ceiling and crashed around my heels with a flurry. I unpinned the pictures. Folded them up, shoved them and the doxing details in my pockets. I started around the room, then, yanked down string after string. I shoved picture after picture into my pockets, infinitely grateful that men's jackets had pockets like the vacuum of space. Jing's picture hung beside a stranger's blurry profile. I didn't see Yates or Daisy anywhere, but I saw Maurice and Jacques from the Delacroix House, and my middle school choir teacher, and a bartender at Dorothy's that always gave me extra lime. I was making a huge fucking mess. I knew in the back of my head that they'd definitely know somebody came through here, that there'd be no question that they'd been robbed, but I couldn't bring myself to care.

Some of the addresses and things were handwritten, like mine had been. They might not all be digitized.

If this fucked them over, even just a smidgen, I'd feel cleaner.

My yanking spree reached the Pythoness Society. I made a mental note of that as I shucked pictures off ropes like grapes. These were women who my mother had known. These were women who I'd maybe met when I was little. These were women who wanted me to drop everything I knew to be with them, which was a crazy, stupid thought I wasn't ready to completely wholesale abandon yet.

I searched, without thinking, for my mother's picture.

She wasn't there.

"Dead witches," I said. "Do you keep pictures of dead witches?"

"We don't photograph corpses." Shiloh had an edge of panic in their voice. "I appreciate the righteousness but if you trash this place, they will absolutely come after us, I'm just saying."

"I'll worry about that later," I snapped.

They yanked open another drawer.

I took a step toward the book on the shrine.

Mr. Scratch writhed around my guts like an eel. *It's dead,* he said, *it's dead, Sideways, it's dead inside of there, I can smell it.*

"What's dead?" I peered down at the book. No label on the cover, like a photo album or vintage erotica. I reached for it, nearly brushed my fingers against it, but couldn't.

Mr. Scratch had hurled a tendril of himself down the length of my finger and strained to hold it still.

The book devil. The strange thing, the thing like me, the thing that I was and am. Mr. Scratch rasped under my nail. *It's dead in there. It's dead between the pages, it can't write anymore. Don't touch it.*

"You survived being burned and abandoned," I said. "What do you mean, it's dead?"

I know, I just know, I can smell it. We don't die, we never die, we cannot even dissolve back into the big broad spiral of unsculpted potential once experience has shaped us otherwise, but there is not life inside that book. The thing like me doesn't remember what it is. It doesn't remember what it's written. It doesn't remember its name. It does not recognize me nor do I know it. I don't think it can feel or think. It's dead, Sideways. It's anathema to me.

"What is this?" I said it to the room, to the pictures in my pockets, to Shiloh, to the sky above the house. "What is this book?"

"It's got the spells we use in it." Shiloh slammed a drawer shut and opened another. They had made it halfway around the room. They breathed through their teeth, chilly and rattling. "Recorded sermons from the founders. Brethren prayers. Cursebreakers. The mimic spell we used on you, it's in there."

"There's a book devil inside it," I said. "Like a proper spell book."

Scratch made a rasping sound inside of me. If he could cough, he would.

Shiloh didn't say anything. They were pulling out boxes from their current drawer, opening them, and tossing them aside. Their elbows cut weird shadows on the floor. They stopped searching for a moment, rubbed their eyes, pressed their hands against their cheeks and stared at the tattered wall.

"Mr. Scratch says it's—"

"I will answer whatever questions you have later. I will tell you everything I know. It's fucked up, everything in this room, this house, this family is rotten. It's bad. It's really fucking bad. That's going to be the gist of the answers to all of your questions. It's bad. They—we—use everything we have to control people, to stalk them and isolate them and destroy them. To compel them to destroy themselves. To disempower and destroy anyone who stands in the path of that mission, including each other, including innocent good-natured neighbors and strangers and the needy and the good. We'll have the rest of our lives for me to explain all the gory bits of witchfinding if that fucking satisfies you, Sideways, but right now I really need you to help. Please."

I took a breath. I wanted to cry or break my hands against the wall.

"Please," they said again.

I turned my back to the dead book and reached for the nearest drawer. It was acquiescing and I hated that, even if they were probably right. I could pitch a fit later. The drawer rattled when I pulled it out to its fullest. I glanced down, mentally prepared myself for deer guts or human teeth, some shit like that.

It was filled with marbles. Glass marbles like you'd play with as a kid. *For mimics,* Scratch said. The deer in the pool in October, of course. One had had a me-colored marble in its mouth.

I shut the drawer, pulled out the next. Crumbly yellowish newspapers filled it like rabbit bedding. The high-lighted passages sensationalized local cool and unexplained phenomena, shit that could be either bunk or magic. Most of them looked a solid decade old, at least. The age of the internet must've usurped the confetti drawer. It was tricky to shut all the way, because papers about a sinkhole that opened under the mayor's house and a woman whose crops were always bagging blue ribbons despite her barely knowing anything about farming kept shoving themselves up in the rollers.

"Lord," said Shiloh.

"What?" My next drawer was full of pliers and vises, which would be a normal thing to find in a drawer if this room didn't have such ripe torture-chamber energy. I felt queasy looking at them. I thought of the stain on the rug outside. I thought about how I was paralyzed upstairs a few months ago, about how Sheriff Chantry was going to come and talk to me. I wondered if he would have brought some of these.

Shiloh was silent. I didn't hear them breathing.

I glanced over, and they were on their knees beside a bottommost drawer. I couldn't see the contents of the drawer from my angle. Shiloh was bent over the drawer, hands pressed against their cheeks, nails pricked against the bags under their eyes.

"Shi," I started.

"I'm colorblind." Their voice was small. It was breathier than usual. Hardly more than a whisper, than a gasp. "I can't do this."

"What are you on about?" I shut the plier drawer and crossed the room, stood over them, glanced down at the drawer they were tending.

My brain misinterpreted. I recalled when I was a kid how museum gift shops always had vats of dyed gemstones.

You'd get a little velvet bag, and you could have as many teal and fuchsia rocks as you could shove in there for five bucks. Made you feel like you had pirate treasure. The drawer that Shiloh had opened was brimming with Technicolor gemstones, all glowing from within, soft and gleaming. But they were not Technicolor gemstones, was the thing.

My head and shoulders howled. My throat and thyroid and lungs and gut.

"I'm blue-yellow colorblind," they said, "and all of these look the same, Sideways. I know what they look like, but I can't pick them out of these. I don't know which ones are the ones that go with the witches I robbed. I don't know. I don't know, I—"

"We'll sort them later," I breathed. I reached down and took a fistful of them. They weren't heavy, barely weighed anything at all, but it hurt to hold them. They zinged through the marrow of my bones like I'd hit something hard, like I'd electrocuted myself. I stuffed the fistful of specter stones in my pocket, reached for more. "It's okay, fucking breathe, help me."

Shiloh scooped some up. They put them in my pockets, too, which I would've teased them about if I didn't think I was about to blow apart into shrapnel. When one pocket was stuffed to the limit, we switched to the other. The specter stones shoved up against the pictures of witches I'd taken. I couldn't feel them. Even piling like this, they didn't weigh my jacket down. When we filled the second pocket, we pulled my jacket open like wings and stuffed the inside pocket that hung over my heart, the one that was supposed to hold your wallet.

"You said you'd only done two," I said.

"That's right," they insisted. "I don't know where the hell these came from, I don't understand," they gasped. "What do we do with them? I have no idea who they belong to, Sideways, I don't know where they're from, I—"

"Later," I insisted. "Let's go find Madeline's."

They nodded, but they didn't get off the floor.

I grabbed them by the elbow and tugged.

Shiloh made a muffled sound, but they found their feet and straightened their back. "Levi's room is upstairs," they breathed. "It's this way, follow me."

I jerked my chin once.

They made for the door. They flipped a light switch on the way out, bathed me and the carnage in darkness. I slipped out before the room itself reached out and grabbed my ankle. I closed the door behind us, but it didn't click and reopened itself, swung ajar like the stag's belly a few rooms down.

We both panted like we'd been running.

They kept them in a drawer together, Mr. Scratch said. *All piled on each other. I want to eat them, Sideways. I want to devour them, I want to melt their bones into cream, I want to eradicate them inside of me, I want them to not exist. How many children? Whose children? Which book devil was their guide and loving guardian? Which version of me was bereft of their witches? Oh, my Honeyeaters, oh, my lovelies, to be thrown in a box, in a drawer, in a bin in the dark with a dead part of my body existential, oh, how I'd vanish those who've done this, oh how I—*

"I'd love to let you, Mr. Scratch," I hissed, "but Madeline is hopefully beating you to it as we speak."

We went through another door, up a few steps, and around a corner.

In the dark, the foyer looked like a cave.

There was a Christmas tree in the middle of the room. It was so tall, so broad that it completely obscured the family crest and the fireplace behind it. Looked like it'd been pilfered from a Macy's. There were expensive, uniform glass ornaments, but homemade-looking ones as well: little bells, organza snowflakes, paper chains, and baked clay angels. The lights on the tree hadn't been unplugged before they left, and it was by its candy-colored glow that we navigated the space.

"I feel like I'm in a mouth." I crossed my arms. "A mouth that smells like pine. I hate this place."

Shiloh kept their jaws clamped shut. They started up the sweeping stairs, and I felt a rush of old fear saw at me. Old fear has long, nasty teeth. I felt chewed. I braced my hand against the railing and made myself climb, made myself go up the stairs that I shouldn't be going up, nobody should ever go up them, holy fuck. I hate heights. I hate these stairs. I hate this house, this place, the people who own it.

I loathe it, I know, I feel your seething and I seethe with you. Breathe, I know it's horrible, but you must breathe, you've got no choice but to breathe, Scratch said. *You can't slow down. Just move. Movement is life.*

Shiloh looked worse than I felt, which didn't seem possible, but even so—they held their shoulders so taut, so square I thought their back might snap from the tension. It was making me double-nervous, how tense they were. If I didn't say something stupid, I'd have a fucking stroke. "Hey, Shi," I said.

They didn't acknowledge me. They waited at the top of the stairs for me to catch up, then kept going, went down the stretch of family portraits and deer bits without turning to look at them. There were, if my suspicion held water, fewer portraits than there'd been last time.

"If you're blue-yellow colorblind," I said, "what color is Squirtle?"

"Excuse me?"

"The Pokémon. You know. Squirtle."

They jerked to a halt so abruptly that I slammed into them. They turned on their heel, looked at me. Their cheeks were striped and shiny. "We've got to stay focused. We need to get to the trailer park before Madeline, right?" They shifted their weight. Crossed their arms. "He looks like a turtle. Stupid question. We weren't allowed to play video games. He's a turtle from hell."

"Hey," I said. "Hey. What's up?"

They hissed in a breath and stared at their feet. "It's stupid." Their jaw clicked, and they looked back at me.

Their eyes were burning. "They put up the tree without me. I always pick it. I'm the only one who cares." They turned around, scraped their nails over their scalp, and kept walking until they stopped again, this time in front of a nondescript door. "This is Levi's room."

They didn't seem to be inclined to walk in first. They didn't move.

I reached for the doorknob and twisted it, gave it a push.

Levi's bedroom looked so normal it felt almost fetishistic. There was an unmade bed with linen sheets, a school uniform draped over an armchair by the desk, a typewriter, a coffee mug that held wooden pens. Entry-level film nerd posters on the wall, and thumbtacked landscape prints, a few poems I made a point not to examine too closely. I shone my phone's flashlight around in sweeping lighthouse circles. He had a monstera. He had an oxblood leather satchel. It wasn't particularly messy. It wasn't particularly anything. It felt like it was trying to sell me something. Made my flesh crawl.

Hell of a place to hold your ex-girlfriend's stolen organ hostage.

"It's in his desk, his sock drawer, or his pillowcase," Shiloh said thinly as they stepped inside the bedroom. They closed the door behind them and leaned on it. "Under the mattress at most adventurous. He isn't original."

"Figures," I said. "You go sock drawer, I'll go bed, we wind up at desk together if the first two fall through."

"Right," they said.

I went for the bed flashlight first. He kept a case of White Claws and a bible beside his headboard, which was unhinged, but not the point. He had two pillows, one stacked on top of the other, and I went for the one underneath first. I scrubbed my tongue over my gums, rolled my shoulders, and dove a hand into the pillowcase's depths. "How are you holding up?"

"I wonder if I've been asked after at the Christmas party," they said. They sounded miserable. "I suspect not."

"You know what," I said, "tomorrow, we'll make a big fuck-off gingerbread house. Gingerbread mansion that's five times cooler than this mansion, less evil and more tricked out. How's that sound?" Something with edges caught my fingertips.

I yanked it out and instantly wished I hadn't. It was a photo booth strip, and every panel was Madeline and Levi, smiling and laughing and tonguing each other. I dropped it on the bed like it was fetid. Childishly rubbed my fingertips on my jeans before I thrust my hands back in the case.

This time, I touched something smooth. I had the irrational sense that it was delicate, and I lifted it with care, like I was sneaking an egg from a robin's nest.

Madeline's soul was violet. I cradled it in my palms.

"I'd really like that," Shiloh said. They looked up from the desk, rubbed their hands together. "Is that it?"

I opened my mouth to say something.

Light bled under the door.

SEVENTEEN

THIS HOME IS NOT MY WORLD

"What do we do?" My lips flew over my teeth, contorted like worms. I wanted to scream but couldn't risk the sound. I shoved Madeline's specter into one of my overfull pockets and took Shiloh by their hands, to hold them, to keep myself from shaking them. "How do we get out?"

"Hush up," they breathed. They pulled themself out of my grip, backed up against the door. I watched their ribs beat under their jacket. They turned their head, braced their temple against the wood. "I don't hear talking."

"Yeah?" I bounced from foot to foot. "What's that mean, Shi?"

"It means there's only one person. They'd never shut up otherwise." They closed their eyes. Their brows twitched inwards, the only motion that broke their steeliness. "Provided they don't know we're here."

Fuck. Fuck, fuck fuck fuck. I rubbed a hand over my skull and made myself breathe, made myself keep both feet planted, made myself not freak the fuck out. Recalled and adopted Madeline's fighter stance. "Is there another way downstairs? How do we—"

"There's a second staircase, it'll take you down to the game room. It's at the end of the hall, to the left, behind a door. There's a bathroom on one side and a linen closet on the other." They made a thin sound in their throat. "Less flashy than jumping out the window, but I don't want the specters falling out of your pockets."

"Think we can wait 'em out?" My bones buzzed.

No waiting, none of that, just leaving, Mr. Scratch hissed. *We have to get out. We have to go go go.*

"No," said Shiloh at the same time as Scratch. "If it's Levi, staying in here is probably the worst thing we could do. We go out and stay down, army crawl along the wall. If we stay flat and silent, they might not notice us from downstairs."

"If they're upstairs?"

"I've got a plan." They smiled. It hurt my teeth to look at. They wrapped their hand around the knob and turned it slow, opened it just a smidgen. "You first," they said. "Get down. No matter what happens, keep crawling and don't look behind you."

"Copy that." I dropped to my stomach. I was worried about the pockets, about them opening and spilling when I moved. "Scratch," I breathed, "help me."

Forever and always.

Shiloh opened the door wider, just wide enough for my shoulders.

I made like an alligator, clawed my way forward with my elbows bent at right angles. Bizarre feeling, the carpet runner on my chest. Adrenaline superseded self-criticism, and I crawled into the light with my heart in my teeth.

The foyer's electric chandelier through the banister's ribs threw stripe shadows over the floor and the backs of my hands. I pressed myself as close to the floorboards as I could manage. I mashed the grit under my palms. I listened for Shiloh behind me, but I couldn't hear them.

Nobody was talking. No rustling, no breathing.

I dragged myself forward by the nails.

End of the hall, to the left, behind the door.

This was a wormhole hallway. For every inch I lugged myself, three more sprang in its place. Scratch shivered in my mouth, and I pressed my tongue to my hard palate in a stupid attempt to console him.

The spikes on this jacket scraped against the hardwood. Hoped they fucked up the varnish. Hoped nobody heard the sound.

We were going to get the fuck out of here, we were going to get the fuck out of here, I was going to get us the fuck out of here. It was going to happen. I was making it fucking happen. This was an incantation. My body was the sigil. We'd get out one hand at a time.

Still couldn't hear Shiloh.

I stopped for a moment, just long enough to press my cheek to the floor. It was hard to see more than myself at this angle. I spied for even just an edge of them, a flash of their blue nails, the edge of a tweed sleeve, anything that told me they were close. That they were on the ground. That they were moving with me. Anything.

I didn't see anything.

Scratch said, *Keep going.* I kept going.

One hand forward, then the next.

I wished that souls were heavy. If they were heavy, I might have any way of knowing whether they were imminently about to spill out and roll away.

There was a sound, then a string of them.

I froze.

I knew that sound. It was heels. High heels were click-clacking across the floor below us. If there were high heels click-clacking now, and there hadn't been before, and the main door hadn't opened and shut in the interim, that meant the person in the heels had been standing still below us. Listening, maybe.

"My husband is the sheriff." Radio voice. Soft, tall, dreamy. "If you thought you were going to rob someone tonight, I'm afraid you've made a poor choice in target."

The heel clicking changed timbre. The notes were higher, hollower.

She was walking up the stairs.

"If you come out," Grace Chantry said, "I can walk you to the door. Be thoughtful about this. It's nearly Christmas—wouldn't you rather be at home than in prison?"

Nearly at the end of the hallway. I started crawling again, faster this time, wriggled toward the corner as fast as my body could carry me. I wanted to run. This felt ridiculous. This was a choreography for shedding skin, not hauling ass.

Grace hummed to herself. Her clicking neared the top of the stairs.

I scrambled around the corner and hoisted myself upright. Gave myself a quick pat down; the specters all seemed to be in place, all my limbs seemed attached to my body in predictable and workable ways. I geared up, hardened my diaphragm, sucked in a breath to run.

The heels stopped clacking.

"Hello, Mother," Shiloh said.

All my sinews snapped tight.

Was this the fucking plan?

No. Absolutely not.

The radiant voice of morality in my head was foaming. I couldn't leave them here. I couldn't leave them with her, I refused to leave them here, I wouldn't. I took them into my home when I hadn't been sure they were good. Maybe they weren't yet, or they were, but they were trying and they were mine, now, they were my friend, I felt the word solidify like a rock in my gut. Friendship, the driving force of my decision-making for the past few months, from whence the Scapegracers were born. I wasn't going to let them be alone here. Not any queer kid, but especially not Shiloh. No.

Sideways.

Could I tornado her over the ledge? Could I twirl her around the chandelier, give Shiloh and me time to run? I grabbed my twister-sigil hand, gave it a squeeze, ignored, then relished, that it made my bruises ache.

You'd kill all three of you in the process.

Deadname, Grace said. "You've come home."

"This isn't home. You threw me out," they said. Their voice was thin, but it didn't waver.

"That was your father's rashness," she said. "You know you'll always be my baby. Oh, come here, come here—"

"You let him throw me out," they insisted. "You watched and you did nothing. All the hideous stuff Dad does, you watch. Watching is assisting. You can't play innocent with me. You're complicit, don't pretend like—"

"Your father is the man of the house." She suddenly sounded teary. "It broke my heart, but I can't go back on his word. Everything he does is motivated by love. If he didn't love you, if he wasn't scared for you, he wouldn't have been so upset."

Sideways, we have to keep going.

"Christ." Shiloh's breath pressed against the walls and the ceiling, banged on them, battered the mortar. "Listen to yourself! I don't want love if it's like that. You also disowned me. If you defended me, things might've been different, but you didn't."

"I'm so glad you're alright," she cooed. "Oh, I was so worried about you. What've you gotten yourself into? Where have you been? Levi said he saw you at school, so I knew you were being good, being responsible on your own. That will impress your father very much."

Smothering somebody with honey to dominate them. Seen that one before. Daisy did it all the time. It wasn't a fucking kindness, and I wanted to rip all my skin off and run around the corner, do something, do anything. Gnaw her ankle. Scream so loud that the house crumbled like Usher's.

Sideways, Shiloh is smart. They're doing this because they want you to escape, you and all the specters. They want them returned. We gave them sigils, you can contact them once we're out, but we have to go. We have to go now, right now, right this instant. I will not lose another daughter to witchfinders. Go.

That wasn't good enough.

It is what we have. Run, now!

"I'm sorry," I breathed, "I am so fucking sorry."

"I'll talk to your father," Grace said. "We'll all sit down as a family."

I bolted. There wasn't much space between me and the door, I crossed it in a stride. The door opened forward, and I slid myself in the gap and hurtled into the darkness behind it. I didn't close it behind me. I didn't watch my step.

I skipped the first step and landed funny on the second. Sour, stinging pain licked up the side of my ankle. *Crunch.* A fucking twist, a little strain, a broken-off foot like Bratz doll shoes, holy mother of fuck it hurt it hurt it hurt. My stomach flattened and sparklers flared in the hinges of my jaw. I grit my teeth, slammed my palms on either side of the staircase—there was a wall, as it turned out, that seemed to follow the staircase down. I stepped down with the good foot. That seemed fine.

I stepped with the other.

Fuck.

Tears needled their noses out of my ducts. "Scratch," I wheezed, "tell me I didn't just fuck up my ankle." I took another bracing step down, but this one was worse than the last, sharper, more vision fuzzying. Not that I could see a damn thing anyway. I was limping through uninterrupted darkness, and I had no idea where the stairs ended, or even precisely where they'd let out. The game room, Shiloh had said. I didn't remember there being another set of doors from the game room, just the hallway with the stain.

I didn't want to go back through there.

I'm sorry, Mr. Scratch soothed, *I'm sorry, Sideways.* He rushed down the length of my leg, circled around my ankle in tight little loops. The loops did nothing for the pain. *I can tell it hurts, but you've got to keep going.*

I forced myself down another few steps. I braced my palms so hard against the walls that I thought I might bust through them, might warp the drywall with the force of my fingertips. I could've cracked the house in half. I went down step after step, until the pain covered my skin like a film. It was like someone injected sour milk into my nervous system— everything curdled, was tart and revoltingly creamy thick. Shiloh had praised my masculinity for its steadfastness, its *loyalty.* I was limping away while they sacrificed themself for me. I failed us. How was I supposed to pedal?

Mr. Scratch's bulk plummeted down my body. He globbed between my sinews. My ankle twitched inside my boot. With a creak and an unspeakably horrible sucking sound, my pain ruptured and became nothing. Ligaments aligned, bone mended, nerves steamed. Mr. Scratch gasped like he'd been drowning. He went limp, fell slack in my heel.

"Are you okay?" I tried my foot. Normal, save for the fact that it sloshed inside. "Scratch, tell me you're okay."

He made a pre-linguistic sound. He wasn't okay. He was beat. Unfucking my ankle had kicked his ass.

If anybody else sacrificed literally anything else for me tonight, I was going to yank the moon out of the sky and eat it.

I ran. I hurtled down the hallway and turned, and I was in the bloodstain hallway, somehow. I went through the far door. The game room lamp hadn't magically turned itself off, and I pelted past the pool table, flew through the fuckboy muck and between the wingback armchairs. I seized the door to the gore room, yanked it open, slammed it shut behind me.

Dark and cold in here.

The open deer glanced over at me and drooled.

No, it didn't. It was a dead deer. It couldn't do that or anything. Its guts were in a bucket and its chest looked like a slipper. Its antlers were tangled with the legs of the metal table. It couldn't move. It didn't.

I patted down my swollen pockets. Souls still there, still straining the seams of the lining. I couldn't hear what was happening upstairs. I couldn't hear Shiloh and Grace. I couldn't hear if they were chatting or screaming or throwing things at each other. I had the specters. I had to go.

I grabbed the door, opened it.

Wind quickened around me in circles. It drew me forward, which I obliged. I shut the door behind me, and the light was gone, and the snow crunched underfoot. The woods, which seemed more densely packed than they had been when we arrived, flushed close against the side of the house. It made a tunnel. Maybe that's why the wind was so insistent. Or maybe it was Elaina?

I grabbed my bike.

I didn't walk it around the perimeter like Shiloh had. I threw it under me, got my feet in the stirrups and pedaled as fast as my body could bear. If my ankle felt like it had earlier, I didn't think I'd make it off the driveway.

It wasn't snowing anymore. It must've stopped just after we slipped inside, because the footprints and the tire tracks were still visible in the snow.

Two sets of footprints.

No matter what Shiloh said, they wouldn't be able to talk the second set of prints out of existence. The bike stripe, neither.

I pedaled harder.

The wind would've been brisk if I *wasn't* biking. On the bike, the wind was like spindrift off the Arctic Circle. It sliced through the seams of my jacket and my body fat, deep enough to rime my bone sponge. My naked fingers were screaming. My cheeks burned red.

The sigils were coming up.

I wished I wasn't too proud for a helmet. I pulled one hand off its handlebar and reached for the necktie, pulled it up until the fabric covered my eyes. My bike lurched a little. I kept it upright but the wind wasn't helping. This part of the road was curvy.

"Scratch, I know you're exhausted," I said, "but I need you to steer, understand me? I need you to keep us from crashing."

I'd burn again before I let you crash. Mr. Scratch sounded ill. He twined up my calf, my thigh, over gut and diaphragm and heart, roped down my arms, made himself snug beneath the gauze. His ink was hot like life, it took the edge off this tundra-breath air. He pushed one hand forward, steered me left. I followed his motion. All the sigils that Madeline carved turned electric against my back. I felt all fourteen of them, felt their shape against my skin like it was a path that ants were crawling. Priya and Iris' sigil warmed my hand, and prickly insistence turned into dull pressure.

Mr. Scratch squeezed the other hand.

I yanked the handles in that direction.

Snow didn't crunch under the tire. I must have been in the trench a car's wheel left. Would've made sense for Grace to have driven home, she couldn't have just appeared in the foyer out of thin air. But why had she come back? Why did she leave the party? Why'd she have to sink her teeth into Shiloh, keep them there?

Are you sure you made the right choice?

"About Shi?" I grit my teeth. "Absolutely not."

If he could be, Mr. Scratch would be panting. I racked

my head for disgusting things to eat. I could eat pins off this jacket. I could eat pocket lint. Matches. A roll of quarters. I needed him to be well. I needed to be symmetrical with him. He didn't say anything else.

My breath turned solid around my face when I breathed out. My teeth chattered and I didn't try to stop them. Turn here, turn there, and the sigils stung less. I was less aware of their buzzing. I felt the supernatural chill stifle itself into coldness.

Forward. Onward.

The front tire struck asphalt, and I stopped. I ripped the blindfold down.

I'd found the normal street. Tires had gashed muddy streaks in the layer of soft white snow, there were streetlights in the distance, and fields that used to be heavy with corn. They'd be soybean fields in spring.

I scrambled for my phone. I'd Maps my way to the trailer park, but I needed to talk to Shiloh, needed confirmation that they were alive, that they were in one piece, that we had a game plan. I'd have Boris come get them at the chapel, maybe. It was close. It was, relatively speaking, safe.

They'd already messaged me.

> **i'm okay mom isn't going back to the party and isn't txting dad yet**

> **i think i'm going to try and steal some of my stuff back. going to take credit for trashing**

the strategy room too, blame it on unprocessed trauma or smth.

yr sigil works a lot i think?? like when she opens her mouth i only hear half of what she says and the rest just makes me feel warm

get yr specter back ttyl

I coughed a breath, which was almost relief, and started a reply.

My phone buzzed again.

Flower emoji.

Daisy Brink.

Hey so I'm sorry. I've been a bitch and text sorrys don't mean shit so I need to see u in person. We can hang out 2morrow just the 2 of us. Or if u want there is a party at my place tonite. Like not a fun party it's too fucking big and fancy and stupid and it's all my dad's friends. Like there are little finger sandwiches and all the rich alcoholics are here making each other worse. I always just stay upstairs because like they just talk about local politics and things that happened in the 80s and infidelity its depressing. But like yates and jing come every year and I thought I'd offer. It always goes until like midnight or 1 am so u got plenty of time if u want to drop

**by and steal some booze or whatvr. I'm
sending u my address consider coming by if u
think it sounds fun. I really need 2 talk 2 u**

Wait.

How many big fancy Christmas parties could there be in
Sycamore Gorge township tonight?

I put Daisy's address in my phone. It was a seven-minute
bike ride from here.

If she just now texted me, that means Madeline hadn't
started yet. I didn't think that murder was something you
texted through. Which meant that the Chantry boys were
all in Daisy's house and she didn't know, because she was
being sullen and antisocial with the Scapegracers upstairs.
And Scratch and I weren't there. And everything was about
to fucking go.

I texted back, **Madeline might be there it might get
violent stick together omw!**

The message attempted to send. It half uploaded and
quit.

"Fuck," I said, whipping down the road on my bike.

Very much so.

EIGHTEEN

MY TRUE LOVE GAVE TO ME

The Brink family McMansion was optically slammed. At baseline, it was a car crash of a house, because it had every kind of window and architectural hiccup in the catalogue going on at once just so that Mr. Brink could materially remind himself that he owned not one but *two* local branches of a shitty credit union, but this was beyond the proverbial pale. The Brink family McMansion looked like a damn mall. There were two Christmas trees outside, tinsel on every slope of ill-advised roof, enough rainbow lights to power a pride float. The drive was lined with light-and-wire reindeer. Their empty deer heads bobbed up and down on a circuit. Cars packed the lawn, stacked tight like tailgaters or music festival attendees. They were all dusted with snow, but the kitschy aura emanating from the Brink household made the real snow seem desperately fake. Soap and oatmeal snow. Gross, sudsy set snow.

Fuck Daisy's dad, but the guy was a master of camp. I got what Shiloh said about pageantry. This felt fruity. Oh, god. Shiloh.

There were enough people inside the house that I could hear the din from the mailbox. Nothing like the drone of two hundred tipsy middle-aged white Anglo-Saxon protestants to set your teeth on edge! Their chatter, and the boom of speakers playing carols louder than was legally allowed, rippled the air around me. Suppose noise ordinances don't apply when you've got the evil sheriff as a guest. It felt like I was approaching a stampede.

I abandoned the bike beside a tree-sized inflatable Santa, tore my hands over my skull, and sprinted up the walkway. My feet throbbed from cold and pounding them on the pavement sent shockwaves up my calves with every stomp. I seized the doorknob, tore it open, threw myself inside.

The cold vanished.

It was hot. Sweltering hot, and smelling distinctly of sweat, booze, pine, mulling spice, and scented candles. And dank? Green dangled from the banisters. I counted not one, but three giant Christmas trees, four green-linen snack tables with cookie tins, finger foods and endless bottles of alcohol, dead-eyed catering waitstaff dressed like elves (bells on their damn shoes, little hats, little shorts), holly boughs, velvet ribbons, a model train set that sped in circles along the edges of the room, candy canes erupting incongruously from every flat surface, paper snowflakes, fairy lights. In the melee, I'd never seen so many bleach-blond bobs in the same place. Red dresses, too, all about knee-length. Just a million Fox News anchor lady misprints. Everybody held their glasses at eye level, like they were Solo cups. The men wore button-downs and blazers, or else hideous Christmas sweaters, and everyone was laughing and dancing and drinking themselves into zombiedom. There were a few people my age, but they were people who were actively on the path toward metamorphizing into the people around them.

The song changed.

Everybody hoisted their drinks and cheered, started singing.

It was "Mele Kalikimaka." Like, the Jimmy Buffett version.

Holy shit. Like, holy fucking shit.

I couldn't see any stairs. There was an upper gallery, but the staircase wasn't in the overgrown foyer/living room/Christmas mosh pit. I took a few steps forward, but the crowd was impenetrably thick.

The sneaking sigil. Right.

I hugged the wall, tried to edge my way around the room without stepping on the model train. It only showed up and whistled when my foot needed to be in that space. It was like some kind of jinx. In this direction, there was a Christmas tree with metallic boxes underneath—because fake presents are exactly what this house needed—and a cluster of catering elves. The elves didn't look at me. They passed around a Juul and whispered smack to each other.

Poor fucks.

I thought I spied Sheriff Chantry across the room. I'd

never seen him out of uniform, but it was hard to mistake
Chantry hair. He had hair like an artichoke heart. He wore
a navy blazer, a white button-down, a "fun" novelty tie with
holly leaves and sleigh bells. People kept clapping him on the
back. He laughed with all his teeth, sucked down a bottle of
beer like it was his job. It wasn't the face of a kidnapper, a
stalker, a murderer, a soul stealer. It wasn't the face of
someone who'd disowned their child earlier this month, left
them to sleep in the cold. It was such a deeply, intensely
uninteresting face. He looked like every third businessman
I'd ever met, or a principal, or a dentist, or some rando
behind me at a checkout line. Or maybe that's what villains
just look like in real life, instead of in movies, where they
tend to be dressed more like me.

Didn't see Madeline.

Didn't see the Chantry boys.

Did see the owner of the fake pizza store dunk a sugar
cookie into his Moscow mule.

Top ten worst rooms for big dykes submission entered,
accepted. Whew, did this suck. I turned a corner, tucked
myself behind the kitsch queen goliath Christmas tree, and
whipped out my phone again. There wasn't a whole lot
behind the tree aside from trash cans and a framed picture
of Daisy with big, swooshy hair and a peasant blouse.

Not my Daisy. Daisy Brink née Stringer. Daisy the
mother, Daisy who named her only offspring after herself
for the honest to god reason of *Gilmore Girls*, Daisy whose
name had been on a necklace in the Delacroix House, Daisy

who died and was found pill bottle still in hand in the garden by her little daughter and her friend.

I chewed on the lining of my cheeks.

The first message hadn't gone through.

Daze I'm at your place where are you???

There was only a millisecond of wait time.

Omg! Its fucking bananas down there, let me come get u! Where are u!

Behind one of the Christmas trees by trash cans

Rite where u belong then lol we'll be right down!!

I shoved my phone back in my pocket and took a step backwards into the tree. Its artificial needles scraped my ears. It felt like being enveloped by a mountain of safety pins.

The whole room slurred the song lyrics in three different keys. It was clear that only about half of the people present knew all the words. There was a lot of *hrmhrmhrm Christmas will be green and bright, hrmhrmhrmhrmhrmhrm and uh stars at night*-ing going around. This song also was going on for a substantially longer time than I remembered it being, not that I spend a lot of time with Jimmy Buffett Christmas albums. Still, though. It had to have been like, at least five minutes. Had someone played it twice? Was it on a loop? Was time all gunked up from all the different weird smells going on in this room? With another glance over, I spotted the pipe I'd suspected earlier. Officer Carter, the cop who worked at West High and had a habit of frisking girls' back pockets, passed it to my old pediatrician. Officer Carter Tasered a kid during last year's junior prom.

I felt insane and kinda goosey.

I put my hands over top of my pockets. The specter stones hummed against my palms. They all had slight variation on texture and temperature. The one nearest my left thumb and forefinger was barbed and icy. The stone next to it, lumpy-molten, was too hot in a way my hand found pleasurable, like feeling fresh-baked bread.

Even though I'd managed to hide myself in the back of a Christmas tree despite not looking anything like a Christmas tree, I still had the acute sensation that there were eyes on my pockets. That people could smell them. These looked like people who poached specters, after all. I mean, fuck. I was in the same room with Sheriff Chantry and his sons with all their filched souls. And they were drunk. And I was surrounded by strangers. And somebody was going to show up soon and kill them. How was she going to manage that? They weren't all in one place and there were witnesses everywhere. Did she plan to pick them off one by one, slasher style?

Where the heck were Daisy and company?

There. She materialized between two laughing men, shouldered between them without so much as an apologetic glance in a tiny blue tennis skirt and an enormous black sweater. Decidedly un-festive. Also, that sweater was mine. She shoved through a cluster of women with Tang-colored tans and frosted tips, Yates and Jing a pace behind her, until she neared the hulking plastic tree. She stopped, then. Scanned around. Her eyes were red, rimmed pinker than Yates' dress, but she didn't look high. Her eyes fixed on me. They got bigger.

"Sideways," she mouthed.

Jing and Yates, who'd been searching in opposite directions, swung their heads forward in the same swooshing motion.

Daisy flew at me. Her arms shot out, hurled around my neck, and all at once she was leaning on me, her full weight across my chest. She'd risen up on tippiest tiptoe. Her hair whirled around my shoulders, her knees knocked close to mine. She didn't seem to mind the spikes against her arms, or even really notice them.

The force of her embrace caught me off guard, and down we fucking went.

Jing and Yates both made huge faces, all open eyes and mouths and nostrils stretched. They threw out their hands with fingers splayed like, *Oh no, oh god, oh shit, oh no.* Their eyebrows stabbed up toward the Balder-killing ceiling. Time smeared; I saw the world with acute clarity in slow motion. Holy wow, this room had a limited color palette that very quickly looked Freddy Krueger-y when one was falling backwards onto a hulking, awful Christmas tree.

My back hit the Christmas tree's itchy green pole spine. Unfortunately, momentum. Daisy kept going. I kept going. The tree started going, and then my vision did some acrobatic cheer flip and we crashed without a bunch of girls in pleated skirts to catch us.

The air clapped out of my lungs.

The world swung like a jackknife. The *thwump* of plastic tree smacking ground, along with the tinkling of cracking ornaments, killed all the drunken jubilance. The conversations halted. Nobody was still singing except Jimmy Buffett. Everybody peered down at us, hands over their mouths, smiling and *oh my god*-ing.

Everything was green for a second. All I could see was plastic tree.

Daisy was a girl-spill across me. She wasn't laughing, so it hadn't been on purpose, but she didn't seem too keen on getting up quite yet either. She braced her hands on my chest. Her fingers wove between the spikes, and she heaved herself into push-up stance. Catching her breath, I think. She mashed the book into me. Her hair covered her face, fell around my chin.

I sucked a breath in. Slapped my pockets, which had been miraculously sealed with a sticky, inky glue. What do people even do without a devil friend? "Thanks," I wheezed. As soon as the oxygen hit my brain, my diaphragm balked, and a laugh shot out of me. I laughed like I was losing my mind. I laughed and my vision went blurry. My floating ribs started to burn.

Everybody was staring.

The Chantry family was staring.

Holy shit, we were so fucked.

"Do you girls need a hand?" The voice was sweet, nonthreatening, an even, low tenor. "That was quite the dive you took." Around the edge of Daisy's hair, I saw his face. Candy-blue eyes, short nose, thin lips dimpling up in a symmetrical billboard smile. Abel Chantry. He beamed down at us. He looked friendly.

I imagined the dead stag appearing behind him. I imagined the lips of its chest parting, its backbone floating to align with his, then the two halves snapping together, swallowing him up like a furry Venus flytrap.

Jing grabbed Daisy around the middle and hauled her upright. She pulled her backwards, out of the way, and then she and Yates reached down and grabbed my hands. I squeezed their wrists, and they heaved me up on my feet. I was dizzy for a second. Kicked a fake present away from me with more force than I intended, it dented and smacked the wall. It landed on the tracks. The train kept coming.

"We're fine," said Daisy. "Duh."

Abel tilted his head to the side. He put his hands in his pockets, didn't drop his smile, didn't blink. "Say," he said. His eyes locked with mine. "Don't I know you from somewhere?"

"Nope." Another laugh ripped out of me. My mouth curled around it, made it sneer-shaped. "You're mistaken."

The song switched. Still Buffett.

People hesitantly returned to their conversations. They

wagged their brows, mouthed things like, *Oh boy* and *Getting a little exuberant with the drinking, are we? Kids, man.*

A man barked orders at the gawking service elves, one of whom had stopped mixing drinks to film this. The orders were to clean this up and resurrect the Christmas tree. The elves looked at each other. This is not what they were hired to do.

Abel took a few strides toward us, toward me.

I took a step back. I sucked my teeth and glowered, bristled under my jacket, reminded myself that trying a twister spell in here would be a massacre. Bugs in a jar with no holes. There were too many people in here. This couldn't be up to fucking fire code. We were smothering each other as-is. My sides ached to screaming. I needed an exit. I saw spots.

"He looks like Levi," said Yates.

"Yeah," said Jing. "Is he bothering you, Sideways?"

"He's his brother." I shook my head. "Get me somewhere I can breathe."

Daisy took my hand and pulled me around the far side of the tree. There was an open doorway, and on the other side stood the kitchen. It opened into a dining room, and while people milled around, picked at yet another snack table that'd been stashed back here, the crowd was substantially thinner. It was thinner still when we bounded around the corner. We climbed a set of carpeted stairs, the four of us nearly on top of each other, and landed in an empty hallway. It was freshly vacuumed and naked feeling.

Daisy released me to shove open a door, and she ushered me and Jing and Yates inside. She shut it behind her, locked it.

We never hung out at Daisy's house. I'd never seen it before.

Daisy's room was a catastrophe. It was almost worse than mine. Actually, definitely worse than mine. I couldn't see the floor because her clothes were everywhere. It looked deliberate. She'd overturned a laundry basket. There were empty strawberry cartons on the foot of her bed, a mountain of stuffed animals, a slick of discarded school papers. Things slurried together like the colors in a rainbow sherbet. In a word: it was gross.

Daisy stomped over to her bed and sat.

Yates sat beside her.

Jing stayed standing. She leaned by the door with her arms locked over her chest.

I collapsed on her desk chair. Something crunched under me, I didn't think about it. My teeth were chattering again, irrespective of the fact that it wasn't cold. I took a breath. Clamped the back of my neck with my hands.

Nobody spoke for a moment.

"So." I scraped the sides of my tongue with my molars. "Did none of you know that the Chantry family was coming over?"

"Everybody in our tax bracket gets invited to these things," Daisy hissed. There was a look on her face I hadn't seen before. Guilt, maybe. Something worse. It unnerved me. "I didn't know. I had no idea. I can't string jack shit together lately. My head's on fire. I'm fucking stupid. I didn't put it together."

"Don't talk about yourself like that," Yates said.

Jing lolled her head back. She looked at me. It felt like slicing me open.

"I was just at their house." My nervous laugh was back. It didn't make any noise. It just shook me. "Me and Shiloh, we were stealing Madeline's specter back. We snuck in because we knew they'd be out. I didn't know this is where they'd be." I looked up at them. I looked at them individually, but I wasn't sure I saw much of anything. My vision was red and smeary. "Grace went home for something, she caught Shiloh. I left them there. I had all these specters, Mr. Scratch said I should go, excuses excuses fuck I'm awful, I ran for it. Then I got your text and realized where the rest of the Chantrys were. I realized they were with you." My throat went dry. "Madeline's gonna be here soon. We need to get back downstairs."

"Madeline," Jing said. She didn't ask me how I knew this, didn't ask about Shiloh or the specters or the Chantry house. Yates looked horror-struck and Daisy had the glaze of dissociation, but Jing looked sharp, she was on it. "Why would she come here?"

"Revenge." I scratched the back of my head. "She's got the whole Chantry clan in one building at one time with no witchfinding booby traps or whatever the fuck they have in that manor house. If she wanted to get them all at once, this is a good way to do that. We got to go back down there. We got to be there when she arrives, or at least catch her when she leaves. I've got her soul on me, we can swap 'em out."

"The Chantry men are down there," Yates repeated. "God, should we leave? Should we try to sneak out?"

"Are they going to kidnap Daisy and her friends from her own party?" Jing looked incredulous. "Sideways is right. We should go back down there. Keep our eyes pricked for Madeline, intercept her."

"If they wanted to kidnap me from this party"—Daisy smacked her lips—"I doubt my dad would object."

Yates and Jing looked a little green.

"There was a fight earlier." Daisy looked at me. The whites of her eyes glowed pink. "These two were lucky enough to score free front-row seats to the Brink family MMA show. Oodles of fun."

"Nobody's going to fuck with you when I'm around," I said. Who cares if we were in a spat? Who cares if she was being weird? I was being weird. Blood oath. Nobody fucks with Daisy.

"We'll see about that." Daisy rose, swayed on her feet. "We go back downstairs, then. So be it."

I rubbed my hand over my mouth and stood back up. I felt wrung out, like I'd been moshing but without the catharsis. The gauze on my knuckles was unraveling. I didn't know how to tighten it properly. I needed Shiloh for that. I needed Shiloh.

Daisy yanked her bedroom door open and stepped out

of it, slinked her way down the hallway faster than I could've spat.

Her father had fought her. Hexes were not enough. I needed to hit him with a holly jolly Christmas tree.

I followed after her. Hustled to keep pace. Jing sped up, walked in step with Daisy, and Yates matched pace with me, reached over to give my hand a little squeeze. I squeezed back, tried to steel my stomach for the umpteenth time. It'd lose its elasticity after tonight. That or I'd never unclench again.

"If we get cornered, what do we do?" Jing rolled her shoulders.

"Drag them outside, I'll handle them there," I said.

"I'm not the best at dragging," Yates said.

"I'm pretty sure Abel would follow you willingly if you asked him real nice." I thought about the knotted thongs on the pool table and felt a little queasy. It was spectacular how little I related to men who were attracted to women. You'd think it'd be like a common link. No. I thought about Shiloh again. I needed to stop thinking.

There was a rustling sound to the left of us. I glanced over, didn't break pace as the Scapegracers marched down the stairs.

Red-eared David Chantry was on the nearby bathroom floor. He was ogling over bottles and scissors and pink-handled razor blades, opening drawers and pulling out everything he could find—pill bottles, which he pocketed, nail polish, which he threw aside in disgust, a pair of period panties, which he brought close to his face with great interest.

I imagined this kid ratting around Shiloh's bedroom, glutting over their diaries. I imagined his bratty kid glee once he found something interesting, imagined the tone he'd take to tell Elias Chantry Shiloh's real name. I remembered the way he'd pushed and prodded at me. How he'd begged to be the one to rip my specter out.

I'd never felt so driven to kick the shit out of a freshman before.

I shook off the thought. He wasn't who we were worried about.

We descended the stairs in lockstep.

The kitchen and dining room were mostly empty. The people talking there seemed wholly enthralled by their conversations, or at least were unmoved by a procession of teenagers, which I couldn't blame them for. Abel wasn't among them. That meant he wasn't lurking by the bottom of the stairs, which was something of a comfort.

We kept moving.

If it wasn't for the crushed ornament glitter still sparkling in the carpet, you might've believed that nobody ruined everything a few minutes prior by body-slamming their friend into a Christmas tree. The crowd had rematerialized its full-blown holiday bliss, and people were dancing, laughing, haranguing the elf waiters again. It didn't take more than a glance around to find the Chantry family, though. They were together now, gathered in a corner. Elias and Abel and Levi, anyway.

Levi looked miserable. He sat cross-legged in a chair by

himself, despondently reading some novel and pouting while Abel and Elias had an animated conversation beside him. They took turns touching his shoulder. Levi shoved them off. He pointedly turned a page.

He wore a holly-leaf bowtie. Had to cover his Chett choker somehow, didn't he?

The rush of animal anger I felt winded me. I've never wanted to strangle someone for being twee before. I'd never so lucidly imagined causing another person permanent bodily harm. I hoped that hex was just non-stop agony.

Abel must've said something that piqued his interest. His shoulders hunched forward. His head perked like a hunting dog's. He swiveled in his chair, and all at once, he and Abel and Elias all looked at me.

After a clap on the back from his father, Abel took a few strides in our direction. He wove between partygoers, cut through groups of drinking men, dissipated clouds of smoke with his shoulders. He was picking up speed.

"We get him outside?" Daisy looked at me. She panted like a racing whippet. Her ribs shook under the sweater. "I can get him outside."

I squeezed Yates' hand tighter. It warmed the twister sigil up.

"Here he comes," Jing sneered.

"Hello, ladies." Abel grinned. "May I have a word?"

NINETEEN

WATCH ME BEAT HOME SWEET HOME

"Do I know you?" Jing put her hands on her hips. "When I'm in the mood for college boys, I don't usually go for weirdo Christian private school fucks."

"How'd you guess? Abel Chantry, it's a pleasure." He extended a hand for her to shake, and when she didn't, he put it back in his pocket. His pupils were notable. Was he high? "Speaking of weird, I've got an odd question. Forgive me, but would the four of you have happened to attend a party in an abandoned house just outside of Sycamore Gorge township limits back in mid-October?"

"Um," Yates blinked, "that's kind of a weird question, but yeah."

"And the four of you are Daisy Brink, Lila Yates, Jing Gao, and Eloise Pike, is that correct?" He flashed his dimples at us, and the pictures in my pockets started itching. "I'd be very interested in talking to the four of you. Should we go someplace more private?"

"I was just thinking the same thing," said Jing. "Care to

step outside with us? If big college boy ain't scared of the cold, that is."

Abel beamed. "That sounds lovely," he said. "Shall we?"

"Can Levi come?" I crossed my arms over my chest, licked my chops, tried to make my shoulders fill up all the ceiling space. He was taller than me, but I leered like he wasn't. The twister sigil on the back of my hand ached. "It'd be more fun to have the both of you."

Daisy shot me a *the fuck do you think you're doing* glance.

First time I did the twister spell, there were four boys. I could take two. Fuck, if Sheriff Chantry came along, I could spin him as well. There'd be mortal fucking consequences for messing with the sheriff, but I would worry about that when I wasn't so livid. He deserved it. Holy fucking hell, he deserved it like no man I'd ever met. Where was Daisy's dad?

"Levi isn't feeling well," Abel said. "Perhaps he'll join us later."

"Poor baby," said Jing. "After you."

Yates squeezed my hand even tighter.

Abel nodded. He turned, whistling along with the cheery, drunken Buffett song, and strolled his way toward the door. The four of us followed close behind him. I felt a lick of joy when a catering elf shoulder-checked him along the way, and I tried to funnel that joy into arrogance. Arrogance was more combustible than confidence and I required fuel. It'd be cold outside.

I shook out my free wrist, stretched my fingers, made a fist.

Abel took the doorknob in his hands. He gave it a little jostle.

Daisy crossed her arms.

Jing sniffed, rubbed the floor with the toe of her shoe.

Yates leaned over to me, brushed her lips by my cheek and whispered, "Is it locked or something?"

"Wasn't when I came in," I said. "Which was what, twenty minutes ago? Could've locked it since then."

Abel couldn't open the door. He gave us all a smiling, apologetic glance, but his yanking got more intense. His arm stiffened up. A vein bounced in his jaw.

"Having a little trouble," Daisy sang, "with the knob, sweetie?"

"It's jammed," he said. His tone matched hers, or would've if he hadn't ruined it by clenching his teeth. "Has somebody locked it?"

"The little twisty bit above, there, that's the lock. Same with the little nipple on the knob itself. See how they're sticking up, not laying down? That means that the door isn't locked." Daisy vibrated with contempt. Her sugar tone could've stripped the varnish off a car. "Which means that I'm afraid you're just going to have to open it with your big witchfinder muscles, or else you aren't ever going to get us alone, and that would be so, so sad."

Hoo, yeah. That did it.

Abel jerked at the door with a rage I associated with day drinkers when their sportsball team ate it. His face burned a meaty red, and he wrenched the door with all his might. His shoulders worked under his jacket. His smile fell into a snarl. He was spitting, snorting like a boar, strangling the handle like he was trying to kill it.

Jing laughed.

Yates didn't. Her eyelashes brushed my temple. "Sideways," she whispered, "you said that Madeline is going to be here soon. What if she's already here?"

I nearly asked what she meant, but I answered my own question before the sound was out of my mouth. The door wasn't budging. The exertion Abel was burning yanking like this, it would be enough to bust some locks, and that didn't even matter because it wasn't locked. Daisy was right. There was no logical reason the door wouldn't open. It should've swung like a saloon.

"Help me check the windows," I said. I had a hunch, and it was a bad one.

Yates detached from my side. She beat me to the nearest window set, slipped her hands between the curtains and felt along the pane. She flipped latches, gripped the ledge, and heaved. Beside her at the adjoining window, I threw the curtains aside less ceremoniously. I grabbed the bottom of the window and pulled. Nothing.

Yates and I looked at each other.

These windows weren't going anywhere.

There were people watching. Not many, but more gathering by the second. Bleary eyes left their drinks and found us. Brows shot high or scrunched down low. The man who had yelled at the catering elves, who I presumed was the elusive Mr. Brink—he'd never gone to a football game to see Daisy cheer and he never picked her up from one of our houses, I'd never seen the man in person before—made a face like mad salami. How could such a toe have produced *Daisy Brink?*

"Daisy," I said. "Do you have a back door?"

"Yeah," she said. She looked between Yates and me. I think she got it; she leaned over, snapped something in Jing's ear, then straight back up. "Patio door's in the kitchen. There's another by the garage, but the garage door is shut."

"Shit," Jing hissed. She took a breath, spun on her heel, and seized Abel by the collar of his shirt. "Peace offering. Let's get her."

"I hate peace like I hate hell and *her*," Daisy snarled. "I don't give a damn about him, but she can't get off easy."

"Don't lose your head." I cracked my knuckles. "Jing's right. Kitchen. Let's move."

"Care to tell me what you're going on about?" Abel barked, gaped down at Jing's hand like a carp. "Get your hands off me, or I'll—"

"Shut up," Daisy barked.

Something crashed across the room and shattered. Punch bowl. Wassail oozed in red fingers across the floor. The elves who tended that snack table all bolted in opposite directions, threw their arms up over their faces.

All our spectators jerked their heads around.

The conversation muddled again. People were less fazed than after Daisy and I fucked up the Christmas trees, because it was hard to beat the spectacle of a plummeting mass of sharp plastic covered with wire and glass, but the locus of attention magnetized to the far side of the room nevertheless.

It was the snack table nearest the kitchen.

A girl in a hoodie stood on the table where the punch bowl had been.

Madeline.

Abel went rigid. He seemed to forget about Jing's hand and its proximity to his throat. He stared overhead with glee and seething abject hunger, the kind of open bloodlust an underfed dog offers to a neighbor's kitten.

Madeline's face stayed shadowed under the hood. I saw her mouth moving, the ebb and flow of her teeth, but I couldn't catch words. It was the same thing, over and over again. Lips, tongue, teeth in a clipped close circuit.

"She's praying," Abel said. "She knows what's coming."

"You are fucking deranged," Jing said. "She's casting."

Something came over me. Follicles prickled. Electricity fizzed between my fat and my skin. My knees went out and Daisy braced a hand against me, kept me upright. I saw her mouth move, saw her ask me what was wrong. I couldn't hear her, though. I couldn't hear anything. There wasn't chattering and Christmas music and the sound of endless bodies breathing. My head cleaved like a hoof.

"Addie!" Levi pushed his way through the crowd, big blue bug eyes swollen and gooey as hot marshmallows. He shoved drinking women aside, knocked an elf waiter's glasses off his tray, fought until he was before her. "Addie, I've missed you, come down and talk to me, oh Addie, I love you, I—"

"He'll break her fucking concentration," Jing said. "We got to get them the fuck away from her, and we need to talk her down before she does anything stupid. If Daisy and I—"

"We'll grab them by the scruff of the neck and hurl them down my basement stairs," Daisy said, "we gotta move quick and—"

"Sideways," Yates said, "we need to—"

Madeline pulled her hood back. There was writing on her athletic tape, she'd wrapped up her wrists and thumbs with it. Sigils and script. The base of her throat gleamed vermillion, like she'd popped a radioactive cherry down her gullet. There I was. I hoped I tasted like battery acid. She clapped her hands over her ears, dropped to her knees, and screamed.

In her head—in our head—she struck a fistful of matches against the rooves of our mouths. We gathered all the liquor up. We sucked in all the gases. We held the sparks inside our mouths, and we slit our cheeks, peeled them back, and breathed fire.

This witch burns back, bitch.

Gold busted up the sides of the room with a roar and a flash of broiling heat. Licks of it jumbled around curtains, lathered armchairs and flats of blue wallpaper—there were tongues over everything, all the tablecloths, the tables beneath them, over the jolly plush Santas they held and the nearby plastic firs, everything inanimate all roasting at once. The smell was thick, consuming, ridiculous. Melting Barbie smell, broken hairdryer, thick in the nostrils and awful.

The alcohol that'd been sloshed on the carpet jumped up as tall as Yates.

Black smoke funneled across the ceiling like a raincloud.

Everybody hollered. They dove over each other, all of Sycamore Gorge township's upper-middle class, all of them tangling, screaming, shoving their way toward the door that Abel Chantry had just failed to open. All those red dresses glowed like embers in the mounting fire. The blond bobs shimmered like light.

There was a sizzle of fear inside of Madeline, inside of us.

The plan was to burn the Chantry family. That was the incantation, to catch their clothes on fire, to burn them where they stood all at once, together.

The house was not the plan.

Sideways' fucking specter. Couldn't it do anything right?

We looked down at Levi. He was too pale for all this light, it made him absorb all the writhing orange and reflect it. Sunshine off a windshield. He stung to look at. Levi wasn't tearing his way over the sea of screaming parents. He wasn't diving toward the doors, wasn't hurling chairs at the windows, wasn't flushing against the walls in attempts to break through them, or else grind himself into gunk. He was standing, screaming up at us. Saying that nickname we hated.

You know what?

Maybe all of us burn to death in here.

So fucking be it.

"Sideways!" Jing and Yates said it at the same time. They yanked at me hard enough that I remembered where my body was. I sucked in a breath, which was a mistake. Breathing was noxious. I jerked my shirt over my nose, shook my head, thrashed my hands out at the wrists.

Mr. Scratch, in my head, was bawling. The fire, it was the fire. He remembered the fire. He remembered the way that fire felt, the way his daughters had smoldered, the sensation of his pages curling up like spider's legs. He remembered his ink boiling. I don't think he could speak.

"Can we break the door spell?" Yates shouted. She wrapped an arm over her head and jumped up and down. Her slippers were flimsy and the carpet smoldered beneath her. "Everybody is going to trample each other and there isn't even a bottleneck, oh my god, oh my god—"

"Stop," Jing shouted back, "we've got to focus, Christ, what if we went after Madeline, if we stop her from casting it might stop—"

"It won't," I said, "it'll keep burning. I don't think she can stop it or control it. I don't think she knows what the fuck is happening, we need to get out of here, that's what we need to do."

Sheriff Chantry was screaming orders that nobody heard.

People pounded on the windows with their fists.

"We have to make a door." There was something about Daisy that I didn't recognize. It was a lucidity that she usually fended off with substance or humor. A hardness. Her witch soul was like gunmetal, I'd somehow forgotten. Her hair strung over her face, her skirt whipped around her knees, but bridges could've been built off her resolve. She seized the hands beside her, Jing's and Yates', and the two of them followed her motion. They grabbed my hands.

"Make a door," Yates said. "How? What are we doing?"

"We could break a wall, or saw through it, or melt it, or something." Jing's resolve flickered. She gritted her teeth, leaned in. "If you have an idea, Daze, say it quick."

"We pick the house off the floor." Daisy looked at me. "Rip the walls off the foundations. Us on the ground, burning rubble in the air. No doors, no windows required. Floor becomes ground. Get it?"

Got it. We'd make it fly.

"We need a sigil," Yates said.

"Fuck sigils, we don't have time," Jing said.

"We're the sigil." I squeezed them tighter. The leather on my back was roasting. The screw-backs of spikes singed like cigarettes. "Your spell, Daze. Chant and we'll amp you up."

Daisy looked at her warping ceiling. Her neck went on forever. She said, "This is Daisy Stringer's house. It'll fly like she did. The walls will rip off the floor and fly, no weight, no rules, no gravity. This is Daisy Stringer's house, and the last thing it'll ever do is fly. Fly like I do. Get its ugly bulk off the face of the Earth."

"This is Daisy Stringer's house," the three of us said.

All I could think about was Dorothy's house snatched by tornadoes and carried to Oz.

"This is my house," Daisy said, "and it'll do as I say!"

Her house moaned inward. Walls bowed, accordioned. The whole structure shrieked around us, cried out with baritone snapping, screeching, the moan of distended wires and pipes. Boards sawed themselves from their bases. Splinters jagged from the floor like whale teeth. Fire rolled up the wallpaper in strips, and fleshy insulation peeked out of gashes like packed meat.

"It will fly like she does," we said.

Magic crackled. Everything crackled. My boots felt hot. The rubber was melting.

Mr. Scratch roused from his exhaustion to scream. Every lick of fire suspended him in unquenchable hysteria. He rasped his soft claws over my shoulders and wailed, screeched like something was being ripped out of him, made sounds in a language that came before language, the text of the swirling blue beyond. Mr. Scratch was the reason I'd been able to cast at all since Madeline robbed me, Mr. Scratch was the reason we could Chett our way through Sycamore Gorge West High's scum, Mr. Scratch was completely unresponsive, and I didn't have the bandwidth to do anything about it.

My jacket felt heavier. It felt like it was weighed down, like I'd pounded the pockets with something heavy. Like I'd filled the seams with rocks. Specter stones. They'd been so light before now.

"Leave earth and get higher," Daisy cried. "You're my house, you'll do what I say!"

"You'll do what she says," said Jing and Yates together.

People hurled themselves at the walls all around us. People crawled over each other, sobbed and shouted, broke one another underfoot. They swayed away from us in a circle. Their bodies contorted into shapes and I imagined those shapes like sigils.

I said, "We're the Scapegracers, I am a Scapegracer, I am the one who liberated you from that basement, from that drawer, from that witchfinder's lair. Help me. Help us. If you don't help us, we'll fucking die in here."

Mr. Scratch hollered, *My daughters, my daughters.*

Light spilled out of my pockets. It poured into the open air, tinged the bottom of my vision with dark iridescence. My skin crawled. The tiny hairs on my head bristled like grasses in a storm. My jaws ached, so I opened them, and the chants that Jing and Yates said fell off my tongue. The burning made my eyes water. I couldn't see the girls around me. I couldn't see the people falling over each other and battering their bodies against windows that wouldn't crack.

"You're my house," Daisy screamed. Her voice broke wet and jagged. "Rise."

"Rise," said us and a dozen dead witches all at once.

The walls lifted like stage curtains. The fire clung to them, shot high in the air like an artificial sun. The shell of the house floated above us, twenty feet in the air, suspended by nothing. Cold air huffed over our shoulders, blew in from every direction. There was no barrier between us and it. Busted, jaggedy boards and a shower of concrete dust hailed down from above. Splinters fell like snow. All the screaming people spilled out into the frigid white night, toppled like tackily dressed dominos.

The furniture blazed around us. It yawned smoke that make my skin feel tight.

Madeline still stood on the table. She hadn't moved her hands off her ears, hadn't found her feet again. She was bowed by the weight of her magic, or maybe her anguish. Maybe those things were the same.

People grabbed each other. Their Christmas sweaters and blazers and festive nice dresses looked covered in chalk. They clamored to their feet, clung to one another, and limped to the lawn and their cars. Outside—not that a place without walls or a ceiling could beg such a distinction—the animatronic fairy-light reindeer kept bobbing their heads up and down. The people who'd spilled out first grappled the reindeer to catch their breath. Someone stumbled into a blow-up Santa, whose billowing voluminousness enveloped them.

Ash and bits of cladding fell over our heads.

I looked up. The house floating high above shone light down upon us. It didn't look house-like from this distance, but I thought I saw the flower of the ceiling fan, and the batwing flapping of half-cremated drapes. It was transfixing. It was like our own, personal meteor. Flecks of it hurtled down around us in burning chunks. The longer I stared, the hazier its shape became. All the McMansion plywood, the staples that held it together came apart.

"When that thing comes down," Yates said, "it's not going to be in one piece."

"It's gonna be like Jenga blocks," Jing said. "It's gonna crush us."

"That's my house," Daisy said. "My room's up there." Her tone wasn't grief, it was something beside it. Drier and stickier. Socks staticky out of a dryer.

I squeezed Jing and Yates as hard as I could.

There was a streak of movement, someone running onto the charred hardwood instead of off it. They weaved between the flaming couch and armchairs, kicked aside a smoldering coat rack, and cut forward to the snack table. They broke for Madeline. White-blond hair. Shock-red face.

Abel Chantry.

He struck Levi, spun on his heels, and grabbed a fistful of Madeline's hair.

"Fuck," I said, "fuck, fuck, absolutely not."

"If we drop hands the house will crash," Jing hissed. "What are we supposed to do, huh?"

"Run," said Yates. Her eyes were huge, I saw the house's glow in them.

"Yeah," said Daisy. She shut her eyes. "Run like your fucking life depends on it."

"Like a burning house is about to crash on your head," said Jing. "Goody."

Abel had Madeline. She snapped to, lashed out against him, screamed a string of pre-linguistic curses and kicked out her heels. Abel yanked her head back. He foamed at the mouth, panted, grinned with all his teeth. He hauled her off the table, and he roped his forearm between her arms and her back. He spat on the floor beside them. "This is your bitch, Levi." His eyes swelled to fill his face, his head, his shoulders with rat-poison blue. "You didn't put her down, so I will. Man up. Come on."

Levi struck a pose of anguish, said, "God forgive me." Then he knelt, grabbed Madeline by the ankles. He didn't look strong, but he didn't budge when she thrashed against his grip. He looked at ravenous Abel, then down at the woman whose soul he stole. "It could have been good. You should've been good."

They dragged her thrashing toward the woods behind the lot, and then they sank between the flickering trees and out of sight, but not out of earshot. Madeline's voice clanged around the dome of my skull, seared through the pink stuff between.

The four of us looked at each other, horrified, nauseous.

A chunk of debris splattered on the flaming couch and went up in a plume of cinders.

"He's supposed to be Chett. We Chett-hexed him. How the fuck can he do that?" Daisy looked between the three of us. She looked, more specifically, at me. "How can he do that, Sideways?"

"I don't know." I curled my lip over my teeth. I thought

of the spell book in that evil room. Curse breakers. Fucking unfair.

"Ready to run?" Jing cracked her neck sideways.

"Yes," said Yates. She bit her lip, sucked in a breath. "On three."

"One," said Yates.

"Two," said Jing.

"Three," said Daisy.

We dropped our hands and sprinted. Fire trucks wailed up the driveway, and in the receding throng of drunk-charred partiers, Elias Chantry screamed, "David, has anyone seen David, where's my son David, oh holy God!"

My boots crunched snow.

The Brink house struck the earth in smithereens.

TWENTY

THE COMEDOWN

Yates and I found each other first. She threw an arm around my neck, and we carried each other around the rubble pile's corner. There was a glimmer of pale hair, and a moment later Jing was upon us, weaving her way into our grapple.

"Where's Daze?" Jing looked at us. There was soot like a slash across her nose. "I can't find her anywhere."

Panic spiked in my stomach. It tasted like curdled milk.

What the fuck was happening to Madeline Kline right now?

"Daisy is an athlete, she outran the crash if we did," Yates insisted. She shivered against me, and I wished my coat didn't have spikes, wished it wouldn't scrape her. A flicker of guilt gnawed me, and I ripped the thing off, cast it around her shoulders. Yates accepted with a nod. She shrank into the battered leather. "We'll keep looking. She can't be far."

"She could've run out the other direction," Jing said. "I checked around the left flank, we'll try the right."

"Let's move." The wind didn't register as cold. I'd been an inch from baking in the house, and the winter that braced me now evened things out. I tingled all over. I was thawing in reverse. I headed to the right, and Jing and Yates kept step with me.

When the house struck the ground, it'd folded in zigzags, like a mammoth, hideous squeeze-box. The mismatched windows wobbled, the tacky gables ridged like a dinosaur's back, the garage door crunched up like old paper. The fire rolled off it, consumed everything with a supernatural hunger. Ash piled on the snow, mixed with it, gave it freckles.

Fuck, there was so much house.

We sprinted around a corner, rounded toward the back.

Firefighters hauled the vipers out of their truck and choked them, pumped water over the wreckage and made it sizzle. Elias was screaming *David, David.* I thought about him ratting around upstairs, crouched in Daisy's bathroom with his fingers in her drawers.

Mr. Scratch coalesced between my radii and ulnae. He throbbed in my arms like a beesting, but he calmed himself down enough to make words. *Do you think he'll understand, Sideways? Do you think he'll understand what is wrought when your children die in fire?*

"I know he won't."

"There she is," Jing gasped. She jolted forward, and I careened after her, grabbed Yates' hand so that we didn't fly apart. Jing was the fastest of the three of us. She got to her first.

Daisy stood with her back against a tree. Her face bled

from a dirty cut that stretched from her temple to the edge of her mouth. It oozed down her neck, it pooled in her collarbone. Clumps of her hair stuck to it. She didn't look at us when we scrambled over. She was looking away from the house, back into the thick of the forest.

"Holy fuck," Jing said, "Daze, you're bleeding, what—"

"I was waiting for you," she said. She flicked her eyes over us, each of us, then looked back into the woods. "Come on."

I heard a howling in the distance.

Madeline.

"Did you hit your head?" Yates was insistent, she grabbed Daisy's sleeve and tugged it backwards. "If you have a concussion, one of us should walk you back around, there are ambulances and—"

"I'm fine," she spat. "Sideways, you wanted the Chantry boys outside, you've got them. Have anything stronger than a Chett hex?"

"I'll do my best," I said.

"Good." Daisy shoved herself off the tree and stalked deeper into the forest.

None of us needed any more encouragement. We followed her in.

The woods swallowed sound. The sirens faded out into a baseline warble, and the crunchy spit of fire staticked to white noise. Snow fell on our shoulders, and we bore forward. Madeline was a singer. She had lungs like a monster. Her screaming was an easy beacon to follow.

Daisy's strides broke into a full-fledged run, and we followed suit, hurtled after her between the naked slants of trees.

The snow on my cheek was hot.

Wasn't snow, then. Funny feeling.

There they were. The Chantry brothers and Madeline, who they'd shoved up against an oak. The boys stuck out like lighthouses in the darkness. It was that blister-blond hair. They looked like fog with shoulders. I couldn't tell them apart from the back. Madeline was howling, and the boys, each one of them with one of her arms in their grip, screamed at each other like children.

"You said you took her specter," Abel snarled. "Clearly you were mistaken."

"I did, I took it, it's at home in my room!" Levi spat at him, literally spat at him. "She's harmless, she's supposed to be harmless, I declawed her!"

"I fucking hate you, I hate you, I hate you," Madeline howled. "I hate you, I hate you—"

"The arson show wasn't proof enough? You're so stupid. You fucked up and whatever happened, whoever dies in this fire, it's your fault, Levi. You're such a fuckup! I can't believe we took care of you after you crawled your way home, bawling like a little girl because mean sluts at a party hexed you. We shouldn't have wasted our time on you. We shouldn't have burned through half the specter store to scrub the curse off. You're such a waste of space, and when we've taken Addie's specter, for real this time, I am going to wring your neck."

"Let go of me, let go of me," Madeline wheezed, "don't touch me, don't you fucking touch me, I hate you, I hate you!" She jerked herself against them, sobbed and sputtered and kicked her feet. They held her like stigmata, and if she kept writhing like this, she'd pop an arm out of socket. "You evil fucks, let me go!"

"You're hurting her, Abel," said Levi, also hurting her.

"She's not a girl, Levi. She's a witch." Abel flattened his tongue over his incisors. "Witches don't feel pain. I'm not taking this with a sigil. I'm not praying over her, laying hands on her. I'm carving it out of her neck with a knife, and you are going to handle the body."

"She's not a witch, I fixed her! I love her! She's my soulmate!"

"I hate you! I hate you! I want you to die!"

"Hey, assholes!" Daisy's blood splashed her shoes. "*Children of the Corn* motherfuckers, I'm talking to you!"

Abel and Levi jolted. They looked at each other, then over their shoulders, mirror images. They didn't let go of Madeline.

Abel clucked his tongue and said, "Behold the Jezebel brigade who broke you in October. That's them, isn't it, Levi?"

"Yeah," said Levi. He fixed his eyes on Yates. "Those are the ones."

"Let go of her," Yates said. She stiffened beside me, squeezed my hand tighter, tossed back her head. The leather jacket brushed the backs of her knees. The patch nearest me read, GRIND THE BONES OF ABUSERS FOR BREAD. "Don't touch her."

Abel laughed, boyish and merry. It was a laugh that sold products in warmly lit propaganda commercials, a laugh that brightened up a boardroom, a laugh that buried accusations. "Lila, sweetheart. You better watch. This'll be you, soon enough, if you aren't a good girl who coughs her evil up willingly. This is for her own good. It looks bad, but that's because you don't know what you're looking at. We're the good guys, Lila. I'm a good guy. Watch and see."

"Fuck off," I breathed. I held my twister sigil hand close to my teeth, grabbed the edge of the gauze, and yanked. Shiloh's wrappings loosened. I sank my nails into my naked palm, cut into the scribbled sigil, and felt Mr. Scratch well beneath my skin.

The trees swayed overhead.

Jing's and Yates' and Daisy's hair flew around their faces, splayed and tossed and rearranged. Dead leaves pulled themselves out from under the snow, cinders billowed, litter danced circles around our ankles.

Abel's and Levi's legs shot out. Their left feet stabbed the earth, and they traced a slow semicircle, stiff as a pair of drawing compasses. Their faces warped—shock, confusion, bewilderment, fury. They lost their grip on Madeline at the same time. They spread apart from each other, spun faster, made their music-box ballerina circuits an inch above the earth. They shouted at each other, but the air caught them and twirled them higher, higher, up where the canopy would be come spring. Levi's arms trailed helplessly. Abel, in a poor attempt to wriggle out of it, bent his arms on either side of his head.

Madeline hit the ground running.

Jing and Daisy were on her at once.

"You've got something that belongs to Sideways," said Daisy.

"You're going to give it back," said Jing.

"Whoa," said Yates. She craned her neck to watch Abel and Levi, put a hand over her eyes, and spoke with a nervous, discordant brightness. Her knees shook. "That's cool! Is this a new spell, Sideways? It's beautiful—what's the sigil look like?"

"It's inherited." I showed her my palm. "One of Scratch's daughters from before us. Her name was Laverne."

"Thank you, Laverne," Yates said. She cradled the back of my hand in both of hers, pressed my palm against her cheek. "Thank you, Mr. Scratch."

"I'm fucking sorry," Madeline growled, "but I need it, I can't be without a specter again, I didn't have a choice—"

"I have your specter," I said.

She snapped her attention to me. "You what?"

"It was under Levi's pillow. Shiloh and I stole it back."

"Where is it?" Madeline froze. She looked at me like she had when we met, like I was something beautiful, a feat of biological architecture unparalleled in other living beings. Like I was something to look at. "Where's my specter, Sideways?"

I turned to Yates, looked at her, at the way Boris' jacket fit her. Holy hell, she was beautiful. I shook my head. I'd put the specters in my pockets. Three pockets, all full of specters. Which one had I put hers in? I stared at Yates, blinked a few times.

"You know where it is," Madeline seethed, "right?"

"We can't do this here," Jing said. "We gotta get going. This isn't a safe spot for this. Sideways, how much longer can you keep them spinning up there?"

"Dunno," I said. "A few more minutes, maybe."

"This place already has ambulances and fire trucks. Elias is here, and so there's gonna be troopers, too, I'd put my life on it." Jing shook her head. "Where should we go?"

"The Delacroix House," said Yates. "It feels safer."

"They'll be open for another two hours." Daisy looked over her shoulder. "If we're going to go, we've gotta go now."

"You can't take me to the Delacroix House," Madeline said. "You can't, they'll be so mad at me, I'll be so, so fucked."

"Delicious," said Jing. "Let's move."

Madeline opened her mouth to protest, but Daisy whirled on her. A drop of her blood splashed against the bridge of Madeline's nose. "You just burned my fucking house down. You tore my friend's soul out, which is the very fucking thing you were going to get revenge on the Chantry boys for, and you *burned* down my *fucking* house. I'm homeless now. You did that. If you want your soul back, Madeline, you better shut the fuck up and follow us. Don't try shit. Don't you even consider it. I swear to god, I'll make your life a living hell. If Maurice punishes you, know that it's a fraction of what I'd do if I was the one picking. Are you coming with us, or are you not?"

Madeline set her teeth in a line. Her eyes went watery. She didn't protest.

"That's what I thought." Daisy about-faced, stomped back toward the house. "My car keys are in the ruins. Jing, say you've got your keys."

Jing felt herself up, pulled the ring from her back pocket. "Yeah, we're good."

"Hey," Yates said. "You can stay with me for as long as you want, okay?"

Daisy didn't say anything to that. She trudged forward, and we followed her in silence until the house was back in sight. In the time we'd spent away, the house had fallen in on itself. Water spouted over the blackened pieces. The two floors condensed into one, and the one tilted like a soufflé.

Jing put a hand on Daisy's back.

Yates rubbed little circles on her shoulder with the hand that wasn't locked with mine.

Somewhere behind us, I heard a snap and an *oof.*

The Chantry boys must've hit the ground.

"Hey, uh." I cleared my throat. "We should maybe run."

"Yeah?" said Daisy.

"Yeah," I said.

We ran. The space we crossed was where the garden would be in summertime; it was framed with tall edges and low piles of thorny vines. The husks of dead-yellow flowers jutted through the ash and the snow.

I imagined the slump of Daisy Stringer somewhere beside us as we passed.

"Daisy!" It was a bark, an order. The man who I assumed was Mr. Brink stomped his way toward us. There was ash in his mustache. "Daisy, I've been calling for you, Jesus Christ. There was a gas explosion. Sheriff Chantry's kid is dead, I've been having a fucking panic attack. Why's there blood on your face? Are you hurt? Hey, talk to me—where do you think you're going?"

"Jing's house," she snapped. She didn't look at him, walked past like he wasn't there. "I'm fine, leave me alone."

Miraculously, he fucking did. He put his hands on his hips and grumbled.

Not the my-kid-nearly-died reaction I would've expected.

Particularly given that, you know, somebody's kid was literally dead.

An awful somebody's awful kid.

Did we do that?

I'd feel something later, maybe. I'd feel something when I had the capacity to think about it. I'd feel empathy because a kid is a kid at some point. Maybe I would. Maybe I was a fucking weirdo whose empathy was broken, because I saw the sheriff bent over a stretcher that the firefighters had hauled out of the house, saw him touch the hair of his burnt-up son. It was just far enough away that they looked tiny, but I heard him. He sounded like the sirens.

He voluntarily kicked out one of his children to fend for themself. To freeze in this storm.

I didn't look at them for long. I looked down and kept moving.

We made our way onto the quickly emptying lawn. Cars pulled out one after another, abandoned the scene's carnage at top speed. I couldn't say I blamed them. One of them backed up into a light-and-wire reindeer, sped away before anybody could accuse them of shit. Assuming they noticed, that is.

Jing's convertible flashed when she smashed the unlock button. She strode up ahead of us, climbed in and started the car. It thrummed. She climbed out to swipe the snow-fluff off her windshield, and Daisy and Yates and I, Madeline trailing, all gathered around the back bumper.

"Who's in the back with traitor?" Daisy jerked her chin up. "Yates, are you game?"

"Yates should sit up with Jing," I said. I didn't want the stones next to Madeline, even if Madeline didn't know they were in there. She was willing to burn herself and an entire party to dust if it meant getting revenge on the fucks who'd ripped her soul out, and I didn't want that energy in arm's reach of the jacket. I didn't trust her not to do something stupid. I rubbed my mouth. "I'll sit in the back with Daisy. Madeline, you're in the middle seat."

Madeline didn't say anything. Her expression was inscrutable.

Yates pulled herself into the front seat, pressed her

cheek against the glass. "This is awful," she said. "Oh, Daisy. I'm so sorry."

I took the right seat, Madeline slid in the middle, then Daisy closed off the left. Our reflections in the rearview mirrors looked cartoon-levels of tense.

"So." Daisy ran her thumbnail along the corner of her mouth. She looked at Madeline, who sat stiffly beside her, with an unfathomably venomous look. "Why didn't you come to us? The Scapegracers spend most of our time hexing abusive jerks. You couldn't have found a group alive more predisposed to helping you. We would've done a lot for you. Instead, you nearly killed one of us, and then you burned down my house with a fifth of the town inside." Her eyes sparkled. "What the fuck were you thinking? Did you think? Did you even consider—"

"You weren't witches when I found you. You were a group of cliquey basics and one witch who'd clearly never seen a proper coven, and hardly knew the half of how magic works. I couldn't ask you for help. I didn't know you." Madeline saw Daisy's ire and matched it. She filled the back of the car with the sheer force of her might, and she peered down at her with unabashed loathing. "Don't you talk to me about shit you don't understand."

"Jesus fucking Christ." Jing cranked up her radio, and she sped out of the lot with a squeal of tires on wet grass. "It's an hour to the Delacroix House and we're going to be quiet 'til then. A kid died and a home is gone. Be fucking pensive. Introspect. Don't run your mouths, capisce?"

"Capisce," said Yates, the only person who Jing hadn't addressed.

"Give Madeline the aux cord," I said. I put my head back against the seat, and before Daisy could protest, I held up my hands. "Death row meal. We listen to whatever music she wants. Sound good?"

"If it shuts all of you up, I'm happy," said Jing.

I thought Daisy would protest, but she didn't.

Yates looked at me, and a flare of warmth burned in my stomach. Approval from Lila Yates so beat approval from god or anything else. Lila Yates was better. She nestled into the coat I'd let her borrow, and yeah, the coat that wasn't mine, but still gave me a weird little head rush to behold. A girl had never worn my jacket before.

Fuck. What about Jing? What about *Can I kiss you?* What about Daisy, who I'd been so fucking mad at, who'd stood up for me and come out and hugged me so hard that we'd ruined Christmas? The only girl in this car I'd ever gone out with was the one who'd organ-thieved me.

I'd get my specter out of her throat soon. I tried to make myself focus on that.

All of you are in a car together, Mr. Scratch said, *driving away from the witchfinders with your souls in your bodies. My daughters together, all breathing, all whole. I am so proud of you. I love all of you so. May I talk to Daisy? Could you pass a bit of me to her?*

"Daisy," I said.

She leaned forward, looked at me with her brows knit up.

"Scratch wants a word." I held out my hand.

She took it, and a spiral of ink bled out from under my fingernail and oozed under her cuticle. Daisy shivered, grabbed my hand as if she needed help balancing, and shut her eyes tight. Mr. Scratch didn't tell me what he told her, but I doubt I needed it like she did.

Madeline stared down at our hands with bewilderment.

"Just play your music," I said. "Don't worry about it."

"Sideways," she said. "I really was planning on giving it back to you. It hardly worked for me, anyway. The fire wasn't . . . that wasn't what I was planning."

"I know," I said. I lolled my head back, flattened my free hand over the dome of my skull. "I saw inside your head every now and then. I knew what you were planning."

She jammed her tongue in her cheek. With the look on her face, I wasn't sure if she had realized that. "I liked you. I really did."

"Whatever." I breathed out once through my nose, hard. "Thanks for the haircut."

Her perpetually half-shut eyes went through every lunar phase in the span of a second.

"Play your fucking music, alright?"

She plugged in her phone obediently. My specter flashed in her neck, pressed itself near me. It strained against her skin. It puckered it, glowed like a spider bite.

Her music flickered on, and Jing cranked it high.

It was her solo song. We all sang it.

✴ TWENTY-ONE ✴

SURGERY FOR FREE

The Delacroix House dusted in snow was a bear trap for Hansel and Gretel. It looked delicious, like its wooden curls and pink turrets would crack between the teeth like wafers, the shingles coated in chocolate, the edging licorice ropes. The place you find when you're cast out and dying and fresh out of breadcrumbs. It *was* a witch house, after all.

It was supposed to be open until 2:00 a.m.

The windows looked dark. No porch lights.

"Fuck," Jing cursed. Literally, maybe. She slammed her palms against the steering wheel, but instead of pulling out of the lot—it was perfect before we'd blasted up, powder unbroken by tires or footsteps—she cut the music and wrenched open the car door. "It's a Friday night, why the fuck wouldn't they be open?"

"Maybe Maurice is traveling, or they've planned a staff in-service or something," Yates tried. "There's still a chance we could swing by first thing tomorrow, right?"

"We're getting Sideways' specter back tonight. Nonnegotiable." Daisy's cheek had stopped bleeding, and the mostly dry gore on her face looked like chocolate tar. It cracked when she spoke and was molten underneath. "I'll pry it out of Madeline on the hood of this car if need be. With pleasure."

"It's fucking freezing out. We're going inside." Jing stepped out of the car. "When Sideways and I saw Maurice in Dorothy's, it was right after we went upstairs and broke that vase. He said we weren't breaking in because anybody with a specter can open the doors. Wouldn't that be true for the front door, or a side door or something?"

"Is it?" Yates peeked back at Madeline.

Madeline didn't say anything. She stared at her hands.

"Worth a fucking try," Jing said. She slammed the car door shut and stalked up toward the house, across the candy-cane-lined walkway and up the broad porch steps. Her purse, which was more like a little backpack than a clutch, reflected the car lights across its heart-shaped face. Her shoulders shrank, then vanished. I thought something against the house went ajar, but Daisy was closer than I was, and my scanty vantage didn't reveal jack shit. "It's cold as a witch's tit."

"I'm the witch," Daisy said. She spat blood.

"You know how to pick a lock, right?" Yates reached back and prodded Daisy in the knee. "You should go help Jing. If the door doesn't magically open, she might really need you. I don't think she'd tap out if it doesn't swing when she says *open sesame*."

"I guess." Daisy kicked open her door and slithered onto the lot beneath it, catching herself just before her chest would've struck the snow. She was more flexible than I usually considered human beings to be. I suppose she had to be, what with all her flippy jumpy cheer stunts that she'd won so many ribbons for crushing. She didn't close the door behind her. She didn't look back, just trudged into the dark with her feet in Jing's footprints. To spare her shoes further damage, maybe. Or for fun.

She deserved fun.

We'd have to have a talk soon.

Being next to Madeline's throat was making me feel rabid. It'd been an hour of sitting next to her, myself inside her, and not clawing my way out. I weighed the benefits of just doing it in the car.

It'd hurt her, and maybe me. Also, I didn't know which of the specters in the jacket was hers, or which pocket it was, and I'd need to spread them out to do a proper search. The dashboard wouldn't cut it. I remembered the minutes between Madeline leaving me and Mr. Scratch possessing me, the time I spent paralyzed on the floor, in the dark, with my nails carving dents in the floorboards. I wouldn't do that to another person. Not when I had a humane option just a few picked locks away.

I made myself look at something that wasn't her neck.

Daisy had left behind a little bloodstain on the seat, so I looked at that. The stain looked like dried peppers, flat and brackenish. There was more of it than there should've been. Face wounds bleed a lot, but still. She maybe should've gone to the hospital, gotten it cleaned and glued up. She could've stayed with the medics while the rest of us came here. There'd been ambulances all over the place, noisy as all hell and strobing like party lights. Somebody had to reinflate all the trampled soccer moms.

You're together again. You had to do this together, as a coven. Splitting off from her would have seemed like rejection, said Mr. Scratch. He sounded strained, still worn, still warped from the fire. *She never would've said yes, and it would've been cruel to make her. It will be alright. I won't let her die.*

Maurice might be inside. He knows some minor healings. Also, it might have escaped your memory seeing as you had significantly larger dolphins to fry, but Maurice was desperate to put me back in a vase and employed a whole bushel of witches to pursue me. They didn't catch me because I am very slippery, and I have you. Still. There's the off chance that he'll want to snatch me up and bottle me again if I'm loose. When you make the switch, I'll have to be stowed in something. I don't want to be bottled up again. I don't want to be up there.

"Don't you worry about that," I murmured. "You're our spell book, now and forever. I wouldn't let anybody get their hands on you. Also, the expression is 'bigger fish to fry,' I think."

Yes! I was embellishing. Is a dolphin not a fish?

Fuck. My brain roommate was moving out and I was going to be alone in this big empty house. Better throw a party or something.

I'll miss you, too. You were an excellent familiar. Is a party inside your body just eating a handsome slice of cake?

"This might be a horrible thing to say," Yates said, "but I think there's a silver lining to her house burning down."

"Silver linings aren't horrible," I said. I couldn't imagine what the silver lining could be, but I was willing to entertain the idea of one existing.

"No house means that living with the three of us, instead of at home, is a possibility. That could be a good thing."

"Is her dad—" I searched for words. My taffy brain was empty of them. "Bad?"

I knew the answer was yes, but I knew none of the specifics. Didn't know the extent of the badness, or its particulars.

"It's bad. It's been bad. I think since her mother's passing, their relationship has been fraught at best. It's not really my story to tell. Anyway, she came out today, and it went over *poorly*. If the big party wasn't tonight, I'm not sure how far it would've gone. As it stands, he's revoked her college fund, has sworn to cut off any and all support after graduation, no inheritance, no nothing. It goes on."

"Right," I said. "Jesus."

Madeline unbuckled herself. She looked down at Daisy's blood. After a moment, she reached down and touched it, crushed it into cayenne between her finger and her thumb.

"I hate fighting," Yates said. "I've seen too much of it this week. I'm really not proud of us, and I hope that we can be friends again like we were. Can we mend and make do?"

I shook my head. "It's fine. We'll be fine."

"Good," she said. She cozied up inside the jacket, scrunched up her nose. "I feel kind of badass in this. Like a video game character." She slipped her hands lower, brushed her fingertips overtop of the pockets. She blinked. "Are you carrying around a bunch of rocks?"

It was like Madeline Kline was activated. Her eyes snapped up. Her energy magnified. She sat upright and her hands twitched. She said, "There are stones in your pockets?"

"Yeah," said Yates as she scooched away from the back seat. She cast her a look, specifically the look she gave men who perked up at the notion that Yates might be in possession of a phone number. Pressed her hands against the seam between dash and door. "Why?"

"Don't," I warned, but whoops. Too slow.

Madeline launched. She threw herself between the driver's and passenger's seat, slammed the gear shift with her elbow and clawed for Yates. She clapped her hands over the jacket. She snarled and swore, battered her hands around the pockets, but before her hands could mongoose around inside of them, Yates yelped and twisted away, swatted at Madeline's twisting wrists.

I seized Madeline by the jacket hood and the loop of her jeans, made my hands into fists and yanked her backwards, hard. She braced for it, but not fast enough. I hauled her across the back seat. The hood-scruffing must've slammed her in the throat because she wheezed and convulsed once, sputtered as she struck the vinyl upholstery. The nape of her neck landed at the edge of what had been Daisy's seat. She gasped. Her left knee slammed against my stomach, and I fell across her, sputtering. She screwed her body under me, beat her forearms into my chest, and I blinked through all the spots in my vision and found her collarbone and heaved my weight against it.

"Get off me," Madeline spat. "You're crushing me, get off!"

"What the hell is happening!" Yates threw her hands up. "We were chill five seconds ago, oh my gosh, stop it!"

"Yates, get out of the car," I growled. "Go stand with Jing and Daze, okay?"

"That's my specter!" She kicked out her feet, tangled them inadvertently with mine. "Give it to me, Yates, it's mine!"

"That's big talk out of you." I repositioned myself, pressed the meat of my forearm across her chest, braced her head in place with my opposite palm. "You lied to me, you fucking lured me upstairs under what pretenses? Huh? Making out with me? We're doing this shit on *my* terms, and that means you're going in the Delacroix House and I'm getting back what's mine, then you'll get yours, then the witches here will do what they think they should with you and that's not my problem, fuck, stop squirming, fuck!" Her teeth glowed against my skin. She clamped hard. Pain flowered in my arm. I didn't let up until the skin broke, and in that moment, she launched herself backwards, out of the open car door with my blood on the edge of her mouth. It was bizarre to be so near to her. To be so near myself. I looked at my bite mark and wanted to laugh.

"I'm not going in there," she spat as she found her feet on the snow beside the car.

"The fuck you are," I said. I wolfed after her, hands and knees until my torso jutted out of the door and my fists were around her waist. I jerked her backwards, lugged her middle toward the seat. "You're not running away, you're going to sit and wait until we've got the door open, then you're going to—"

"Shut up," she hissed. She bashed her hands against mine, clawed at my bruised knuckles, pinched and squeezed and jammed them. "Shut up, shut up, I can't believe I liked you, I—"

"You tricked me into thinking you wanted to be my girlfriend," I said, "so that you could mug the soul out of me! Holy fuck, Daisy's right, it's a damn good thing that we're letting Maurice decide what happens—"

"Do you think that he's smarter than you? Kinder than you? Maurice is an art dealer who lets covens store their shit in his attic, Sideways. Nobody is in charge here. There aren't laws and there aren't rules and there aren't parents who'll take care of you. Maurice is going to call my coven, is what he's going to do."

"You have a coven?" I balked, pulled her back harder. In the back of my head, I recalled Jacques mentioning that she was a Corbie, and remembering only made me angry.

"Where the hell are they, then? Hasn't he called them already? Shouldn't they be on your rescue mission, shouldn't they have helped you so that you didn't have to rip me up? What the fuck is wrong with you that your own coven wouldn't help you?" I curled my lip. "I can't believe this."

"Jesus fucking Christ, Sideways! I fucked a witchfinder, and I stayed when I knew what he was," Madeline cried out. "Everybody who knew excommunicated me. If people at the Delacroix called the Corbies, that means they didn't care to look for me, but now that somebody's gone ahead and caught me for them? God, I hate this. I hate witches, I hate you, let go of me, I just want everything to go back to *normal*, I want to fucking play basketball and go to prom and ruin my life for teenage reasons, they'll kill me, Sideways, they'll fucking kill me. Let me go. Let go!"

My throat felt hard. Maybe Scratch was calcifying inside it.

"I'm sorry, Madeline." Yates perched herself up by the windshield, as far from the tussle as she could feasibly be. There were tears on her face. They dripped stripes down her chin. "I'm so sorry about all of this, about everything."

"What's going on?" Jing's voice.

I snapped my head up.

Jing and Daisy descended on the car together. They must not have been running long, but they'd broken into a sprint as soon as they saw the struggle. They closed in. Each grabbed one of Madeline's wrists, and something in Madeline's posture changed. All the tightness down her back went slack. The slackness followed all the way down the backs of her legs, and in an instant she was boneless. She noodled in our grip, and Jing and Daisy heaved to keep her upright. Jing pulled one arm over her shoulders, and Daisy mirrored with the other.

I let my hands fall off her.

I felt a smack of something nauseous.

Guilt, maybe. Something like.

"She tried to make a break for it," Yates said.

"Yeah?" Jing peered in the car. Her eyes fixed on Yates' face, specifically the rivulets that marked her from socket to jaw. "You're crying. Did Madeline hurt you?"

Yates whipped her head *no*. She rubbed the back of her wrists over her face, smeared the tears around until they formed a glossy salt mask. "She didn't touch me."

"She better not have," said Daisy. She looked down her bloody nose. "We got the door open. The main door had a specter lock, so that was fine. The screen door had a traditional lock but I picked that shit, no problem." They'd taken a while. I felt like it'd been a problem. "Let's go. It's time to put your guts back, Sideways."

I nodded. I felt thawed. Joy and dread, love and repulsion.

"Come on," Jing said. She started forward, and Daisy matched her pace. They lugged Madeline up the walk. Her feet being limp as they were meant that her heels were level with the candy-cane heads, and I kept waiting for them to tilt, hook her ankles.

"This is a good thing," I said. "I'm getting my specter back. We're doing the right thing."

"It's a good thing," said Yates. "It's the only thing."

It is, Mr. Scratch assured. *It's not the part that ought to concern us come morning time.*

I bit my tongue. Looked up at Yates, who'd climbed out of the car and was walking in the same direction as Daisy, Jing, and Madeline, save for the fact that she'd hesitated and waited up. Looked over her shoulder back at me. Raised her brows like, *Are you coming?*

I shoved myself off the car and took a few strides forward.

Yates linked hands with me.

"You're amazing and everybody loves you," I said. Snow flaked down from the sky again, fine and crushed-glass bright. It dusted her curls. We made our way up the walkway, and my stomach dropped.

I was getting my soul back.

I was going to be myself again, unshattered.

Up ahead, Jing and Daisy lugged Madeline into the shadowy house. The toes of Madeline's sneakers were the last thing to disappear into the darkness, dragging and squeaking until they vanished from sight. Even then, the squeaking lingered.

"We all love you, too," she said.

We walked up the steps. They sang underfoot rather than creaking.

Yates pushed open the door, and we passed through one by one.

Jing and Daisy bickered in the dark. Vagaries about whether or not they should turn on a lamp. Upside: it wouldn't be dark. Downside: people might know we're in here. Rebuttal: we are obviously in here. Objection: that doesn't mean we should flip on all the lights and make the house into a giant beacon of having been trespassed. The house having been trespassed should not show that shit off.

"Was that a fucking ablative absolute? Unbelievable," said Daisy.

"I literally have no idea what that means," said Jing.

Yates tugged the chain of a Tiffany lamp. Light flooded through the stained glass, revealed Jing and Daisy and Madeline all on the floor in the tinted pink and indigo glow. They each held one of Madeline's arms down, not that it seemed necessary. Madeline wasn't moving. I don't think she was in her body properly. Her eyes focused on nothing. They were unreflective and small-pupiled.

The Delacroix House had changed up its display a bit since last I'd been here.

An enormous painting of two naked sailors, dappled peachy in impressionist brushstrokes, floated up above us like a pair of embracing angels. There were flowers on every surface, lurid orchids and big wilting peonies, and fabrics too rich for casual display. Velvets that might've lived in the Vatican once. Heavy cream silks, crunchy brocade, translucent linens that folded like plaits of hair. The DELACROIX HOUSE neon scrawl flickered on without our say-so, and it wrung prisms from the crystal chandelier.

Madeline had been slammed on the ornate carpet, and the patterns around her head looked like little moving animals. Madeline shut her eyes and panted.

"Sideways." Daisy made eyes at me. Her face was a horror show. I don't think it'd ever be quite the same. "I'm ready for this night to get better."

"Yeah." I bounced from toe to toe. "Yeah, we should be ready."

"Where does Mr. Scratch go?" Jing jerked her head to the side, an attempt to flip her hair out of her eyes that failed. Chunks of stringy, ash-splattered blond clung to her cheeks and nose. "Once we put you into you, he's gotta go somewhere, doesn't he? Shouldn't he go first?"

"Yeah," I blinked. The idea of doing this without Scratch inside me was horrifying, but it made sense and I felt myself bending to it. He made soothing sounds in the back of my head. Sounds that reminded me that my Scape-gracers could cast for me, that I just needed to move the sigil on my hand around, that I wasn't going to be gasping alone in a broken-up attic. I was going to be fine. Mr. Scratch deserved it. I thought a little harder and it hit me. "Fuck, I don't have a book on me." Without a book, he'd have nowhere to go. It was light in here, now. He hated the light. It'd be torture, making him just linger around on the carpet without a vessel to hold him. He was a liquid creature. He was sort of squiggly useless without a shell.

Jing let go of Madeline. She pulled her purse off her back and unzipped it, stuck her hand in the little holographic pouch and rooted around. While she was rummaging, Daisy positioned herself at Madeline's head, put one of her hands on Madeline's upper arm where Jing had just been pressing. A second later, Jing pulled something out of her purse. It was a small something, cardboard and marbled.

"A composition notebook?" Daisy snorted. "Seriously?"

"It's brand new. I bought it for cramming this weekend, so that I might have a chance of actually passing my Chem final." Jing stretched her hand out, offered me the notebook. "I know it's boring, but it's what I have. What's Scratch think? Would he mind?"

No, Mr. Scratch said. He curlicued over my shoulders and made a purring sound. It massaged a bit. Almost tickled. *I wouldn't mind in the least.*

"He's cool with it," I said. I tucked the book under my arm, then spun around to face Yates. "Hey, so uh." I cleared my throat. "I need the jacket back."

"Okay." She pulled it off, folded it in half, and tossed it to me.

The spikes shimmered in an arch.

I caught the jacket wrong. My hand closed around the bottom half of it, which meant the top half swung down by my knees like a banner. It hung upside down, and out of its pockets rained an endless onslaught of specter stones. They crashed around my feet, skittered out across the hardwood floors, shot under the legs of antique furniture and clattered against walls. The picture papers I'd stolen, the ones with names and addresses, managed not to flake out on me. They stayed in the jacket, even when I threw it aside in a moment of abject horror.

"What the fuck?" Jing recoiled from the hailstorm I'd wrought.

I dove to my knees, pawed around for the stones, tried to rake them toward me like coins in a scraper arcade game. They kept slipping through my claws. I grit my teeth. "Shi and I found these in a drawer in the Chantry house, we just took the lot, I figured, I mean I thought that, *boy* these are slippery."

"There it is." Madeline sat up so abruptly that she tore herself out of Daisy's grip. She toppled forward, shot on her stomach under the welcome podium. She jammed her hand underneath and snaked it around. None of us moved to stop her. She pulled herself free a moment later, held her violet specter between her first and second fingers. She grinned like a maniac. Choked a sob. "It's here. I'm here."

I got off my knees. I made myself stand up, crossed to linger beside her. I leaned down. My body screamed at me, screamed that it would be sore tomorrow, or maybe for the rest of my life. "It's yours. It's going to be yours. Can you lay down so I can give it to you? Take what's mine, too?"

She looked up from her specter, looked at me. Her eyelids, ever glossy, caught the sheen of the neon sign above. It matched her. Something shifted. "Yeah," she said after a moment. The edge was gone, and she was back to that rough, raw honey tone she'd used the night I met her. She didn't protest when I took the specter from her. She didn't lash out at me, didn't bite or spit. She crawled back over to the carpet, sat in the middle, and collapsed backwards. "Be gentle."

I weighed her soul in my hand, but there wasn't anything to weigh. It was lighter than the air around it. If it hadn't been for the throbbing, the urgent need for home, I doubted I would've known it was there at all.

"We going to do this?" Daisy returned her hands to Madeline's shoulders, braced her in place again even though Madeline wasn't struggling. Madeline had her eyes shut like a sleeping-curse-drenched princess. Daisy shoved her down more as a rhetorical point.

"Yeah," I said. I felt the atmosphere of the room change, felt it get heavier across our backs. Static mussed my hair up. My guts turned to marmalade. I stood over Madeline, her soul in my fist, strangers' souls littered all around us. I pushed my tongue to the gap in my teeth. "Let's begin."

TWENTY-TWO

BORN-AGAIN BASTARD

The other Scapegracers circled us. Their clasped hands cast triangular shadows down over Madeline and me. They chanted. I didn't catch the words but I felt their reverberation with every part of my body that touched the floor. It was like the crash and rumble of a pep rally, where the bleachers in the gymnasium soaked every nascent vibration in the room and amplified them, sent them pounding from your toe bones to your kneecaps, your pelvis, your breastbone, your skull. I held Madeline's soul in my teeth to keep my hands free. I knelt, with her permission, directly over her, shins on either side of her hips. It was the position she'd struck when she pulled my soul out—ribs close to mixing, spines an acute angle. Somebody could accuse it of being a sexual pose. They'd be wrong but their case wouldn't be weak.

I held the empty composition book in my hands. This was going to be the roughest. I tried to shake the brain out of my head, tried to flip down all the governing switches. I wanted to run on the chanting's pulse alone. My vital systems could tick by their measure for a while, at least until the thing was done. I opened the composition book to its inside seam, the place where the double-wide papers were folded for standard pagination's sake. I pressed that seam against my belly, then slid it up higher, along the place where my ribs met.

Mr. Scratch came tendril by tendril down the wings of my collarbone. He purred there, nuzzled against my sternum. He shot a feeler out of my chest. The gooey black string struck the book's cotton binding, glossy as drool, and tethered. He shot more. Strings of his body joined every binding stitch. His strings thickened. He leaned on them, oozed through my shirt like tar or honey through a cheese cloth. It made a wet, low sound. He seeped out of me, kept saying, *Oh, my daughters. My darling Sideways. Hold fast.*

Feeling him deplete from my chest was like losing a baby molar. There was this emptiness in my chest cavity that couldn't go unnoticed. My organs flushed against his absence like, *Where'd he go? He was keeping us warm.*

Mr. Scratch was crowning. Whichever one of the Scapegracers stood nearest to my left side stopped chanting for a moment, too distracted to continue. She caught herself, but I felt the pause cleave the magic. It chafed against the back of my neck. I couldn't blame her, though, because the sight of Mr. Scratch heaving the thickest part of himself, a part that ballooned out of my chest and looked like an aspic or a particularly decadent slime mold, a molasses-born squid, was a lot. He billowed out of my sternum and *shlunk*ed into the composition notebook. It vibrated. The cover's consistency changed in my hands, got thicker, coarser, marbled like alligator skin. All the black splotches in its pattern raised like scales, the white slivers receding and growing metallic-slick under my fingertips. The spine fuzzed like velvet. It beefed up, got blockier. The pages thickened, the blue stripes snapped and snaked around the pulp's surface with wormlike abandon, then settled in ornate margin scrolling that would've made a Medieval monk man weep.

The bulk of him was out. Left in my body were his delicate roots. Those thinned and frayed and became liquid, bubbled through my pores. They came out of my chest. They looked like black baby ferns, like little axolotl ear wisps. They left me, and I was empty. Bereft of my devil and myself. Panic raised in my throat like bile. I bit down on Madeline's specter harder. A bright taste filled my mouth. Hot blood and peppermint candy.

Madeline shuddered underneath me.

I pulled the book, which was a slightly different book than it had been before, away from my chest. I shut it, leaned to place it above Madeline's head. It rested on a Scapegracer's hot-pink toes. My hand tremored the whole time. My grip strength was gone. No force behind my movements. There wasn't firmness in my core, all my muscles were stretched-out bands. I fought the sudden overwhelming desire to fall apart. We had enough specters to pick up after this. Didn't need to be scraping me off the rug, too.

The specters organized themselves around our circle in shapes I didn't recognize. Planetary symbols gone crooked, interwoven, and elaborated in patterns that defied meaning. None of us had moved them there. Most of them hadn't been on the rug at all when I dropped them, had skittered off across the floor in random directions. I blinked and they rolled an orbit around us, switched themselves with their neighbors to shape new sigils. They had their own light and threw rainbows around the ceiling. I wonder if they'd burn holes in the rug.

I shook my head. Looked down at Madeline. My necktie brushed her chest. I picked at the last of my gauze, uncovered the sigil on my palm I'd made for her. *Surrender and take back.* Serpentine and crosshairs. The pen marks looked faint, and the sigil was ribbed by the lines in my palm, but it stung against the open air like a lesion.

Madeline nodded. I don't know what she was affirming, but I braced myself low on my right forearm, which I placed beside her head. Her short hair looked good on her. It made her look like Peter Pan. I tried to hold myself upright, tried to keep my weight off her. Fit my hand on the side of her neck.

The chanting changed around us. It was lower, harsher, sweeter, faster.

I felt my soul in her neck. I felt it pulse against my palm, thrilled for me, molten and ridged like a peach pit. It would saw its way out of her, gnaw through sinew and gristle and jugular to get back to me. It would do anything for me, it *was* me, I wanted to suck it out like a thorn. Breathing was hard. I buckled, fell on her, but she didn't say anything about it. Her eyes rolled back in her head. How'd she do it for so long? Go without her specter? I would crumble. I'd turn into gravel.

Surrender and give back, said the Scapegracers all around me.

Madeline let out a scream. It was broken, low and jagged, but it wasn't pain. It was a vent. It was a sound that'd been building for months, calcifying behind the specter, and now that I'd dislodged it, it gushed forth. She'd said that my soul was like swallowing barbed wire. I was prickly and full of hooks and fanged loose voltage. I'd hurt on the way down. Maybe I hurt on the way up. Maybe that was fair.

The specters all around us seized and bloomed like party lights. They flashed between the Scapegracers' legs, illuminated Madeline's face in shifting Technicolor. Violet still flickered from above. A counterpoint to all the spinning candy colors, something that suited her more. It made her features hard to see. The borders of her body, and of mine, were blurred out by the polychrome motion.

Her soul tasted like a bitten tongue in my teeth. Coppery and sweet, I mean. Sharp and unclean in some vivacious, unchangeable way. There was enough verve in her that my stomach burned. It felt like hard liquor. It made my linings raw.

I pulled my hand higher. Folded it under her jaw.

Something red flashed in the back of her throat. It flew

up, struck the roof of her mouth. It blazed so intensely that it shone through her closed lips. It X-rayed her teeth. She opened her eyes and looked at me, looked at the rock in my mouth. She grinned at me. She swung an arm up, clapped her hand against the back of my neck. Her hand was dead cold against my scruff. She held me firm.

The Scapegracers didn't stop chanting but I felt them buckle for a moment. A barely resisted urge to peel us apart before we tussled again, maybe. Mr. Scratch would have something to say about that, but he wasn't in my head, he couldn't whisper to me like he used to.

Madeline brought my head down and at once rose up to meet me.

She jabbed her tongue between my teeth.

The same motion thrust my soul into my hard palate and snaked the violet out from between my teeth and back through hers. It was quick, but my nerves slammed and dragged the second out, broke it into fractals that expanded forever. My soul on her tongue in my mouth, her soul in my teeth in her lips. I kissed her.

Then my specter struck my throat and all my thinking fizzled out.

She was right. I was prickly. I scraped my way down, cut myself up like gargling saltwater. I was a shot of vinegar, a throated pepper, a mouthful of pineapple whose enzymes wanted desperately to eat you back. I hurt. I was delicious. I fell down my gullet, descended into my chest with more heat than I thought by body could hold. I was searing. I was

Daisy's house on fire. I was the black hawthorn outside my foster mom's house, struck by lightning in the rage of a midsummer storm.

I collapsed beside her, battered my hands up and down my sides, searched for the places where I fit inside me again. The gravel became a whole granite slab. Or, at least, it made itself like tesserae and lumped into a mosaic approximation of what I'd been before. What the fuck had I been before? My head swam with redness. My vision was Jing's convertible, it was Yates' nail polish, it was rocking my knuckles against my wall and showing Shiloh how you could use lipstick for cheek blush and a nosebleed that woke me up with dreams of drowning. I was red, everything was red. It was viscera and ripe fruit. Hickies and cherry tomatoes. I dropped further inside myself and my insides gaped to greet me. All my organs swirled around, wrestled themselves loose from their dots so that they could slither around my specter, unravel it like a book devil unravels an eye in the mouth. It felt like that, anyway. It was an enormously red feeling. I had no explanation, just a pseudosynesthetic thrill that I couldn't shake.

It hurt. It hurt all over, it jangled every single nerve ending and made my synapses ruck with maenadic frenzy. I was the fork stuck in a light socket. I was the light socket. My eyes were screwed-in bulbs that threw cherry-colored light. Wind howled outside the windows. The pipes groaned. A storm must be blowing. I loved the whole wide world.

The Scapegracers dropped their hands and flew beside me. I felt hands on my shoulders, on my head, on my upper arms. Somebody took me into their lap—I expected it to be Yates, so when I opened my eyes and saw Daisy, I had to blink a few times. All of them panted. They peered down at me, shoulders heaving, ribs aflutter like they'd just downed specters themselves. Sweat pearled, makeup ran, ashes sparkling in twists of hair. There were one hundred and twenty human ribs in this room, and all of them were flagging. A riptide of breath. A murmuration.

"Sideways!" Jing was all teeth. She beamed at me, seized my hand and squeezed it. "That was such a head rush—how are you? How do you feel?"

"Do you feel high? I feel high," Daisy said. Her blood-crunchy face flaked down on me as she smiled. "It's never felt like that before."

"Look." Yates pressed something to my hands. I tried to scrunch myself upright, but I didn't get far before Daisy hoisted me up higher. She put her chin on the top of my head, and my gaze fell on the book I'd been handed.

It was still a composition notebook. Mostly, anyway. It was a vampy sissy villain fever-dream composition note-book, ridged and glossy, velour-backboned, chalked with glitter at the edges. Gorgeous. When I thumbed it open, the cotton binding was gone. It was something finer, shinier, red and purple and gray and blue. My hair. He'd eaten all my hair after I'd shorn it off and stuffed it in that bag, a fact I'd mostly forgotten in attempts to block the memory of how it felt to shove all my hair in my mouth. Like depraved cotton candy. It was maybe disgusting. I should've thought it was deeply creepy, should've thought about the other things that must have made their way into the material of this book, about the things I'd had on my tongue for Mr. Scratch's sake. I didn't give a fuck. It was wonderful and it made me feel like a kid again, like receiving my first *VMM*.

I wouldn't need those anymore.

Mr. Scratch opened between my hands. Every spell we'd already made, along with a smattering of spells labeled with the names of Honeyeaters, filled the first few pages. I thumbed through all of them, the illustrations of Chett dolls, of levitating girls, of unlocking doors and shoes stuck to pavement. Our sigils, as perfect as if he'd sucked them off the walls and scanned them. The instructions were written in an odd amalgam of all our handwriting, the i's dotted with hearts, the vowels spiraling, the tails of the f's and y's sharper and longer than they had any right to be. Yates' practice equations, my shitty doodled stars and eyes, Jing's book quotes and Daisy's daisy sketches marked dividers between spells. The dividers were blue, made of the flushed ink that'd shaped standard notebook lines. They didn't seem to be cognizant of who made what spell, or at least were rather impartial. It was equitable and random, ours interwoven seamlessly with Priya and Iris' spell, Laverne's spell, Elaina's charm for looking through your own soul, and all manner of inherited spells I hadn't tried yet. I passed over the last one, and the pages were blank.

Well then? The words scrawled themselves into existence, flourishing in a handwriting a tad loopier and more flamboyant than the previous type. *Are you impressed?*

"You're fucking gorgeous," I breathed. I pulled the book close and pressed a kiss to its cover.

I'm flattered. Please flatter me. Also, I'm a proper volume. Title me. I'd like to give myself a cover page. I feel naked without one.

Daisy swallowed, which felt funny against the back of my head. "Why can't we call you Mr. Scratch?"

"Yeah, I like calling you that," said Yates. "It would be weird to completely rename you. You're a whole, I mean, not a *person*, but you're a whole autonomous being. You should pick your own name."

"Yeah, but his name isn't the name of the book, per se." Jing pulled a hand through her hair, then leaned down to stroke her finger along the edge of the page. "I agree that he oughta pick, though. Fair's fair."

You're no fun, Mr. Scratch teased. The pages fluttered through my hands, flying backwards until we were at the front of the book. The page was unadorned. Then he bloomed under it, rose up through the pulp and spread into letters. *THE SCAPEGRACERS' SCRATCHBOOK,* it read. Daisy's blood flecked down on it, and it absorbed into the paper, filled in the loops of A and R and P and O with bright scarlet.

I hugged the book to my chest. Daisy hugged her arms around my shoulders, and Jing and Yates embraced the two of us, and we all sat on the floor and rocked together, all of us around our grimoire, our scratchbook.

Madeline got up beside us. She tossed her hood up, stretched on tiptoe so that every bone in her popped and creaked in place. She stood there for a moment, breathing, feeling the life in her fingertips. Then she ran.

Jing watched her go without untangling herself from the girlweb. She touched my shoulder. "Should we go after her?"

Daisy's hair swooshed on either side of my cheeks. It smelled, under the burning house and gore, like bubblegum. "Say *sic* and I'll drag her back in five seconds flat."

"No." There wasn't any room for concern in my system. My bloodstream was overloaded with victorious wholeness. The feeling might crash later, and my pancreas would punish me for the unabashed happiness, but who gives a fuck about their pancreas? I leaned backwards into Daisy, pulled our scratchbook closer to my chest.

"Yeah," said Yates. "Let what comes next be in her hands."

The door swung ajar. Wind spiraled in fistfuls of snow, thick and big as thumbprints, like rose petals at a wedding. Madeline had those basketball-player legs. She could've vaulted over a skyscraper with them. Her kneecaps were up near Yates' hipbones. Hyperbole, but like, not really. Madeline was long gone, and the cold took her place. It floated over us, frosted the tips of our breath. The four of us scooted in closer to each other. We hid our noses in one another's arms or necks.

"There's a motel not too far from here," Jing said. "Do you think we should crash there instead of driving all the way home? I'm not a gambling man, but if that's the amount of snow that's blowing inside with a porch in its way, I'd wager the roads are absolutely fucked."

Daisy snorted. She shouldn't have snorted. The floodgates of her face opened, and down poured the sticky red.

"Ack!" Yates untangled herself, made a yacking sound in the back of her throat. "Jesus, Daisy! We have to find you a first aid kit, we're not going anywhere until we do. Are you sure we shouldn't Maps our way to the nearest hospital or something? That's a really nasty cut."

"I'm fine," Daisy snapped. She pulled me closer in a defensive motion, like I was a human shield, or a wall to hide behind. A lezzie teddy bear. Her blood sloshed over my shoulder. "I don't need to go to a fucking hospital, I'm absolutely fine. Duh! Soap and water. That's it, got it?"

"Daze, I love and admire your stubbornness, but know that if your house hadn't just gone up like a marshmallow, I would be so annoyed right now." Jing unfurled herself as well. "Come on, Yates. There's got to be a first aid kit in the bathroom, or in the kitchen maybe. Sideways, gather up all the specters so we don't trip on them. Wouldn't that be a hell of a way to end the night?" She stood up, took a few strides toward Yates, and leaned down to whisper something in her ear. The neon sign made her blond look lilac. Whatever she said made Yates cover her mouth and laugh.

An engine roared and abruptly died. A car door slammed. Low conversation, indistinct, coming closer.

"Shit!" Jing spun around. "What are you doing on the floor? Get up, we've gotta scram and find someplace to hide."

"Hide?" Yates balked at her. "There is blood everywhere and souls all over the floor. How exactly are we going to hide, Jing?"

"Jesus fucking Christ," Jing said. She jumped on her toes, whipped her head around like she was searching for something to throw. It was the stance of somebody who had run from the cops at a raucous party more than once. Several times. Many, many fucking times. "We can't just stand around, that's ridiculous, we're sitting ducks."

"I'm not standing around. I'm sitting." Daisy leaned back. She tilted her head to the side, directed the stream of blood down her neck. It pooled in my collarbone, slipped down between my cleavage, caked the rim of my bra and slipped further. I must look such a mess. What else is new?

"And you, Sideways?" Jing looked between us. "You gonna do something?"

"Daisy hasn't let go of me. I'm trapped." I shrugged my shoulders. My specter was back. Come, peril.

"Relax, Jing." Daisy shot her a horrible smile. "We've had a long night. Go limp in the fist of god, would ya?" Then, in my ear: "We've got to talk."

Two men filled the doorway. They both wore pinstripe

suits. The taller man removed his hat. They tipped their snowy shoes on the welcome mat, and Maurice Delacroix and a man carrying Maurice Delacroix's bag entered the Delacroix House. The lenses of Maurice's browline glasses flashed. He looked around the room, then down at my girls on the rug. "Pardon me, children. What the fuck is going on?"

✳ TWENTY-THREE ✳

FRUITY BODIES

I supposed this was Maurice's office. It didn't look like an office. The walls were felted with red pentacles, the desk was a flat-topped casket, the carpet was the pelt of an unidentifiable animal. Upon closer inspection, it appeared not to be an animal at all, but a series of faux-fur coats that had been sewn together to shape the body of a chimeric monster. There were fountains in the far corners, and Roman busts adorned with smudged lipstick and used false lashes. Annotated playing cards, matchbooks, mounted sickles. Altars, everywhere. Maurice and I sat across from one another in matching zebra-stripe armchairs on either side of the casket-desk. The specters arranged themselves in arrays across the surface. Jing sat beside me. Yates sat with Daisy on a chaise lounge behind us, serving as moral support as the stranger charmed her head wound shut.

"So. We call you, tell you not to pursue Madeline, that we were calling in experts to come and handle matters for the safety of everybody involved." Maurice smiled at us, folded his hands together. "Now, your specter is in your throat, hers in hers, your friends are bleeding in our atrium, and there are upwards of two dozen disembodied specters in my office. Help me understand what happened. Quickly, if you'd please."

Jing and I looked at each other.

"I, uh." I cleared my throat. "We went after her. Clearly. It was reckless but you have to understand, I was desperate."

"I understand that you disobeyed because you were desperate. Continue."

"We didn't find her," I said, "but the motel gave us a lead. I decided to pursue her on my own, without my coven."

"And what coven would that be?" Maurice lofted a brow.

"The Scapegracers," Jing said. "That's us. We've got our own spell book and everything. We're a coven."

"I see." He rested his cheek on his fist.

"I went alone." I didn't want to tell him about Shiloh. Oh god, Shiloh. I needed to text them ASAP. "I had a hunch that her specter was in the Chantry house."

"I had little doubt it was." Maurice sighed. "There's an incantation that all witchfinders share, one that bars a witch from crossing property lines once their detached specter has been anointed for repurposing on the premises. It would explain why Madeline couldn't fetch it herself, and why you found so many. They become physically irretrievable by the witch to whom they belong."

"These were all in their house," I said. I ghosted my fingertips over the tops of the specters, some withered, others plump and ripe and yielding. "I gathered them, and as many of their materials on individual witches as possible." I reached into my pockets—I'd donned the leather jacket again—and pulled out a few of the pictures. "These won't correspond to the specters, I think. They didn't seem to have them for the witches they've already robbed."

Maurice and Jing both looked a little ill.

Maurice picked up a picture, uncrunched it, and held it close to his nose. He looked at it with a tangle of fascination and horror. "Jupiter," he said. His voice was thin. "Come see this."

"Just a moment." The man, who'd finished patching Daisy up, stood. He handed the rag to Yates, and she took his place with a nod, pressed the cloth to the line of mended skin. "It'll scar, but only just. I'm sorry I couldn't have gotten to it sooner."

"I'll survive," Daisy mumbled.

Yates mouthed something at her.

Daisy shrugged her shoulders. "Thanks," she said.

"My pleasure." Jupiter strode our way. He stood beside Maurice, pressed a kiss to his forehead, and leaned down. He fixed his gaze on the picture. He threw a hand over his mouth. "God in heaven, that's Pearl."

"Pearl," Jing repeated.

"They're a server here." Jupiter looked between the two of us. "They haven't picked a coven yet. They're sixteen. Where was this picture?"

"In the Chantry family's basement." My tongue felt a little thick. "Do you want me to keep going?"

Maurice and Jupiter nodded in tandem.

"I found these, stole them, and went to Daisy's house. Her father was having this Christmas party, and the Chantry family was in attendance. Madeline came. She caught the house on fire. We got nearly everybody out, and we got her away from the Chantry brothers and brought her here. We thought we should do our specter exchange in the Delacroix House instead of the woods or our car or something. We thought it would be safer here." I sucked my teeth, tried to read their expressions. They weren't looking at me, though. Maurice and Jupiter were looking at the specters on the desk, and the picture of Pearl they held in their hands. "I'm sorry that we broke in and bled on your rug. Again. Desperate."

"The house is always open to witches. If you'd called us, we would've come and opened it." Maurice put the picture down. He ran his hands over his face, folded his hands into a prayerful position, and pressed them to the sides of his mouth. "I've never seen so many disembodied specters. Never, in all my life. We have to call the Sisters Corbie about Madeline, but I think we'll need to call *all* the covens to whom these specters could conceivably belong. Every major coven in the nation. They need to be able to sift through these, reunite them with the few witches who've survived this long, respectfully bury the rest."

"It'll take a few months to get them all here," said Jupiter. He cocked his head to the side, looked between Jing and me. "You four could've died tonight."

"Yeah," said Jing. "I know."

"It's about time we have young, proactive witches." Jupiter took a breath. "I don't think it's a wise idea for the group of you to drive back tonight. Daisy and Yates mentioned a motel—we have boarding rooms upstairs that you might find to your liking, free of charge. You can drive home in the morning when the roads are clear. Maurice pulled over to charm our tires on the way here, that's how questionable the interstate is right now."

I eyed Jing, who I suspected would be the most likely out of all of us to object. She didn't, though. She nodded, reached out a hand in thanks. "We'd like that."

"I'll show you to your room," said Maurice. He stood up, pressed his fingertips against the desk. "Do any of you have questions for us?"

"What happens to Madeline?" Yates looked up from Daisy's face, which she was currently scrubbing with baby wipes. "I don't want anybody to hurt her or anything."

"She'll be pursued in earnest. She isn't magically volatile anymore, not with her own specter returned to her. The Sisters Corbie will seek justice. It isn't my decision," Maurice said. He sounded like he wished it was. "I would be surprised if her own coven hurt her. She has made some *grave* missteps, and I imagine they will have reprimand in mind, but they're a family. Families don't do that."

Jupiter shot Maurice a look.

I felt wildly nauseous.

"Is that a casket?" Daisy leaned over to catch a glance. "Seriously, is your table a casket? Is there a body in it?"

"Yes." Maurice smiled. "Let's ascend."

✳

The bedroom had two queens, like a hotel room. That was where the similarities ended.

All the walls were draped with heavy curtains. It felt like a burlesque stage. Pulled back, they revealed a pastoral mural that bloomed over every inch of wall. There were lots of prancing nymphs in the mural, and lambs grazing through wildflowers, and napping long-lashed twink shepherds, satyrs, baby dragons. The beds looked squishy, enticing with their handsome red duvets. The carpets felt hypnotically plush against my naked, screaming toes. There was a claw-foot bathtub in the corner of the room. The bathroom attached to the room had two sinks and a shower, which raised questions to me about the bathtub in this one. It had feet like a manticore.

All of us tossed our shoes in a pile. We stripped off our coats, our sweaters, anything caked with blood gunk or flakes of Daisy's house. Jing went for the carved walnut wardrobe as soon as we entered the room, and there she found creamy silk bathrobes. Three of them had huge feather-boa lips around the sleeves and the collar. There were two smoking jackets as well, and a housecoat that looked like the smoking jackets save for the fact that it was floor length. Slippers, too. A mortar and pestle and a set of paintbrushes that we didn't question.

Daisy called dibs on one of the bathrobes. Jing called another. Yates put a hand over her phone midway through explaining to Julian that we were alive and okay, said she wanted the feathery white one. Feathers are itchy. I went for the Hugh Hefner housecoat. I mean, fuck that guy and his rotting bones, but damn, it was a cool jacket. I felt like I owned a casino and smoked cigars and had four pet rottweilers and an army of albino peacocks. We shucked our clothes to the skin. The layers had gotten crunchy, chalky, disgusting to the point of mournfulness. The sweater Daisy had been wearing, the sweater that had been mine, was so heavy with blood that it squelched when it hit the floor. I would've normally been self-conscious, stripping down like this, but there was something catastrophically not weird about it. It was like drama. No shame in a costume change. If anything, letting my skin breathe a minute felt amazing. I wanted out of my bra, out of all the things that hugged me too tight. We'd look like Vincent Price and the Hammer Horror girls like this. Wasn't that a thought?

Yates shouldered on her amazing, ridiculous white coat and called her parents, then Jing's parents, then mine. She said soft little nothings to all of them, assured them that we were alive, that we were well, that we were together. I wondered if she was casting.

Nothing felt real. This was a dream. How could everything be fixed right as everything shattered?

I could hex myself awake. Should I?

"That's everybody," Yates said.

"Not everybody." I tied the housecoat around my hips and leaned against the wall. I grabbed my phone off the counter. Nearly dead, but not quite. Not yet. I thumbed up Shiloh's contact, and I hit call. Tucked the chin against my cheek.

Please pick up.

They didn't.

I shut my eyes, rolled my head back, and fought the urge to scream. I redialed. I waited.

They picked up on the last ring. "Sideways?"

They sounded funny. Too quiet.

I ran my hand over my hair. I felt filthy. "Hey, where are you? How are you?"

"Did you get your specter back?"

"I did," I said. "So did Madeline. I've brought all the specters you found to the Delacroix House, too. They're going to get them to the covens, try and return them as best as possible."

"Good." They took a breath. "That's really good."

"How are you?" Cracks spiderwebbed the ceiling. The mended world was flaking. I felt like I should pin my head between my knees. "Shiloh, talk to me."

"Did you kill my little brother?"

I opened my mouth and couldn't shut it.

"David is dead." Their voice cracked. The name fluttered high in their register, and I braced my free hand against the wall behind me, flattened my palm so that it didn't spasm and hit something. "Father's so distraught that he's hardly noticed I'm here. Abel's throwing a tantrum. Levi's locked himself in his room. They haven't found out about the room in the basement yet. I need to be here when that happens. I don't think I'm in danger, you don't have to worry about that. I don't know. I don't know. Look, I'll call you in the morning, okay?"

"Promise you will?" My flat hand curled up. It scraped at the mural. The paint on the shepherd twink's eye broke under my nail. "If anything happens, text me, okay? Please text me. Please promise. Please come back home."

"I promise. I'm going to get some sleep, Sideways."

"Take care of yourself, Shi."

Sorry about David.

There was no air in my lungs.

The phone clicked. I dropped it on the counter and made myself breathe.

Everybody was looking at me.

"Shiloh's okay." They're not. "They're going to call me in the morning." Would they?

Yates' expression cracked. She turned away from me, braced her hands against the mattress. Jing inhaled sharply. I saw her thread David's death and Shiloh's location together. She looked grim. She looked, I thought, mad at me. Daisy, meanwhile, was expressionless.

Daisy said, "In the morning, call them on speaker. We'll rescue them."

I nodded. My head swam.

"They're yours," Daisy said. "So, they've got to be fine.

We'll make the conditions for them to be fine. That's what our coven does."

＊

At nearly five in the morning, all of us lay in bed. None of us were sleeping. I don't know if we could. We'd managed to fit all of us in the claw-foot bathtub, which was wonderful until we had to get back out of it. We'd toweled off, donned our robes once more, shoved the two beds together, and laid on top of the blankets. There was a strangeness about this night, a fullness to it. I was afraid of rupturing it with sleep. I had to ride it out. Only a few more hours until sunrise.

We'd killed a fourteen-year-old. None of us knew how to talk about that.

Jing whispered into Yates' shoulder. I wondered if Jing was still in love with her. Who wasn't in love with Yates?

Daisy bit me. Sharp and wet on my arm. It was weird but not outside of the realm of standard Daisy antics. I eyed her, nudged a stray hair off her forehead with my knuckle. "Daze?"

"I got jealous." Her eyelashes tickled. "You were somebody else's haven. Somebody I didn't trust to be around you. How dare you."

I craned my neck to look at her. She evaded direct glances. "I'm your haven?"

"Duh." She nodded, which felt like a nuzzle. "It was hard to be around you sometimes because when I was around you, everybody was like, *Ooh, Daisy's finally done it. She's finally crossed the lezzie threshold.* People thought I was gay just for being beside you. What a stupid reason to be right. I resented you for it. I resented that you made me feel like myself because I don't always like myself. I hate that bitch, frankly. But I like you. I took it out on you. That wasn't fair."

"It's easier to be your haven when you keep me around." I felt light-headed. I hooked an arm around her shoulders. I looked at the ceiling. "Thank you for coming out for me that morning. For defending me."

"You'd do it for me." She bit me again.

"Can you keep a secret? Just between us?"

She nodded, still biting me. That hurt. Oddly grounding.

"I'm not a girl. I'm a lesbian but I'm not a girl. I'm just butch. A they/them butch." I breathed in hard. "It's not a huge jump from where I'm at. But the distinction matters. It's meaningful to me."

She took her teeth out of my arm and whispered, "Cross my heart."

"Finals are gonna kill me," Jing said. She addressed all of us, the ceiling fan, the stars beyond. She sounded worn. I wanted an arm around her, too.

"Yeah," I agreed. "On the edge of fully flunking."

"I'm only worried about Physics," said Daisy. "Fuck Physics."

Yates didn't add anything, because she was set to be the

valedictorian unless something profoundly wrong happened. She rolled on her stomach and rested her cheek on my unbitten arm. "We still have a little time until Christmas."

"Yeah?" Daisy yawned.

"Meaning"—Yates propped her chin on my elbow—"we could still do Secret Santa. I *love* Secret Santa. And it being so short notice would make it exciting! It'd be a nice surprise for the end of finals week. A celebration of having one semester left of high school. Come on, please?"

Daisy and Jing exchanged a glance.

"Yeah," I said. A smile slid over me. My eyes fell shut. My Scratchless head felt dry, weightless. Itchy. "Yeah, we can do a Secret Santa."

Jing and Daisy made affirmative noises.

"Great!" Yates gathered herself up and slipped off the bed. She padded over to the pile of her clothes, rummaged through her things until she found her wallet. Our names were on slips of paper inside, the same slips that she'd torn the first time we'd tried this.

"Did you just carry those around?" Jing sat up and stretched. "Why?"

"Good luck." Yates beamed. She folded the slips and drifted back between the beds, held the four pearl-crumples in her cupped hands. Sunlight bubbled behind the blinds. "If I had them in my wallet, Secret Santa wasn't ever canceled. Just postponed. Call that magic. I was right! Now, everybody chose."

We all put our hands in hers.

ACKNOWLEDGMENTS

This book wouldn't exist without Sarah, who generously let me crash at her place the summer that this was drafted. A few passages still taste like nectarines.

Thank you to the innumerable people who've kept me kicking.

Thank you to my mentors back home, non-exhaustively but notably Anita, cris, Patrick, Margaret, Steve, Rhonda, Jeremy, and Sara, who influenced me and this story by extension. Thank you to the mentors I've found since then, most notably Hilary and Bill; I am wiser and kinder for having known you. Thank you to my mother, for everything.

Thank you to Dakota, for taking care of me. Thank you Em and Hannah for fielding all my revision woes. Thank you Sneha, whose insights are invaluable, and without whom I'd be lost. Thank you, Meg and Caymen, for allowing me to rave in your kitchen about books you've yet to read, and thank you, Christina, for your fearsome compassion. Thank you to Asya for being so wonderful, and for making me want to make.

Thank you to Marty for being an anchor through a series of storms, to Viengsamai for literal years of wisdom and friendship, to Cass and Sarah for your kindness, quickness, generosity, and patience, to Anka and Dana for making these books so gorgeous, to Liz for having taken a chance on me, to Kat, Leah, and NaNá for having shaped this book from there, to Isa and Sepi for their faith, and to Abby for having championed me for so long. Thank you to the workers who produced the materials that comprise this book, the workers who printed and bound this book, and the workers who transported this book to bookstores and libraries and one significant headshop. Thanks, booksellers! Thanks, librarians! Thanks, everyone who helps along the way.

Thank you to people who've bought this book for queer and trans teenagers in their life. Thank you to queer and trans elders for showing me that we grow up and demonstrating our vast communal capacity for uncomplicated happiness. Thank you to the countless musicians and the filmmakers and the writers I adore, sinners all, who make art feel alive; your genius renews my devotion to the form. Thank you to everyone who's brought me into my butchness. Thank you each and every fagdyke angel. Thank you Christmas, I love you Christmas. Thank you chain-link fences, thank you honeysuckles, thank you to Spike who has been returned to earth, thanks fireflies, thanks fireworks, thanks promise of tomorrow. I am going to keep writing about you.